PETER'S EYES WENT WIDE WITH AUTHENTIC TERROR . . .

"*Viktor* is *Lucifer. Lucifer* is *Victor. He* is the Evil sent to destroy the world! He comes from Hell, I tell you!"

Suddenly Peter's head was bolt upright. He began to shake uncontrollably. "Listen!" he whispered. "Here it comes . . ."

The whole ship shuddered with the sound of an explosion. The lights flickered twice, then went out completely. In a second, the CIC was filled with black, acrid smoke. The crackling of flames could be heard in the next compartment.

The man called Peter let out a long, agonizing scream, then sank back to the darkened floor . . .

TOP-FLIGHT AERIAL ADVENTURE
FROM ZEBRA BOOKS!

WINGMAN (2015, $3.95)
by Mack Maloney

From the radioactive ruins of a nuclear-devastated U.S. emerges a hero for the ages. A brilliant ace fighter pilot, he takes to the skies to help free his once-great homeland from the brutal heel of the evil Soviet warlords. He is the last hope of a ravaged land. He is Hawk Hunter . . . Wingman!

WINGMAN #2: THE CIRCLE WAR (2120, $3.95)
by Mack Maloney

A second explosive showdown with the Russian overlords and their armies of destruction is in the wind. Only the deadly aerial ace Hawk Hunter can rally the forces of freedom and strike one last blow for a forgotten dream called "America"!

WINGMAN #3: THE LUCIFER CRUSADE (2232, $3.95)
by Mack Maloney

Viktor, the depraved international terrorist who orchestrated the bloody war for America's West, has escaped. Ace pilot Hawk Hunter takes off for a deadly confrontation in the skies above the Middle East, determined to bring the maniac to justice or die in the attempt!

GHOST PILOT (2207, $3.95)
by Anton Emmerton

Flyer Ian Lamont is driven by bizarre unseen forces to relive the last days in the life of his late father, an RAF pilot killed during World War II. But history is about to repeat itself as a sinister secret from beyond the grave transforms Lamont's worst nightmares of fiery aerial death into terrifying reality!

Available wherever paperbacks are sold, or order direct from the Publisher. Send cover price plus 50¢ per copy for mailing and handling to Zebra Books, Dept. 2232, 475 Park Avenue South, New York, N.Y. 10016. Residents of New York, New Jersey and Pennsylvania must include sales tax. DO NOT SEND CASH.

WINGMAN

THE LUCIFER CRUSADE
BY MACK MALONEY

ZEBRA BOOKS
KENSINGTON PUBLISHING CORP.

Chapter 1

The F-4 Phantom jet fighter touched down on the deserted runway and taxied towards a nearby row of hangars.

Just off the landing strip, next to the aircraft parking area, the remains of a MiG-21 were still burning. Another MiG had crashed through the roof of one of the hangars, and the resulting fire had burned down half the building. Still another Soviet fighter had crashed into the base's only radar antenna, scattering pieces of the huge, once-revolving dish all over the tarmac.

Smoke from the three smoldering fighters had spread out over the small airbase like a dark and dirty fog.

The F-4 came to a halt in front of the burning hangar and its pilot popped the airplane's canopy. Standing up in the open cockpit, Captain "Crunch" O'Malley removed his flight helmet and looked around.

"Welcome to the Azores," he muttered.

Crunch's rear-seat weapons officer, a lieutenant named Elvis, also stood up and surveyed the damage. "Do you think he's been here?" he asked

5

Crunch.

"Well, we got three MiGs shot down here and two more burning on the beach," Crunch said. "All apparently iced by one person. Only one pilot I know that could do that."

Then Elvis noticed an odd thing: through the smoke and next to the burning hangar, he could see a man tied to a chair. "Captain," he said pointing toward the bound and gagged man. "Who the hell is that?"

The two pilots climbed out of the F-4 and cautiously walked toward the man. Crunch was armed with an M-16, Elvis with a 9mm pistol.

The man sat silently as they approached. The only noise was the jet's engine winding down and the crackling of the three MiG fires. Directly above, the noon sun was beating down unmercifully.

Crunch took out a knife and immediately cut off the man's gag.

"Gracias, señor," the man gasped, taking a quick succession of deep breaths. He was about sixty years old, with a slight build and wearing the sweaty remains of a mechanic's overall. The two pilots, themselves clad in sleek dark-blue flight suits, towered over him.

"How long you been here, Pops?" Crunch asked, hesitating to undo the ropes holding the man's hands and feet to the chair.

"Two days," the old man answered, with a slight accent. "They come. Wreck my home. Wreck the base. Look at that hangar. It's ruined. Burnt. I'm an old man. I cannot repair it myself."

"Who wrecked this place?" Crunch asked, deciding the man was harmless enough to untie. He quickly undid the ropes.

"Air pirates. Russians. I don't know," the man

answered, rubbing his wrists made raw by the twine.

"Russians?" Elvis asked, catching Crunch's eye.

"*Si*," the man said, stretching his arms and legs. "Russian air pirates. Bounty hunters. They land here, three days ago. Five MiGs. They don't call ahead. They don't contact me in control tower. They just land, with no permission. Steal my fuel. Steal my food."

"This sounds interesting," Crunch said, wryly. "Go on, Pops, tell us the whole story."

"Start by telling us who you are and what the hell you're doing here alone," Elvis added.

"My name is Diego de la Crisco," the craggy-faced man began. "I run this base. Used to be four hundred men. Now just me. Airplanes, flying from America, used to stop here all the time. For fuel, food, ammo. Now not as much. But those who stop, I sell to them food. Fuel. Maybe fix an engine blade sometimes.

"Three days ago, the MiGs came. The pilots, they bust in, slap me around. Keep me locked up. They don't talk my language, but I can tell they are waiting for someone."

"Who's that someone?" Crunch asked.

"The American pilot," the man said. "He is my friend. He saved me. He is the man who shot them all down."

Crunch and Elvis exchanged winks. "Go on, Diego," Crunch said.

"The MiG pilots," he continued, "they knew the American was coming. They are very excited as there is a reward for shooting down the American's airplane. They wait until he shows up on radar, then they take off, all five of them. They plan beforehand how they will attack him. Like an ambush.

"Ah, but the American, he's way too smart for the

7

MiGs. He knows somehow they are waiting for him. He has more Sidewinders on his jet than anyone I have ever seen. The MiGs jump him, right over the base. But he flies like a demon. Twisting. Turning. Diving. One minute he's here. Next second, way over there. One by one, he blasts all five MiGs from the sky. I watch the whole thing, cheering. My throat still stings I cheer so much. Trouble is, the wrecked MiGs, they fall on my base."

"After the battle, did this American land here?" Crunch asked.

"Well, of course, *señor,*" Diego said, slightly taken aback. "This American is now a very good friend of mine."

"Did he tell you what his name was?" Elvis asked.

"Yes," the old man said with a sly smile. "But I know who he is before he even lands his airplane. I have heard of this American pilot. He flies a red, white, and blue jet. The powerful F-16. I know my airplanes. I know no one flies the F-16 anymore, except for this American."

"Was his name Hawk Hunter?" Crunch asked.

"*Si, señor,*" the man said excitedly. "But I know him by his other name. He's the pilot they call The Wingman."

Crunch and Elvis looked at each other and nodded.

"The Wingman stays only a day," Diego went on. "Then he says he must go."

"So, if you and he are such good friends," Elvis asked, "who tied you up here?"

"The others, *señor,*" Diego said, anger coming back into his voice. "The others land hours after Hawk Hunter leaves. They too are looking for him."

"Who were these 'others'?" Crunch asked. "More Russians? Were they flying Russian jet fighters?"

"No," Diego answered. "They come in only one airplane. An American P-3. Big, four propeller engines. Old U.S. Navy. But these men are not Americans. They are Arabs, I think. The plane is painted all black. I know they stole it somewhere."

"And they were also looking for Hunter?" Elvis asked.

"Yes," Diego continued. "They come and *they* slap me around. I'm an old man. I can't take all this. They are mad that Hunter has shot down the MiGs. These men have paid for the MiGs to shoot down Hunter. Now they are mad that it is the MiGs that have crashed."

"So they tied you up and left you out here?" Crunch asked.

"Si, si, señor," Diego said, spitting for emphasis. "They are *pigs*. They could have just shot me. But they leave me to die the slow death. But I knew that either Hunter or his friends would rescue me."

"What else did these other men say?" Elvis asked.

Diego shook his head. "They say a big battle is soon to happen. Out in the eastern Mediterranean. Out in the desert. These men, like the MiGs—they are on the bad side. But they are afraid."

"Afraid?" asked Crunch. "Afraid of what?"

A wide smile creased Diego's face. "They are afraid, *señor,* that they will have to fight Hunter."

They gave Diego some food packs from the F-4 and also a cask of brandy they always carried. The old man ate heartily and drained the brandy, then immediately went to sleep. Retreating to the base's control tower, Crunch and Elvis discussed their mission so far.

They were looking for Hawk Hunter. He, like

they, belonged to the Pacific American Air Corps, the air defense arm for the territory formerly known as the states of California, Washington, and Oregon. Hunter was one of PAAC's commanders, and in a strict military sense their commanding officer. But he was more their friend than anything else, and an unusual friend at that. Formerly a pilot in the Air Force demonstration team known as the Thunderbirds, Hunter was also a genius (certified at a young age), a doctor of aeronautics (at seventeen, being the youngest student ever to graduate MIT), and had trained to pilot the Space Shuttle.

He was also widely regarded as the best fighter pilot who had ever lived . . .

There were many stories about how Hunter had fought so bravely in World War III. But no one was more bitter than he when America was tricked into signing an armistice with the Soviet Union — supposedly to end World War III, a non-nuclear struggle that the U.S. and NATO had won on the battlefield of Western Europe. But no sooner was the ink dry on the treaty — and the traitorous U.S. Vice-President safely transported to Moscow — when the Kremlin ordered a devastating surprise nuclear strike against the center of the American continent. It was the most dastardly sneak attack in the history of mankind.

Mortally wounded, the US had no choice but to accept Russia's terms. The punishment was called The New Order. Its major demands had the US Armed Forces immediately disarmed and their weapons destroyed. Then the US itself was dismembered — broken up into a mishmash of countries, republics, and free territories. Dividing the continent down the middle was The Badlands, the radioactive netherworld that stretched from Oklahoma to the

10

Dakotas, courtesy of the Soviet ICBMs.

Ever since they were broken up, the many American states and countries had frequently been at war with one another—wars started in large part by Soviet agents and their agitating terrorist allies. The latest battle had pitted the democratic forces of the West against a Soviet-infiltrated, cultish Eastern army known as The Circle. The leader of The Circle had been a Soviet agent named Viktor Robotov. Hunter had successfully led the air forces for the West in defeating The Circle, despite the fact that Viktor's Russian allies had secretly infiltrated thousands of SAM anti-aircraft batteries and troops into the American Badlands.

The victory was a costly one for the West, though. Many major cities as well as small towns had been destroyed in the fighting. The vital air trade routes between Free Canada and Los Angeles—plied by convoys of airliners now turned into cargo carriers—had been disrupted for a long period of time. Shortages of all kinds had been felt on both sides.

What was worse, thousands of Americans on both sides had died in the civil war. And this was the *real* reason Viktor and the Kremlin had started The Circle War. Their aim was to continue the distablization of America, thus forestalling any notions that the American states and territories might have about reuniting and carrying out their revenge on Mother Russia.

But the fighting aside, The Circle War had had a very personal effect on Hawk Hunter. Before the war broke out, Viktor had kidnapped the pilot's true love, a stunning Bardot look-alike named Dominique. He had drugged her, forced himself on her, and used her viciously—through a kind of pornographic psychological warfare—to control his Circle

11

troops. Hunter had finally rescued Dominique, literally crashing in on a party being given for Viktor atop one of New York City's World Trade Center buildings. Once she was safe, Hunter had made arrangements for her to live in the relative security of Free Canada.

But he could not let Viktor get away with his crime. The man had violated the two things that meant the most to Hunter—his country and his woman. Hunter had vowed to track Viktor down.

He was gone the day the war ended. Somehow, he had gotten to New York City and retrieved his F-16 from its hiding place at the abandoned JFK Airport. Then he had set out across the Atlantic in pursuit of Viktor. Crunch and Elvis had no idea how Hunter knew Viktor had headed for the Mediterranean after The Circle War ended. *He just knew.* The fact was that Hunter had been born with an amazing aptitude for ESP. Hunter's extraordinary abilities were particularly acute in detecting enemy aircraft. Besides being the ultimate fighter pilot, Hunter was also a kind of human radar. But he also had an astounding sixth sense about many things. Knowing where Viktor fled to after the war was one of them.

Everyone—from the Russians to the PAAC pilots to the air pirates that roamed the North American skies—knew that a man of such intelligence and skill as Hunter was an automatic threat to those who ran The New Order. These Soviet puppets, firmly ensconced in the Bahamas, had put a price of $500 million on Hunter's head. He was wanted—dead or alive—for "crimes against The New Order." Crimes such as carrying an American flag. Or espousing reunification of the states. Or even even uttering the words "United States of America."

But Hunter had decided long ago that if these

were the kinds of crimes that made The New Order put a price on his head, then he would continue to commit them freely and openly.

Besides, the amount of money a bounty hunter could get for his hide was source of amusement for the pilot. He would tell people that he wasn't worth even half that much.

He was, however, very valuable to PAAC and all the democratic peoples who wanted to reunite America again. That's why his overall commander at PAAC, General Dave Jones, had sent Crunch and Elvis after Hunter. Crunch and Elvis made up one half of a free-lance F-4 fighter unit known as the Ace Wrecking Company. They were, in effect, under contract to PAAC. So General Jones was their employer. Jones knew Crunch, a veteran F-4 Phantom pilot from way back, was best suited for the mission. At best he and Elvis could convince Hunter to return to America. At worst, they could give him protection in his search for Viktor.

But they would have to find him first.

"Well, we know he was here in the Azores two and a half days ago," Crunch said, looking at a large map of the Atlantic and Mediterranean. "He could be in Portugal, Gibraltar, maybe North Africa by now."

"Well, he had no trouble icing those MiGs," Crunch said, shaking his head in admiration. "Maybe he doesn't need any help in tracking down Viktor either."

"Well, I agree that Hunter is the best to ever fly, and so he's very valuable to PAAC right now," Elvis said. "But I also know him pretty well, as you do, captain. And when he gets something set in his mind, it's impossible to talk him out of it. Viktor fooled with his lady big time. Screwed up the country too. That's playing with fire as far as Hawk is concerned. I don't blame him for going after Viktor. And he could probably track down the creep better if he is alone."

Crunch ran his fingers through his hair, then continued. "Hunter's a good friend of mine and a good friend to all the guys in PAAC. But Jones is the boss. He says find him and drag him back. So we find him."

"Well, it's not the finding him that will be difficult," Elvis said. "It's the 'dragging him back' part that worries me."

Chapter 2

The skies over Casablanca were busy the night Hunter arrived.

He had seen the lights of the city from seventy miles out, reflecting off the atmosphere and the nearby Atlantic. Now, as he descended from 55,000 feet, the city's blue-green glare got brighter, shining out like a beacon on the otherwise pitch-black Moroccan coastline.

Fifty miles out, he brought his F-16 down to wavetop level and throttled back to a 350-mph crawl. The jet fighter's terrain-radar-acquisition system had painted an infrared picture of the city's airport onto one of his control panel's TV screens and he had been studying it with much interest.

He had assumed that the airport—and the city— would be deserted. But just the opposite was true. In fact, there were so many airplanes circling Casablanca, it looked like a typical stack-up over Chicago's O'Hare in the old days.

Suddenly, his radio crackled.

"Casablanca control to approaching aircraft," a high-pitched voice sang over the static. "We have you on our radar screens. You are on an unauthorized landing pattern. Break off! Break off!"

Hunter calmly pushed his radio transmission button. "Casablanca Control, this is an aircraft of the Pacific American Air Corps. I am requesting emergency landing clearance. I am low on fuel."

"Break off," the shrillish reply came back. "We are at over-capacity. Our airspace is at the critical point. We have no open landing zone for you. You are unauthorized."

Hunter checked his instruments. He was twelve miles off the coast. He tapped the back of the throttle bar twice, slowing the F-16 down further.

"Casablanca Control, I am down to a hundred pounds of fuel. I must land."

"We have no fuel for you," the air controller came back. "You are unauthorized . . ."

Hunter was carefully watching the action over the airport on his TV screen. The aircraft were stacked up ten high over the airport. More than forty airplanes at various altitudes were traveling around and around on the same lazy circling pattern. At the same time, other aircraft were taking off every thirty seconds from the airport's single runway.

Hunter could tell that most of the air traffic was made up of airliners. 747s, 707s, DC-10s, Airbuses. Some appeared to be riding on each other's tails. Airplanes were taking off just as incoming aircraft bounced in. The radio chatter was a storm of pilot's voices, yelling out their coordinates and doing everything they could to avoid a midair collision. It was the most confusing aircraft handling pattern he'd ever seen. But somehow the overworked air controllers were making it .work.

He checked his instruments again. Ten miles out, fuel getting lower. Time to negotiate.

"Casablanca control," he said into his microphone. "What is your 'landing authorization' fee?"

There was only the slightest of hesitation, then the answer came back. "Small aircraft. Jet fighter. One bag of gold, or five silver."

Steep, but expected. But he didn't intend to pay anywhere near that just to land.

"Casablanca control," Hunter called just as he reached the coastline. "I have one bag of silver. It's yours if you give me landing okay."

"Two bags," came the reply.

"Bag and a half," Hunter said.

"Land clear on seven," the controller said, his shrill voice rising yet another octave. "Right behind the Air-India Jumbo."

Welcome to Casablanca.

Hunter inserted the F-16 into the melee of landing and departing airliners. A fog bank in the night sky over the airport made the approach even more hazardous. He dodged at least a half-dozen airliners, nearly clipped the tail section of a stray 727, and actually landed *ahead* of the red Air-India 747. As his wheels touched the ground, a DC-10 was lifting off no more than 500 feet ahead of him.

He followed the line of yellow runway lights to a taxiing path lined with blue. The number of aircraft above the airport was nothing compared to what was on the ground. The place was a traffic jam of airliners.

"What the hell is going on here?" he asked himself as he rolled up to a very thin empty station point near the bustling terminal. There were people everywhere—some carrying luggage, others just bags on their backs. Men, women, kids. They were in the terminal, on its roof and walkways, even on parts of the runway. There were flashing lights everywhere and he could hear sirens even over the noise of his jet engine.

He noticed there was a slight twinge of panic in the way the crowds were behaving. The loading of a nearby DC-9 was not going at an orderly pace. People were pushing and shoving each other — *squeezing* themselves up the loading ramp and into the airplane. Fistfights were breaking out near other airplanes.

This isn't just another busy night at the airport, he reasoned. It looked more like an evacuation . . .

He shut down the 16 and punched up his exotic anti-theft computer program. Once it kicked in, the airplane was not only theft-proof but, thanks to a zapping electrical charge that ran throughout its body, it was also tamper-proof. Convinced the airplane was secure, Hunter popped the canopy, grabbed his M-16, and climbed out.

The noise was deafening. He walked across the crowded tarmac, avoiding the crowds as best he could. He could see desperation in their faces, but they weren't a refugee rabble. They looked well-fed and mostly well-clothed. Yet people were battering each other to get on the airliners. But why? He noticed another curious thing: the incoming aircraft were not discharging anyone. They were flying in empty, loading up, and taking off without so much as a wipe of the windshield.

There were a lot of bad vibes in the air. He felt like a full-scale panic could break out at any moment.

Instinctively, he looked around for some kind of police force or military presence. There was none.

Nor were any of the aircraft of non-civilian design. His F-16 was the only military aircraft in the airport.

He made his way through the confusion to the control tower and found it too was a madhouse. There were more than forty air controllers, all barking orders into the microphones and frantically looking into their radar screens. The place was strewn with plates, half-eaten meals, pots of bubbling tea and coffee, and more than a few empty wine bottles. Hunter felt lucky he had made it down in one piece.

He was here to pay his landing fee, and perhaps get a little information. He sought out the head of the place, figuring this would be the man who should receive his "authorization fee." A man sitting at a desk slightly away from the pandemonium seemed to fit the bill.

Hunter threw a bag and a half of silver onto his desk. The man looked up immediately from the Arabic-language newspaper.

"I own that F-16 that just came in," Hunter told him.

The man looked him over. "Aren't you *Hawk Hunter*?" he said with a surprised look.

Hunter was taken aback slightly. Who the hell knew him way out here?

"Yes," he replied, looking into the older man's steel-black eyes. He was completely bald: a small, tough, a very distinguished-looking Arab. "My name *is* Hunter. I'm from the Pacific American—"

"—from the United States Air Force," the man said, cutting him off knowingly. "And the Thunderbirds. And the Northeast Economic Zone Air Patrol."

Hunter was speechless. He knew he had made somewhat of a name for himself back in America.

But had news of his exploits carried all the way over to North Africa?

The answer was no. However, a less-than-flattering mug shot of him had made the trip. The man reached inside his desk draw and came out with a bounty poster. It was for Hunter. His old service ID picture was on it, as were these words:

ONE BILLION DOLLARS IN SILVER OR GOLD FOR THE CAPTURE OR PROOF OF DEATH OF HAWK HUNTER, CRIMINAL WANTED BY THE NEW ORDER. COLLECTION POINTS: PARIS, THE BAHAMAS, MOSCOW.

"One billion?" Hunter blurted out. "Christ." He knew The Circle had put a price of a *half*-billion on his head about a year ago. *But a billion?* Apparently the New Order had doubled the pot.

This would only mean more trouble for Hunter.

"I could shoot you right now and collect, major," the man said.

Hunter had his M-16 off his shoulder and ready in an instant.

"But I won't," the man quickly added.

"What's the matter? You don't *need* a billion dollars?" Hunter asked defiantly.

"No, it's because I know who you *really* are, major," the man said, confidently lighting a long, dark cigarette. He was a native Moroccan. Hunter could tell by his accent. "And I know you're not a criminal."

The man rose, gathered in the silver, and motioned Hunter to a miniscule office at the rear of the control tower. They went inside and the man closed the door, effectively blocking out the noisy confusion of the air controllers.

"Said el-Fauzi," the man said, introducing himself, extending his hand. "It's an honor to meet you, major."

Hunter shook his hand. "Really? 'An honor'?"

"Yes, major," el-Fauzi said, producing a bottle and pouring out two drinks into miniature, porcelain cups. "I worked with U.S. Naval Intelligence during the war. We—everyone—knew of your F-16 squadron and the big air battles. After the war, the Russians let everyone know that you and your squadron were officially 'war criminals.' That's what you get for kicking their asses."

"But you also knew about the Zone Air Patrol," Hunter said.

"You mean ZAP?" el-Fauzi said. "Oh, we hear a lot of things here, major. All the time."

The office's window looked right out onto the tarmac. Hunter couldn't help but be distracted by the pandemonium outside.

"What's going on here?" he asked.

"Those people?" el-Fauzi said, sipping his drink. "Well, they're escaping, of course."

"Escaping?"

"Yes, major," el-Fauzi said, looking surprised. "Escaping. Getting out. Flying to South America. All of them. Before the war breaks out again."

"That seems to be on everyone's minds these days," Hunter said, tasting the thick, ultra-bitter liquor. His friend, Diego on the Azores, had talked about the imminent war.

"As well it should be, major," el-Fauzi said. "But isn't that why you are here in Casablanca?"

"To fight?" Hunter asked.

"Why, yes," el-Fauzi answered. "To join The Modern Knights."

21

"I don't know anything about any Modern Knights," Hunter said, reaching into his pocket. He produced a picture of Viktor.

"I am chasing this man," he said, handing the photo to el-Fauzi.

El-Fauzi took the photo and instantly dropped it as if it were on fire. "That's him!" he nearly screamed, his unflappable manner temporarily leaving him. "That is Lucifer!"

"Lucifer?" Hunter said. "Who the hell is Lucifer? That man is Viktor Robotov. He's a Russian agent. Caused a rather large misunderstanding back in America—one that left a couple hundred thousand or so people dead. So now I'm tracking him. Heard he might have passed through here."

"This man is the one they call *Lucifer,*" el-Fauzi said, downing his drink and pouring another. He was slowly regaining his composure. "He passed *over* us, some time ago."

" 'Passed over'?" Hunter asked.

"Yes," el-Fauzi said. "In his horrible black airplane. He had several free-lance fighters with him. Ran right through our airspace, shot down several planes, simply for being in their way."

Sounds like Viktor, Hunter thought.

"But, we know him as Lucifer," the Moroccan continued. "He's the most powerful man left in the Mediterranean. Europe. The Middle East. Anywhere. His allies hold every piece of major territory east of Tunisia all the way to the Sinai. He controls everything east of that. It is *he* who is to make war on the rest of the Mediterranean. People know it's coming. They're trying to get out now."

"And that's what this is all about?" Hunter asked, motioning towards the mass of humanity outside trying to fit onto the waiting airliners.

22

"Yes," el-Fauzi said, refilling their cups. "World War Three, major, is about to heat up again."

Hunter shook his head. That's just what Diego had said. He still couldn't believe it.

"Where is this Lucifer?" he asked. "Where's his base? His headquarters? Where is he right now?"

El-Fauzi laughed, then quickly became dead serious.

"He is *everywhere*," he whispered.

"You mean, his spies are everywhere?"

"Spies too," el-Fauzi said. "But the man himself. He walks among us, they say. He's seen frequently. Here. In Tunis. On Crete. Cairo. And farther east. Spreading terror. People are afraid just to look on his image. The poor believe him to have god-like powers. His face appears in the night sky, they say. Even looking at his photo can cause death."

Hunter closed his eyes and clenched his teeth. He realized that he hadn't been giving Viktor enough credit. He had sown his seeds of fear and hysteria in Europe and the Mediterranean just as effectively as he had in America.

"Who knows where he *really* is?" Hunter asked.

El-Fauzi laughed again. "One man, in town," he said. "The Lord. He'll tell you. He knows where *everyone* is. Come. I'll take you to him."

Chapter 3

A half-hour later they were in a jeep bouncing over a cratered highway, approaching the city of Casablanca. Or at least Hunter assumed it was Casablanca.

The city before him was brilliantly lit up, like a neon oasis in the middle of the desert. In fact Hunter felt it was *too* bright. A dozen multi-colored searchlights dashed across the night sky. From this distance, every building seemed to have all its lights on at once. Everywhere was blazing electricity. No wonder the light of the city could be seen from seventy miles out.

But, as a city, it also looked, well . . . too small to Hunter.

El-Fauzi, behind the wheel for the breakneck trip, roared into the city. Almost immediately the jeep was forced to slow down to a crawl, so crowded was the street. Everywhere were shops, eating places, gambling dens, rug stores, whorehouses, and cafes. And despite the late hour, the streets were filled with people, some dressed in authentic-looking Moroccan clothes, others wearing strange, 1940ish styles.

And everything was so goddamn bright!

Hunter had to shield his eyes to look at some of the streetlights. Finally he saw one that was broken and he realized it was a Kleig light, an ultra-powerful piece of illuminating equipment used for filming movies.

Then he noticed the buildings were very authentic. *Too* authentic. Nothing seemed out of place. That was the problem. From the stucco-type construction to the grand Arabic and English lettering, the "perfect" buildings looked more like movie props.

El-Fauzi knew what he was thinking. "It *is* a movie set," he explained. "Years ago, right before the war broke out, a Hollywood movie company came here, built this place. The real Casablanca was destroyed in the war. It's over the next hill—or what's left of it."

"Are you telling me that all these people are living on a movie set?" Hunter asked.

"That's right," el-Fauzi said. "Oh, they've added to it. And it's barely one-tenth the size of the real city, and that's only counting downtown. But when the war cooled down, there were a lot of people passing through this part of the world. We had a fairly serviceable airport, and we knew if it were operational, we could make money and survive. And why build another city? Hollywood built this one for us!"

"God, this place is wired," Hunter said, seeing mules of thick electrical cables stretched everywhere. "How can you afford to burn this much juice?"

" 'Juice' is one thing we have a lot of, major," el-Fauzi said, turning a corner and heading for the center of the small prop city. "Natural gas. It's everywhere. Under the ground. We've got gas turbines. A bunch of them. They drink the stuff. It's pure and they love it. They run like charms. So we

25

got more electricity than we need."

It was all starting to make sense to Hunter. The crazy kind of sense that served as normalcy in the New Order world.

The jeep screeched to a stop in front of a well-lit cafe. Crowds of people were streaming in and out. Many of them were beautiful women. A piano tinkled inside. A bright neon sign above the place featured a flashing palm tree and the establishment's name: "Rick's American Cafe."

"I think I've seen this movie," Hunter told el-Fauzi.

"We all have." El-Fauzi laughed, jumping out of the open jeep. "That's why they built this place. They were going to film it again!"

They went into the cafe and el-Fauzi hugged the *maitré d'*. They were soon escorted to the best table. A bottle of champagne appeared out of nowhere. Normally, Hunter would have felt silly. Most of the women present were wearing evening gowns; many of the men were in tuxedos. He was dressed in his flight suit, baseball cap on his head, flight boots on his feet, his helmet dangling from his belt, and the M-16 on his shoulder. Yet no one seemed to notice he wasn't exactly formal.

There were many soldiers there too. Officers mostly, wearing a wide range of dress uniforms, most with flashes of medals on their chests. Each officer appeared to be holding his own personal court with two, three, or four women. Those fancy uniforms did it every time. Most of the officers appeared to be unarmed. But Hunter could see their bodyguards lurking in the shadows, drinking at tables on the periphery of the action.

The air was thick with the smell of incense, hashish, cooking food, and sweet liquor. A beautiful young woman was singing on a stage nearby. A courtly black gentleman played a flawlessly moody piano. Again, everything was script-perfect.

El-Fauzi knew half the people who walked by the table, rising and kissing most of them once on each cheek. A waiter appeared, said nothing, and snapped his fingers. A searing rack of lamb materialized an instant later.

Hunter was legitimately hungry, and apparently so was el-Fauzi. The man attacked the piece of smoking meat with vigor. That's all Hunter needed. He started carving off pieces of the lamb for himself.

They sat and ate and drank two bottles of champagne. The band played, people danced. Hunter spent half the time eyeing the many, many beautiful women in the place—the other half wolfing down his meal.

They finished off the lamb in about twenty minutes. The meal cleared away, they sat sipping after-dinner drinks. Suddenly el-Fauzi said, "That's him."

Hunter turned to see a large man, wearing a white suit and a fez, stroll into the cafe and head for a dinner booth near the wall. Within seconds, other dark figures moved toward the booth. Some stopped briefly to whisper something to the large man, then hurried on their way. It was obvious he was some kind of top dog.

"That's the Lord," el-Fauzi told Hunter. "Lord Lard. Very rich. Very powerful. He's big in arms sales. He can get fighters, tanks, SAMs, ammo. He has connections. No one is sure just where. Italy, some say. Some say Sicily or even Sardinia. But he sells to anyone, any side, any leader, any flag. Deals only in gold, no silver."

"And this is the guy who's going to tell me where I can find Viktor?" Hunter asked.

"If anyone knows, Lard does," el-Fauzi said. El-Fauzi rose and walked over to the man. A second later, he was motioning Hunter to join them.

Hunter squeezed into the man's booth and found a martini sitting in front of him. El-Fauzi whispered something to Lard, then turned to Hunter. "You'll excuse me," he said, with a wink. "There's an old friend of mine—a stewardess—whom I must absolutely buy a drink for. We'll talk later."

El-Fauzi's quick exit seemed designed to leave Hunter and Lard alone.

"So you're the famous criminal, Hawk Hunter," Lard said, a smile wrinkling his plump face. His accent was vaguely British. "What's the asking price for your head these days, major?"

"I understand it keeps going up all the time," Hunter replied.

"Not many criminals will The New Order pay a billion dollars for, Hunter," Lard said, swigging his martini. "A man could buy a country and rent an army with that kind of money."

"Spoken like a true businessman," Hunter told him.

Laud laughed. "But I understand you are not here to fight, Hunter. This surprises me. There are probably more mercenaries per square mile between here and Algeria than anywhere, ever, in history."

"Well, there's never been a shortage of mercenaries," Hunter said. "The world can get along without another one."

"Oh, major, this is no time to stick to your lofty ideals," Lard said. "Do you realize that when this war starts up again, half the troops on both sides will be paid mercenaries? Hundreds of thousands of soldiers, millions of dollars. You, Hunter, alone could make millions, probably hundreds of millions.

If you're worth a billion dollars to The New Order, you're worth at least half that to whoever wants to win the most when the war kicks back up."

Hunter reached inside his flight suit and pulled out the picture of Viktor. He passed it to Lard.

"Who is this guy?" he asked.

Lard produced a monocle and examined the photo. "Ah, Hunter," he said, handing it back to him. "Don't tell me you've got yourself tangled up with the almighty 'Lucifer'?"

"Forget this 'Lucifer' bullshit," Hunter told him. "I know this man as Viktor Robotov. I'm damn sure he's a Russian agent. He was recently in America engineering a war that set us back four to five years. He's a master terrorist."

"Terrorist? Oh, but he is also a 'god,' this Lucifer," Lard said mockingly.

Hunter was getting aggravated. "Look, I know he's a manipulator and a genius for brainwashing the masses. But pumping this guy up like he's a god — it's a joke. Who the hell can believe it?"

Lard laughed again, and gulped down the rest of the martini. "Major Hunter, get with it. This is The New Order. Look at yourself. You're sitting in a movie set that people have turned into a *real* thing. *They* believe it. So it's real. They'll believe anything. People want to follow gods, major. 'Lucifer' makes sense to half of them. And he's paying the other half."

Hunter didn't want to waste any more time. "Where is he?" he said. "Where's his HQ?"

Lard opened his mouth as if to say something, but only one word came out. It sounded like "Algiers." Then a bloody foam flowed up from his throat and out his mouth. His eyes turned up and his head slammed down on the table in front of him with a loud "wham!"

Lard was dead. Poisoned. Probably by the martini. Luckily Hunter had never cared for the petrol-tasting gin bombs, and he had left his untouched.

The sound of Lard's head cracking on the table had been loud enough to stop the singer singing and the piano-player playing. Two soldiers — undoubtably Lard's hired security people — appeared and helplessly shook the body. They knew they'd fucked up. Someone should have been testing the drinks.

More soldiers appeared. Guns were being drawn. All of a sudden it seemed as if everyone in the place was carrying a piece. Hunter turned around and tried to catch sight of el-Fauzi, but the man was long gone. He immediately had the sinking feeling that either he or the big fat slob on the table in front of him had been set up.

Hunter knew it was time to leave. A dangerous tension ripped through the cafe. Suddenly the lights went out, and that's when the lead started flying. Women screamed, men yelled as there was a mad dash for the darkened door. Guns were going off all around him, though he never figured out who was shooting at whom, or why. He had dropped down to the floor at the sound of the first gunshot, glad he was carrying his flight helmet. He quickly put it on and checked the clip in his M-16. As usual it was filled with tracer rounds.

He made his way along the line of tables, feeling in front of him with the snout of the M-16. The only light around him was coming from the many gun flashes erupting all over the club. Soon the place was thick with the smell of spent gunpowder.

He spied the front door and noticed that most of the crowd had made good their escape. However, an unhealthy barrage of pistol fire was coming from very close to the exit. It was concentrating on some unseen enemy located at the back of the room. Bullets were pinging and ricocheting around the darkened cafe, sometimes accompanied by a groan or a scream when one of them found flesh. This was no place to be, he thought. Still, he couldn't help thinking that this sort of thing must apparently happen quite often at the cafe.

He decided to create a distraction, something that would cause everyone to take cover and give him the precious four or five seconds he would need to make a break for the front door.

He raised the M-16's nose until it was pointing at the ceiling, then ripped off a long burst of tracers. The bright trails of white-hot phosphorous illuminators lit up the interior of the cafe brilliantly. The bullets scraped the plastered ceiling, causing a rain of cracked and sparkling material to fall. The chatter of the automatic weapon filled the walls with a loud, echoing, dangerous sound. Immediately all the gunmen dove for cover.

Hunter was out the door in three seconds . . .

He found the jeep unattended outside the cafe. El-Fauzi was nowhere to be seen. Despite the gunplay in the club, the people in the streets of the movie set town seemed unaffected. Hunter started the jeep and headed back for the airport, glad to be out of the strange place.

The airport was even more crowded, more confused, more desperate than before. The F-16 was sitting untouched. He resisted the temptation to go looking for el-Fauzi; whatever the man's motives had been, Hunter was sure he would be impossible to find. Besides, with the situation at the airport deteriorating rapidly, he wanted to get off as quickly as possible. His search for clues to Viktor's whereabouts would have to continue in some other place.

He climbed aboard the F-16 and started to warm up the avionics. A wave of a bag of silver was all that was needed to flag down a passing fuel truck, and soon his tanks were full. Without bothering to contact the control tower, he taxied out onto the runway and took off on the tail of a battered Brazilian 707.

Minutes later, he turned northeast. Lard's last word had been "Algiers," and Hunter figured that was as good a place as any to resume his search for Viktor.

Chapter 4

Hunter was glad to get away from Casablanca. The place was just too weird for him. Movie-set towns. The airborne evacuation. El-Fauzi. Lard. The gun battle at the cafe. All the talk of war and armies of mercenaries waiting to go at it was particularly disturbing. So was the billion-dollar bounty on his head. He'd have to be extra careful about watching his tail. That poisoned drink could very well have been meant for him instead of Lard. And he was sure that word would spread quickly that he was in the area. It all had such an unreal atmosphere about it.

And he couldn't help thinking that the spectre of Viktor — or Lucifer — was lurking behind it all.

He set a course low over the Moroccan desert, heading for Algeria and the unknown. He had to expect the unexpected. Play it smart. If war were about to break out in the region, he'd have to assume that any population center would be equipped with SAMs, maybe interceptors. Both of which he wanted to avoid. The sand-skimming course over the desert seemed to be his best choice.

Suddenly he *felt* trouble. His well-developed sixth

33

sense — particularly attuned to nearby hostile air-craft — had his body tingling. He checked his long-range radar, which soon confirmed his feelings. There were two fighters approaching him from the northwest. They were moving fast and they were heavily armed.

He instinctively checked his instruments. Everything looked good until he went to test-fire his specially designed "Six Pack" of M-61 Vulcan cannons in the nose of the F-16. To his surprise, a push of the trigger produced nothing. Another push, still nothing. According to his panel lights, everything was in order. Strange . . . He quickly rerouted the fire command through his flight computer. Still nothing.

Someone *had* tampered with the airplane while it was parked at Casablanca, he knew it. He punched up his air-to-air missile-arming program. It too was drawing a blank. Sabotage! He should have expected it, although the electrically charged alarm system had never failed him before. An expert had done the dirty deed. But he'd have to figure out who the culprit was later. Right now, he needed to concentrate on the approaching interceptors.

He booted the 16 up to full military speed and was glad to feel the afterburner kick in so smoothly. The saboteur had apparently only tinkered with his armaments and not the airplane's power plant. He stayed down low, hoping to skirt the look-down radar the interceptors might be carrying. His pursuers were just twenty miles behind him. He was sure he could outrun them to Algiers, but what would happen then?

"F-16, F-16." His radio suddenly burst to life. "This is the Gibraltar Defense Force. You are in an unauthorized air zone. Prepare for interception."

He was "unauthorized" again. Yet he didn't feel threatened. The voice on the radio was British. Oddly, it did not sound hostile. Just serious. Hunter felt instinctively drawn to trust it.

"Gibraltar Defense," he radioed back. "This is Major Hawk Hunter of the Pacific American Air Corps. I was unaware this was restricted air space. Request permission to leave the area at once."

"F-16." The voice came back. "You are not only in a restricted airspace, you are also traveling at illegally high rate of speed. You must be cited. We are tracking you with long-range missiles. We will fire if we have to. Please reduce speed and prepare for interception."

High speed? Cited? What the hell was this?

Hunter decided to slow down and let the interceptors catch up to him. He was unarmed, and although he knew he could have outran the long-range air-to-airs, with all the twisting and turning required more than half his fuel would be burned up uselessly. Anyway, the interceptor pilots didn't sound menacing.

They were Tornados. Impressive fighters that had been made back in the old days by a group of European companies. Hunter had seen many of them during the air battles over France. They were a rugged, versatile, even-flying aircraft, one of the best in the world.

They came up on either side of him. They were definitely British—both airplanes had Union Jacks painted on their tail sections. One moved in closer to his port wing and gave a gentlemanly wave.

"Sorry, F-16, but you'll have to follow us," he radioed over. "Course seven-two-niner Tango. Our base is thirty-four kilos northwest."

Hunter waved back. Something about the British.

No matter what, they always *sounded* so civilized.

The Tornados pulled ahead and turned northwest. Hunter followed.

The air base was actually a small, straight stretch of abandoned highway with a half-dozen large tents on either side. A long fuel truck sat off on the edge of the makeshift runway; jeeps and personnel carriers moved about. Several Rapier anti-aircraft missile batteries ringed the base. Two other Tornados were parked on metal plates that served as temporary parking stations on the highway shoulder.

The two British interceptors landed in formation and Hunter came in right after them. They taxied to their assigned metal plates, while Hunter rolled along to the center of the base. Several men waited there. A ground mechanic directed him in with a pair of red flags and gave him the thumbs-up when he was in the correct parking position. He shut down the engine, popped the canopy, and climbed out to meet the men.

They were all officers of the Royal Air Force, dressed in the correct desert fatigues. As one, they snapped to a perfect opened-palmed salute. Hunter returned it as best he could. One officer stepped forward—a man with bright red hair and an enormous mustache to match. He walked over and shook Hunter's hand.

"Captain Stewart Heath," he said in a slight Cockney accent. "Sorry about all this, Major Hunter."

"Well, it's been a hell of a long time since I've got a speeding ticket," Hunter said.

Heath pointed to the two taxiing pilots. "They're just young bucks, major," Heath said. "Just a tad, shall we say, 'enthusiastic'?"

Hunter smiled for the first time. "They're just doing their job," he said.

"I'm glad you see it that way, major," Heath said with a grin. "Now there will be a smallish fine. But not too much. Say, a quarter bag of silver. And if you pay it up right now, I can invite you to have breakfast with us with a clear conscience."

Hunter reached into his flight-suit pocket and came up with a small bag of coins. A lieutenant appeared, and Hunter handed him the bag. He returned the gesture with a salute.

Heath clapped his hands once loudly. "Smashing," he said, beaming. "Now, major, please. Will you join us?"

Although it seemed as if he had just finished his roasted lamb feast at the cafe, Hunter found himself hungry again. Plus he genuinely liked the Brits.

"Okay," he agreed. "Could always use a little more chow."

The entire group of officers, along with the two intercepting pilots, adjourned to a large tent where a meal of scrambled eggs, rolls, and tea was already waiting for them. Everyone helped themselves and settled down at the cafeteria-style benches to eat. Heath sat next to Hunter.

"We've heard of you, of course, Major Hunter," Heath told him. "When our boys radioed in they were tracking an F-16, well, there's only one F-16 flying these days, so we're told."

"What are you guys doing way out here?" Hunter asked him.

"It's a long story," Heath said, sipping his tea. "After the war cooled down, we—our wing of the RAF, that is—came into possession of the land on both sides of Gibraltar. We must patrol this far, to watch our southern flank. The speed-limit rule is simply one more way we can control the airspace. It keeps the troublemakers out, plus if we see anything coming our way at full boot, well, we'll know he's an enemy, won't we?"

Hunter couldn't argue with the typically British logic.

"Are you here to join the war, major?" one of the other officers asked across the table.

Hunter shook his head. "Believe it or not, the answer is no," he said. "In fact, up until a short time ago, I had no idea this war — or any other war — was going on."

"Oh, but you are out of touch over in America," Heath said. "It's not the 'quick jump over the pond' that it used to be."

"How true, captain," Hunter agreed. "We are very isolated. And we're embroiled in so many of our own problems, we don't have time to catch up on what's happening over here. But, by God, I would never have thought the big war was still going on."

"Well, in fairness to you Americans, the war did calm down a bit for nearly two years," Heath told him. "Became sort of a 'phony war,' actually. The Soviets were too weak to lift a gun right after . . . well, after the dirty bastards nuked you. Many countries had entire armed units still intact. Most settled where they stood. We were at the RAF base on Gibraltar when the armistice was declared. We sat there — on our base — for close to seven months. No one came to disarm us. Only then did we realize the Russians couldn't throw together five working divisions in Europe on a bet. So we started, well, moving about a bit."

He courteously refilled Hunter's plate with eggs

and his cup with tea. Then he continued.

"It was about a year ago when we realized that the Russians were suddenly desperately light on the surface-to-airs. That's when we started flying long-range patrols. With nothing to shoot at us, we were flying as far north and east as Berlin. For the most part, we didn't see any appreciable Russian strength anywhere."

"You said they were short on SAMs," Hunter said.

"Yes, it was the most curious thing," Heath said. "We had our eyes on them, of course. And we were in contact with other RAF bases. And it seemed as if their SAM forces just dwindled overnight. It was such a strange thing for them to do, leave themselves open like that. They gave up whatever control they might have had over the European airspace. And there weren't enough MIGs around to make much of a difference. Plus a lot of their men defected."

"They withdrew their SAMs and sent them to America," Hunter told him. "They tried to split the continent right in half. Came close to doing it too. We just got through with them. It was rough."

"By God, major, are you serious?" Heath said. "We had no idea you were having a go with the Russkies over there."

Hunter settled back and told them the whole story. The formation of The Circle, the SAMs hidden in The Badlands, the ferocious battle between the democratic Western Forces and the fanatical, Soviet puppet armies of The Circle. The British officers were at once fascinated and flabbergasted by the tale.

"They took a huge risk," Heath said at the end of the story. "They were so intent on keeping you Yanks down."

"Well, they've set us back," Hunter said with bitterness in his voice. "And that's why I'm here."

He reached inside his pocket and pulled out the picture of Viktor.

"I've been tracking this man," he said, handing the photo to Heath. "He's responsible for the whole Circle War."

Heath looked at the photo. "Why, this is the Lucifer bloke," he said. "The Madman of the Mediterranean. He's behind all the war talk right now."

"Well, he's the one who formed The Circle," Hunter said. "We know him as Viktor Robotov. He's a Russian agent, obviously high up on the ladder. He's the guy that got the Soviets to sneak in their SAMs."

"Well, he's quite dangerous," Heath said. "He's got almost a cult following. I've seen videotapes of him. Religious, socialist, anarchic rubbish. It's all jibberish. But he's pushing the right button in the lowest common denominator, if you will."

"He did the same thing in America," Hunter said. "That's why I'm on his tail."

Heath stroked his fiery red mustache. "Well, you've taken on quite a task for yourself, major," he said. "I believe Lucifer is busy relighting World War Three right now. I'm not so sure he'll have time for you."

Hunter only smiled and said, "We'll see."

Chapter 5

He enjoyed talking to the Brits. They offered to give him a look at one of their Tornados, an invitation Hunter readily accepted. He loved airplanes and airplane design. He'd go anywhere, anytime, and talk airplanes with just about anyone.

After he went over every inch of the British fighter, it was time to turn his attention to his own airplane and its sabotaged firing system.

It took him less than a minute to find the problem. The saboteurs had been clever. They hadn't tripped the electric-shock alarm because they hadn't touched the airplane's body. Nothing was tampered with, no wires were cut. Instead the saboteurs, most likely using a small laser, had cut through a thin seam on the side of the airplane's radardome located on its snout. Once through, the laser zapped the hundred or so semiconductors attached to its sophisticated logic center. The result: no weapons.

Hunter could fix the problem, but only by hot-wiring all the systems back to the power generator—a slow, time-consuming, two-day job at the least. But it was clear he couldn't go on without his defenses. He decided to take advantage of being in a friendly base. The Brits told him he could stay as long as he liked.

That night he lay in the visitor's tent, wrestling with his bug netting. An hour before, he had finished eating a hardy meal with the Brits, downing several cold Algerian beers along the way. Now the desert was cooling down and Hunter was looking forward to a good night's sleep.

Having finally solved the bug net, he lay on his bunk thinking. He reached inside his flight-suit pocket and took out a small flag. He unfolded it and fingered the material. It was his most prized possession: a small American flag. He carried it with him everywhere — ever since he'd taken it from a citizen he saw shot in war-torn New York City right after returning from the European theater years before.

The flag meant so much to him. It was the last symbol he knew of that reached back to the days before the big war started. Back when his country was called The United States of America. Back when there was that special unity found in all Americans. Back when it wasn't illegal to carry this flag. It was a law he defied every day of his life. He would gladly die fighting for his right to carry the Stars and Stripes. For his right to remember what it used to be like. For his right to dream what it might someday be again . . .

Also inside his pocket he carried a picture of Dominique. What was she to him? His girlfriend? His lover? His soul mate? She was in Canada now, in friendly hands, recovering from a terrible two-year ordeal in which Viktor had kidnapped her and used her shamelessly for his twisted, brainwashing

Circle War campaign.

Hunter's heart started thumping whenever he thought of her.

He was handsome. Taller than most fighter pilots, and slightly quiet. He had been a certified genius as a child, a doctor in aeronautics from MIT at seventeen, and flying Air Force fighters by nineteen. He was recognized as the best fighter pilot that had ever lived — a reputation helped in great part, he knew, by his amazing sixth sense and the way it integrated into every action he performed while flying. Hunter didn't just *fly* an airplane — he became one with it.

Some women found him dashing. He enjoyed them all. But no one — no one — affected him like Dominique. Ever since that day they'd met in war-torn France, she'd been with him. They had lived together briefly, but he had sent her away because it was too dangerous to remain where they were. Then she had been spirited off by Viktor's agents, and would still be with the madman today if Hunter hadn't rescued her.

But now, here he was, separated from the woman he loved, chasing some brainwashing lunatic across the top of Africa. His life had never been simple, and he didn't expect it to change anytime soon.

Hunter had been in a deep sleep for three hours when he suddenly sat bolt upright . . .

Missiles. Fired from way off. Coming this way . . .

He was up and running in a matter of seconds. Across the sand, across the highway-runway, toward the only tent at the small base that still had a light burning in it. It was the Scramble Tent, where two pilots waited on call around the clock.

43

Hunter burst in, startling the two British officers, who had been sitting calmly playing a game of cribbage.

"Missiles!" Hunter said. "There's three of them coming this way!"

The two pilots looked at him as if he were mad. "I say, major," one drawled. "Are you sure?"

He didn't hang around long enough to reply. He was running again, this time to his F-16.

The 16 was the fastest-warming airplane in the world. Unlike other fighters, it could be started unassisted by the pilot and rolling for takeoff in under forty-five seconds. Hunter routinely cut that time to less than a half minute.

He fired up the F-16's engine and moved out onto the runway. He could *feel* the missiles coming in from the northeast, probably launched by an aircraft somewhere out of the Med. He switched on his radar and immediately got three clear readings. They were sophisticated "fire-and-forget" missiles — deadly flying bombs that locked into a target from far off and homed in unerringly over distances of up to 100 miles or even more. Hunter knew these missiles were just 50 miles from the British base and closing fast.

He roared off the runway, noting out of the corner of his eye that the two British pilots were running to their Tornados.

Hunter was still unarmed, his firing system still disconnected. But he knew he had to stop the missiles somehow. He turned the 16 in the direction of the oncoming rockets and booted in the afterburner. He had a visual sighting on them in twenty seconds.

They were flying in a straight line separated by a mile apiece — mindless instruments of destruction all too reminiscent of the Nazi buzz bombs of World

44

War II.

Hunter would have to work fast, and still he doubted if he could stop all three of them.

The night was pitch-black and the inside of his cockpit was ashimmer in the green light of his TV screens. He put the 16 into a wicked 180-degree turn, the G-forces stretching the muscles on his face into a grim smile. He got on the tail of the third trailing missile and quickly calculated its exact speed and altitude. He pumped the numbers into his flight computer and pushed a button. More lights flashed as the computer went to work. Instantly, the F-16 moved right up beside the missile. He took over manual control of the jet again and maneuvered the 16's wing towards the short control and steering stub of the missile. Deftly, he moved the airplane up a little. Then more to the right. Now down a touch. It was a dangerous, delicate maneuver—both he and the missile were traveling at 400 mph plus. One wrong move and they'd be picking him up in little pieces all over the desert.

He took a deep gulp from his oxygen mask and slid the 16 in closer to the missile. With an irritating scraping noise, the F-16's right wing moved up and underneath the missile's. He knew he could only hold the precarious position for a few seconds. With the flick of his wrist, he jerked the control stick to the left. The F-16's wing bumped the missile's stub just enough to upset its predetermined course. The missile's gyro-system immediately overloaded, causing its targeting system to go blank. The missile did a complete flip-over, then plunged into the sands below, detonating in a huge explosion.

But Hunter didn't even see the flash. He was already moving up and into position on the second missile.

He didn't have time to be so fancy with rocket number two. The base was just ten miles away. He caught up with the missile and pulled ahead and slightly above it. Then he gradually brought the F-16 down until the jet engine's hot exhaust was blowing directly into the missile's air-intake duct. Instantly the missile's fuel-combustion chamber became overheated by the F-16's aftersmoke. Hunter bit his lip and held the risky position for seven long seconds before sharply veering away. Just in time, as the fuel ignited and the missile self-destructed in midair.

But there was still one missile left and now, with the base in view, he knew he would not be able to stop it.

The missile impacted exactly where his F-16 had been parked, causing a large blast of fire and dust. Luckily the two scramble pilots had warned the rest of the base before taking off in the two Tornados. The explosion was far enough away from the base's other two airplanes so as not to cause any damage. However, as he streaked over the base and watched helplessly, Hunter could see that three of the base tents—those holding their valuable supplies—were burning ferociously. The base's water supply was also hit.

He landed by the light of the fires and taxied to the far end of the runway. Without water, the base's personnel were helpless in fighting the flames. They could only move as much equipment as possible away from the blazing supply tents.

Hunter jumped out of the F-16 and ran to meet Heath, who was directing the emergency operation.

"That was a bad one, it was," Heath said, looking at the base's supplies going up in smoke.

"You've been attacked like this before?" Hunter asked.

"Twice," Heath said grimly. "But only by one missile at a time. Three missiles at us means someone was serious this time. If you hadn't stopped those other two, we'd have all been killed."

But Hunter wasn't taking any bows. The one rocket that made it through had impacted exactly where the 16 had been parked.

"They might have been going for me," he told Heath. "The New Order has a hefty price on my head and I think someone is trying to collect."

"Don't be crazy, old boy," Heath said, smiling and giving him a reassuring pat on the back. "There's no way you can be certain that missile had your name on it. As I said, we've been attacked before. They're trying to soften us up before the war starts up again. Anyone trying to start trouble in the Med knows they have to deal with our Tornados. They were just being a bit, well, 'preemptive,' I'd say."

Hunter appreciated Heath's effort to cheer him up, but he also knew the officer was wrong: those long-range missiles could definitely be targeted down to the last inch. All it would have taken was for a spy atop one of the sand dunes overlooking the base to send a message back to the launch crew in the Med, pinpointing the exact position of Hunter's F-16. In fact, all three missiles could have been targeted for the F-16. If it hadn't been for his own "early warning system," his precious jet would be a piece of charred wreckage right now. And Hunter would be the first to admit that taking out his airplane was the next best thing to putting a bullet between his eyes.

Still, he couldn't be absolutely certain the missile attack was an assassination attempt.

"Okay," Hunter said, knowing it was smart to consider all possibilities. "Do you think this is the work of Viktor—or Lucifer, if you prefer?"

"More likely one of his many rotting allies," Heath answered. "Those missiles were probably launched somewhere off Melilla or near the coast of Algeria. Off a boat, I'd say. You might have guessed airplanes, but we don't find many airborne free-lancers in these parts. There's a definite shortage of working fighters.

"That's why our Tornados—and your F-16 there—are so valuable."

A junior officer ran up to them. "They got the radio, sir," he said smartly. "The bugger fused together when the missile hit."

"Blast!" Heath said. "I needed that radio to report this and to request more stores. Well, I guess now we'll have to jump in one of the Tors and go tell Command personally."

The flames started to die down. The sun was just peeking over the sand dunes. Already, the cold desert night air was beginning to warm up.

"Let me help," Hunter said. "You'll need an escort. I'll gladly go along."

"Well, that's sporting of you, Hunter," Heath said. "I accept. I know my commanders will want to talk to you anyway."

"Talk?" Hunter asked. "About what?"

Heath looked at him and grinned. "Oh, about this Lucifer," he said. "The war. Maybe some employment."

"Well, I'm not looking for a job," Hunter told him.

Heath let out a hearty laugh. "I must warn you, major," he said. "My commanders can be very persuasive . . ."

Chapter 6

Hunter had never seen the Rock of Gibraltar before. The goddamn thing was four times as big as he'd imagined it to be. It was one of the world's most important crossroads: the tip of Europe, the beginning of Africa. The only entrance to the western end of the Med and traditionally a strategic piece of real estate, Gibraltar was even more vital in the New Order world.

The trip up to the RAF base took only a matter of twenty minutes for the two supersonic jets. Hunter accompanied Heath after quickly jury-rigging two of the F-16's six nose cannons. The British officer told him it would be easier and quicker to fix the rest of his Six Pack along with the Sidewinder launch system at the main Gibraltar base.

They had flown out over the Atlantic and approached from the west. The landing pattern brought them in right next to the big rock. Hunter could see the Brits had put gun and SAM emplacements all over it, as well as some long-range missiles near its peak. A battery of radar dishes was spinning at its absolute summit, and a swarm of helicopters looked to be in perpetual orbit around the massive chunk of stone. It was defense in depth. Anyone unfriendly—either floating or flying—who attempted to enter the Med would find themselves at the mercy of the British guns and missiles.

Within minutes, Hunter found himself down and taxiing up to a camouflaged terminal building. Heath had been right when he said jet fighters were in short supply in the area. Hunter saw only a few Tornados, a Sea Harrier jet minus its VTOL Pegasus engine, and an ancient Jaguar. Not surprisingly, a crowd gathered around Hunter's F-16 as soon as he pulled up to his holding station. Next to the Tornados, the jet was the most sophisticated piece of equipment to fly through the base in two years.

Heath joined him as he climbed down from the cockpit and together they walked to the base's command center. Hunter couldn't help but notice the harbor base was buzzing with activity.

"All this is preparation for Lucifer?" Hunter asked Heath.

"You might say that," Heath said, an air of mystery in his voice.

They entered the building and bounded up the stairs. Everywhere people were bustling, moving about. There was a smell of urgency to it all.

Heath knocked smartly on a glass office door and let himself in. Hunter followed him into the office, where six men—all RAF officers—stood around a large map located in the center of the room.

"Heath reporting, sir!"

"Heath," the oldest of the officers responded. "Good to see you, man." The officer who spoke was about fifty, wore a neatly trimmed mustache, and was obviously tough as nails. "We weren't expecting you, although we couldn't raise you in the Marconi earlier this morning."

"Had a bit of trouble, sir," Heath told the man. "Some bastard tried to take us out last night, sir. With three missiles, sea-launched, I suspect."

"Really, Heath?" the man said, walking from around the table and towards them. "Anyone hurt?"

"No sir," Heath replied. "Only one missile made it through. Caught three of our supply tents and the water supply, sir. Melted down the radio when it hit too, sir."

"Three missiles and only one hit?" the senior officer asked.

"Yes, sir, thanks to Major Hunter here," Heath said, by way of introducing Hunter.

The officer looked him over. "Hawk Hunter?" he asked.

"Yes, that's right," Hunter answered, shaking hands with the man. Hunter was thinking he was maybe *too* well known in these parts.

Heath politely completed the introduction. "This is Sir Neil Asten, commanding officer of the Royal Gibraltar Defense Forces."

The three men walked to a private office off the main conference room. Heath quickly filled in the officer on how Hunter had come to land at the desert highway base.

"Odd how these things happen, Major Hunter," Sir Neil said, settling behind the office's desk and rummaging through its drawers. "We heard you were in Casablanca and we've been trying to locate *you* ever since. Now, here you walk right in on us."

"You were trying to contact me?" Hunter asked. "Why?"

Sir Neil gave Heath a wink and then grinned

51

broadly. He pulled a bottle out of his bottom drawer, along with three shot glasses. He quickly filled each glass with what looked to Hunter to be bathtub gin.

Taking his glass and raising it in toast, Neil said, "To the Crown!"

"To the Crown!" Heath joined in.

"Cheers," Hunter said, "I guess."

All three men knocked back the gin in one motion, then sat down.

"Yes, major, we were very interested in getting in touch with you when we heard you'd landed at Casablanca," Sir Neil said. "You're a brave man cavorting about North Africa with a billion-dollar price tag on your head."

"I'm going after the man you've come to know as Lucifer," Hunter told him, quickly retelling the story of the Circle War and Viktor/Lucifer's hand in it. "He succeeded in disrupting our rebuilding efforts back in America, and he did it with a lot of Soviet help. I'm tracking him down to make sure he doesn't get away with it."

"Well, I'm sure my officers have told you that Mister Lucifer is rather . . . preoccupied now," Sir Neil said.

"So I've heard," Hunter replied. "But I can't let that stop me."

"And it shouldn't!" Sir Neil said enthusiastically. He gave a conspiratorial look to Heath. "In fact, major, I think our goals are similar. We too want to stop Lucifer before he re-ignites this never-ending war again."

Hunter wished the Englishman would get to the point.

"We would like to offer you a proposition, major," Sir Neil said, refilling their glasses. "A 'consulting' job, you might say."

Hunter held up his hand and said politely: "As I told Captain Heath, I'm not looking for a job. I am on a mission—technically speaking, for the Pacific American Air Corps—to apprehend Lucifer. I know the dangers involved. It's almost like trying to kidnap Hitler, I suppose. But this is what I'm here for. I feel I have to work alone on it."

Sir Neil thought a moment, then said, "Once again, major, I must say that I admire your courage. Lucifer has committed a huge crime against America in starting that Circle War, and obviously you Yanks want to make him pay. To that I say, 'Here! Here!'

"But you must be realistic, major. We are on the brink of a major war here too. One that will affect America as much as it affects us here in the Med. In fact, it will likely affect the entire world as much as the Big One did.

"You see, when we say that World War Three never really ended, it's not just a matter of historical note. We never signed any armistice agreement with The New Order, and in our opinion, neither did you Yanks. You were betrayed, pure and simple. And that stopped the major fighting. But the war—its causes, its aims, its effects—did not end when your traitor Vice-President signed away your country. It provided a lull, major. A satisfying lull for the Reds, as they were so beaten—and still are—they could barely lift a finger to pull a trigger.

"But look at what they *did* do. Weakened as they were, they still gambled and brought the battle to you back in America. Sure, they were using Lucifer in order to disrupt your rebuilding efforts. But don't you see? Mr. Lucifer was also using *them*. He's a war profiteer of the highest, ugliest order.

"It is not the first time in history, major, that a

war has started and had its direction, its motives, its eventual winners and losers change midstream. We British are maybe more sensitive to it than you Americans, because our history is longer and, I'm almost ashamed to say, more militant. Centuries ago, we fought wars that went on for years — decades — even more than a hundred years. These wars were a constant shifting of alliances, with many prolonged lulls in actual battles too, I might add.

"Things are no different here, major. Yes, World War Three started when the Soviets gassed Western Europe. Yes, huge battles were fought around the world, battles that NATO and the democracies won. And, yes, your Vice-President was a traitor and he signed America off. But that did not end the war, Hunter. In fact, you could look at your Circle War as just one more campaign of World War Three."

Hunter knew Heath had been right when he said his commanding officer could be very persuasive. The Wingman had never thought of The Circle War as being anything more than just that — a war for the American continent, just like the Battle for Football City. But putting it in the larger context of a *continuation* of World War III made some sense. It also served to light yet another fire deep down inside Hunter. Simply put: if World War III was not yet over, then the United States didn't really lose.

Not yet, anyway.

"You see, major," Heath said. "Those countries and states left in Western Europe are just now beginning to recognize the evil and destructiveness this Lucifer represents. No one had even heard about him until a few months ago. But obviously he's been planning this war all along, even while he was devastating your country.

"Only now are the Western Europeans in the

process of raising armies. But it's not like the old days, when governments could issue a draft or call-up. Much of Europe now is similar to the feudal societies that prevailed hundreds of years ago. Not the strictly lord-over-peasant rubbish. But in most cases, the people work for the person who owns the land they live on or the factory they work in. Remember, while a good part of Western Europe's population was killed in the Soviets' gas attack, many of the buildings and factories were left standing. Indeed, that was the Russians' aim! Kill the people but preserve the industry, the very spoils of war.

"Now some of those factories are back up and working. And the workers owe allegiance to the factory owner or whoever. It is these rather wealthy people who are raising their armies to try and stop Lucifer. They are known by the rather grandiose name of The Modern Knights.

"But you see, Hunter, we were already in place here. When the specter of Lucifer rose, The Modern Knights contacted us and asked for one thing: time. Time for them to raise, equip, train, and—most important—move their armies. We immediately saw their point and, knowing full well the critical situation, we agreed. Now they have agreed to fund our operation—with certain qualifications, that is."

Sir Neil poured out three more drinks. Gradually, Hunter was becoming fascinated by this contemporary history lesson. Still, he had no desire to be caught up in anything which would steer him away from his very personal goal: the pursuit of Viktor.

Sir Neil lifted his glass in another toast, but this was confined to a quick and unelaborate "Cheers" before the man drained the shot. Hunter and Heath did likewise.

"We have a plan, Major Hunter," Sir Neil continued. "One that could thwart a large part of Lucifer's war-making sickness. One that could strike a pre-emptive blow and delay this new phase of the war long enough for The Modern Knights to move their armies. But it is a bold plan. One that needs all the help we can muster. This is why, when we heard you were in the area, we wanted to contact you, major."

Hunter once again began to speak up. "I find this all very interesting, but —"

Sir Neil raise his hand. "Please, major, let me at least tell you of our plan. I think you'll see that our cause and your goal are one in the same."

He paused for a moment, then continued. "Our idea is to strike quicker than Lucifer. Seize and hold a very important strategic point just a few days before The Modern Knights and their armies arrive."

"Where is this strategic point?" Hunter asked.

Sir Neil looked at Heath, then back at Hunter. He was heartened that the American was showing some interest. "You realize, major, that this is all very, very hush-hush."

Hunter nodded. "Of course."

"And that if we bring you into our confidence you will become one of only about twenty individuals who know our intentions."

"Yes, I understand," Hunter said. His curiosity — or was it the gin? — was getting the best of him.

Once again, Sir Neil smiled broadly.

"Okay, Major," Sir Neil said, rising and pulling down a map on the wall behind his desk. It showed the entire Middle East and Africa region in detail. "Let me preface this by saying that the majority of Lucifer's forces — The Legion, he calls them — are concentrated in what used to be called Saudi Arabia.

That country was hit pretty hard during the first clashes of the Big War, and not just by neutron bombs either. The government was wiped out, and so was most of their oil production facilities. All that was left was their land, and Lucifer took it.

"He recruited many radical religious freaks, terrorists — and, of course, mercenaries. There are close to one million men in all. For the past year, they have been training in his new Arabian Kingdom for the Holy War against the democracies. And, by the way, that Kingdom includes the Persian Gulf."

"And all that oil?" Hunter asked.

"Yes," Sir Neil nodded. "All that oil."

Hunter let out a long, low whistle. One thing that stayed constant in the New Order world was the axiom "Oil is power."

Sir Neil continued. "What makes this all the more dangerous for us is the number of allies Lucifer has bought throughout the Med itself. His confederates are operating all over. His tentacles are everywhere.

"But in all this disputed area, there is one point that has yet been claimed. One very important strategic position. The army that holds it will in fact control the flow of the war to come. And the race will soon be on. Our plan is to seize this strategic point. Our intelligence agents tell us that Lucifer covets it too."

Hunter studied the map. Using the little information Sir Neil had told him, he had already guessed where the all-important strategic point was.

"The Suez Canal," he said.

Sir Neil clapped his hands. "Right on! Major," he said with obvious glee. "Suez. He who controls it can tighten or loosen the screws as he wishes. He can move his army through the canal and he's assured of his oil supply once he breaks out into the

57

Med."

Hunter thought for a moment, then asked, "Do you know just what it is that Lucifer wants?"

Sir Neil shook his head. "A good question," he said. "We've asked it ourselves many times. The answer apparently has to do with what exactly Lucifer's deep-down intentions are. Here is a man using the name of the Devil himself. He's not building an army as much as he is building a cult. He is attracting the most radical religious elements in the region to continue to fight this war. They are, for the most part, a rabble. Armed fanatics, just as you explained the Circle Armies were. The only difference is they receive extensive training in terrorist tactics. But there are certain limitations one must address when you have men in arms in quantity, but not quality."

"Just like back in America," Hunter said. "He never really believed that he could take us over per se. He was happy enough just keeping us destabilized."

"Exactly, major," Sir Neil said. "It's all part of the same plan. Keep the whole world off balance. Until someone — be it the Russians, or some entity even more evil — can rise up and take over. Lucifer is more than just a Soviet agent. He is a master terrorist. He does what he does purely for the terror of it."

Hunter's head was spinning, and now he couldn't blame it entirely on the gin. It seemed as if the world had become Lucifer's deadly playground.

"The man is a monumental egomaniac," Hunter said. "And he has to be stopped. But wouldn't it be easier just to track him down? After all, that's what I'm here for."

Sir Neil shook his head grimly. "There are two problems with that approach, old boy," he said.

58

"First, we know though our intelligence agents that Lucifer has an extremely elaborate chain of command, manned by Soviets or Soviet puppets and designed, no doubt, in Moscow. It's a highly intricate system and is quite the opposite of the rabble he calls his army.

"The central purpose of this command is not to win battles or even the coming war — although this is high on their list, of course. No, their major aim, we have learned, is to continue the fight even if Lucifer is killed or captured. They are expert propagandists. They are well-prepared to make their leader a religious martyr if they have to.

"In fact, it wouldn't be beyond them in the least to *fake* Lucifer's death at just the right time. Look at your own experience back in America. You said there was a point where you and many others thought Viktor might be dead. And what happened? Only the veterans in his army were dissuaded from fighting. The brainwashed young soldiers fought on."

"That's true," Hunter agreed. "We know he was putting 'feel-good' drugs into their chow."

"Exactly!" Heath said. "The difference here is that the drugs have been replaced by the traditional religious fanaticism of the region. He doesn't have to dope these soldiers."

"The second problem is finding Lucifer if we wanted to," Sir Neil said. "His command headquarters is continually on the move. They have many secret locations in southern Saudi Arabia — a place so desolate even the old Saudis called it *Rub al Khali* or 'The Empty Quarter.' But he does have several major seaport bases on the Red Sea."

Sir Neil quickly splashed out three more drinks. This time the formality of toasting was dispensed

59

with; all there men drained their glasses simultaneously.

The British commander continued. "Lucifer is also very well guarded. It would be very hard for a single assassin to find him and get close enough to him. Even if that assassin is flying an F-16."

Hunter thought for a moment. The situation was so bizarre, it took a minute to sink in. Finally he said, "I'm still not so sure that I can give up what I came over here for. But I have to admit I'm fascinated."

He saw Neil and Heath exchange winks.

"Okay, so what is your plan?" the pilot asked. "How *do* you intend to seize the Suez Canal?"

Sir Neil smiled once again: "We thought you'd never ask . . ."

... ... as you ...
... ...

Chapter 7

"Do you really think Hunter could have made it out of this place?" Elvis, the Weapons Systems Officer, asked.

Captain Crunch O'Malley shook his head. "This one might even have been beyond Hunter."

Standing on the wing of their lopsided, stuck-in-the-mud F-4 Phantom, the two pilots were looking out on the astonishing mass of humanity that covered the Casablanca airport. The nervous air evacuation to South America of forty-eight hours before had turned into utter chaos.

Now there must have been 100,000 people crowded into the square half-mile-sized base. Few were carrying anything more than the clothes on their backs, although rifles and sidearms were much in evidence. There were so many people, they were lining the runways, standing no more than twenty feet from where monstrous 747s and DC-10s were roaring in and out. Thousands more were crushed inside the airport's terminal, and overflowing onto its outside walkways, its roof, and its window sills. The area surrounding the T-shaped structure was thick with people, all of them trying to do one thing: get on an airliner and get the hell out of Casablanca.

The problem was the airliners were landing with much less frequency now. The aerial traffic jam had cleared up the night before; airliners coming in now were given a clear shot at landing immediately. And most of them were landing more for want of fuel than a desire to join the dangerous confusion. Plus, once the airplanes were down, it was taking them two hours or more to pass through the crowds and get from the taxiing strip to the terminal building.

Fewer airliners meant fewer seats to freedom. And the price of the ride was going up—drastically. Where two days before five bags of silver or one bag of gold would have meant at least a seat at the rear of the plane, now greedy aircrews were now charging as much as six bags of gold just to sit on the cabin floor. The quick hike in air fare led to some disagreements. The sound of gunfire, once distracting in its infrequency, was now a constant background noise.

But as bad as the crowd was *inside* the airport, it paled in comparison with the mob that waited outside the airfield's fence. O'Malley estimated there were close to a quarter of a million people surrounding the facility.

"This is ridiculous!" O'Malley said to Elvis. "A thousand 747s couldn't carry all these people out!"

The Wreckers had arrived just minutes after a gruesome catastrophe. Many of the fences around the airport were no longer strong enough to hold back the burgeoning crowds. Several had already broken down. One of those remaining was the barrier on the north side of the airport, closest to its last operating runway. Its supports finally gave way just as a beat-up Swedish National Airline 747 Jumbo jet, smoking and desperately low on fuel, made what was technically an unauthorized landing.

Just as the big airplane came in, the weight of the thousands pressing against the fence made it collapse. Those leaning on the fence when it snapped were forced to run in all directions, the crush behind them was so great. Several hundred were forced right into the path of the landing 747. The airliner's pilots, horrified to see the people on the runway, were too low to abort. The big plane plowed through hundreds of terrified people head on, flipping many up and over its wings and horribly sucking others into its jet-engine nozzles. The pilots had immediately reversed the big jet's engines in an attempt to halt the airplane's screeching roll and stop the unbelievable carnage, but the action only caused the airliner to skid off the runway and plunge into a larger crowd of people. A fire quickly broke out and the airplane exploded, killing its crew, and more than a thousand others.

O'Malley and Elvis had arrived just two minutes later. They found the runway littered with bodies. Only O'Malley's skill allowed the fighter jet to land without colliding with a corpse. Still, in steering the landing aircraft around the bodies, O'Malley was forced to swerve the plane off the runway, and now it was stuck up to its right wingtip in sand and dirt that had turned to mud at the end of the runway.

O'Malley reached inside his flight suit, dug out six bags of silver coins, and gave them to Elvis. "Try to bribe someone with a towline and a vehicle, will you?" O'Malley asked him. "We've got to winch this bird out."

"Roger," Elvis said, taking the silver and bounding off the jet's wing.

O'Malley reached into the F-4's cockpit and came up with an M-16. "Here, better take this too" he said, handing the gun to Elvis. "And better keep your helmet on."

"Where you headed, captain?" Elvis asked.

O'Malley looked out onto the mass confusion of the airfield, then checked his .45 automatic sidearm pistol.

"I'm going to the control tower to find out if anyone's seen an F-16 around here."

Chapter 8

The RAF Nimrod reconnaissance aircraft took off and gracefully climbed to 20,000 feet. Although there was bad weather off to the northeast, it was a beautifully clear morning over Gibraltar.

The big plane turned toward direct north and was soon over the coast of Portugal. Hunter and Sir Neil were sharing a large window near the plane's navigator's console, both enjoying the view of the shimmering early morning Atlantic and inviting lushness of the land below.

The pilot called back a reading and Sir Neil checked a navigation chart. "All right, major," he said with a sly smile. "We are soon to cross over Lisbon. If you look down into their port facilities, I think you'll see something very interesting."

Hunter moved closer to the window. Despite a bunch of puffy clouds, he could begin to focus on the port of Lisbon below. Immediately, he saw what Sir Neil was talking about.

"Jeezuz," Hunter exclaimed. "I've never seen so

many ships in one place in my life!"

The port and the surrounding waterways were crowded with ships. Freighters, ocean liners, warships, large ferries. There must have been at least 200 of them. They were anchored side by side in a line that stretched for miles. All of them were painted with the same drab, gray-green color scheme.

"Those are the ships of The Modern Knights," Sir Neil said, a touch of boast in his voice. "Two hundred and forty major vessels. It is a fleet to rival only Lucifer's."

"I should say so," Hunter said, fascinated at the sight of concentrated power.

"But, it's what will be riding in those ships that's important, major," the Englishman continued.

The airplane turned east. Soon, they were flying over what Hunter recognized immediately as a massive military complex close by a mountain range.

"This is *Montemor-o-Novo,*" Sir Neil said, rolling the word perfectly. "This is the major staging facility for The Modern Knights. They have hired hundreds of thousands of mercenaries. From all over western Europe. There's another facility like this at Plymouth in the UK. It is these troops, traveling on those ships, that will go against Lucifer's Legions. This undertaking rivals the invasion force put together for the Normandy landings back in World War II."

While the Nimrod circled, Hunter studied every aspect of the huge base. It *did* look like a scene out of the movie on D-Day. "Just when will these troops be ready to move out?" he asked.

"We are hoping they'll embark just a few days after we do," Sir Neil said, slowly. "Trouble is, the logistics of such an operation are monstrous."

Hunter looked back at the Englishman. For the

first time since meeting Sir Neil, Hunter heard a hint of uncertainty in his voice.

An hour later, Sir Neil was seated at the navigator's control station with Hunter peering over his shoulder. The Englishman fiddled with the bank of touch-sensitive buttons that controlled the airplane's sophisticated "look-down" radar.

The Nimrod had climbed to 50,000 feet and headed northeast. They had hit the bad weather just before crossing over the Pyrenees. Now, even at this height, rain pelted the jet, and strong headwinds buffeted its wings.

"We'll be over our second 'target' in a few minutes," Sir Neil said, working hard to get the jumble of lines on the video screen in front of them to properly shape themselves to the contour of the earth below. "This weather gives us a good hiding place, Hunter, but it also plays daffy with the TV imaging."

Sir Neil gave the control panel a well-placed slap just above its fuse bank. The screen blinked twice and then became crystal-clear. Where there had been hundreds of lines of wavy static before, now there was the sharp, neon-blue-and-white image of the snow-capped mountain range.

"Ah, yes, the Pyrenees," Sir Neil said happily by way of explanation. "Used to take the wife skiing there before the war. She's in Free Canada now, thank God."

Hunter couldn't help but think of Dominique; she too was in Free Canada.

The TV screen was beautifully registering the ground ten miles below, despite the poor weather. The image was so clear, it almost looked like it was being shot by a television camera, not a ground-imaging radar.

"Great piece of equipment, this," Sir Neil said, fine-tuning the picture even more. "It's a LORAL TK-1Q imager."

"Next best thing to being there," Hunter agreed.

Slowly the image of the mountain faded and was replaced by the swaying lines of the ocean.

"We're over the Gulf of Lions now," Sir Neil said. "That's Marseilles up ahead."

The airplane bucked once, hard. The video screen protested with a brief burst of static, then returned a faithful picture of the southern coast of France. Hunter turned to look over the heads of the Nimrod's pilots and out the cockpit window. The rain was getting heavier, the air more turbulent. The pilots had the airplane's windshield wipers working overtime, and were taking turns wrestling with the controls in an effort to keep the airplane level.

"Here it comes!" Sir Neil called out, drawing Hunter's attention back to the screen. At the same time, the Nimrod's pilot called back to them. "Toulon is clear, Commander."

Hunter knew the pilot had just done a routine electronic-weapons sweep of the ground below and found no hostile SAMs waiting for them. Now, as Hunter studied the TV screen, he saw the outline of the once-famous French Riviera come into view.

An anxious jolt ran through him. The most important element of the Brits' plan to capture the Suez was soon to come into view below. The closer they got, the wilder the British plan was becoming to Hunter.

"Just a few seconds now," Sir Neil told him. "Just the other side of Nice and we'll see it . . ."

Sir Neil and his men were convinced the only way to seize control of the Canal was with air power. Warplanes were rarer items in the Med than in America. Lucifer's Legions had very few, although the madman's allies in the area boasted some small but formidable air forces. These were mostly local air units, satisfied with their role as air terrorists in Lucifer's employ, doing occasional air pirating or free-lance bombing jobs on the side.

On the other hand, the RAF, with its major air facility at Gibraltar and a few outposts like the Highway Base scattered throughout the Western Mediterranean, could muster as many as thirty aircraft, of varying types and quality. And unlike the air raiders, the Brits had a coordinated air-command system; their units frequently did training exercises together, with the entire command carrying out extensive maneuvers several times a year.

The trouble was the British air power found itself confined to the western Med. The RAF airplanes rarely ranged much beyond the airspace west of Sardinia. There were no friendly air fields that would serve them if they did. These days, going from west to east on the Med was like sailing up the proverbial River of Fools. The further one traveled, the more bizarre and unpredictable things became. All kinds of dangerous characters plied the waters of the central and eastern sea, as well as sometimes prowling the skies above it. Appropriately enough, the miscellaneous madness peaked right around the Suez Canal. And just 250 miles beyond that lay the outer reaches of Lucifer's evil empire.

Just as in America, where Hunter and democracies stopped a larger land army with a small but effective air force during The Circle War, the Brits felt that if they could project their air superiority—quickly—to Suez, they could seize the canal and the air above it. Thus, the skies would be in friendly hands when The Modern Knights arrived a few days later.

"We're like the air commandos who go in just before the big invasion," Sir Neil had told him. "Get there before the enemy. Hold him off with our air power. Deny him use of the canal."

The question was: how to move all that air power?

The answer lay directly below the RAF Nimrod.

"Here it comes," Sir Neil said, adding in all proper English seriousness, "Major Hunter, this will be one of the most beautiful sights you will ever see."

Hunter focused his eyes on the radar-imaging screen. The big jet—still rolling and pitching in the severe weather—was over the once chic city of Nice. He could see the miles of shoreline, the glamorous beachfront buildings he knew were casinos. It evoked memories of the happier, exciting time of the prewar world.

Suddenly the Nimrod hit a violent air pocket, driving the aircraft down and causing another wave of static to burst onto the video screen. "Bloody—" Sir Neil murmured as he tried to revive the video screen.

Hunter readjusted his flight helmet, which had been knocked almost 180-degrees around his head in the latest jar. By the time he fixed it and could see again, Sir Neil had the TV screen back up and working. "There it is!" Sir Neil was yelling. "Isn't it tremendous?"

That's when Hunter saw it. It was so big it filled the radar screen even though they were ten miles high.

70

"Jezzuz," he whispered. Suddenly everything started to make sense. The Brits couldn't fly their air armada to the Suez—so they were going to float it there instead.

"It's an aircraft carrier," Hunter said.

"It's the USS *Saratoga,*" Sir Neil informed him.

"It's an enormous aircraft carrier."

"Well, you see, it looks very big because it's run aground," the Englishman explained with glee. "You're seeing a lot of what's usually below the water line.

"It's still the biggest *goddamn* thing I've ever seen."

"That's quite true—it *is* one of the largest you Yanks ever built," Sir Neil told him. "It was converted to nuclear power. Had a proud war record too. Until it washed up here anyway."

The pilot had put the Nimrod into a turn. The bad weather was still shaking every nut and bolt in the airplane, but nowhere near enough for Hunter's eyes to be distracted from the TV screen.

The ship was about an eighth of a mile off the sandy beach of Villefranche, just east of Nice. Its titanic draft being what it was, it appeared to be firmly stuck in the mud. "How did it get here?" Hunter asked.

"We're not sure, actually," Sir Neil said. "We know it saw a lot of action off the Balkans during the Big War. It was fighting off the coast of Italy when the armistice was signed. After that, we don't know what happened. Like a lot of other ships, it probably drifted until supplies were out. Then, it was abandoned."

"Most important," Hunter said, excitedly, "where the hell are the airplanes?"

Sir Neil shook his head. "Again, no way to know,"

he said. "They're gone, of course. F-14s, A-6s, A-7s, a few SA-3s also, don't you think?"

"F-18s too," Hunter said. "That's a bunch of pretty hot airplanes to be on the loose." For the first time in as long as he could remember, Hunter was legitimately worried. In America, his F-16 was undisputedly the hottest fighter around. One of the reasons for this was that it was the *only* F-16 around that he knew of. In fact, it was the most advanced fighter still flying—the rest of the continental American air corps were relegated to flying older, though no less lethal, fighters.

But these missing Navy jets were a problem. A monkey wrench thrown into the works. Forty highly sophisticated, state-of-the-art aircraft in the wrong hands was clearly troublesome, not to mention ego-bruising.

"Wherever they are," Sir Neil said, "it's not anywhere around here. One story has it they were washed overboard. In the storm that grounded her, you see. Another—more romantic—tale goes that the pilots simply took off and flew until their fuel ran out, at which time they dropped patriotically into the sea."

"That's hard to believe," Hunter said, his eyes leaving the TV screen for the first time.

"I'll say," Sir Neil continued. "Of course, there is one other rumor. Some say they were flown down South America way."

South America. He'd been hearing a lot of mention of the continent lately. Hunter filed it all away and let the matter drop. He turned his attention back to the radar screen.

"So you intend to refurbish her, put your aircraft aboard, and sail to the Suez," Hunter asked.

"That's correct, major," Sir Neil said. "We can

adapt about twenty-five aircraft — fighters mostly — to set down on her. She'll need work on the catapults, but we're sure we're up to it."

"Have you been down to her?" he asked.

"No," Sir Neil said. "The area is not exactly . . . secured, shall we say? But two of our commandos dropped in and had a look a few months ago. She's seaworthy. Her holds are secure."

"What shape are the reactors in?" Hunter asked.

"Oh, they're in fine shape," Sir Neil told him. "Trouble is, there's no nuclear fuel. Perhaps the sailors were smart and dumped it into the ocean before she was beached. Of course, then again, perhaps someone stole it all."

Another bit of unsettling news.

"So," Hunter said, trying to fit in the last remaining pieces of the Brits' plan, "do you have replacement fuel?"

"No, no," Sir Neil said, almost laughing. "We don't have any fuel. Nor do we have anyone who would know how to get the thing running if we did. We were with you Yanks in nuclear-power subs, but nuclear-powered carriers just weren't our game."

Hunter ran his hand over his chin. "Well, if you can't power the thing to the Suez, how the hell are you going to get it there?"

Sir Neil laughed again. "Simple matter, Hunter, my good man," the Englishman said flawlessly. "We intend to *tow* it there . . ."

Chapter 9

Hunter steered his F-16 toward its final landing approach to the Algiers airport. This day too was crystal-clear and bright, the sun so hot he could feel it even in his air-conditioned cockpit. In front of him the two single-seat British Tornados were lowering their landing gear and activating their air brakes. Hunter routinely disengaged his flight computer and took over the airplane manually for landing. All the time his radio was blaring with excited Arabic coming from the Algerian air controllers.

The F-16's weapons systems were fixed. With the help of a mile of electrical wire, Hunter had been able to hot-wire both his Vulcan cannon Six Pack and his Sidewinder launchers back into working condition. But it had been a long, arduous process. He renewed his vowed revenge against the saboteurs many times. No one—but no one—could screw around with his airplane and get away with it . . .

One day after overflying the aircraft carrier, he

and Sir Neil had come to an understanding. They had agreed that, no matter how different their approach, their goal was the same: stop Lucifer. Whether Hunter did it by tracking down the super-villain (admittedly a difficult mission), or the Brits did it by securing the Suez for The Modern Knights (also very difficult), the effect would be the same: the madman's plans would be put asunder. And as crazy as the Brits' idea was, Hunter was always a sucker for a noble cause. In the end, he knew they needed his help.

So Hunter decided to take a two-option approach. He would help the Brits get their aircraft carrier floating, loaded up, and moving towards the Suez. Then, and only then, would he make up his mind whether he would press on to the East by himself to find the elusive Lucifer.

This flight to Algiers fit right into his dual approach. The Brits needed manpower—friendly, employable manpower—to serve both as the USS *Saratoga*'s crew and as a protection force once they reached the Suez. Algiers was the site of the largest mercenary encampments in the entire Med and the Brits were here to buy. Hunter had agreed to accompany Heath and the other Tornado pilot to the Algerian city for their shopping spree. They were carrying millions of dollars in gold—good soldiers didn't come cheap—and needed someone of Hunter's caliber to watch their backs in the volatile arms-and-man bazaar.

But Hunter also had a more personal reason to make the trip. Just before he died, the last thing Lord Lard had said to him was, "Algiers." Hunter took this to mean that some clue to the whereabouts of Lucifer could be found in the coastal city. So, while he was riding shotgun for the British, he would also have his eye out for something—any-thing—that could lead him to Lucifer . . .

He set the F-16 down right behind the Tornados and together they taxied to their assigned holding stations. Unlike Casablanca, the Algiers airport was totally devoid of citizens. The place was crowded, but with soldiers. Soldiers of many countries and allegiances, wearing every possible combination of uniform and carrying many different types of weap-ons.

The pilots emerged from their airplanes just as a squad of red-uniformed men appeared. Each of the men was over six-five, heavily armed, and black.

Heath approached the man in charge. "Hum-dingo, my friend," the British pilot said, greeting the soldier. "Good to see you, brother."

The man grinned. "Heath, it's been more than a year since you've visited your friends in Algiers. We thought you had forgotten about us."

Hunter smiled. The man was obviously a member of some tribe from the middle of Africa, yet he spoke English with the flair and accent of someone who had graduated from Oxford.

Heath introduced Hunter and the other Tornado pilot—a Captain Raleigh—to Humdingo, explain-ing, "Humdingo used to be a chief. Big chief in the Congo. That's before he found his way to England and learned our nasty ways."

"This is true," Humdingo said in a booming voice. "I learned that the British refuse to believe the sun has set on their Empire. And that they will go to great lengths trying to prove it! Me? I just like their food."

Heath laughed. "Humdingo, you're the only person in the world who actually likes English food."

They got down to business. Heath produced a bag of gold. "We shouldn't be gone for more than twenty-four hours," he told Humdingo, handing him the gold. "By all means, shoot anyone suspicious who comes near these airplanes."

"An F-16?" Humdingo said, admiring Hunter's sleek jet fighter. "Never guarded one of these before."

Heath turned to Hunter. "These guys are specialists," he told him. "Nothing will happen to our aircraft while we're gone."

As if to emphasize the point, Humdingo barked out a sharp order in Congolese and his squad snapped to. With crack precision, the soldiers two-stepped to their positions. In ten seconds they had formed a protective circle around the three jet fighters. Hunter couldn't imagine anyone wanting to tangle with the two dozen well-armed black warriors. He left his F-16 in their hands, enjoying a certain degree of peace of mind.

Humdingo also provided the trio with a jeep. With Heath behind the wheel, they roared off toward the city of Algiers.

They called the fortress *Maison de la Guerre*—Place of War. Hunter's first glimpse of it had been misleading. They had driven through Algiers proper, reached the hills beyond its limits, and found the authentic-looking fort sitting atop a rise on the edge of town. It looked like it was right out of a Foreign Legion movie, except that from the top of its parapets flew literally hundreds of flags. The two soldiers of undetermined origin guarding the front gate eyed them suspiciously as they pulled up in front. A few gold pieces from Heath's hand to their pockets made them instant allies.

The pilots climbed out of the jeep and walked through the huge gate the guards had opened for them. "Here is where we will find our crew," Heath told Hunter.

Inside, the fort's front courtyard was no less authentic. Soldiers were milling around, as were some camels and a scattering of civilians selling a variety of black-market items. Rifle ammunition looked to be the biggest seller.

They moved on to the fort's noisy center courtyard and found more than a hundred elaborate recruiting booths set up in neat rows. This was the Mercenary Supermarket.

It was a combination exchange and recruiting post. The merchandise was paycheck soldiers. Business was brisk. Each booth had a banner flying from it, and two or three soldiers sitting in residence. Most also had customers with them, vigorously discussing the one thing that mattered in the place: price.

The two Brits began shopping, Hunter began to wander. He walked through the courtyard viewing the various advertisements hanging on the booths. "Sappers—Italy's Finest," one placard boasted. "Underwater Demo Is Our Speciality, Free French Navy," another announced. There were booths and ads for regular infantry, mountain soldiers, ski troops, seaborne assault forces, installation protection services, artillery specialists. Others boasted "Complete Package Deals" such as a battalion of infantry, two squads of artillerymen, sappers, scouts, and combat engineers. Each group for hire claimed allegiance to a certain country or territory—some such as Nepal, Greece, Italy, and Free Yugloslavia Hunter recognized. Others such as the First Central Empire, the Red Coast Territories, and the Sunset Islands he had never heard of.

He walked through the bazaar and out toward the back of the fort. He had one question: where were all these soldiers the ads bragged about?

Even before he had a chance to contemplate it, he had his answer.

He stepped out the back of the fort to find a grassy valley. It was slight and perhaps three-quarters of a mile across. In this valley were thousands of troop tents and tens of thousands of soldiers. It was the home of the combatants for hire of the New Order world.

Hunter looked out on the sea of soldiers. Some were training, doing exercises, or involved in target practice. Others were sitting near their tents, cleaning weapons or attending to other equipment. Still others were lounging about underneath the valley's many trees. The most popular spot in the valley was a large watering hole in its center. It was an authentic oasis, surrounded by a thick collar of palm trees and makeshift open-air barrooms.

Here too hundreds of flags fluttered in the breeze above the individual encampments. French. Swiss, Swede. Thai. Angolan. Irish. Hunter's keen vision picked out a number of familiar patterns.

Then his head started buzzing. His mouth went dry. Off at the far end of the valley, too far out for even his keen sight to zoom in on, one flag in hundreds stood out. It seemed to be flying slightly higher, slightly stiffer in the breeze. He reached to his breast pocket, to the bulge of folded cloth he always kept there. He felt a lump in his throat.

Could it be?

Hunter started running. Down one dusty path to

another. On to the dirt road that ran through the valley, skirted the watering hole, and led to the far end of glen. He was breathing heavily, his flight helmet clinking at his side. No one paid him much attention to him—he was just one soldier in thousands.

He kept his eyes fixed on the flag flying at the end of the valley, getting closer to it with every step. He started to make out its design. Still he ran on, avoiding collisions with jeeps, jogging squads of soldiers, and smelly camels. Soon he could pick out the definite shapes on the flag—the lines, the pattern. He ran faster. About an eighth of a mile away, his eyes started to water. He could see the flag more clearly. The stars, the stripes, then the colors . . .

There were red, white, and blue.

Chapter 10

Hunter saw his first Americans before he even reached the camp underneath the fluttering American flag. There were six of them, walking nonchalantly down the road toward the watering hole. They were wearing green overall fatigues, baseball hats, and sneakers. Each man had a patch sewn onto his uniform's left shoulder. It too was an American flag.

Hunter ran up to them.

"Are you guys USA?" he asked.

"Yes, sir," one of them answered.

Hunter pulled out his own small American flag and said, "So am I."

The Americans immediately eyed his major's bars and instinctively snapped to a salute.

Hunter quickly saluted back. He wasn't interested in such formalities now.

"I'm Major Hunter, formerly of the US Air Force," he said, with pride evident in his voice. "What *are* you guys? Army?"

"No, sir," one spoke up. "Just the uniforms are Army. We are US Navy, sir."

"Navy?" Hunter asked. "What *kind* of Navy?"

"Most of us are submariners, sir," another told him.

"Atomic or diesel?"

"Atomic, sir," was the answer.

Bingo.

"Who's your commanding officer, guys?" Hunter asked, already moving towards the American camp.

"Lieutenant Yastrewski," one yelled.

"Just ask for 'Yaz,' major," another called out.

Hunter reached the American camp, his eyes fixed on the large American flag that flew above its main tent. The flag *was* bigger and higher than those of other camps. It was the biggest one Hunter had seen since The New Order went down. The American camp, though much smaller than many of the bivouacs, was also more elaborate. He spotted a number of sophisticated weapons and a lot of top-shelf communications gear dispersed around the ten-acre site. He also noticed that members of other armies were present in the camp, mostly gathered around Americans near the state-of-the-art hardware. It appeared the Americans were instructing the other troops.

Hunter identified himself to the camp guards and was ushered into the camp's HQ.

A small man—typical of submariners—came in to meet him. Unlike his men, this officer was dressed in Navy blues.

"I'm Lieutenant Yastrewski," the slightly younger man said, shaking hands with Hunter. "First American Seaborne Assault, Repair and Support Group."

"I'm Major Hunter, Pacific American Air Corps," Hunter said. Immediately he knew his title sounded as strange to the submariner as "First American

. . ." did to him.

"I'm a pilot for the territory that was once called California, Washington, and Oregon," Hunter clarified.

"There's no more California?" the man asked.

Hunter shook his head. "Probably not as you remember it." He was not surprised that the man didn't know what was going on in New Order America.

"When's the last time you were stateside, lieutenant?"

The man shook his head. "Not since the war, sir. I was stationed in Norfolk, Virginia. I suppose that area's changed pretty much now too."

Hunter nodded. "The whole country has changed," he said.

"We hear bits and pieces," the officer told him. "But not much."

Hunter looked around the HQ tent. It was jammed with some of the most advanced electronics and communications gear he'd ever seen since the war. "Quite a setup you got here," he told Yastrewski.

"Well, we try, major," the Navy man replied. "Are you here to contract some help?"

"Well, friends of mine are," Hunter told him. "Some Brits I hooked up with may be looking for some sailors with experience in nuclear operations."

The officer was quiet for a moment, then asked, "Could I offer you a cup of coffee, major. Or a drink?"

Hunter smiled. "How about both?"

Five minutes later, they were sitting inside the camp's chow tent, mixing muddy Algerian coffee with even darker Algerian liquor. A large pot of noodles, boiling in a creamy wine sauce, appeared. The lieutenant scooped out two bowls for them.

"How many men do you have, lieutenant?" Hunter asked between bites.

"Three hundred and seventy-six," Yaz replied proudly. "We're the smallest group here, but we are by far the best-equipped.

"Most of us were aboard the USS *Albany* when it went down off Ireland on the last day of the war. We made it to shore and a bunch of us stuck together. We kicked around for a year or so, doing some protection work. Then made it over to England. Got work driving a bunch of ferries back and forth over the Channel. Eventually we moved to France, then here. Been camped about five months now."

"How did you know to come here?" Hunter asked.

"Because of all the war rumors," Yaz told him. "People said a big one was coming, or, actually, that World War Three was about to heat up again. They said they would need soldiers, equipment, weapons.

"Well, we're not combat soldiers, at least we weren't trained to be. But we *are* technicians, engineers, specialists. We've found that very few people in the Med know how to operate a lot of the high-tech stuff that's floating around these days. We do. We know what a semiconductor is and what it does. We understand laser-sighters, gate-arrays, tele-guidance. We had the skills. So we came here and opened for business. On one hand we repair some of the stuff that comes in. On the other, we teach people how to use it once it's fixed."

"Sounds like a very enterprising idea," Hunter said, swigging his drink.

"Well, we need the money," Yaz continued. "We're trying to get enough cash to get a boat or an airplane or something to get everyone back to the States."

"It's a lot different over there now," Hunter told him. "Some might think it's not much to go home to."

The lieutenant nodded. "I know," he said slowly. "We hear different things. Never enough to put the whole picture together, though. We know it's changed. But we still want to go back. It's our country."

Hunter instantly admired the man.

"Do you guys hire out like the rest of the people here?" he asked.

"We've never been approached," Yaz said. "Rarely does anyone need us more than two or three at a time. Most of the stuff we do is strictly one-man, one-job."

"Could your guys sail a big ship?" Hunter asked him.

Yaz thought a moment. "How big?"

"The biggest," Hunter said.

"A carrier?" Yaz asked, his eyes going slightly wide. "A nuke?"

Hunter knew he could trust the man. "Yes, but a disabled one," he told him. "No juice in the reactors." He quickly explained what the Brits' plan was and why he had flown to Algiers.

"This Lucifer guy is supposed to be one tough weirdo," Yaz said after taking it all in. "I mean, he's the guy behind the big war that's coming. I'm glad someone's going to try and stop him before he blitzkriegs his way to the Atlantic."

He stopped and drained his drink, then said, "But actually towing a carrier through the Med to the Canal? That's one very crazy idea."

"In your best Navy opinion, *can* it done?"

Yaz thought it over. "I doubt it. There are a thousand things that could go wrong."

"But is it impossible?"

Yaz looked him in the eye. "Well, nothing's impossible, major. At least that's what they taught us in Naval Officers training."

Hunter nodded and took a long swig of his drink. "The Brits came here to buy protection forces and hoped to scrape up some sailors in the process," he told him. "But these are RAF guys. They don't have the foggiest idea how to move the ship and they'll be the first to admit it. And, believe me, they're paying good money."

Again Yaz gave it some careful thought, then said, "Well, you know, even if the reactors aren't running, the ship could still be powered up enough to run the weapons and to have some lights, I suppose. If we can rustle up some generators, that is. Or, better yet, get the gas turbines running."

"Can your guys handle it?" Hunter asked.

"I think so," Yaz said. "We live and breath electronics here. But getting that carrier where they want it to go will take more than just lining up the circuits right. It will need a lot of coordination, teamwork more than anything else. That I can convince them of."

Hunter was already convinced.

That night the British pilots had arranged for a secret conference to be held in a village nearby. The site was the back room of a rundown cafe. The Englishmen had interviewed more than forty different mercenary groups during the day and now they asked seven group leaders to join them at the session. They were anxious to talk to the Americans too.

The meeting started precisely at midnight. Hunter, seated at the left of Heath and Raleigh, studied the other men who sat around the table in the smoky backroom.

The man directly to his right represented a group of Frenchmen who specialized in ship defense. They would come equipped with a dozen Phalanx Gatling-style machine guns — weapons so quick and powerful, they could send up a wall of lead so intense, no antiship missile could penetrate it.

The man next to him was a captain in the Australian Army. His 900-man battalion, a mixture of Aussies and Gurkha troops, was well-trained in special weapons and tactics. If the carrier ever actually made it to the Suez, these soldiers would come in handy.

Next came a colonel in the Free Spanish Air Force. His group had been originally attached to a NATO early-warning radar unit. Now they hired out as an air-defense team, complete with portable shoulder-launched, antiaircraft Stinger missiles from the US. Appropriately enough, they were called Rocketeers.

A man in a black, flowing robe and a turban sat to Spaniard's right. He represented the Free Moroccan Brigade — a group of 7500 men. They were very versatile combat soldiers, well acquainted with desert warfare as well as seaborne assaults. These troops would serve as the carrier's strike force, large enough to seize and hold moderately sized objectives. They were also *very* anti-Lucifer, despite the fact they, like many in Lucifer's Legion, were devout Moslems. The Brits knew this to be an important point.

An Italian sat next to the Moroccan. The man

87

headed up a small unit of communications specialists. These men would be in charge of getting the carrier's sophisticated radio and radar systems up and running.

Next came the Norwegian Naval Commander, a man named Olson. He operated a squad of fifteen swift frigates. These vessels would provide the carrier with sea defense and escort and also would be called on to do scouting duties.

Then there was the Irishman. Small and red-faced, the man, authentically named Paddy O'Brien, also brought a very important aspect to the party — maybe the *most* important. He owned a fleet of twenty armed tugboats, each boasting a crew of ten. They would be the ones responsible for the actual "pulling and pushing," as he put it of the USS *Saratoga*. O'Brien could also arrange to have an oiler — a refueling ship — join the venture.

Finally there was Lieutenant Yastrewski, US Navy. His specialists would run the ship.

The purpose of the backroom meeting was to hammer out contracts. The negotiations were intense. The Brits had plenty of money, courtesy of the wealthy Modern Knights. But they were rock-solid on the prices each group would be paid. Beyond money, though, the Brits had to make sure everyone in the room was of a like mind. There were no negotiations on this point. To a man, the group leaders agreed that Lucifer had to be stopped. The Moroccans were the most adamant. So it was not just for gold that the participants agreed to join the bold adventure. Freedom was also a factor. "My kind of people," thought Hunter.

The conference was still going strong when the sun came up. All the deals had been struck before dawn. Now a multitude of logistics had to be planned: equipment and supplies secured, pickup points for the groups arranged.

Hunter was more impressed with the Brits all the time. Throughout the meeting, Heath and Raleigh had calmly addressed each concern, negotiated firmly but fairly, then assigned the units their responsibilities. All groups took their assignments with cool professional élan.

"Then it's settled!" Heath said, after discussing the final points. "Gentlemen, if I had a drink, I would toast to you — all of you. What we are about to undertake will undoubtedly affect the balance of power in this area — if not the world — for many years to come. God — *Allah* — help us all . . ."

The road back to the airport was clogged with soldiers returning from a wild night in Algiers. Hunter was stretched out on the rear seat of the jeep, trying to relax before the return flight to RAF Gibraltar. Up front, Heath and Raleigh were enthusiastically discussing the forces they had just hired. They were much relieved. The first very important step had been completed. Hunter was only mildly troubled by the fact that he hadn't been able to uncover any inside information about Lucifer. He admitted to himself that he was getting caught up in the Brit's Great Suez Adventure.

Hunter sensed trouble just seconds before the rocket-propelled grenade landed in front of the jeep.

He had been able to sit up and yank Heath around the neck, causing the British driver to hit the brakes and thus avoiding what would have been a direct hit on their vehicle. The grenade exploded ten feet in front of them, filling the air with deadly shrapnel, which killed several soldiers unlucky enough to be walking on the road.

An instant after the grenade landed, Hunter, Heath, and Raleigh were out of the jeep and under cover in a trench next to the road. A cliff on the left side of the roadway looked to be the most likely spot for the ambushers to hide. Hunter had his M-16 up and ready, his extraordinary eyes scanning the ledges for any sign of the attackers. All around them, hungover soldiers, their weapons also at ready, had also taken cover, none of them sure who had fired the grenade and why.

Hunter had a couple good guesses . . .

"Someone up there doesn't like us," Heath said, his own 9mm automatic pistol at the ready.

"Either we've been betrayed by someone at the meeting, or Lucifer's people heard we were in town," Raleigh said.

"Could be someone trying to make a little extra cash," Hunter said. "After all, the person who turns in my hide is in for a billion dollars."

Just then he heard the distinctive whoosh of an RPG being fired.

"Here comes another one!" Hunter yelled loud enough so everyone in earshot could hear him.

Another shell crashed down three seconds later, landing twenty feet from the jeep and sending out another cloud of flaming shrapnel. Thanks to Hunter's warning, no one was hurt in the second blast.

An instant after the shell exploded, Hunter was up and firing his M-16 towards a point two-thirds of the way up the cliff. He had detected a telltale puff of smoke from the grenade launcher and was now spraying the point with tracer-laced M-16 bullets.

The two Brits and many of the soldiers caught along the road did the same thing. But, at the same moment, a powerful machine gun opened up from another part of the rocky bluff. Then another and another.

Within seconds, a full-fledged firefight had broken out.

Hunter still concentrated his fire on the point where he knew the RPG launcher was. After his fifth barrage, he heard something hit home. There was a loud explosion on the side of the cliff and a rain of rocks and metal showered down onto the roadway. Hunter's fire had not only found the RPG operators, it had hit their ammunition. Two bodies came down the bluff in the small avalanche, both landing with a bloody splat in the middle of the road.

The machine-gun fire intensified. Still, Hunter had to find out who the attackers were. To the shock and amazement of the two British pilots, he was up and running toward one of the attackers who had fallen from the cliff. With bullets splashing all around him, the Wingman dragged the fallen ambusher back to the trench.

Even Hunter was amazed that the man was still breathing, though he had only seconds to go. His body was cracked and bleeding from a number of points. The pilot studied the man. He was wearing a nondescript black uniform, with a turban and a cloth covering most of his face. Each breath the man took resulted in a exhalation of blood, which spurted out of the cloth covering his mouth. Still, his eyes were open.

"Who are you?" Hunter demanded. "Who is your boss?"

The man actually managed a laugh. "Hunter . . ."

he gasped. "You fool . . ."

His eyes then went up into his head. A gush of blood came out of his mouth and he was dead.

Hunter, surprised that the man knew him by name, slowly unwrapped the bloody cloth that covered most of the dead man's face. He recognized the man's features right away. It was el-Fauzi, the man he had met at the Casablanca control tower.

"Do you know him?" Heath asked, crawling over to Hunter and the dead man.

"Believe it or not, I do," the pilot replied, searching the body. "He led me to a character named Lord Lard in Casablanca. Lard's the guy who told me to come here, to Algiers. They must have been setting me up."

"That's what it looks like, old boy," Heath said, ducking away from a barrage of machine-gun fire. "But the question is: were they just after that billion-dollar bounty or are they allies of Lucifer?"

Hunter looked at el-Fauzi's broken body.

"Maybe I'll never know," he said to himself.

The fire from the cliff intensified. Hunter pushed aside the body and concentrated on the rest of the attackers. There were spits of fire coming from at least a dozen locations on the side of the cliff as well as at its peak. Meanwhile, many of the mercenaries who happened to be on the fringes of the ambush had withdrawn, leaving only Hunter, Heath, Raleigh, and three bystanders square in the line of fire.

The good news was that one of those bystanders had a radio . . .

Fifteen minutes later, Hunter heard the chopper approaching from the west. It was a Westland Lynx, the British-built helicopter originally built for anti-shipping operations. As the copter came into view, Hunter could clearly see its bright yellow-and-green markings as well as the half-dozen TOW missiles jimmy-rigged on its belly.

"Humdingo came through for us," Heath said to Hunter.

They had crawled over to the mercenary who happened to be carrying the radio and called back to the Algiers airport control tower. For the promise of a bag of silver, a runner carried a detailed message to Humdingo, who was on duty guarding the F-16 and the Tornados. Humdingo then arranged to have one of the airport's many free-lance helicopter gunships fly out to the site of the ambush.

The fire from the cliff had intensified in the ensuing time, but now it was redirected when the helicopter arrived. The Lynx ignored the barrage of bullets being thrown up at it by the ambushers and, in workmanlike fashion, swooped in and deposited a TOW missile directly on the top of the cliff. The resulting explosion caused a small landslide—two more bodies landing on the road amidst the debris.

The Lynx circled around and fired two more missiles into the side of the bluff. Again, the two explosions caused minor avalanches as well as three tumbling bodies. The chopper made two more passes, both times firing its dual machine guns. Even above the racket of the chopper blades, Hunter could hear the shells puncturing flesh. One more TOW missile strike and all fire from the cliff ceased. The attack was over.

The trapped soldiers emerged from the trench just as the Lynx was setting down on the road. Heath made a point of giving a bag of silver to each of the unlucky mercenaries trapped in the ambush, including a half-dozen gold coins in the bag of the man who had been carrying the lifesaving radio.

The mercenaries went on their way as Hunter, Heath, and Raleigh approached the Lynx. Humdingo himself stepped out of the aircraft, his grin even wider than before.

"Heath, old man," he said in perfect Queen's English. You are lucky you have such a good friend as Humdingo in Algiers."

"Amen, chief," Heath said, with much relief.

The Lynx pilot — he looked like a Greek to Hunter — stepped out of the chopper and approached Heath.

"Who pays?" he asked, nonchalantly.

"I do," Heath said, reaching into his satchel to what Hunter was beginning to believe was an endless supply of money. "How much?"

The pilot stroked his thin beard. "Let's see," he said, doing some quick calculations. "Four TOWs, six belts of ammo, fuel, and landing fees. That's four and a half bags of silver."

Heath took a look at the battered jeep and dug out five full bags of silver coins.

"I'll throw in another half bag for a lift back to the airport."

The Greek pilot gave him the thumbs-up sign. "Done," he said with a smile.

Chapter 11

"Iron Fist" was the name of the group that controlled the territory once known as the French Riviera.

The Fist was an offshoot of a radical anarchist group that had once carried out terrorist bombings in prewar France. Back then, its members, although publicly described as "left-wingers," were actually pseudo-political troublemakers, the sons and daughters of rich Gallic industrialists who grew bored with being wealthy and decided to kill and maim innocent people in the name of some hair-brained "People's Revolution." Their dream came true with the start of World War III; the Red Armies deposited their "revolutionary" SCUD poison missiles in the middle of Europe on Christmas Eve, killing millions. Members of Iron Fist were crushed right alongside their bourgeois countrymen in the Soviet onslaught that followed. Many of its surviving members simply cowered in hiding places while the real armies fought the war.

Only when the guns fell silent and the beaten yet victorious Russians withdrew did the members of Iron Fist emerge from their holes and claim the once-posh Riviera as their "Liberated Zone of the People." The comical thing about it all was that the only "people" living in the territory were the members of Iron Fist itself.

Such grade-school revolutionary foolishness was more than an inconvenience to the Sir Neil and his British adventurers. The USS *Saratoga* was beached 2000 feet off the territory controlled by Iron Fist. The problem was that the British Intelligence people believed Iron Fist had made some "new friends" lately. Namely, a notorious motorized division known as The Red Army Faction. They too were a band of terrorists before the war. But unlike members of the Fist, The Red Army Faction had gotten into the free-lance military business in a big way. And more than a few observers believed the Faction was supported in some part by the warlords in Moscow.

Recruiting many surviving Warsaw Pact soldiers and recovering much of their battlefield equipment, the Faction became a modern-day equivalent of the Goths — 20,000 well-armed barbarians on wheels. Their specialty was sacking cities. Their military formula was simple: attack, rape, pillage, carry off slaves, and move on. They had been terrorizing central Europe since the end of the first Great Battles. No one on the continent had had the ambition to take them on. Thus, the Faction added to the instability that Moscow craved.

The Brits had suspected for some time that the Faction wanted to grab some territory in the warmer climes, at least during the European winter months. As with any army, its troops needed a place to take R&R. The Riviera was a natural choice — it gave them an outlet to the sea, plenty of living accommodations, plus an ally in Iron Fist that at least shared some of their revolutionary fervor, if in name only. And the Fist was weak enough that they could be crushed at first whine.

As it turned out, The Red Army Faction also had plans for the USS *Saratoga*.

If The Faction intended to make the Riviera its R&R billet, it would need some security, especially in air defense. When the two RAF commandos had first reconnoitered the carrier, they had found that someone had stripped away about a third of its ship defensive weapons, including its important antiaircraft systems. The Brits knew such an operation was beyond the limited know-how of the pampered revolutionaries of Iron Fist, yet well within the technical expertise of the Faction. When many of the missing carrier guns and SAM launchers started showing up in recon photos sitting atop the formerly luxurious casinos and mansions from Nice to Monte Carlo, the Brits knew the Faction was serious about vacationing in the south of France.

"Now, they take potshots at passing aircraft every once and a while," Sir Neil was telling the group of officers, including Hunter, as they studied a lighted map of the Riviera. They were in the control room of a Norwegian frigate, one of four anchored in a small port on the deserted Mediterranean island of Majorca, several hundred miles to the southwest of France. "They got two airliners last week. Either their troops get bored very quickly and like playing with the ack-ack guns or it's the Faction's way of telling everyone that they've claimed some exclusive beachfront property."

Hunter shook his head. He wondered if the battle-hardened soldiers of the Faction sat up all night playing roulette with the pussies of Iron Fist.

"The trouble is that we have very little hard information about the area," Sir Neil continued. "We have to assume that, besides whatever Iron Fist can do, there might be at least a couple battalions of Red Army Faction soldiers lounging around the city."

Three days had passed since Hunter, Heath, and Raleigh had left Algiers. As per their contract, four of the fifteen Norwegian frigates had arrived in Gibraltar during the night, where they had picked up a British Special Air Services battalion and a hundred of Yaz's men and proceeded to Majorca. RAF airborne combat engineers had already secured a landing area and docking facilities on the island. The frigates arrived the following night, shortly before Hunter landed his F-16 at the island's secret airbase, along with six heavily armed Tornados.

Now, for what seemed like the one hundredth time, Sir Neil meticulously went over the plan to retrieve the *Saratoga*. Those in attendance in the control room with Sir Neil and Hunter included Heath, Raleigh, two SAS officers, Yaz, and the Norwegian commander—Gjaff Olson, who was also the skipper of the command frigate.

"We have to do three things before we can even think of moving the carrier," Sir Neil explained. "One, we have to suppress the antiaircraft guns in Villefranche. Two, we have to secure the beach—we'll call it Gold Beach—near where the *Saratoga* is stuck. And three, we have to secure the *Saratoga* itself.

"Three Tornados will be responsible for the first objective. They will attack the town's SAM sites. Don't worry about whether we have justifiable provocation—remember those bastards have shot down airliners full of innocent people. As for securing Gold Beach, we'll use the landing crafts on frigates one, two and three, and put about 600 men of the SAS battalion ashore. The choppers from those ships will stand by for any rescue duties.

"Once there, the SAS will set up an aggressive beachhead and occupy the three blocks of buildings right on the shoreline. This should give us a reasonable buffer zone and prevent anyone from Villefranche from getting close enough to accurately fire on the carrier.

"The 300 remaining SAS troopers will be in charge of boarding the *Saratoga* itself. We've got one helicopter to work with, so two squads of SAS will chopper right onto the deck of the carrier. If there is anyone aboard—either Fist or Faction—these troops will have to deal with them. The rest of the 300 will be on board this vessel, frigate four. They will move up alongside the carrier and go up on ropes provided by the chopper squads. By that time the ship should be secure.

"Once we are certain that the carrier is in our hands, we'll chopper about a hundred of the Yank sailors aboard. We'll be running the whole operation from right here in frigate four."

The room was quiet while Sir Neil let the information sink in.

"As you know, we'll have to hold the beach for at least six hours until the Yanks can get the carrier's primary systems running," he continued. "Captain Olson's men will help the Yanks install the main towlines so when O'Brien's tugs arrive at midnight, we'll be set to pull her off."

The moon was with them—the tides would be ideal to float the big ship, providing everything was ready. And one of the first tasks Yaz's men would perform would be to get the carrier's aircraft-retrieval systems in order. Once that was done, Hunter, his F-16 already equipped with the necessary belly-attached arresting hook, would be able to land on the USS *Saratoga*'s flight deck. Important task number two would be to get the carrier's aircraft-launching catapult systems working.

Hunter knew the recovery plan was solid. But he also knew all too well that the best-laid plans are usually screwed up by an uncalculated variable. Sir Neil read his mind.

"The Fist shouldn't be that much of a problem," he said. "But as far as the Faction soldiers on R and R, well, we have to expect the unexpected. We have to assume that they bring their equipment on liberty with them, and as they are a motorized division, this means tanks and personnel carriers. Plus they can just as easily pick up a radiophone and buy some free-lance air cover or heavy warships.

"That's where you come in, Major Hunter. We'll have to rely on you to counter anything unexpected, either in the air, on the sea, or on the ground."

Hunter knew it was a tall order. But the cause was worthy.

"It's going to take some practice to set the Tornados down on the carrier," Sir Neil continued. "We won't be able to do it during this operation. So only you and your F-16 have the agility to do it with so little preparation. Plus it will probably be dark by the time we get the arresting cables working. So you'll be looking at a nighttime landing. But, for at least the time being, you'll have to be our only recoverable aircraft. Let's just hope the sea stays calm and it doesn't get too sticky."

Yaz turned to Hunter and with a wide grin said,

"Welcome to the Navy, major."

Hunter shook his head. "This is what I get for betting against Army all those years."

The six Tornados swept in at wave-top level, rising up to 500 feet only when they were in sight of the coast of southern France. The crude radar system of the Iron Fist picked up the incoming blips about a mile out to sea. Anti-aircraft guns opened up almost immediately after the airplanes passed over the first row of beachfront casinos of Villefranche. The British pilots expertly maneuvered around the deadly bursts of smoke and proceeded to select targets of opportunity. It was an hour before dusk. The opening shots in the plan to free the USS *Saratoga* had been fired.

Three of the Tornados split off and were soon over the beach near where the USS *Saratoga* lay. The three remaining British jets repeatedly twisted and turned their way above the city, firing at the ack-ack guns and lining up the not-yet-warm SAM sites for laser-guided bombs.

A little more than 10,000 feet above, Hunter orbited in his F-16. He was able to watch the action around Villefranche via his terrain-radar video system. It was like having a TV camera hovering over the battle. Meanwhile, he could see the three Norwegian frigates as they dashed for Gold Beach, their cargo of 600 SAS troopers waiting on the decks to be loaded onto landing craft and put ashore. The remaining frigate, carrying Sir Neil and the command staff, circled the *Saratoga*. The immobile aircraft carrier, its stern pointing directly toward the beach 2000 feet away, was a huge, imposing sight, dark and ominous in the middle of the now-frenetic activity.

His radar picked up the blip of the approaching RAF helicopter. This would be ferrying the SAS troops to be dropped onto the carrier.

So far, so good, he thought.

Hunter moved the F-16 directly over the carrier just as the Sea King chopper was setting down on the deck. He knew twenty-four SAS men were leaping out, and by the chatter on his radio he also knew that the landing on the carrier was unopposed.

He could now see the first of the landing crafts being disgorged from the frigates. Soon the first of the SAS beach troops would be splashing ashore. The trio of Tornados were methodically roaring up and down the beach at 1000 feet, carefully watching for any opposing troops. Less than a mile away, fires were beginning to erupt in the town of Villefranche as the bombing Tornados were finding targets.

That's when Hunter felt it. *Enemy aircraft.* Coming his way. Six of them. Approaching from the northeast. Moving at just under Mach 1.

His hands were immediately a blur of movement. He started pushing buttons, flicking switches, punching in computer codes. A mental checklist went off in his head. Weapons systems on. Fuel reserves switched, external tanks dropped. Flight computer set for intercept. Sidewinders armed. Test-firing of his nose cannons successful.

He was ready. Now, who the hell was the enemy?

He found out soon enough. "Christ," he murmured, looking at his radar screen. The jets were still forty miles away, but he could tell by their radar signatures that they were Dassault-Breguet Super Etendards. The airplanes were originally French-built naval strike craft, but obviously they were operating from a land base somewhere in central

Europe. The Red Army Faction had indeed made the call for some free-lance air support.

"Of all the goddamn airplanes to show up," Hunter cursed. It wasn't the performance of the jets that bothered him. The French airplanes only had a top speed of 745 mph. His F-16 could do two and a half times that without breathing hard. Rather it was what the airplanes were armed with that was troubling. He knew Super Etendards could only be carrying one weapon: *Exocets*.

The Exocet was an anti-ship missile of the deadliest order. It could be fired from long- or short-range, depending on the ability and the motives of the pilot. It was programmed to deliver a 364-pound warhead of high explosive into a ship while traveling 600 mph. The missiles had made their murderous debut years ago in the Falkland Islands War. A few years later, an American frigate had been hit by one in the Persian Gulf. They flew again in the opening battles of World War III. Now Hunter knew at least six of them were heading his way.

Just as he was about to call in to Sir Neil on the Norwegian command ship, he heard one of the Gold Beach Tornados break in on the line.

"We've got trouble on Gold," the cockney-accented pilot reported. "Tanks moving on beach highway from Villefranche. Looks like a gang of them — T-62s. Thirty at least. Also BMPs . . ."

Goddamn! The Faction brought their tanks with them on holiday. Thirty *Soviet*-built tanks to boot.

Hunter flipped his radio-send switch and was immediately talking to Sir Neil. "We got six Super Etendards coming your way," he told the British officer. "They're probably loaded with Exocets."

"Christ, Hunter," the reply came back. "Who are they and what's their bloody position?"

"Probably free-lancers, coming in a two-seventy Tango," Hunter said, noting the aircraft were now just thirty miles away and staggering their flight pattern into three groups of two. The enemy planes were starting a long arc out over the sea. "They are getting in their attack positions now. You'd better red-alert everyone on the ships. Once those Exocets are launched, they'll hit the first thing that configures to their computer 'ship-ID' profile. And that includes the carrier."

There was a burst of static, then Sir Neil's voice came through: "Hunter, can you hold them, man? We've got tanks moving toward the SAS guys on Gold. All six Tornados are being vectored there right now!"

"Roger," Hunter replied, turning toward the Super Etenards and kicking in his afterburner. "You take care of the tanks. I'll go after these guys . . ."

Almost immediately the red alert was flashed to the Norwegian frigates. Their crews started to take countermeasures. The Exocet was a radar-homing missile. Hundreds of ship profiles were locked into its computer memory. Once a profile took hold via the missile's on-board radar, the rocket would set a course right for its center. To counteract this, the Norwegian sailors started firing chaff rockets — small projectiles containing millions of ultra-thin, metalized, fiberglass wires. The cloud of chaff was designed to confuse the Exocet's radar-homing device by mimicking several attractive radar targets. It was a good idea, but in reality the chaff defense worked about half the time.

Hunter put the 16 into a screaming dive and was instantly in the airspace between the attacking airplanes and the ships. Already he knew the lead Super Etendard had released a missile. The mini-blip on his radar screen confirmed it. He coolly set a path directly for the oncoming computerized projectile. The F-16 was traveling at 1100 mph and the Exocet was coming at him at nearly 650 mph.

"This won't take long," he thought.

Sure enough, five miles away he saw the telltale trail of smoke coming from the sea-skimming missile heading straight at him. He held the F-16 steady, barely flicking the aircraft's side-stick controller. Now the missile was just three miles away. He counted off 1-2-3, then squeezed his cannon trigger. The Vulcan Six Pack roared in response, sending up a wall of lead. The missile and the cannon shells met a split-second later head on. A huge yellow explosion lit up the late afternoon sky. When the smoke cleared, nothing was left but cinders.

Even before the Exocet exploded, Hunter had launched a Sidewinder at the lead Super Etendard. The missile raced toward the attacking aircraft. An explosion off on the horizon ten seconds later confirmed the lead airplane had been hit.

Hunter turned his attention the second lead enemy airplane. It too had launched a deadly missile. Then, like a true hired hand, the pilot had turned his airplane around and fled the area. Hunter instantly had a clear visual sighting on the missile it had launched. Trouble was, it was moving too fast for him to shoot it down.

He knew the Exocet's radar-homing computer had selected the circling Norwegian command frigate as its target. It was much too late for him to radio the ship to take evasive action. There was only one way he could prevent the missile from hitting its target. Hunter booted the F-16 until he was flying on an intersecting collision course with the missile. He kicked the 16's engines once more and flashed right in front of the rocket, at the same time boosting up the power in his three cockpit radar sets.

The missile took the bait. Its on-board computer instantly "went dumb," forgetting about the frigate and instead homing in on all the activity in the F-16's cockpit. Hunter smiled, yanked back on the side-stick controller, and put the jet fighter into a merciless, straight-up climb.

The missile followed as advertised, but the speed of its target and the strain of the hellish climb were too much for its on-board circuitry. Wires began to melt, fuel began to heat up. Its electronic brain went crazy, instructing the missile's steering systems to begin rotating. This caused the warhead to be jolted against its protective casing. A spark resulted and this ignited the warhead. The missile exploded an instant later.

"Two missiles down . . ." Hunter whispered. "Only four to go . . ."

He flipped the jet onto its back and found himself directly above two more incoming Super Etendards. Instinctively his fingers pushed the Sidewinder launch trigger and two missiles shot out from under his wings. They flew unerringly toward the slower attacking airplanes. One was sucked up into the trailing Super Etendard's rear exhaust pipe. The airplane was instantly obliterated. The second Sidewinder caught the other jet right in the cockpit, exploding the chamber and ejecting the lifeless form of the pilot out through the smashed canopy glass. The aircraft went into a crazy spin and slammed into the sea with a steamy crash.

He found the last two remaining Super Etendards roaring over the top of the small fleet of three troop-carrying frigates, their Exocets still under the wings. He knew the pilots were trying to spin about and attack from the east, thereby giving them the option of attacking some of the SAS landing crafts in the process. But the gunners on the frigates interrupted those plans. The Norwegians sent up a wall of lead that impressed even Hunter. The SAS troopers on the beach were also firing at the enemy jets. One of the Super Etendards was caught square in a cross-fire, its fuel tank taking hundreds of hits before it finally split and erupted into a ball of flame, taking the aircraft and its pilot with it.

The remaining jet, its pilot inordinately plucky, roared out into a wide turn and started back toward the small fleet.

"Send up chaff! Quick!" Hunter yelled into his microphone.

Almost before the words were out of his mouth, he could see a wall of chaff come flying up from the frigates. But the attacking jet was too far away from the close-to-shore frigates. The pilot launched his missile and immediately fled the area. Hunter instinctively wanted to chase the retreating airplane, but there was a much more immediate threat.

The Exocet was heading right for the *Saratoga* . . .

Without an instant's hesitation, Hunter launched a Sidewinder, although he was not in a line-of-sight position. It was the only chance he had, and a risky one at that.

He was hoping the Sidewinder would get to the Exocet before the Exocet got to the carrier. It would be missile against missile. The Sidewinder was infra-red, the Exocet was radar-targeted. The Exocet was an anti-shipper, the Sidewinder an air-to-air. The Exocet was bigger, faster, much more powerful — its warhead could damage the carrier beyond repair.

The Sidewinder was more nimble, but it was carrying only enough explosive to shoot down an aircraft. Plus it would have to make one hell of a maneuver to get to the Exocet. But Hunter knew the Sidewinder had at least one advantage: it could take out a target head on. He crossed his fingers and watched the drama unfold.

The Sidewinder twisted down toward the Exocet, homing in on its infra-red target. Urging it on with body English, Hunter watched as his missile executed the necessary 120-degree turn. The Exocet was now less than 500 feet off the bow of the *Saratoga*. Gunners on all four frigates were throwing up a wall of bullets in the enemy missile's general direction hoping a lucky shot would hit the missile. Even the SAS men on the deck of the carrier were firing at the oncoming missile with their rifles as it came right for them. "Christ," Hunter whispered. "This is going to be real close . . ."

The Sidewinder won the race . . .

Just 100 feet off the side of the carrier, the smaller American-made weapon caught the front fin of the Exocet, clipping it and causing its warhead to explode before it hit the carrier. Pieces of near-supersonic debris still carried on into the side of the *Saratoga,* but with much less force and resulting damage than if the missile had impacted intact. A small fire broke out on the carrier, but Hunter, streaking by the big ship, knew it was manageable.

He heard a burst of cheers from his earphones. "Good shooting, Hunter!" Sir Neil's voice came through, so loud it caused his ears to ring.

"Don't thank me," Hunter said, only half-jokingly. "Thank the guys who built that Sidewinder so many years ago. That's what it means to be 'Made in the USA.' "

But now there was a new threat.

While Hunter was taking on the Exocets, a major battle had erupted on Gold Beach. Approximately 500 SAS troops were ashore and they were battling many of the T-62 tanks that had moved up from the town. Another group of about a dozen tanks were firing directly on the frigates, which were aggressively firing back.

The Tornados were strafing the tanks firing at the beach soldiers, but already one of the jets had been shot down by a shoulder-launched SAM. Two other Tornados were low on fuel and ammo and would shortly have to return to Majorca.

But in his highly trained mind's eye, Hunter knew the battle would soon change. It was getting dark, and right now the night would be the Recovery Force's best ally. He swooped in over the beach and started strafing the T-62s. Meanwhile, shells from the frigate's deck guns were finding targets in the enemy column. The SAS troops were also joining the fray, sending mortar shells crashing on to the enemy-controlled highway near their beachhead.

Two more passes over the tank column and Hunter saw the predicted change in the battle. The tanks were withdrawing to the side of the road where their crews would dig them in. They could continue to shell the beachhead from these stationary positions, but the battle had reached a point where the tanks needed to be resupplied.

As darkness quickly enveloped the area, the shooting on both sides died down to just scattered exchanges. Both sides hunkered down for the night.

Chapter 12

"OK, F-16," the voice crackled through the radio, "you are cleared for landing."

Hunter began a final turn over the USS *Saratoga*. He'd been circling the carrier for nearly an hour, using every trick in the book to preserve his precious fuel. Now he had about five minutes' worth of gas remaining.

It was nearly completely dark. A full moon was rising, and with it the tides. The SAS beachhead troops were exchanging scattered fire with the Faction tanks. The three Norwegian frigates were sweeping up and down the shoreline, battering both the tanks and the city of Villefranche itself with their small but powerful deck guns. Meanwhile the SAS carrier contingent had secured the *Saratoga* and Yaz's men were on board. They had been able to fix two of the four arresting cables on the carrier's deck in record time, setting up a bank of temporary floodlights in the process. Now it was time to test the cables.

Hunter had never attempted a carrier landing before, but he had hooked onto arresting cables on many occasions. He brought the F-16 down low as he made the final turn to the carrier. The floodlights that bathed the carrier deck gave it the appearance of a football field at night. He lined up the centerline of the deck with his HUD display and brought down his landing gear. The carrier was listing at a slight angle, but not enough to bother him.

Yaz himself was on the radio, his voice calmly calling out the wind direction and the all-important distance-to-ship measurement. The Navy man confirmed that the F-16's arresting hook was fully deployed.

Hunter was now 500 feet out. He caressed the F-16's side-stick controller. Flaps were lowered, air brakes engaged. 300 feet to go. He pulled the nose up slightly. A cross wind came up, causing him to dip the starboard wing slightly. 200 feet. Down a little more. His speed was just 120 knots. He throttled back on Yaz's suggestion. 150 feet out. He could see the two arresting cables now. He would try for the first one. Missing that, he could always hope to snag the second one. If that were unsuccessful, he would be swimming for his life in the dark waters of the Med.

"OK, major," Hunter heard Yaz say. "You're looking good. Down just a hair. One hundred feet to go. Throttle back. Back. Steady. Nose up a little. Good!"

Hunter's F-16 hit the first cable. There was a great screech and a burst of friction smoke as the arresting hook grabbed the cable, stretched it to its full limit, and snapped back. The F-16 shuddered all over, its engines screaming. Hunter was thrown forward in the cockpit, then slammed back against his seat. What a rush! he thought. He was down. The airplane was safe. From 100 mph to a dead stop in a second and a half. No wonder the Navy guys likened carrier landings to "having sex in a car wreck."

The 16 was immediately surrounded by Yaz's men, who started attaching securing lines to the aircraft and bolting them to the carrier deck. He could see other sailors were already draping the heavy-wound towlines over the stern of the carrier in preparation for O'Brien's tugs. Hunter popped the canopy and climbed out. Heath and Yaz were waiting for him.

"This might be a first," Yaz told him. "An Air Force plane landing on a Navy carrier . . . unopposed, that is."

Hunter checked over the fighter and, once he was convinced it was in relatively good shape, he, Heath, and Yaz headed towards the *Saratoga*'s Combat Information Center or CIC, the central nervous system of any warship. As they walked along the ship's passageways, Hunter could see SAS men and Yaz's sailors running throughout the ship performing their prearranged tasks.

"The beachhead is in good shape," the British officer told him. "Our SAS guys have occupied the shoreline buildings and have a good defensive perimeter set up. We're lucky because the Faction are not known as night-fighters and the Iron Fist people are probably cowering under their beds."

"How about the ship's launch system?" Hunter asked. "Can we get it working?"

Yaz raised his hands to display two sets of crossed fingers. "We got electricity to the primary controls," he said. "And the hydraulic pumps for the steam catapult are fixable. If the steam tanks don't leak and the pipes take the pressure, we could launch in less than three hours if we had to."

Hunter felt a jolt of pride for the Navy guys. He

knew the jobs Yaz had described would usually take at least a day to complete.

"No trouble when your chopper guys landed on board?" Hunter asked Heath.

Heath shook his head. "The ship was nearly empty," he said.

"Nearly?"

"Except for one person," Heath said. "I'll introduce you."

They reached the bridge to find a squad of SAS men surrounding a strange figure. It was an old man, dressed in rags and sporting a dirty, gray beard and long, stringy hair that nearly reached his waist. He was wearing a sackcloth tied at the middle with a piece of electrical wire and dilapidated combat boots on his feet. A dozen garishly colored strings of beads hung around his neck. He looked like both a hermit and an out-of-date hippie. The man was sitting in an old pine box that looked to be a cross between a bed and a coffin. His eyes closed as if he was meditating.

"Who's the old guy?" Hunter asked.

"His name is Peter," Heath said. "Or so he tells us. We found him here, in this box. Says he's been living here for a while. Also says that he's been 'expecting us.' "

The man opened his eyes and looked at Hunter. The pilot could tell right away the man was a little crazy.

"It's him!" Peter started yelling. "He's come!"

Hunter looked at Heath. "Who the hell is he talking about?"

"I think he's talking about you, major," Heath answered.

Peter bounded out of the box and into a kneeling position. He started chanting loudly in gibberish, pausing occasionally to look up at Hunter and let out an insane laugh.

"Christ," Hunter said. "This guy's nuts . . ."

"Maybe so," Heath said. "But look at this." He picked up a notebook and gave it to Hunter. "The SAS guys found him writing away in this when they came aboard."

Hunter recognized the book as a typical ship's log. He was surprised to find the writing inside was not only extremely neat and readable, it was almost stylized, like that in a Bible.

Hunter started reading the log and felt a wave of astonishment pass over him. There, on the first three pages, was a completely accurate version of what he and the Brits had been doing in the past week. From the bombing at the Highway Base to the trip to Algiers to their attacking Villefranche to their boarding of the *Saratoga*. It mentioned Sir Neil, Heath, Hunter, and even Yaz by name. The whole story — right up to the section titled "Peter Meets the Pilot" — written as if it were already history.

"How the hell did this guy know all this?" Hunter asked, plainly shocked.

Heath could only shrug his shoulders. "We don't have the foggiest idea," the Englishman said. "A bit spooky, don't you think?"

"Spooky?" Hunter said. "It's damned scary!"

Hunter looked at the man called Peter. He was now lying prostrate on the floor, his soft moaning muffled by his wild hair and beard.

"He says he's been living on ship for a long time," Heath continued. "Waiting for us. Hiding from the Fist and the Faction whenever they came aboard. He apparently knows the ship like the back of his hand. He might even be a member of the original crew,

114

though from all that mumbling he's doing, it's hard to pick out an accent."

"Yeah, he also looks pretty old to be a regular crew member," Yaz said. "He could be a CPO or even an officer, though."

Hunter knelt down beside the man. "Hey, pal," he said in a soothing, coaxing tone. "Who told you we were coming?"

The man looked up at him, his shaking hands brushing the hair from his face. "I knew . . ." he said in a trembling voice. "I've known for years . . ."

Those eyes, Hunter thought. He saw madness behind them, but also a flicker of intelligence. "What else do you know?" he asked.

The man gathered himself back up into a kneeling position and closed his eyes tight. "Women! I see painted women," he said through gritted teeth. "Beautiful women. You'll see them to! And flowers! Green flowers floating in the ocean!"

Hunter caught Heath's eye. The Englishman was shaking his head as if to confirm that he believed the man was nuts.

Still, Peter went on, his voice going low. "I see a face in the sky," he croaked. "I see the ocean burning. I see you, the pilot, alone in the desert. And I see Viktor . . ."

"What do you know about Viktor?" Hunter asked him quickly.

Peter's eyes went wide with authentic terror. "Viktor *is* Lucifer. Lucifer *is* Viktor. He is the Evil sent to destroy the world . . ."

"Well, he's got that part right," Hunter said.

Peter then stretched upward and put out his arms as if he were hanging on a cross. *"Lucifer!"* he bellowed, startling everyone in the room, including the battle-hardened SAS men. *"He* is the Antichrist!"

"Oh, brother," Hunter said, instinctively backing away from the man. "Not this . . ."

"Lucifer is the real thing—he comes from Hell, I tell you!" the old man screamed, his voice tortured and cracked. "He *is* six-six-six . . ."

"The man is over the edge," Heath said.

Suddenly Peter's head was bolt upright. He began to shake uncontrollably. "Listen!" he whispered. "Here it comes . . ."

Those in the room could hear a faint whistling sound, quickly getting louder.

"Incoming!" someone yelled.

Bang!

Suddenly the whole ship shuddered with the sound of an explosion. The lights flickered twice, then went out completely. In a second, the CIC was filled with black, acrid smoke. The crackling of flames could be heard in the next compartment.

Instantly, the room was a scene of controlled confusion as those inside tried to make their way in the smoky blackness to decks above.

The man called Peter let out a long agonizing scream, then sank back to the darkened floor . . .

Chapter 13

Hunter was already on the carrier deck before the second shell hit the *Saratoga*. He had recognized the distinctive whistling sound of the howitzer and could tell by its pitch that it was being fired at the ship from a position somewhere near Villefranche.

Heath and Yaz were right behind him when he reached the deck. Off in the distance they could hear the thumping of the three howitzers firing simultaneously.

"I hear them but I don't see them!" Yaz said trying to locate the howitzers' positions.

"They're hidden in the town, probably close to the shoreline," Hunter said. "Those are the only kind of guns that could possibly have the range to do us some damage."

"Jesus, I didn't think the Faction had such heavy-duty stuff," Heath said as one of the shells crashed into the sea just 100 yards off the port side of the carrier.

"Maybe they don't," Hunter said. "They could have got lucky and hired a free-lance howitzer group that was camped nearby."

The shoreline was now a portrait of flames and

smoke. The beachhead had yet to be attacked by the howitzers. Whoever was firing the ten-mile-range guns was zeroing in on the carrier. The first shot had been a lucky hit right against the side of the ship near the CIC. Fortunately, it made more noise than anything else, and Yaz's men were already fighting the small blaze that had broken out. But other shells were now landing dangerously close. Two of the frigates were moving into position off Villefranche in an attempt to locate the howitzers' hidden positions. One of them was the command ship carrying Sir Neil and the Recovery Mission planners. But Hunter knew the frigates' gunners would not be able to get in close enough to find out where the big guns were.

Just then one of Heath's men yelled to him from the bridge on the carrier's conning tower. "Sir! The tugs are here!"

The trio whirled around to see a group of red and white blinking lights stretching across the dark horizon. "Well, well, Mr. O'Brien," Heath said. "You've arrived ahead of schedule . . ."

"And just in time," Yaz added.

"We've got to get this show on the road," Hunter said. "Yaz, get on the horn to Sir Neil, will you? Tell him the tugs have arrived and we've got to start pulling the SAS guys off the beach now."

"Where you going, major?" Yaz wanted to know.

Hunter and Heath were already running toward the big Sea King helicopter sitting on the carrier deck. "We're going to find those howitzers!" he yelled back.

The Sea King was armed with two outdated but still effective 40mm grenade launchers. Heath had automatically jumped behind the controls of the big chopper and Hunter had strapped himself into the side-door gunner's seat. They were airborne less than a minute later, taking off just as a howitzer shell had come crashing down on the deck, dangerously close to where the F-16 was parked.

Hunter hung out the open bay door of the chopper as Heath steered the Sea King toward the shore. Already a frigate was moving toward the SAS beach-head, preparing to take off the first contingent of troops. Sir Neil's command ship was still looking for the howitzers, but now the entrenched T-62 tank crews—probably awakened by the resurgence in fighting—were beginning to take shots at the Norwegian ship. Soon the night sky was filled with hundreds of crisscrossing shells.

"Let's drop in by the back door!" Hunter yelled to Heath. The smiling Englishman with the enormous red mustache gave Hunter the thumbs-up signal and put the chopper into a steep bank. Soon they were away from the battle and over the dark hills of southern France.

Heath brought the chopper inland about twenty miles, then he turned south again, the fires of Villefranche providing a good beacon for them. Hunter studied the outline of the town. Then, amidst the smoke and the flames, he saw one, then two, then three telltale muzzle flashes. He yelled to Heath and pointed. The howitzers were mobiles—huge tank-like vehicles capable of firing, then moving to another position. Right now, they were on the far outskirts of the city, partially hidden by a seawall and practically impossible to see from the frigates. Heath gunned the Sea King in their direction.

The chopper was over the city by the time Hunter had figured out how to fire the grenade launcher. He had to guess at the fusing mechanisms, though. Twisting the timer on one grenade, he loaded one of the launcher's twin tubes. Below them they could see soldiers running helter-skelter in the streets of Villefranche. The frigates had resumed shelling the city itself, hoping they'd get a lucky shot at the howitzers. These shells were causing much panic among the Iron Fist soldiers, clearly visible in their yellow designer uniforms. Fires from the Tornados' bombing hours earlier were still burning unchecked. The noise and confusion were so intense no one noted the Sea King passing overhead.

Within seconds they were close behind the howitzers' position. Hunter had a clear view of the big guns, lined up along a sea wall methodically pumping out shells towards the carrier. Heath slowed the chopper down and hovered about 100 yards away from the closest mobile gun.

"Hold her steady, captain," Hunter yelled to the Englishman. He eye-sighted the grenade launcher and pulled the trigger. The launcher shuddered and belched a small cloud of black smoke that nearly asphyxiated Hunter.

Through red eyes, he followed the path of the grenade as it impacted on the turret of the first gun, blowing off a chunk of the tank-like body.

"Direct hit!" Heath yelled. "Good shot, Hunter old boy!"

Already Hunter was lining up a shot on the second big gun. But by now, the howitzer crew had spotted the chopper and were training their smaller mounted machine guns on Heath and Hunter. Plus some courageous antiaircraft gunners in the nearby town had started firing at the Sea King.

Despite a murderous barrage being fired at him, Hunter calmly loaded the launcher and line-sighted the second howitzer. He launched a second grenade. This one hit the rear of the mounted cannon, igniting its fuel supply. Within two seconds, the howitzer was engulfed in flames.

"Jesus, what a lucky shot!" Hunter yelled out.

"Should we try for three?" Heath yelled to him, straining to be heard over the noisy clatter of the chopper blades as well as the intense fire from below.

"No! Back off!" Hunter yelled to Heath, who needed no further prompting. The Britisher bolted the Sea King around and flew back over the city and out of range of any brave antiaircraft gunners.

"We won't be able to surprise them like that a second time," Heath told him as soon as they had cleared the area.

"We won't have to," Hunter said. He had sensed the approaching aircraft. It was two of the Tornados, returning to the action after refueling and rearming back on Majorca.

Heath was already on the radio, giving the Tornados the coordinates of the howitzers' position. Hunter and the Englishman watched from a distance as the swing-wing fighters swooped in and took out the last howitzer with two well-placed antipersonnel bombs. Then the Tornados turned east and strafed the revived tank emplacements.

"Those boys have the situation under control," Hunter called out to Heath. "Let's head for the beach."

The Englishman steered towards the SAS beachhead and soon the Sea King was down on the shore. Landing craft from the Norwegian frigates were busy ferrying SAS men off the beach, despite an occasional tank round landing in the sand or in the shallow water.

Hunter jumped out of the copter and quickly found the SAS beachmaster. He knew that if the SAS force had taken some casualties, the Sea King would be the fastest mode of transporting them to the medical unit on the command frigate. But the SAS casualties had been surprisingly light.

However, there were other "passengers" the SAS men wanted Hunter to evacuate . . .

"Right after we landed we moved into this small hotel near the highway road," the SAS beachmaster, a Scotsman named Montgomery, told Hunter as the two men walked toward the three blocks of buildings the SAS had temporarily occupied. "We were using it as an observation post when we heard screams coming from the cellar. We found a bunch of, well, *citizens* down there."

"Citizens?"

"Aye!" Montgomery said. "The Fist was using it as a jail or some such thing. Had these people under lock and key. Some were chained to their beds."

Reaching the hotel, Montgomery led him to a room off the lobby. Hunter sensed there was something unusual about the liberated citizens. He was right. Inside sat twenty-four beautiful, if slightly disheveled, women. The women were too busy eating the K-rations the SAS men had given them to notice Hunter and Montgomery had walked in.

"Ladies of the night, they are . . ." Montgomery explained. "They say they've been held hostage here by the Fist for better than two years. Been, should we say, 'servicing' them and the Faction soldiers all that time. Not getting a dime for it either."

Beautiful women? Painted ladies? Revolutionary mistresses? Hunter thought.

"They've been a great help to us," Montgomery continued. "Pointing out enemy positions and so on.

Those bastards will kill them all if we leave them behind."

One of the women, slightly older, yet no less beautiful, came up to Hunter and the beachmaster. Her name was Clara, Montgomery explained, and she was the House Madam.

"Can you take us with you?" Clara asked Hunter, her hand strategically resting on his chest. "The boys told us you are swiping that big ship out there. Well, swipe us too!'

Clara oozed sensuality. She, like the rest of her troop, was dressed in a 1960s-style miniskirt, low-cut blouse, dark stockings, and high heels. Despite her "ordeal," she was in good shape, as it were. *Very* good shape . . .

"We'll go anywhere, *do anything,* just to get out of here," she said, with a well-practiced, innocent smile.

Hunter turned to Montgomery. "Who's the senior man here?"

Montgomery, a field captain, shifted uneasily. "Well, sir," he said, slowly. "The colonel took a bullet in the groin and he's already been sea-lifted back to the ship. Our Sergeant-Major was killed by a tank shell. All that's left are captains and a few lieutenants.

"I guess that makes you the senior man, suh!"

Hunter detected a slight smile on the Scot.

Why do these things always happen to me? Hunter had to ask himself.

Outside, the sporadic sounds of gunfire suddenly flared up. An artillery shell, fired from somewhere near the Faction T-62 emplacements a half mile away, crashed down on the street outside the hotel. One of the Tornados streaked low overhead, rattling the hotel from top to bottom.

"Sounds like things are heating up outside, major," Montgomery said.

Hunter was still wrestling with the question of what the Recovery Force could possibly do with the twenty-four prostitutes when another tank shell landed right outside the hotel, shattering the few remaining intact windows in the place. A few cries came from the assembled ladies.

"Okay," Hunter said, making his decision. "We'll lift the girls out in the chopper. Captain, you'd better start withdrawing the last of your men."

"Aye, aye, suh!" Montgomery said, flashing a smile and an authentic opened-palmed British salute.

Clara's arms were around Hunter in a half-second. "Thank you, Major," she cooed. "We are very . . . grateful."

Ten minutes later, a very surprised Captain Heath was helping Hunter load the two dozen women onto the Sea King. The last of the SAS troopers were climbing aboard their landing crafts even as a new barrage of tank shells came crashing down on the beach. The rejuvenated attack was too little too late. The temporary SAS occupation was coming to an end, their mission successful.

Heath gave Hunter and the women a thumbs-up signal and lifted off the beach, plotting a course to the command frigate. Passing the *Saratoga* on the way, Hunter could see that Yaz's men had already attached heavy-wound lines of rope to twelve of O'Brien tugs. Eight more of the tugs were circling nearby. In the light of their salvage beacons, Hunter could see each tug had an enormous shamrock painted on its deck. They looked like huge green flowers, floating on the sea. The work appeared to be proceeding so smoothly, Hunter estimated the carrier would be moving before sun up.

He caught Heath stealing glimpses of the women crowded into the helicopter compartment. "Wait until Sir Neil sees this," Heath yelled.

But even the presence of the two dozen beauties was not enough to distract Hunter from his deeper thoughts. He just couldn't get the words the old man Peter had spoke out of his head . . .

Chapter 14

The F-4 Phantom turned high over the desert highway base and came in for a landing.

Gone were the tents and temporary buildings, the water tanks and antiaircraft batteries. No Tornados sat on the pavement runway or patrolled the nearby air space. All that remained of the RAF highway base was a weatherworn desert mobile house trailer, three fuel tanker trucks parked side by side, and two elderly reservists of the Gibraltar Home Guard.

Captain Crunch rolled the jet fighter to a halt and popped the canopy. The two reservists, their game of gin rummy interrupted, walked over to the jet as the airplane's engine was just beginning to wind down.

"Are you here for fuel, lads?" one of the reservists, a man named Smythe, yelled up to Crunch and Elvis, a flexible silver ladder under his arm.

"Yes, if you have JP-8," Crunch yelled back.

"We do," Smythe called back. "Have yer got gold or silver?"

"Silver," Crunch said, holding up four bags. "We're close to dry. Can you give us enough to make the next big base?"

"Twenty minutes from here on afterburner," Smythe answered, his words easier to hear as the F-4's engine spun to a halt. "Are you Canadians here for the war?"

"We're from America," Crunch called back. "We're looking for another American. A pilot named Hunter."

"Hunter, you say?" Smythe called back. "Does he fly a fancy jet airplane? Red and white and blue?"

"That's the man," Crunch said, standing up in the Phantom's front seat. "Have you seen him?"

"He was here," the other reservist said. "Back when this place was a working air base."

Both Crunch and Elvis looked around. They had assumed the base had always looked like this: two stretches of straight highway with the reservists' trailer and the fuel trucks.

"You mean this was once more than just a fuel stop?" Elvis asked.

"Aye, lad," Smythe said as his partner headed off to start one of the gas trucks and begin the refueling. "A few weeks ago, this was a major base for the Gibraltar Defense Force, that being formerly a part of the RAF."

Smythe unfolded his ladder and put it up against the F-4. He slowly climbed up until he was eye level with the two pilots. Unstrapping a bottle of ice water from his belt, he passed it to the pilot.

"You look like you got a bad wing there," Smythe said looking at the Phantom's starboard side.

"We did a skid back in Casablanca," Crunch told him, taking a long swig of ice water, then passing the bottle back to Elvis.

"Casablanca!" The old man laughed. "Well, you boys are lucky you made it out of there with just a twisted wing!"

127

"You saw Hunter?" Crunch asked.

"No," Smythe answered. "But we heard about him. He saved this base he did. Stopped two out of three missiles from blowing the place off the map. What a corker! Flipped the bloody things right over, they say."

Crunch eyed the scarred portion of the highway-runway where the third missile had fallen, then asked, "Do you know where Hunter is now?"

"Yes I do," Smythe told him. "He's gone. Gone with the rest of them. Gone to fight the war."

Crunch looked at Elvis, then shook his head. "Do you *exactly* where?"

Smythe laughed. "Aye, haven't you blokes heard? He and the RAF guys are sailing a carrier to the Suez! Going to stop that Lucifer character right where he lives, the arse!"

"An *aircraft* carrier?" Crunch said in disbelief.

"It's a grand-sounding adventure isn't it?" Smythe said. "*A Crusade* they are calling it. I'd be with them if I wasn't seventy years old. They all left — days ago. Sent Roger and me here. Just to top off the tanks of the regular customers we get through here. Things have been slow, though, mate. The war is coming. People are afraid to fly, even this far west."

Roger had arrived with the fuel truck and began filling the F-4's wing tanks. Smythe pulled out a piece of beef jerky and started chewing on it.

"Course they haven't got a prayer, the poor bastards," he said.

"Who's that?" Crunch asked.

"Well, your boy Hunter and the heroes of the RAF, I'd say," Smythe replied. "They're sailing to an early death if you ask me. Why, they'll be lucky if they make it past Crete. Do you know what the Med is like these days, lads? Blimey. It's filled with

Russians, terrorists, Lucifer's allies, and Lord knows what else. And that's even before you get to Lucifer's Kingdom. Who knows what's floating around out there.

"Aye, those RAF guys. Brave. Filled with courage they are. And your boy Hunter too, of course. Brave fools, laddies."

Roger had completed filling up the F-4's tank. Crunch turned over four bags of silver to Smythe.

"Where can we find out more about this crusade?" Crunch asked, flipping his standby switches and turning on the F-4's generator.

"You're heading there, mates," Smythe said, taking his bottle and descending the ladder. "Gibraltar, lads. Been having trouble raising them on the radio this morning. But don't worry. They'll tell you all about it in Gibraltar . . ."

With that, Crunch lowered the canopy, gave Smythe a wave, and taxied the jet slowly to the end of the highway runway. The two reservists watched as a spit of flame erupted from the back of the F-4. Then, its engine screaming, the Phantom roared down the runway, lifted off, and disappeared over the horizon.

Chapter 15

Hunter brought up the throttle on the F-16 and made a final check of his instruments. Everything was okay. He gave the thumbs-up signal to one of Yaz's men standing next to the aircraft, then leaned back in the fighter's seat and braced himself. A long thin wisp of steam rose up in front of him as he counted down:

". . . three . . . two . . . one . . . Now!"

He was slammed against the seat with such a force, his ears started ringing. The carrier deck whipped by in a blur and next thing he knew, he was out over the open sea. The F-16 had gone from standing still to 120 mph in less than three seconds.

"Jeezuz!" he thought as he yanked back on the side-stick controller and gained altitude. "No wonder those Navy pilots are all crazy."

The first catapult launch in a long time from the deck of the USS *Saratoga* was a success.

They were now more than fifty miles away from the Riviera and heading east. Moving the *Saratoga* proved to be just another few hours' work for O'Brien's tugs. The Irishman and his men had pulled and pushed and pulled some more with their twenty extra-large tugboats. Just as the sun was coming up, O'Brien got all of his tugs working together and, sure enough, the carrier slipped off its sandy resting place and out into deep water once again. All the Faction tank gunners could do was lob a few angry but meaningless shells into the sea as the *Saratoga* and its strange attending fleet of tugs and frigates sailed away.

Yaz's guys had the steam catapult working soon afterwards, and by nine o'clock Hunter was ready to attempt a takeoff. The *Saratoga* needed air protection quick; it was still moving fairly slowly and would be a sitting duck for a well-placed Exocet missile. So Hunter began what would be the first of many combat air patrols.

The carrier's first destination was the coast of Algeria. That was where they would pick up the bulk of their hired fighting force, plus meet the oiler that O'Brien had arranged for. In the meantime, the six Tornados and the two dozen other aircraft that Sir Neil's men had commandeered from their RAF units would begin the risky business of learning how to land and takeoff from a carrier deck.

As Hunter soared to 10,000 feet, he was both fascinated and amused by the sight below him. There was the *Saratoga*, from stem to stern nearly a quarter-mile long, looking magnificent against the sparkling water of the Med. The amusing part was the twelve tugs that were pulling and the eight that were pushing the majestic ship.

It was at that moment that Hunter had to stop and remind himself just what the hell he was doing. *Towing* a lifeless nuclear aircraft carrier across 1500 miles of God-knows-what all the way to the Suez Canal? In the vanguard of a modern-day crusade? Only in the New Order world could such an outrageous enterprise make sense. And only an Englishman could have talked him—or any of them—into joining up. The question was: would it lead him to Lucifer?

Another thing worried Hunter. The conglomeration of jet aircraft the RAF had assembled for the adventure ranged from eleven state-of-the-art Tornados to four shitbox Jaguars, aircraft built way before Hunter was even born. Sure, there were three Harrier jump-jets he could count on, plus an American-built S-A3, but most of the aircraft were more suited for ground support. His 16 was the only real fighter-interceptor in the bunch.

The problem was weaponry: the RAF had managed to buy a fair quantity of bombs—from napalm to antipersonnel bomblets and everything in between—that could be fitted to most of their aircraft. But for Hunter, the only real dogfighter in the group, there were only three Sidewinders to be had. He had previously rigged his F-16 to carry as many as twenty at a time. Should any real trouble happen—such as another Exocet attack or an air strike on the carrier—Hunter might expend three Sidewinders in a matter of seconds.

He wrestled with these and other thoughts as he slowly orbited the *Saratoga*. They were cruising on a slow southeasterly course, in the general direction of the Algerian coast, but also close enough to Majorca so the four helicopters at their disposal could ferry equipment out from the island. Now, as he watched from above, two Tornados, arresting hooks newly installed on the underbellies, approached to practice landing on the carrier.

O'Brien's tugs had slowed the carrier down to a dead stop and turned her into the wind. A stationary target was much easier to land on than one that was moving. But it was crucial that they get all twenty-four airplane pilots up to speed on carrier landings within the next thirty-six hours. Beyond that, aircraft flying out from Majorca would have to stay there, because they would be beyond their operating range and to wait for them would disrupt Sir Neil's rigorously planned timetable.

Hunter watched as the first Tornado came in for its initial try. The Norwegian frigates were strategically placed around the carrier in case one of the RAF airplanes went into the drink. The Sea King helicopter hovered nearby, ready for sea-rescue duty if needed, as were O'Brien's idle tugs. The Tornado came in hard, bounced on the deck, and received the wave-off. The pilot gunned its engine and the plane screamed for altitude. After a long arc around the carrier, the Tornado tried again. But this second attempt only resulted in a higher bounce on the *Saratoga*'s deck and another wave-off.

"Come on, Redcoat," Hunter murmured. "Set it down once and you'll be doing it in your sleep in two weeks."

The Tornado's third attempt was successful, and everyone breathed easier. His wingman made it on board in two attempts. As soon as their airplanes were cleared away — via the carrier's huge and now-working mid-deck elevator — two more Tornados appeared on the horizon. They too received several wave-offs before finally setting down. That's when two elderly Jaguars arrived, and to just about everyone's delight set down perfectly on the carrier, each on the first try.

For the next hour they came: seven more Tornados, two more Jaguars. Then came the unusual American-made, S3-A Navy antisubmarine aircraft, a small, twin-engined airplane that looked like a minibomber. This airplane — contracted from an Australian pilot — was painted entirely in garish punk pink.

Somehow, the RAF guys had got a hold of four SAAB JA37 Viggens, veterans of the Swedish Air Force. Because these ground-attack airplanes were custom-made to operate from highways and very short airstrips, setting them down on the carrier proved to be no problem.

Finally, the Harrier jump-jets arrived, each one setting down on the carrier deck vertically. Now, all the airplanes were aboard. Within minutes, O'Brien's tugs gunned their engines and began the pull-push process once again.

Before he prepared to land, Hunter put the F-16 into a steep climb. He soared past 30,000, 40,000, 50,000 feet. The atmosphere was extraordinarily clear, the sun bright as he had ever seen it. A good feeling washed over him. What the hell? So they're towing the goddamn carrier across the Med. They'll have twenty-five jet fighters, and more than 8500 soldiers on board. Plus the frigates and the armed tugs—it all made for a formidable fleet. *Maybe it would all lead him to Lucifer . . .*

He turned the jet over and pointed it to the east. Instantly he felt the euphoria drain from him. Off on the eastern horizon was a cloud bank so dark it looked like the onset of night. Long, mile-high spirals of churning black and gray cumulus clouds washed over the sky like huge, nightmarish, slow-motion tidal waves. Hunter knew an omen when he saw one. This adventure would be anything but a leisurely cruise across the Med. God help us, he thought.

He put the F-16 into a dive and headed back for the carrier.

Chapter 16

Hunter brought the F-16 in for a now-routine carrier landing. His approach was slightly distracted by a group of people standing on the lip of the flattop's deck. Strangely, at first, he thought they were aiming a gun at him. In an instant though he realized it wasn't a gun at all—it was a movie camera.

The 16 screeched to a halt and Hunter jumped out, leaving the aircraft in the capable hands of Yaz's sailors. As he stepped down onto the carrier deck, he noticed the camera crew had rushed to the side of the jet and that they were faithfully recording his every movement.

"Hold it right there, we got some dramatic light," the man who seemed to be the leader of the film crew yelled to him. "Give us a salute, major!"

Hunter awkwardly saluted, then hurried to the nearest hatch door. Sir Neil was coming out just as he was going in.

"Hunter, old boy!" the Englishman said with a mile-wide grin. "I thought all you Yanks were keen on being in the flicks? Hollywood and all that."

"You'll have to talk to my agent," Hunter said, removing his flight helmet and running his hand through his longish sandy hair. "Where did you dig up the camera crew?"

"They were a BBC unit attached to our base when the Big War started," Sir Neil said, walking with him toward the ship's mess. "We were stuck with them, and they with us, when the big battles were going on. Got some incredible footage of the first few days of fighting, they did. When the war died down, they had nowhere to go. So I commissioned them and they've been with us ever since."

Hunter guessed the rest from there. "And you're recording our mission to Suez then?" he asked.

"Yes," Sir Neil said. "I can't resist. They were able to dig up some fairly high-tech video equipment somewhere around Casablanca a few months ago, and miles of blank videotape. So I figured, 'Why not?' Whatever happens to us, it will be preserved for posterity. They got some great stuff of our recent engagement with the Fist and the Faction, especially your removal of those howitzers."

Hunter shook his head in admiration of the robust British commander. For Sir Neil, the mission to Suez was more than a preemptive action spearheading for the Modern Knights and their armies; it was a high adventure, and Sir Neil had the kind of love for a bold undertaking that was in every English soldier's blood since, well, since there was an England.

They arrived at the ship's mess, where a temporary kitchen had been set up. They waited in line with everyone else, old-fashioned tin cups in hand. Once served, they sought out an empty table. The fare for the day was nothing more than a watery stew, slightly peppered with a rare piece of vegetable floating around.

Hunter took one sip and grimaced. "God, we've got to do something about the food," he said.

"And the aircraft fuel situation," Sir Neil said, coughing himself on the bitter-tasting stew. "And the electricity. Yaz's guys are straining the two generators we have on board."

"And ammo for my 16," Hunter said, continuing the list.

"Aye, Hunter," Sir Neil said, finally giving up on the stew and reaching instead for a stale piece of bread. "I know we're not exactly flush in the Sidewinder department. And we could use some more antiaircraft and antimissile defenses. Not just for us, here on the carrier, but for O'Brien's tugs too. They're as valuable to us as anything."

"Will we be able to afford some of this stuff on the black market when we reach Algiers?" Hunter asked, attacking a piece of bread himself.

"Afford it, by all mean, yes," Sir Neil said. "But whether it will be available is the real question. Raleigh is back at Algiers now, organizing the pickup of our mercenaries. He called in to say that most of the top arms are being bought up — both openly and secretly — by Lucifer's allies. The neutrals are getting into the action too. The rumor is the people who are holding all these weapons — the behind-the-scenes blokes — are turning off the spigot for a while. Driving the prices up. An artificial shortage. Raleigh says there probably won't be very much left when we get there."

"It's a problem," Hunter said. "We know things can get hairy after we pass through the Strait of Sicily. According to the schedule, that could be as soon as a week from now."

"We probably won't have to worry about it, major," Sir Neil said, taking one last brave sip of the stew before pushing it away from him. "The food will kill us long before that . . ."

An hour later, Hunter was inspecting the carrier's newly acquired air arm. He was particularly impressed with the Tornados, even if they were of the two-seat, ground-attack design. (The single-seat version was quicker and built for the interceptor role.) The Tornado was the only fighter aircraft made containing reverse thrusters. It could land on a dime. So the carrier landings would be soon quite routine for their pilots.

The SAAB Viggens too were durable aircraft, and Sir Neil had spoke highly of their Swedish mercenary pilots. The Harrier jump-jets would be the most handy, and the ancient Jaguars—well, he admired the pluck of anyone who would dare fly them, let alone fight in them.

But besides his F-16, it was the S-3A that would be the most valuable. The S-3A—owned and operated by an Australian pilot named E. J. Russell—had a vast array of sophisticated reconnaissance gear on board as well as "standoff" missile-attack and antiship capability. So this airplane could act as the *Saratoga*'s scout plane.

Many of the pilots knew who Hunter was, and as he walked amongst the aircraft they came up and introduced themselves. As Hunter was the overall air commander for the mission, it was up to him to coordinate the air arm's priorities and procedures. The first thing he did was schedule a meeting later that day for all of the pilots at which tactics and strategies would be discussed. His second act was to schedule a poker game to follow the first meeting.

He was in the middle of inspecting one of the Tornado's unique radar systems when the ship's intercom system barked out: "Major Hunter, please report to the bridge, immediately."

It was the first time the intercom had been used since the ship was liberated and it startled a number of people below the deck.

"Well, I'm glad they got that working," he said to one of the Tornado pilots as he climbed down from the Tornado and headed for the *Saratoga*'s bridge. "I think . . ."

The man called Peter was sitting in the chair normally reserved for the Captain when he was on the bridge. Surrounding the bizarre little man were Sir Neil, Heath, and Gjiff Olson, the commander of the Norwegian frigates.

"Hunter, you've got to hear this," Sir Neil told him as he walked in.

Peter was fighting with a long, slimy drool that was drenching the beard immediately around the sides of his mouth. His filthy hands were pulling at his tangled hair, which Hunter now noticed was falling out in clumps. The man was babbling as usual, staring off into space, alternately laughing and crying. But it was those eyes! Madness. *Craziness.* But windows to an intelligence that had not quite completely diminished but that could also apparently see what no others could see.

"Eyes in the sky!" Peter was yelling in between his unintelligible ranting. "*Follow me!* They're all gone to the orgy. We can *sneak* in. Caesar! Caesar! Beware the eyes in the sky . . ."

"What's going on?" Hunter asked.

"Be patient with us, major," Sir Neil said. "He's

139

been saying some very interesting things. He could be coming around to them again soon."

"Virgins! Sacrifice her! *Sacrifice her!*" Peter laughed, tears rolling down his craggy cheeks. "They've all gone to the party. Sidewinders. *Yes, Sidewinders!* More than I've ever seen!"

"Did he say Sidewinders?" Hunter had to ask, trying to make some sense out of the gurgle.

"Yes," Heath answered. "He's been saying it over and over for the past twenty minutes."

"Perhaps he knows something we don't?" Sir Neil said to Hunter.

Hunter shrugged and moved close to the man. "Peter," he said calmly, "where are the Sidewinders?"

The man turned and looked into Hunter's eyes, his gaze triggering a jolt that ran through to Hunter's brain. "You," he said. "You are The Wingman, aren't you? I know you are. I've been waiting for you."

Once again, Hunter was startled by one of Peter's revelations. Even in his spookishly accurate ship's log prophecy, he had never mentioned Hunter's "other" name.

"The Sidewinders, Peter," Hunter repeated. "Where are they?"

He grabbed Hunter's sleeve and pulled him close. The man looked as if he hadn't bathed in a decade or so, and now Hunter's nose confirmed it.

"You know I dream . . ." Peter said, his voice a raspy whisper. "I see many things . . . I know you see many things too."

Hunter couldn't argue with the man. He *did* possess a certain degree of extrasensory perception.

"They're all gone to the orgy," Peter continued. "Let's go! We can *sneak* in. We can *steal their Sidewinders!*"

140

"Where, Peter?" Hunter asked him, staring deep into those blue pools of madness. "Where are the Sidewinders?"

Peter drew himself up straight in the chair, brushed back his gooey hair, and said: "Cagliari . . ."

Chapter 17

The S-3A passed over the coast of Sardinia and turned southeast. The Australian pilot named E. J. Russell was at the controls; Hunter was strapped into the side-by-side copilot's seat, working the sophisticated surveillance gear. The airplane had recently received a coat of Navy gray to cover its former punk-pink color. It was flying at 56,500 feet, higher than any SAM that might be lurking on the western coast of the island, and hopefully beyond the reach of the radar they assumed was operating on the eastern edge.

Cagliari was the largest city on Sardinia, the island that sat below Corsica, and less than 200 air miles west of Rome. After the Big War started, the Italian Navy evacuated the civilians from the sparsely populated island as they were easier to protect back on the mainland. As the war intensified, all that remained on the island were the tens of thousands of goats that lived there — and the American troops stationed at the massive air base at Cagliari.

Cagliari's air base was built by the Americans in the 1980s for two good reasons. First, as a possible launching point for air strikes against the looney-tunes that once ruled Libya, and second, as a modern weapons-storage facility for NATO. Sardinia's central Mediterranean location and small population made it ideal for storing armaments that could be needed anywhere in the region. When fighting broke out in Europe, the aircraft stationed at the big base were instantly dispatched to the front. They never came back. Soviet SCUD missiles, carrying poison gas, hit the airbase soon afterward, killing every living thing on the island, including all of the base's ground personnel.

After the major battles of the war were over and done with, and the whole of Europe became a strange kind of netherworld, unseemly elements drifted down from northern Italy, sailed back to Sardinia, and claimed it as their own.

What they found was a huge military complex, an air base still virtually intact—containing, everything except the airplanes. There were many deep, underground, concrete bunkers containing thousands of weapons that were never used. It was an arms bonanza. So, the new Sardinians—deserters and war criminals, most of them—set up a large arms-wholesale operation.

At the same time, they wrapped the island—and their enterprise—in a veil of secrecy. They were wise to the point of knowing that the less said about what they had, the better. So they sold their wares through an army of middlemen, with entangled webs of backdoor deals and money passed in the night. They quietly reaped incredible profits. Though few of the buyers knew it, many of the weapons bought in the bazaars of Algiers—especially air weapons—originated from the underground warehouses just across the Med at Cagliari.

As a result of this strictly enforced code of silence — *omerta* was a tradition in the region — very few normally informed sources in the Med knew what was going on with the people running the Cagliari base these days. But the reports that filtered through — via rumors, travelers' stories, and gun-running braggadocio — added up to one strange situation.

The arms marketeers had quickly conquered Corsica to the north and set up a territory majestically called The Holy Sardinian Empire. And they took their ancient Roman history seriously. They reportedly paraded around in togas, accompanied by modern Roman-Legion-style guards. They acquired slaves and with the free labor built a slew of pseudo-Roman-style buildings — palaces, temples, coliseums, meeting houses, bathhouses, and aquariums. By raiding nearby Italy — now in the throes of anarchy — the Sardinians were able to capture their most prized possessions — their "virgins." These young girls — hundreds if not thousands of them — were used by the twenty central figures in the Sardinian government in a never-ending frenzy of lust and perversion. Not a day started on Sardinia without the obligatory virgin sacrifice, and the sado-masochistic rituals carried on all day and well into the night. The Sardinian rulers were apparently gluttons (they had appropriately built vomitoriums), living a satyr's life of endless food, wine, and sex with young girls. All of it was fueled by the profits they made selling the nearly bottomless supply of weapons held in storage in the underground warehouses at Cagliari.

How Peter knew there was a major celebration in the works for Sardinia was anyone's guess. But by using the S-3A's long-range, video-imaging, look-down radar, Hunter was able to confirm the strange man's prediction. Crossing over the center of the island, he could clearly see that preparations for some kind of holiday were going on inside the city of Cagliari itself even though it was the dead of night. The adjacent air base was all but unlit and apparently deserted. By monitoring local radio bands and using the small amount of Italian at his disposal, Hunter was able to ascertain that the celebration — The Day of the Kings, they were calling it — would take place in forty-eight hours.

The pilot Russell pulled the S-3A to the south and started a long sweep around the bottom of the island. Here Hunter got his first good look at the defenses surrounding the base at Cagliari itself. In a word, they were heavy.

"Christ, these guys have air defense in triple depth," Hunter said to Russell as he watched his video-imaging screen from the side jump seat of the S-3A. "It's all American stuff too. Hawks. Rapiers. I'm sure they must have hundreds of Stingers lying around too."

"They're like kids in a candy store, mate," Russell said, taking a peek at the video screen. "But how can they possibly have enough guys willing to man all that stuff? No one's ever attacked them — and with all that young stuff tied down and waiting for them, who'd want to sit in front of a Rapier screen all day?"

"That's a good question," Hunter said, sharpening the image on the video screen. "They must have a central firing station somewhere."

"You mean someplace where one or two guys can watch over the whole thing?" Russell asked.

"Possibly," Hunter said, unfastening his oxygen mask and stroking his two-day beard. "They would

145

see a blip coming and push the right buttons. Or maybe push *all* the buttons and hope they hit something."

The S-3A streaked on into the night, Hunter watching the video screen carefully for anything likely to be the base's central firing-control station.

Then he saw it. "Take a look at this, E.J.," Hunter told the pilot. "The place looks like a small temple of some sort. It's got a lot of what look like phone lines running into it."

"Yes, and it's up on a hill," Russell commented. "Good command of the sky in all directions."

Hunter pushed a bank of buttons and turned some fine-tuning knobs. "Bingo!" he said. "I got a lock on a radar dish. A big one too. Right next to the temple. But it's only operating at half power."

"They probably have to make their electricity locally, maybe with gas-driven generators," Russell said. "It would take a big one to run all those SAMs, though."

Hunter scribbled down a barrage of notes, then told Russell, "Okay, let's head for home."

"You got an idea, major?" the Aussie pilot asked.

"Not yet," Hunter said, smiling. "But I'm working on it."

Hunter lay awake on his bunk, thinking. He and Russell had landed the S-3A just an hour before; Sir Neil's BBC crew was all set up when they arrived to capture their landing on videotape. Now he was trying to catch some shut-eye before he briefed Sir Neil and the others on what they'd seen on Sardinia.

Of all the strangenesses going on, it was the man Peter that stuck in his mind. The *Saratoga* could use all the weapons it could get, especially Sidewinders.

146

The original plan was to buy anything they could on the Algiers black market, or get it by some other means. But even Sir Neil had admitted that he hadn't considered the armaments at Cagliari until Peter had gone into his trance on the bridge. The only well-known fact about the island empire was that it was considered too well defended to fool with. But Peter's prediction that "they'll all be at the orgy" seemed to be confirmed by Hunter's interception of radio signals concerning the "Day of the Kings" celebration. And if Peter's tip that the Sardinians could be caught with their pants down was true, it might signal an opportunity too good to pass up. Especially since Raleigh had reported that the flow of arms into the Algerian markets was quickly drying up.

The question was: did they dare risk an operation on the word of a crazy man?

Sir Neil and Hunter had had a lengthy discussion earlier on what to do with Peter. When he wasn't blathering on the bridge, he could be found blathering in his pine box, which Yaz and his guys had judiciously moved to an empty cabin. If Peter had been just an ordinary wacko, Sir Neil would have had one of the choppers set him down on the nearest dry land and that would have been it.

But obviously, Peter was not just a run-of-the-mill lunatic. Hunter had reread his prophetic ship's log three times and was chilled each time by its uncanny, *unearthly* accuracy. Names, places, events, all were exact. And, as far as anyone could figure out, Peter had simply pulled it out of the ether and scribbled it into the log.

Even in Peter's drooling ramblings there could be gems of prophecy. One obvious example: Hunter knew the "flowers on the sea" Peter ranted about were, in fact, O'Brien's shamrock-adorned tugs arriving just in time off the Riviera. Then there were the painted ladies . . .

So Sir Neil and Hunter decided that they couldn't just cast the loon off. Though they also agreed that he be watched by at least four SAS men at all times.

Hunter took a deep breath and rubbed his tired eyes. He could feel his bunk vibrating in the never-ending pull-push motion of the carrier as O'Brien's tugs worked endlessly into the night. His mind felt as if it too were in a pull-push mode. Was all this worth it? Did his mission even have the slightest chance of succeeding? Or was he just caught up in the adventurism that had nobly gripped the Brits? And still the major question nagged him: was all this swashbuckling eventually going to lead him to Viktor?

Like many events in his life, this one was getting very, very strange . . .

He closed his eyes and let his thoughts take off in a million different directions, a usual exercise before he drifted off to sleep. He knew several crucial events would dominate the next few days. They were soon to rendezvous with the rest of Olson's Norwegian frigates. Then the carrier would have to be put in its best defensive condition. But the first priority would be their arrival off the coast of Algiers to meet the oiler and the Moroccan desert fighters, the Aussie Special Forces, the French ship defensemen, the Spanish air defensemen, the Italians, and the rest of Yaz's men.

There was still a long road ahead . . .

He unconsciously reached into his pocket and felt the reassuring bulge of the folded American flag and the dog-eared corners of Dominique's photograph. He wished for a moment with Peter's perceptive power to look the thousands of miles to the west to where Dominique was. "I love you, honey," he whispered, his eyes closed tight. "I'll be home someday . . ."

Suddenly there was a knock at his door. The hatch swung open, and in the dim light Hunter could see the unmistakable form of a female. She came closer to him. It was Clara, the Madam.

She sat down on the edge of his bunk and nonchalantly put her hand on his upper right thigh. Although she was dressed in a one-piece mechanic's uniform, her zippered front was open to her navel and her perfume smelled like sweet air.

"Mister Hunter," she whispered seductively, "I have something for you."

"For me?" Hunter asked innocently, trying to hide a slight shaking in his voice.

"Yes, *monsieur*," she continued. "I had a very long talk with Sir Neil earlier tonight."

"And?" Hunter asked, very well aware that Clara's hand was inching its way up his leg.

"And he's agreed to let us — my girls and me — stay on board," she said slowly. "For the time being . . ."

"He has?"

"Yes, my love." Clara laughed. "Over wine and candlelight, I can be quite persuasive." On cue, her hand moved closer to his crotch.

"So how's this . . . uh, involve me?"

"Oh, *Monsieur* Hunter," Clara said, leaning over to whisper in his ear. "He told me that it was you that requested we stay on board. He said it was an American tradition, is it not? To have women on board ship? To help, of course."

"Help . . . ?"

"Yes, major," she said, leaning even closer and stroking his long hair. "As therapists . . ."

"Therapists?"

"Yes, major. This mission you are going on will be very stressful, no?"

"It could get, uh, stressful . . ." His excitement level was reaching the bursting point.

"Well, then, major. When was the last time you had a deep, relaxing massage?"

She didn't give Hunter time to answer. She snapped her fingers and another female slipped into the room.

"This is Emma," Clara said. With that, she stood up and led the other woman to his bunk. Then she gracefully left the room.

Hunter could sense the other woman's shyness, but he had yet to see her face. He reached up and clicked on the small light over his head. Their eyes met for the first time.

Hunter was thunderstruck . . .

She was young, beautiful, and looked hauntingly reminiscent of Dominique . . .

She didn't speak. She reached up and turned out the bunk light. Then he felt her hands slowly work up his arm to his shoulder. To his neck, down his chest, to his waist, and back up again. He wasn't about to fight it. His hormones were flying about his body in afterburner. Nature takes its course, he thought.

Emma's hands worked his tired thigh muscles, front and back. Then she undid his flight boots—he usually wore them to bed to be ready in an emergency—and let them drop to the floor. His flight suit came off next.

Then she stood and removed her own coverall. In the dim light he could see her lovely silhouette. Small, delicate breasts. Beautiful shape. Shapely rear and outstanding legs. Best of all, the long, blonde hair. He closed his eyes and imagined it was Dominique. Younger, before the War, when he didn't even know her. Emma lay down beside him and caressed his shoulders and chest. His mind was working the fantasy overtime.

After what seemed like hours of foreplay, they made love. His psyche was reeling, his brain exploding. It was wonderful. Emma was perfect for him. Even Dominique would understand . . .

It was only much later that he realized that Peter had even had a hand in this.

Chapter 18

It was nearly midnight when the tug slipped into the small Algerian cove and tied up to a rickety dock. The tide was high and a full moon was shining above. The harbor was deserted except for a lone figure, dressed in Arab robes and a turban, who quickly helped tie up the tug, then came aboard.

Sir Neil himself greeted the man with a warm handshake. It was Raleigh, the British officer who had helped arrange the mercenary deals with Heath and Hunter. He had returned to Algiers to facilitate the transactions. Now the time had come for the Brits to take delivery.

While it was no secret that the English had contracted for the nearly 10,000-man multinational force, the exact time and place of their departure from Algiers had been kept especially confidential, as had been their mission. Sir Neil knew full well that they could never keep an operation like towing an aircraft carrier the length of the Med a secret for very long, but the longer it remained covert, the better.

So Raleigh had arranged to have most of the Aussie, French, and Spanish mercenaries trucked to a small coastal village twenty miles from Algiers, and it was from there the paycheck soldiers would be shuttled to the *Saratoga*.

"Everything is ready, sir," Raleigh told the British Commander. "The Moroccans are loading on a freighter right now, back in Algiers. The oiler is also standing by. They'll both move just as soon as we transmit the go-code. Everyone else is waiting up in the hills."

"Well done, Raleigh, old boy," Sir Neil told him, leading him to the stern of the tug. "See that pair of red lights out there?"

Raleigh strained his eyes to make out two faint crimson lights on the dark horizon. "Yes, I see them, sir."

"That's the *Saratoga*, man," Sir Neil continued. "O'Brien has twelve tugs waiting to come in and start ferrying the troops aboard. Once we've got the majority of them on board, we'll radio the Moroccans and the oiler to make their move."

"I understand, sir," Raleigh said, pulling his hood over his head again, walking towards the gangplank. "Tell the tugs to come in. We're ready for them."

Hunter sat dozing in the cockpit of the F-16. The jet fighter was secured to the carrier's catapult system, ready to rocket the aircraft off the deck at a moment's notice. Should any trouble arise that would interfere with the pickup of the mercenaries, Hunter would be airborne first to counter the threat.

He was beat. The day's preparation for the midnight pickup off Algeria had been brutal. Hunter's role was to check, double-check, and then triple-check each of the carrier's aircraft, then document a lengthy status check on every available pilot. Without the modern conveniences he once enjoyed way back when with the regular Air Force, the combat evaluation procedure turned into a long, arduous process.

Once the ferrying operation got underway, the air arm would be responsible for providing air cover. The job called for helicopters, and the Sea King had had to be left behind on Majorca. But because the *Saratoga* had linked up earlier in the day with the eleven additional frigates of Captain Olson's Norwegian fleet, Hunter was now flush with choppers. Each frigate carried one—mostly British-built Bell Sea Scouts. Under agreement with the Norwegians, these copters were at Hunter's disposal.

He was also tired because his pleasant liaison with Emma had lasted well into the morning and very little of that time had been devoted to sleeping. She had finally opened up and talked to him, though, about herself and about Clara's girls. Far from being street hookers, the women had actually been the highest-priced group of "mistresses" on the prewar European continent. They had specialized in escorting jet-setters—both men and women, as it turned out—and all their clients had been fabulously wealthy. Clara had insisted on it: every client had to have at least $10 million in the bank before Clara even returned their calls. It was her way of protecting her girls—along with stringent medical tests. Small wonder Clara's girls had charged—and were gladly paid—as much as $20,000 for just a single night of bliss.

The odd thing about it all was that Emma realized she looked like a younger version of Dominique. Clara had told her so. But how did Clara know? Hunter had asked during the love session. Emma's answer stunned him. She said the man Peter had

Or had the Soviets learned about the carrier's m[ission] and were they attempting to disrupt it? May[be t]he airplanes were being flown by mercenaries, a[l]hough it's a rare occasion when the Soviet Air For[ce] permits free-lancers to fly its equipment while st[ill] carrying the old Red Star. Then there was anoth[er] way-out possibility: could the bombers actually be on [a] bounty-hunting mission, with Hunter and the bi[ll]ion-dollar reward as the prize?

The last thought shook him slightly. But whatev[er] he case, Hunter knew the airplanes would have t[o] act soon.

"Hunter?" Heath called. "Do you think you[r] [f]riends up there might chat on the radio?"

"Only one way to find out," Hunter said, turnin[g] [o]n his UHF band radio and closing to within a mil[e] of the bombers.

"Ilyushin-28 flight commander," he began. "Thi[s] is Major Hunter of the . . . Allied Expeditionar[y] Force." He had just made up the name. "You ar[e] . . . Please identify yoursel[f]

come to Clara and told her that Emma was the girl for Hunter. Once again Peter's perceptive abilities chilled him. He was both mystified and amazed that Peter could look that deep into his soul.

There was a constant chatter of radio traffic bouncing around in his headphones and it was getting mixed up with his half-awake dreams of the beautiful Emma. Suddenly he got a message that didn't come by way of his on-board radio. *Aircraft approaching!* his senses told him.

And they ain't friendly . . .

Hunter was wide awake in an instant. He knew there were four of them — bombers, flying way up there and coming in from the east.

Reacting fast to his sixth sense, he simultaneously hit his engine-engage switch and radioed the carrier's control tower that he was launching immediately. The F-16 was warm in less than thirty seconds, long enough for the ever-vigilant BBC crew to crank up their lights and catch the action on video. Hunter waved to the launch officer and two seconds later the 16 streaked off the carrier deck, its exhaust flame lighting up the dark Mediterranean night.

Hunter put the fighter into a steep climb, mentally setting a course to intercept the incoming aircraft. He climbed to 30,000, 40,000, 50,000 feet, all the time listening to his own inner voice guide him toward the unidentified airplanes.

His radar picked them up less than a half-minute later sixty-five miles out.

"Christ," he whispered as he interpreted the blips on his screen. "They look like Ilyushin-28s."

The Ilyushin-28 was a Soviet-built, medium-sized, two-engine jet bomber, from the 1960s. He knew it carried fairly sophisticated equipment which enabled it to find and hit a target accurately, but not from this high an altitude. Another strange thing, these four airplanes must have converted to night-fighting duty, not exactly a routine retrofit.

Hunter was within twenty miles of them in a minute. From there he could clearly study the aircraft on his video-imaging radar and try to ascertain what they were up to. They *were* acting suspicious — one clue was the fact they were "flying quiet," that is, under radio silence.

He radioed in to Heath, who was manning the CIC on the *Saratoga*. "We've got trouble," he reported. "Four Ilyushin mediums, in preattack formation, but right now flying too high to hit anything."

"Any idea what their intentions might be?" Heath asked through the static. He knew, as well as Hunter, that a bomber formation flying around the volatile Med region wasn't all *that* unusual. They just couldn't go around shooting at anything that flew by, without making a lot of unnecessary commotion or enemies. Plus Hunter had his Sidewinder shortage to think about.

"They're flying in pairs right now," Hunter said, arming his three remaining Sidewinders. "Judging from their course, two could be heading for Algiers, the other two could maybe break off, dive, and go for our tugs. But these guys have to get down on the deck for their bombing runs."

There was a short silence. Both Hunter and Heath evaluated the situation.

Then Heath broke in. "We calculate that at their present course, speed, and altitude, they'll have to break off and dive within the next ninety seconds if they expect to hit us.

"In other words, if we wait, they could just fly over and keep on going. But —"

"But, if we wait, they could come in and s[ ] punch us," Hunter finished.

There was an annoying burst of static, then [ ] said, "Can you ID them, Hunter?"

"Well, I'm sure they've seen me on their r[ ] Hunter answered. "No point in keeping it a se[ ]

He throttled up and streaked passed the [ ] flying bombers. As he flashed by, he was able t[ ] a good look at the markings on the bombers. [ ] he was surprised. On the side of each airplane[ ] the unmistakable red star of the Soviet Air F[ ]

Hunter radioed back, "You'd better get son[ ] else up on deck and ready to take off. These[ ] look like genuine Soviet Air Force."

"I say, Hunter," Heath called back. "Did I[ ] Soviet markings?"

"Roger," Hunter confirmed. "I'd know tha[ ] [ ] star anywhere. I put them only forty miles from the carrier and the tugs right now, and even closer to the port at Algiers."

A half-minute went by. It was agonizing [ ] were belligerent, th[ ]

"But, if we wait, they could come in and sucker-punch us," Hunter finished.

There was an annoying burst of static, then Heath said, "Can you ID them, Hunter?"

"Well, I'm sure they've seen me on their radar," Hunter answered. "No point in keeping it a secret."

He throttled up and streaked passed the slow-flying bombers. As he flashed by, he was able to get a good look at the markings on the bombers. Even he was surprised. On the side of each airplane was the unmistakable red star of the Soviet Air Force.

Hunter radioed back, "You'd better get someone else up on deck and ready to take off. These guys look like genuine Soviet Air Force."

"I say, Hunter," Heath called back. "Did I copy? Soviet markings?"

"Roger," Hunter confirmed. "I'd know that red star anywhere. I put them only forty miles from the carrier and the tugs right now, and even closer to the port at Algiers."

A half-minute went by. It was agonizing. If they were belligerent, the Soviets would have to go into their attack mode within forty-five seconds. If they had decided to mind their own business, they would just keep on flying.

Hunter had never been in this position before. In the past, any Soviet airplane he spotted was immediately judged an enemy and immediately attacked. Things were done differently in and over the Med.

His radio crackled to life again. "We have two Harriers warmed up, Hunter," Heath responded. "And Sir Neil is now aware of the situation."

The aircraft were now only thirty seconds from the port of Algiers and the small harbor where the ferrying operation was taking place. Were the planes—although Russian—simply flying through?

Or had the Soviets learned about the carrier's mission and were they attempting to disrupt it? Maybe the airplanes were being flown by mercenaries, although it's a rare occasion when the Soviet Air Force permits free-lancers to fly its equipment while still carrying the old Red Star. Then there was another way-out possibility: could the bombers actually be on a bounty-hunting mission, with Hunter and the billion-dollar reward as the prize?

The last thought shook him slightly. But whatever the case, Hunter knew the airplanes would have to act soon.

"Hunter?" Heath called. "Do you think your friends up there might chat on the radio?"

"Only one way to find out," Hunter said, turning on his UHF band radio and closing to within a mile of the bombers.

"Ilyushin-28 flight commander," he began. "This is Major Hunter of the . . . Allied Expeditionary Force." He had just made up the name. "You are flying in a restricted area. Please identify yourself and your intentions."

He flicked the radio switch back to "Receive." Nothing.

"Flight commander," he tried again. "I am prepared to attack if you do not ID yourself."

Again, nothing . . .

He flew right up on the tail of the trailing aircraft.

"Ilyushin flight commander, please ID . . ." The words were barely out of his mouth when he suddenly yanked the F-16 to the right. Just in time he had dodged a burst of gunfire from the tail gunner of the last Ilyushin.

"Jesus!" he yelled. "They just took a shot at me!" He was more surprised than anything; very few Ilyushin-28s carried tail gunners.

Just then the airplanes split up. The first pair dove through the clouds and toward the port at Algiers; the other two veered to the west, increased their speed, and went into a similar dive. These two were now pointed right towards the small village where O'Brien's tugs were just starting to pick up the mercenaries.

"Launch the Harriers!" Hunter yelled into his radio. "Get them vectored towards Algiers! And someone better warn that Moroccan troopship . . ."

With that, he took off after the pair of bombers that were heading for the tugs.

Down below, O'Brien's tugs were churning up the sea between the Algerian village harbor and the *Saratoga*. The ferrying operation was proceeding very smoothly when Sir Neil had first gotten word about the approaching Soviet aircraft. All of the tug crews were just receiving the word to go to battle stations when they heard a horrifying scream of engines coming from the east.

First to burst through the 1500-foot cloud cover was a shiny silver Ilyushin-28. It was heading for a group of three tugs that were just a mile away from the *Saratoga*. All of them filled with mercenaries. Sir Neil, watching from a tug a half-mile from the action, saw the bomber level up and going into a bombing-run course.

"Bloody Russians!" he screamed, "Those tugs are sitting ducks—"

But just then, another aircraft broke through the clouds. It was smaller, quicker. It was painted red, white, and blue.

"It's Hunter!" he yelled. "He's right on the bastard's tail!"

The three tugs attempted to scatter, but the jets were moving too fast. The crews on the other tugs away from the action could only watch as the F-16 pulled right up on the rear of the Ilyushin while the Soviet airplane prepared to drop its first rack of bombs. All the while the Soviet tail gunner was blazing away at the fighter, and Hunter was blazing away at him with his Vulcan Six Pack.

Sir Neil knew something had to give. In this case, it was the entire tail section of the Ilyushin. Hunter's six-knuckle, 20mm-cannon punch was too much for the old Soviet airplane. The 16's cannon shells found something explodable in the rear of the Soviet airplane and ignited it. The tail was instantly incinerated. The bomber, its rear quarter completely enveloped in flames, did a slow flip and plunged into the Med, with a great fiery crash of steam and smoke.

A cheer went up from all those on the tugs. "That's Hawk Hunter in that F-16." The word was passed. "That's the guy they call The Wingman!"

But the danger was far from over.

Off in the distance, the other Ilyushin had emerged from the clouds and was streaking along the wave tops, going in torpedo-bomber-style on the carrier itself. It passed two of the Norwegian frigates on the way—both ships sent up a wall of anti-aircraft fire that lit up the overcast Mediterranean sky. But somehow the Soviet airplane made it through.

Hunter was there in a flash, streaking around the bow of the *Saratoga* and facing the Soviet airplane head on. The Six Pack opened up with a burst of orange flame that was clearly visible on the tugs more than a mile away. The two jets barreled on toward each other, neither giving quarter.

"Stay with him, man!" Sir Neil said under his breath as he watched the drama. "Hang in there, this high an altitude. Another strange thing, these four airplanes must have converted to night-fighting duty, not exactly a routine retrofit.

Hunter was within twenty miles of them in a minute. From there he could clearly study the aircraft on his video-imaging radar and try to ascertain what they were up to. They *were* acting suspicious — one clue was the fact they were "flying quiet," that is, under radio silence.

He radioed in to Heath, who was manning the CIC on the *Saratoga*. "We've got trouble," he reported. "Four Ilyushin mediums, in preattack formation, but right now flying too high to hit anything."

"Any idea what their intentions might be?" Heath asked through the static. He knew, as well as Hunter, that a bomber formation flying around the volatile Med region wasn't all *that* unusual. They just couldn't go around shooting at anything that flew by, without making a lot of unnecessary commotion or enemies. Plus Hunter had his Sidewinder shortage to think about.

"They're flying in pairs right now," Hunter said, arming his three remaining Sidewinders. "Judging from their course, two could be heading for Algiers, the other two could maybe break off, dive, and go for our tugs. But these guys have to get down on the deck for their bombing runs."

There was a short silence. Both Hunter and Heath evaluated the situation.

Then Heath broke in. "We calculate that at their present course, speed, and altitude, they'll have to break off and dive within the next ninety seconds if they expect to hit us.

"In other words, if we wait, they could just fly over and keep on going. But—"

come to Clara and told her that Emma was the girl for Hunter. Once again Peter's perceptive abilities chilled him. He was both mystified and amazed that Peter could look that deep into his soul.

There was a constant chatter of radio traffic bouncing around in his headphones and it was getting mixed up with his half-awake dreams of the beautiful Emma. Suddenly he got a message that didn't come by way of his on-board radio. *Aircraft approaching!* his senses told him.

And they ain't friendly . . .

Hunter was wide awake in an instant. He knew there were four of them — bombers, flying way up there and coming in from the east.

Reacting fast to his sixth sense, he simultaneously hit his engine-engage switch and radioed the carrier's control tower that he was launching immediately. The F-16 was warm in less than thirty seconds, long enough for the ever-vigilant BBC crew to crank up their lights and catch the action on video. Hunter waved to the launch officer and two seconds later the 16 streaked off the carrier deck, its exhaust flame lighting up the dark Mediterranean night.

Hunter put the fighter into a steep climb, mentally setting a course to intercept the incoming aircraft. He climbed to 30,000, 40,000, 50,000 feet, all the time listening to his own inner voice guide him toward the unidentified airplanes.

His radar picked them up less than a half-minute later sixty-five miles out.

"Christ," he whispered as he interpreted the blips on his screen. "They look like Ilyushin-28s."

The Ilyushin-28 was a Soviet-built, medium-sized, two-engine jet bomber, from the 1960s. He knew it carried fairly sophisticated equipment which enabled it to find and hit a target accurately, but not from

Hunter!"

Finally, those aboard the tugs saw a flash erupt from underneath the 16's port wing. A streak of light and smoke followed, traveling a path straight and true towards the onrushing Ilyushin.

"He's launched a Sidewinder!" Sir Neil called out.

Before the words were out of his mouth, the missile caught the Ilyushin face on, crashed through the plexiglas nose, and traveled on to the cockpit, where it detonated. A bright orange ball of flame appeared and seemed to hang in the air for one long moment. Then what remained of the bomber slammed into the sea, just 300 yards from the carrier.

"Blimey, that was close," Sir Neil whispered. "Too close . . ."

The ferrying operation was still going on when the sun popped up, large and red, the next morning.

Watching the sunrise from the deck of Olson's command frigate, Hunter was reminded of the old saying "Red sky in the morning, sailor take warning . . ."

Just 200 feet off the starboard bow of the anchored carrier the frigate's crew was lifting the wreckage of one of the destroyed Ilyushins out of the water. The ship's crane snared the airplane under its tail wing and swung it up and over, allowing a deluge of seawater to escape through the many perforations in the plane's skin. Then the crane operator gingerly lowered the battered fusilage onto the frigate's empty helicopter pad.

Hunter was the first one to approach the wreckage. Heath and Sir Neil followed. They watched as the American headed straight for the Ilyushin's bashed-in cockpit. There wasn't much left that the Sidewinder hadn't destroyed, but Hunter was just looking for clues. Clues to prove his suspicions about the origins of the air attack.

Crawling through the sharp, tangled mess of metal and wires, Hunter finally reached the pilot's compartment. Sir Neil and Heath were right behind him, though moving a little slower. When they got there, Hunter was examining what was left of the airplane's controls.

"Same as the two bombers the Harriers greased?" Heath asked.

"Exactly," Hunter said. "And that's what worries me."

Sir Neil shook his head in disbelief. "No bodies," he said. "No pilot. No crew."

"No bombs," Heath said.

"They didn't need any crew," Hunter said, wrestling with a black box attached on the airplane's main control board. "These airplanes were flying on some kind of an ultra-sophisticated autopilot. More like a remote-control unit. I'm sure the guts of it are in this black box."

"Autopilots, I can understand," Heath said, trying to reason it out. "But why no bombs?"

"This might give us the answer," Hunter said, struggling with yet another piece of smashed, tangled equipment.

"Is that what I think it is?" Sir Neil asked, looking at the almost unidentifiable chunk of melted metal and wires.

"If you are thinking TV camera, you're right," Hunter told him. "These airplanes weren't on a bombing mission at all. They were sent here simply as TV spyships, getting closeup pictures of us and the ferrying operation and transmitting them back to whoever was watching at the other end."

"And radio sensors triggered the tail guns?" Sir Neil deduced.

"I'm sure of it," Hunter said, turning the destroyed TV camera over in his hands. "They were flying so *strangely.* The Harrier pilots noticed it too. They got to those Ilyushins before they even dived on the Moroccan troopship."

"Well, that's how a lot of Soviet pilots fly," Heath observed. "Rather robotic bastards, aren't they?"

Hunter nodded, then said, "Whoever sent these airplanes really knows our way of thinking. They know we're not going to shoot down everything that comes close. They know we have to intercept and ID anything before taking action. So they keep us guessing as to who is flying these things. Then, when I got too close, they have the tail gunner open up on me."

"Pretty elaborate scheme just to take our picture," Heath said. "Kind of spooky having someone up there watching us. Especially someone flying Soviet Air Force bombers."

"Christ," Hunter said softly, something clicking in his mind. "Wasn't Peter going on about something like 'eyes in the sky'?"

Both Sir Neil and Heath looked at him. "By God, man," Sir Neil said. "Peter called this one too?"

Hunter didn't even hazard an answer.

"Peter or not," he said, "the lid is really off now."

Despite the strange Ilyushins episode, the mercenary pickup was completed without further incident shortly before noon that day.

The 200-man, red-bereted French air-defense contingent was busy installing its Phalanx air-defense guns at various points around the ship. When used properly, the Phalanx was an awesome weapon. Using bullets made from depleted uranium, the Phalanx's mission was to automatically destroy incoming antiship missiles, such as the Exocets. Each 20mm gun contained a search-and-track radar, a magazine holding tens of thousands of bullets, and a hundred or so pounds of electronics. The Phalanx gun had the ability to identify and attack any high-speed target approaching the ship. It did so by simply throwing up a wall of bullets—at a rate of 100 shells *a second*—in the path of the oncoming missile.

No matter how good the attacker's guidance system was, nothing could get through a Phalanx barrage. Ships such as the Norwegian frigates usually carried just one Phalanx; a carrier the size of the *Saratoga* might carry two. The French mercenaries would set up a total of six Phalanx guns around the ship—two on the stern, two on the bow, and two on the *Saratoga*'s center superstructure. When it came to fighting off Exocets, Sir Neil wasn't taking any chances.

Nor was he neglecting air defense. The Spanish air-defense team was also busy. The group boasted twenty-five two-man Stinger missile teams. These deadly antiaircraft missiles were launched from a bazooka-like tube held on one's shoulder. The Spaniards were so good at firing the American-made missile, they actually held highly competitive target-shooting contests among themselves—using authentic, fully armed missiles for ammunition.

The Spaniards had built mobile launching platforms for the missiles and were shoehorning their weapons anywhere and everywhere possible around the carrier. Meanwhile, the ship's superstructure was crawling with Italian radar and communications experts. They were installing no less than four antennas: one air-search radar at the highest point on the conning tower, with a bulbous Mk-2 fire-control-system radar right beside it. They wired up a SLQ-32 radar-warning and electronic-countermeasures system to the island's rear, next to a Separate Target Illumination Radar set that would help the French and Spanish gunners track multiple targets. The Italians were also working on setting up a long-range communications antenna which, when operating, would allow them to listen in on transmissions originating from the east end of the Med all the way deep into Lucifer's Arabian Empire.

Once their equipment was installed, the Italians would join the rest of Yaz's men in refurbishing the most important unit on the *Saratoga*—the Combat Information Center. It was in this CIC room that all the carrier's communications, radar, and defensive systems were coordinated.

At the far end of the ship, most of the Australian Special Forces team were on deck, doing their midday calisthenics. Some of the Gurkha troops sat nearby, cleaning their famous machete-like long knives and watching the Aussies do jumping jacks.

Off the portside of the carrier, a large sea freighter was docked. This was the *El Ka-Bongo*, the ship that served as a ferry for the 7500 Moroccan desert fighters. It too would become part of the fleet, just as the oiler anchored beside it.

Watching it all from the highest point on the *Saratoga*'s superstructure was Hawk Hunter. The sun was now at its highest point in the sky. The blue-green waters of the Med were shimmering in the noontime radiance. He watched as the dozen tugs in front of the carrier simultaneously started their smoky diesel engines. The waters churning in their wake, the tugs fanned out until their thick towlines attached to the front of the carrier became taut. Hunter felt their pull. Then, from the rear of the carrier, he heard the familiar bump of the eight trailing tugs nudging against the rear of the ship. This was the push.

The carrier didn't move for more than two minutes. But then, slowly, the combined forces working on the enormous ship started to take effect. Hunter could feel a light breeze on his face—a slight wind caused by the movement of the huge carrier. They were moving. The ship—like the small fleet of frigates and tugs around it—was alive. Breathing with adventure, sailing toward the east. Toward the unknown.

Chapter 19

Hunter uncorked the wine bottle and poured out three glasses. He was sitting in the *Saratoga*'s CIC room, studying reams of transcripts just given to him by the head of the Italian communications group, Captain Giuseppe d'Salvo.

"So this is what our friend Lucifer is up to," said Sir Neil as he reached for his wine glass. "I'm glad the long-range communications antenna is working so well. Giuseppe, your guys have done a great job."

The Englishman raised his glass in a toast. "To our Italian compadres!"

Hunter and the Italian officer raised their glasses and each man downed the small glass of *vino*.

"This is invaluable information," Sir Neil continued. "But it is also quite frightening. Lucifer is definitely on the move."

It was fascinating stuff. Giuseppe's men had been able to identify Lucifer's main radio frequencies. Although the broadcasts were mostly in Arabic, Giuseppe's men had had no problem translating them with help from the Moroccans. Within hours of setting up their long-range antenna, the Italians had come up with some extremely valuable intelligence.

Lucifer's troops—close to fifty divisions in strength—were going through their last paces of training. The reports indicated that the madman was contracting ships of all types to sail to the port of Ashara, formerly part of South Yemen. From there the armada would sail up the Red Sea, through the Suez Canal, and break out into the Med. At that point they would link up with their local allies and start a sweep across both the northern and southern shores of the sea. It was a campaign that would rival everyone from Alexander to Rommel.

"It's strange," Hunter said, looking at the transcripts. "Lucifer is not much of a military leader. He made mistakes during The Circle War. Letting his troops move out in the open, not sending critical messages in code. Things like that. They gave us the breaks we needed to defeat him."

"As we figured before," Sir Neal said, "he's more of a cult leader than a battlefield general. Sending messages like these, uncoded—I take it as an act of arrogance. I'm sure he knows what we are up to, although he probably doesn't know where we are or what our exact plans may be. And I'm sure he also is aware of what The Modern Knights are doing—his spies are everywhere, after all."

"So what he's doing is underestimating us," Hunter said, hoping at the same time that the *Saratoga*'s small force actually had something to be underestimated about.

"Let's hope so," Sir Neal said with a wink. "One thing is for sure, Lucifer will be moving his troops within a few weeks. Once they are aboard those ships and sailing, nothing will stop them. That's why it's imperative that we beat him to the Suez. And that we have enough weapons to fight them with when we get there."

Hunter and Giuseppe nodded. The race for the canal was on . . .

The two friends of Anna, Chloe and Claudia, reached the outskirts of Cagliari and began taking off their clothes. Below them, down the road about a quarter-mile away, they could see the city streets were lit up and decorated with banners, streamers, and thousands of multicolored balloons. It reminded Chloe of the Mardi Gras she had once attended in Rio.

Quickly both women discarded their overalls and donned a toga-like garment that they had sewn together from bedsheets. They wore sandal-like shoes on their feet. Each woman was also carrying a small derringer-like gun, loaded with three bullets, to be used only in emergency.

They both checked their garments. After judging them to be authentic enough, they embraced, kissed each other's cheek for luck, then began to walk into the city.

It wasn't long before they saw just what kind of celebration The Day of Kings was meant to be. They came upon a roadblock, manned by six men carrying M-16 rifles. But the sentries didn't even bother to give Chloe and Claudia a second look. They were too busy having sex with six women they had conveniently tied down on tables inside the guardpost building.

Chloe and Claudia moved on, occasionally passing similar scenes along the way—soldiers having their way with young girls and women, some of whom were actually enjoying it.

But these isolated instances were nothing compared to what the two call girls saw inside the city itself.

"My God," Claudia said after walking through the unguarded city gates. "It looks like—"

"Sodom and Gomorrah," Chloe finished for her.

It was true. The city was in the throes of a lust frenzy. Everywhere—on street corners, in open houses, in small parks that lined the roads—there were people committing sexual acts on each other. Even two people as worldly as Choe and Claudia couldn't believe the extent and the intensity of the orgy-like goings-on.

They saw men screwing one, two, three women at once. Women making love to other women. Two men on one woman. The variations went on and on. Age didn't seem to matter—and the wine was flowing as if from an endless supply.

They neared the center of town, trying to take everything in. An arena of some kind had been set up and bleacher-style seats erected around it. They wandered up to the side of one of the seating galleries and peered inside. It was like a gladiator's ring, but with one important difference. There were sexual games going on in the arena. At that moment, one man, armed with a net and a length of rope, was attempting to lasso one of five screaming young girls who had been placed in the ring with him. As Chloe and Claudia watched, the man finally netted one of the girls and instantly tied her up like a calf caught in a rodeo.

The victim, just a teenager, was pleading with the man to let her go. But her captor only laughed. Each scream resulted in a great cheer from the crowd. More cheers erupted when the man ripped off his clothes and entered her, jamming her violently. The man was quickly spent. He stood up, raised his hands to the crowd for one last cheer, then

170

slowly walked out of the arena. As soon as this happened, another man was let in to chase one of the four remaining girls.

Chloe and Claudia knew they had to move on. They walked around the side of the arena and toward the center of town. Here they saw the grandiose Roman-style structures the Holy Sardinians had built for themselves. Huge, pillar-supported affairs, all of white gleaming marble. In these buildings, and even on the buildings' steps, they could hear and see people having sex. Occasionally they would come upon a still body—maybe dead, maybe just unconscious. But they never stopped to find out.

They were almost to the far edge of the town when the mob met them. There were about seventy men, walking toward the main celebration in the center of the city. They caught Chloe and Claudia unaware. The leader of the gang was a tall, burly, animal-like man wearing a long beard, a loin cloth, and nothing else.

"Ah, more pussy to join our party!" he said, grabbing Claudia. He instantly began stripping off her toga and fondling her breasts. Chloe was next. She was thrown into the crowd of men. Her clothes were also ripped off. Both women were then passed from man to man, each one fondling or sucking their breasts, or jamming their fingers into their privates. As soon as each man had had his due, he would rejoin the mob that was moving toward the center of the town.

Chloe felt as if she were in a dream. So many hands were on her at once, her senses were reeling. Most men tried to use their hands to penetrate every orifice, while some were trying to force her to her knees to perform oral sex on them. She was bouncing from man to man, and could see Claudia doing the same thing out of the corner of her eye.

It was absolute insanity. She wanted to cry, but at the same time she wanted to laugh. She was repulsed by the crude men, yet excited by the multitude of hands swarming all over her body. She felt as if something were going to explode inside her. Her head felt light, her eyes started to close, she gasped once, twice, then nearly fainted.

Then it was over. She and Claudia had passed through the crowd of men and now the crowd was gone. The women looked at each other in amazement for a few moments. They had never thought to use their small guns.

They quickly gathered up their clothes, what remained of them, and hurried out of town.

"Chloe!"

The young woman instantly recognized the voice as Hunter's. She and Claudia had walked the mile and half from the city of Cagliari to the abandoned U.S. air base and ammo depot. Now she knew that Hunter and a strike force from the *Saratoga* were hiding nearby, ready for the second phase of their operation to begin.

Hunter emerged from a large, long hedgerow and quickly embraced her. Chloe was Anna's best friend, so Hunter felt a special attachment to her.

"Are you okay?" he asked with some anxiety in his voice. Her mission with Claudia to reconnoiter the strange Sardinian town had been extremely dangerous, but critical to the operation.

Hunter was relieved to see she had made it in one piece. In fact, he couldn't help but notice the slightly blissful look she had about her.

"There are no soldiers that we could see in the

city," she reported as Hunter led her to the side of the dusty road near the base. "No SAMs either. It appears that anyone who is able to have sex is having it—plenty of it—in that city tonight."

It was just what Hunter wanted to hear.

Earlier in the evening, a strike force made up mostly of Australian Special Forces troops and Spanish rocket teams had helicoptered into a remote part of the island from six Norwegian frigates off-shore. Hunter was the strike force leader, while Sir Neal, itching for a bit of action, had come along as the overall commander. With the twenty-five tough Aussie troops at his disposal, Hunter hoped to locate and airlift out as many Sidewinders and other weapons that he could find in the Sardinians' ammo bunkers. Sir Neal, along with a half-dozen Spanish rocketeers, would guard the strike force's rear from any threat, whether it be on the ground or in the air.

Hunter knew that the mission had to be done quickly. While the two women provided a diversion for any guards at the base, he and the Aussies would sweep into the weapons bunkers, locate what they needed, then radio back a special code to the six helicopters waiting nearby. The choppers were already outfitted with cargo nets. The strike force would have to drag out as many cases of weapons as they could and load them onto the chopper nets. If things went very well, Hunter thought they might be able to load up four of the six choppers. Of course, he knew there would always be unpredictable elements to contend with.

The strike force, wearing black coveralls and old Marine guard helmets they had found on the carrier, advanced cautiously up the narrow road to the front gate of the weapons-storage site. A small guard-house stood next to the entrance, a single light burning in its window. Off in the distance, the lusty revelers back in Cagliari had begun setting off fireworks, unintentionally adding to the strike force's cover.

Hunter motioned for the Aussies to take cover on either side of the road, then called Chloe and Claudia to the front of the column. They quickly went over their prearranged plan. Then, checking their small guns once again, the two women headed for the guardhouse.

The five soldiers inside the guardhouse were surprised when they answered the knock on their door and found Chloe and Claudia standing there. Both women had expertly made themselves look disheveled. Claudia's toga was nearly completely torn off, and both of Chloe's breasts were exposed. Both women were wearing their best professional smiles, which, when mixed with the smell of the alcohol, made for a powerful combination.

"Parlez-vous francais?" Chloe asked the burly man who answered the door.

"Oui, madam," the soldier answered, a strange look coming across his face.

"Your comrades in town sent us to you," Claudia said, snuggling up against the man. "They felt bad that you were up here missing out on all the festivities."

"Our comrades sent you?" another of the soldiers asked, getting up from the card game the men had been playing.

While Claudia was talking to the men, Chloe was taking in the equipment the soldiers had in the guardhouse. Several rifles were leaning in the corner. An elaborate radio set was off to one side. A large pane-less window opening dominated the rear of the house, allowing a clear view of the city a mile and a

174

half away.

"Can we come in and join you?" Chloe asked.

Hidden in the bushes twenty feet away, Hunter and Sir Neal watched the two women go into the guardhouse, the door closing behind them. Hunter turned to the leader of the Aussie troopers and gave him the thumbs-up sign.

"Go to it, Hunter," Sir Neal said, patting him on the back. "We got your asses covered."

With that, Hunter and the Aussie force slipped passed the guardhouse and down into the depression that contained a large underground weapons-storage bunker and several smaller ones.

Staying in the shadows and moving silently, Hunter and the troopers inched their way toward the bunkers. Once he was sure that there were no guards patrolling the inside of the facility, he gave the Aussie leader a prearranged signal. Meanwhile, off in the distance, the Sardinians were continuing their fireworks display.

The strike force began splitting up. A dozen men took up positions around the facility's perimeter. The remaining soldiers divided into two-man teams, each headed for a small bunker. Their task was to force open the door, get inside, quickly determine what weapons were on hand for the taking, and then report back to their group leader. Hunter and two Aussies, meanwhile, would head for the main storage building that dominated the facility. He was certain that the Sardinians kept most of their Sidewinders there.

That's when the strange feeling came over Hunter. Something wasn't right. He could feel it. Reaching the large housing, he quickly picked the simple lock and, together with the help of the Aussies, pried the huge iron door open. Clicking his flashlight on,

Hunter and the two troopers entered the bunker.

Hunter took one look and swore, "Christ!" he whispered angrily. "After all this . . ."

"Well I'll be damned," one of the Aussie soldiers said.

The bunker was empty . . .

Hunter ran outside and found the Aussie group leader coming towards him.

"Turning up negative all around, major," the Aussie leader, a man named Dundee, told him. "None of my guys have found a bloody thing."

"Nothing here," Hunter said, bitterness in his voice. He was mad at himself. While this certainly wasn't the only weapons-storage site on the island, it was the one furthest from the city, and therefore, in Hunter's mind, the easiest target. But undertaking the dangerous operation for nothing was not good military planning.

So the Sardinians were smarter than he thought. For some reason they had moved all the weapons out of the storage facility, apparently some time ago.

Quickly and quietly, the Aussies began moving their way back toward the guardhouse. Hunter was hoping that Chloe and Claudia had already been able to knock out the guards. They would have to get the girls out and make their way back to the choppers waiting two miles away.

But now he felt a second strange feeling come over him. The fireworks in the town had stopped. For the first time since they had landed on the island, there was complete silence all around them.

Hunter knew that meant trouble.

They reached the guardhouse. While Dundee went on to tell Sir Neal of the empty bunkers, Hunter and two Aussies went to retrieve Chloe and Claudia.

Hunter cautiously approached the guardhouse,

only to see his worst fears had come true. The guards had not been knocked out; he could plainly see two of them walking around the sentry post. What was worse, they were carrying rifles with them.

Something had gone wrong and now Hunter knew there would have to be gunplay.

He crept up to the side of the house and peered inside. For some reason the guards hadn't gone for the girls' ruse. Chloe and Claudia were tied up back to back on two chairs, while the soldiers paced around them anxiously. It could only mean one thing: they had reported the girls' presence to their superiors in the town. Hunter was sure someone was coming to investigate.

Two more Aussies joined Hunter and the others around the house and, on the count of three, they burst in. Hunter himself came through the open window, his M-16 blazing. Two more Ausssies kicked in the door and sprayed the interior of the shack with bullets, while two other troopers dove towards the girls, knocking them down and covering them with their bodies.

It was over in a matter of seconds. All of the guards were dead. But it had been noisy. Too noisy.

"What happened?" Hunter asked Chloe.

"The soldiers knew that their comrades didn't send us," she answered in a slightly frightened voice. "They told us they had no use for women."

"No use for women?" Hunter said. "You mean they were—"

"Eunuchs," Claudia said. "Apparently most of the lowly guards here are."

"Well I'll be damned," Hunter said. "Just like in the old days . . ."

Suddenly a shot rang out, followed by the sound

of an explosion. Hunter, the Aussies, and the girls were out of the guardhouse in a second, making their way down the road to the main group. Sir Neal and Dundee were there to meet them.

"We're gong to have company very soon," Sir Neal said, pointing back toward the town. Hunter could see he was right. A convoy of trucks was making its way up the pass towards the weapons facility. An American-built Bradley Fighting Vehicle — a kind of half-tank, half-personnel carrier — was leading the way.

As they watched, its weapons officer was pumping out mortar rounds in their direction.

"Let's go!" Hunter yelled as the shells started to crash down around them. The strike force troopers needed no further prodding. The small band took off through the brush and out into the open fields.

Chapter 20

They ran into more trouble right away. Another enemy force, this one containing foot soldiers plus some trucks, was making its way toward them from the north. If Hunter didn't act quickly, the strike force would be cut off from both sides and squeezed by the advancing Sardinians.

Hunter had no choice—he had to call for the choppers. The strike force made its way down into a gulley and found an abandoned farmhouse and barn. The enemy approaching from the town had momentarily lost sight of them, but began lobbing mortar rounds into the gulley nevertheless. The foot soldiers looked like they were heading to link up with the column. Then they all would search the small valley together. Hunter figured the strike force had about twenty minutes tops to be evacuated by the frigate copters.

The Aussie troopers formed a defense perimeter around the farmhouse, while the Spanish rocket teams readjusted their warheads for use against the ground troops. Chloe and Claudia took refuge inside the farmhouse while Hunter and Sir Neil helped with the defense preparations outside.

Hunter sent a one-word message to the chopper pilots which he knew would bring them into the general area. Then he would be forced to send up two flares — the predetermined signal for trouble — and hope the chopper pilots would think quickly and come in for the rescue.

Five tense minutes passed. Mortar shells were landing nearby, but the strike force held its fire so as not to give away its position.

Using one of the Aussie troops' nightscopes, Hunter could see the two Sardinian forces had linked up about three-quarters of a mile away and now were slowly starting to descend into the small valley, a Bradley Fighting Vehicle in the lead.

That's when he heard the choppers approaching . . .

He quickly informed Sir Neil.

"Let's get the ladies out first, Hunter," the Englishman said. "I hope we'll be able to hold them off for long enough."

Hunter knew it was going to be close. Already the sound of the six rescue choppers was beginning to fill the air. Trouble was, the Sardinians heard them too. Within seconds, the night sky was filled with tracer bullets, all directed toward the approaching helicopters.

It was now or never. Hunter took out his flare gun and let two rockets fly. This marked their hiding place for both the choppers and the enemy troops, now a half-mile away.

The mortar shells started dropping closer to the farmhouse. The Aussies opened up on the approaching Sardinians, while the Spanish rocketmen fired on the lead Bradley Fighting Vehicle. Their first shot glanced off the front of the vehicle and careened into a group of soldiers unlucky enough to be nearby. The converted Stinger missile exploded, killing many of the soldiers.

Now the firefight was going at full fury. The Sardinians looked like expert terrain fighters. They were crawling through the underbrush, and some were soon only a quarter-mile from the Aussies' defense line. At the same time, other enemy troops were firing at the approaching helicopters. The gunners on the air ships were now also returning the fire.

"Boy," Hunter said to himself as he added his M-16 to the fray. "Did this idea get screwed up!"

The first chopper came down right in the front yard of the farmhouse. Hunter and Sir Neil hustled the two women out and literally threw them on to the chopper. Three of Dundee's men who had been wounded went next along with their stretcher-bearers. Then Dundee sent aboard another six men and gave the pilot the lift-off signal. The big British helicopter belched a large cloud of black smoke and then roared off, amidst a shower of tracer bullets.

Thus the rescue began. The withering fire from the Aussies, the pinpoint accuracy of the Spanish Rocketeers, plus the fire from the chopper gunners held off the enemy long enough for four more choppers to come in and pick up troops.

Soon there were only Hunter, Sir Neil, and a squad of Spanish rocketmen on the ground. The plan was for them to go out on the last chopper.

But this sixth helicopter was going nowhere. Even before it touched down, a mortar round came crashing down right into its main rotor blade, blowing it off. The chopper yawed to its left, then came down hard right onto the abandoned farmhouse. Hunter and Sir Neil just barely ducked away from the scythe-like chopper blade as it spun over ahead, clipped a tree right off at its roots, and proceeded to chop up some Sardinian troops who had been crawling down in back of the strike force's position.

Hunter ran into the burning farmhouse and yanked the injured chopper pilot out of the burning machine. The gunner was dead. Sir Neil was beside Hunter to help, and together they managed to carry the pilot to safety before the entire house went up.

Now, with no means of escape by air and a wounded person on their hands, Hunter had to think quick.

"We've got to get the hell out of here," Hunter said to Sir Neil, who had already rigged up a makeshift stretcher for the wounded pilot. Hunter told the Spanish rocketeers to send a barrage right into the enemy positions, then get prepared to fall back. With one great *whoosh!* the Spaniards let fly six rockets in unison, splattering the road and enemy vehicles with flame and causing the enemy infantry to take cover.

Given the moment of diversion, Hunter, Sir Neil, and the six Spaniards took off into the bush, carrying the wounded pilot. The entire farmhouse, barn, and surrounding area was now a mass of flame and the enemy troops were still lobbing mortar shells and tracers into the conflagration. Despite the delay of having to carry the stretcher, the tiny band successfully melted away into the hedgerows at the end of the valley and into the farm country beyond.

Chapter 21

They hid out on the island for the next day and night, moving only in darkness, hoping for a chance to signal one of the frigate helicopters that they knew would be looking for them. However, the Sardinian army troops kept on their tail the whole time, obviously under orders to capture the raiders dead or alive.

The wounded pilot was now at least conscious, although his legs were pretty banged up. In addition, Hunter and the band had no provisions, no gear, no medicine. Hunter knew that by sunup the second day they would have to find some kind of transport if they were to finally shake their pursuers and get up into the hills of Sardinia in the north.

The next morning, they got lucky, or so Hunter thought. Reconnoitering from a small hill, he spotted an enemy truck parked near the side of the road. The crew was bundled up in sleeping bags and sprawled on the road's shoulder. Hunter guessed it was either some kind of long-range patrol, or perhaps a construction squad that traveled around the island checking on things such as radio lines. No matter. Whatever the case, the crew looked to be lightly armed and the truck was obviously in working order.

While three of the Spanish rocketmen stayed with the wounded pilot, Hunter and Sir Neil took the three others and slowly worked their way down to the roadside. A number of empty wine bottles lay about their camp, a clue to why the crew was sleeping so soundly.

"Looks like they had a bit of a party last night," Sir Neil whispered to Hunter as they closed in on the truck. "Perhaps they're eunuchs too and can only get what they are looking for in the old grape, what?"

Hunter had to laugh at the Englishman. Swaggering, swashbuckling — that was Sir Neil. Christ, they'd been lost out in the Sardinian wilderness for a day and a half, and Sir Neil looked as if he had just done nothing more strenuous than giving his polo pony a morning workout. His uniform was still neatly pressed, his beret adjusted on his head at the correct angle. His boots were even spit-shined. The ever-present cigarette and holder completed the scene. Hunter shook his head. He had come to greatly admire Sir Neil. The Brit reminded him very much of both Seth and Dave Jones — the Air Force officers who were Hunter's mentors. Yes, the Jones boys would have liked Sir Neil. Brave, professional, great sense of humor, as well as a great sense of purpose.

Yes, Hunter told himself once again, only an Englishman could have talked him into this adventure.

Hunter turned to the Spanish rocketeers and gave a hand signal which indicated that they would simply knock out the sleeping soldiers. Killing them wouldn't be necessary. Then Hunter gave the signal to move out.

They crept up on the side of the road and quietly broke into two groups. Hunter and two Spaniards moved towards the Sardinians' encampment; Sir Neil and the other rocketeer would check out the truck itself.

Hunter and his partners improvised a system for knocking out the sleeping soldiers. One Spaniard would shake the man awake, while Hunter held his hand over the victim's mouth. The third rocketeer would hit the man square on the head with a satchel he'd filled with rocks. Because the soldiers were sleeping off a drunk, none of them woke up unexpectedly as Hunter and his companions moved through the camp. Within a minute, they had put seven soldiers out of action.

Meanwhile, Sir Neil and the other Spaniard had crept up to the truck. While the Britisher was peeking in the cab, his partner checked underneath it. Finding nothing, Sir Neil and the Spaniard walked around to the rear of the truck.

With a flick of his hand, Sir Neil pulled open the back flap of the truck.

Behind it were two men, wide awake, manning a small-caliber machine gun. Sir Neil just caught a glimpse of the gunner's finger pulling the trigger . . .

Three bullets caught the Englishman square in the shoulder and the chest. Another sliced through his scalp carrying off the beret in a burst of cloth, hair, and blood. Sir Neil dropped immediately. The stunned Spanish mercenary raised his gun, but too late, as he caught a full burst square in the face. His head nearly obliterated, the Spaniard stood upright for two long, spooky seconds before falling over onto Sir Neil's crumpled form.

Hunter had seen the whole thing happen. Even now, as he and the two other rocketeers sprayed the back of the truck with gunfire, he felt a lump come up in his throat. Sir Neil was down, lifeless, covered in his own blood and that of the headless Spaniard.

He was up and running towards the truck immediately, at the same time yelling for the other rocketeers to bring the wounded pilot down from the hill. The gunfire would bring company. He knew they would have to make good their escape now.

Hunter reached the back of the truck and dragged the Spaniard's body off Sir Neil. He turned the Englishman over and felt for a heartbeat or any signs of breathing. There were none. He stuck his hand down the man's throat and cleared his passageway. Then he began giving him mouth to mouth resuscitation. He stopped and beat on the man's heart.

"Come on, you Limey bastard," Hunter said as he furiously pumped on the man's chest. "We need you!"

By this time the other rocketeers had reached the truck and were loading on the wounded pilot. One Spaniard got behind the wheel and started the truck. Another helped Hunter load Sir Neil in the back.

"Go North!" Hunter yelled to the driver, who immediately pulled a five-point U-turn and gunned the truck's accelerator. Within seconds they were roaring down the dusty road.

Somehow, bouncing along the road, Hunter had managed to raise a heartbeat in the seriously wounded Sir Neil. His breathing was irregular and he was losing a lot of blood, yet the Englishman was still alive.

They dressed his wounds as best they could, yet the plucky Brit was losing a lot of blood and getting whiter by the minute.

"The sea . . ." Hunter said suddenly. "We've got to

186

get him to the sea."

Less than thirty minutes later they came upon a seaside villa. Its name was Casillino and, by the looks of it, it had once been a fancy, high-priced resort area.

But it wasn't the expensive-looking hotels or the fancy yachts abandoned in the harbor that caught Hunter's attention. It was the medium-sized freighter that was tied up to its pier.

"That's our ticket home, boys," he said.

But it wouldn't be easy. As they approached the town, Hunter could clearly see that the entrance to the harbor area was guarded by Sardinians. He could also see several soldiers on the freighter itself.

"Okay," he yelled up to the driver through the cab's access window. "Just pretend like we are the guys who were supposed to be driving this truck."

The driver nodded and headed straight through the abandoned town and right up to the main gate. Two soldiers were sitting in a guardhouse, and as soon as they saw the Spanish driver's uniform, they knew something was amiss.

It didn't matter. Hunter ripped a hole in the truck's canvas siding and was spraying the guard hut with M-16 fire. The Spanish driver then hit the accelerator and the truck bolted into the harbor area.

"Head right for the ship!" Hunter yelled to the driver, while he reloaded his M-16. The driver spun the truck around and they were soon roaring down the dock going toward the freighter. They were beginning to take some return fire now but, judging by its intensity, Hunter determined there were only a dozen or so soldiers guarding the otherwise deserted resort docks.

They reached the ship and quickly piled out of the truck, taking pains not to unduly upset Sir Neil or the wounded pilot.

Hunter and the Spaniards shot their way up the gangplank, causing the soldiers who were guarding the ship to jump overboard instead of shooting it out with the wildmen from the truck.

But then Hunter saw that the force of Sardinians that had been tracking them for two days had just appeared at the far end of town.

"We need a diversion," Hunter said to one of the rocketeers as soon as they were all aboard. Just as soon as he said it, he saw exactly what he needed. It was a fuel tank, not very large, but conveniently placed between the ship and the entrance to the docking area.

Using his M-16 on single-shot, he started peppering the fuel tank's top ringer valve. After about a dozen shots, he had managed to start a small fire. That was all he needed.

With the rocketeers returning the guards' fire and the two wounded members of the party safely put aboard, Hunter went about the task of trying to get the freighter underway. He knew some—but not much—about how to get a ship of this size moving. Luckily, the vessel was fairly modern and had a number of automatic start-up controls. It was also equipped with electronic start motors that revved the ship's main screws and jump-started its main engines at the same time. What the hell, Hunter thought, he would simply drive the ship out of the harbor on these electric motors—no doubt burning them out in the process, but at least they'd be underway. He yelled to the Spaniards to cast off the lines. Then he pushed some buttons, turned some dials, and—to his surprise—the ship actually started to move.

By this time, the pursuing Sardinians had arrived on the dock just as the fuel tanks he'd set ablaze blew up. The dock area was suddenly awash with flame. That put an end to the enemy fire.

"Now all I've got to do is figure out how to sail this thing," he said to himself.

As it turned out, he wouldn't have to. The wounded pilot, a Norwegian named Olaaf, hobbled to the center of the bridge and volunteered to steer the ship.

"I used to be a skipper," he told Hunter. "This is all automatic anyway. May I?"

Hunter gladly stepped aside and let the Norseman take over. Soon they were sailing quickly out of the harbor, Olaaf having gotten the main engine to work.

Hunter checked Sir Neil. He was stable but still in bad shape. He leaned over and said in the man's ear, "Don't worry, sir, we're out now. We're heading back to the *Saratoga*."

He thought he saw the slightest look of acknowledgment on the Englishman's face.

Just then one of the rocketeers came forward and indicated to Hunter that he should follow him.

"Big, sir," the Spaniard kept saying. "Big. What we need."

Hunter followed him into the hold of the ship and flicked on the lights.

"Jesus H. Christ," he said, stunned.

Inside the hold were at least a hundred crates marked "SIDEWINDERS."

Chapter 22

The F-4 circled the Gibraltar air base five times before finally coming for a landing. Although the base's landing lights, radar dishes, and other equipment were operating, Crunch had gotten no response to his repeated attempts to radio the control tower.

"I got a very bad feeling about this," the pilot said as he rolled the airplane up to a hardstand. No ground personnel appeared to greet them, as would normally be the case at any airfield. "Did everyone take the day off?" he wondered.

"I can't believe they all went off on this crusade," Elvis said.

"Well, if they did," Crunch said, looking around, "they left a lot of equipment on."

Suddenly Elvis called out, "Christ! What the hell are those things?" Crunch turned to see Elvis pointing at something directly over them. The pilot looked up and saw a dozen or more huge birds lazily circling the base.

"Are they what I think they are?" Elvis asked.

"Jesus, I'm afraid so," Crunch said, slowly. "God-damned vultures."

He rolled the ship around to the back of the

. "Most likely with one of Lucifer's allies. [...] to be used against us."

[...]at's the case, we were more than dumb lucky [...] on that freighter," Heath said.

[...]t," agreed Hunter. "Not only did we get [...]idewinders than we need, we kept them out of [...]nfriendly hands."

[...] Saratoga once again starting sailing to the [...]n earnest. They entered the Strait of Sicily the [...]wing evening—a night during which Hunter [...]y examined the cornucopia of weapons they'd [...]d aboard the Sardinian ship. Hunter counted [...]e than 150 Sidewinders in the cache, which were [...]ed to the ammunition magazine aboard the [...]rier. There were also a number of antipersonnel [...]mbs, small napalm rockets, and a few dozen [...]rike antiradar missiles, as well as more standard [...]n bombs and high-explosive devices.

[...]Hunter immediately wired up six Sidewinders to [...]s F-16, and began configuring the Harrier jump-[...]ts to do the same. Of all the jets on the carrier, the [...]arriers could most easily adapt to the fighter-[...]nterceptor role.

Hunter later took an hour off to visit the ailing Sir Neil. The Englishman was confined in the carrier's version of intensive care, the two Italian doctors hovering over him. He was heavily bandaged from his waist to his head. Still, the Brit was conscious and typically plucky.

"Hunter, old bean," the man said when the pilot entered the room. "I hear our mission was a success in the end."

"I would have given it all back if we could have avoided this," Hunter told him, examining his

hangar, and it was there they made a gruesome discovery. Not only were there several dozen bodies scattered about, there were also five or six dead vultures lying nearby.

At once Crunch and Elvis were both glad that they hadn't popped the F-4's canopy and removed their oxygen masks.

"These guys were gassed," Crunch said. "We could probably find a SCUD missile casing around here somewhere if we looked hard enough. Painted with a big red star on its side, no doubt."

"The gas killed the people, then the poison in the people's blood killed the vultures," Elvis said.

"That's it," Crunch replied, looking back up at the buzzards circling overhead. "And those guys up there are still trying to figure it out."

Crunch rolled the F-4 closer to the bodies. They looked like base help as opposed to RAF personnel. He was sure that other groups of bodies in twos and threes could be found around the base. But then Elvis pointed out something.

"Captain, look at the bodies closest to us," the Weapons Officer said. "Their pockets have been pulled out. Like they were searched or something."

"Either that," Crunch said, "or they got some pretty smart vultures in this part of the world."

"Who the hell would want to go through the pockets of a bunch of stiffs like these?" Elvis asked. "Looters of some kind?"

"Either that or whoever greased this place was looking to kill one person in particular," Crunch observed.

They were quiet for a moment, then Elvis asked, "Do you . . . do you think they were aiming to kill Hawk?"

Crunch had been thinking the exact same thing.

"It would be difficult to say," he answered. "But there is a possibility that's exactly what happened.

"Remember, our boy has a billion-dollar price tag on his head. And I believe the Russians would gladly supply some wacko everything he needed to bump off our good buddy. Even SCUD missiles.

"Or they'd probably take on the job themselves. I don't think the New Order boys would mind turning over a billion dollars to the gang in Moscow."

"It's probably their money to begin with," Elvis said.

Crunch fired up the engine and rolled the F-4 toward the runway.

"I've seen enough," he said to Elvis. "I think it's time to call home and tell them what's going on over here. Between some nutty crusade and the fact that every other weirdo in Europe is looking to bump him off, I think Mr. Hunter is going to need a little more help than just you and I can provide."

Chapter 23

They were at sea for only an hour befor met by two of the Norwegian frigates saili northern end of Sardinia. The ship's cho instantly used to evacuate Sir Neil bac Saratoga, where two Italian doctors—men the communications group—could attend to ous wounds. Although Hunter and the rocketeers had been able to stem the bleeding the Englishman's wounds, Hunter knew the sw ing Brit would never be the same again.

The loss of Sir Neil was tempered somewha the discovery of the load of weapons in the hold the small Sardinian ship. Back on the Saratoga o again, Hunter met with Heath and Yaz and cussed the mother lode he had found.

"Either they were hiding their most valuable wea ons in that ship or they were just about to make huge arms deal and we happened to hijack the delivery truck," Hunter said as he battled his way through yet another plate of ill-prepared food. "Not only are there Sidewinders, but also Shrike antiship missiles and dozens of other weapons."

"If I had to guess, I'd say they were doing a deal,"

Yaz said
Probabl
"If th
jumping
"Rig
more S
some

The
east i
follo
close
four
mor
mov
car
bo
Sh
ir

h
j

wounds.

"Rubbish, Hunter!" Sir Neil replied, his weakened voice rising a notch. "We needed the weapons, man! We couldn't very well sail into the Gates of Hell with a popgun now could we? And an unloaded popgun at that."

"But we need you, sir," Hunter said. "You were the brains of this outfit."

"And what the hell makes you think I still can't be!" the wounded officer said, nearly ripping his head bandage. "What do you intend on doing? Casting me adrift in the Med and going on without me?"

"Wouldn't think of it, sir," the pilot said with a grin. "You'll have to stay here and eat this rotten food with the rest of us."

Sir Neil managed a smile, then motioned Hunter to come close. Speaking in a voice low enough that his doctors couldn't hear, he said: "Aye, Hunter, when you get a chance, please slip me a bit of the grape, wot? Just a small bottle would do. Some of Giuseppe's good stuff. Just to get the blood flowing in the right direction?"

At that moment, Hunter was certain Sir Neil would survive his wounds.

The sun was just starting to break the eastern Med horizon when one of Yaz's men started pounding on Hunter's cabin door. He was sound asleep at the time, wrapped very comfortably in young Anna's arms. But he was up and at the door in a second. He sensed that something was up.

"Sorry, major," the young sailor said, catching a peek at Anna's naked breasts out of the corner of his eye. "But CIC reports a large flotilla of ships

195

heading our way."

"Jeezus," Hunter cursed pulling on his flight suit and boots. "What kind of boats, any idea?"

"Well, the blips on surface radar indicate that they're fairly small," the sailor said. "But there's more than a hundred of them."

Hunter was up on the flight deck in a matter of minutes, glad to see that Yaz's guys had his F-16 fired up and ready for launch.

He met Heath just as he was climbing up the 16's access ladder. The BBC film crew was nearby, recording everything.

"They're about twenty-five miles to the northeast," Heath told Hunter. "Definitely coming right for us."

"What kind of small boats are floating around here these days?" Hunter asked him as he put on his flight helmet. "Do they make PT boats anymore?"

"Could be anything, Hunter," Heath told him. "Armed trawlers perhaps. Maybe converted minesweepers."

"Can you get the Harriers warmed up?" Hunter asked just before he closed his canopy. "If there are more than a hundred of these guys, I'm gonna need help."

With that, the F-16 roared off the carrier in a burst of steam, climbed, and streaked off toward the northeast.

Hunter clicked on his "look-down" radar and located the fleet of ships immediately. He checked his cannon ammunition indicator. It showed all six of his M-61 Vulcans were full. His computers indicated that no sophisticated weapons were aboard the boats—yet he knew torpedos wouldn't necessarily trip the computer's sensors.

He took a deep gulp of oxygen and put the 16 into a dive.

He broke through a light cloud cover at about 5000 feet and found himself right on top of the flotilla. The fleet was spread out for almost two miles. He wasn't surprised that the boats were all different shapes and sizes — trawlers, pleasure yachts, ocean ferries, even a few armed tugboats similar to O'Brien's.

Hunter *was* surprised however when he saw that most of them were flying white flags.

He dropped down to 500 feet and slowed the jet down to a crawl, certain that there were no antiaircraft missiles ready to fire at him. He tipped the 16 to its portside to get a better look at the boats. They appeared to be crowded with armed men — irregulars, he theorized. No specific uniforms. And, far from appearing hostile, they were all waving and cheering as he flew by.

He buzzed the fleet a few more times, noticing several of the boats were carrying radio antennas on their masts. On a chance the boats were carrying modern communications equipment, he searched both his VHF and UHF bands to try to pick up any signal. At the end of the UHF band, he started to pick something up.

". . . *Liberte Marina* calling," the heavily Italian accented voice called out through a burst of static. "We are compadres. Please do not attack. We are the *Liberte Marina* . . ."

Liberte Marina? Did that translate into Freedom Navy? If so, what the hell was the Freedom Navy?

Two Harriers arrived on the scene a few minutes later, and luckily one of the pilots was conversant in Italian. As Hunter orbited above monitoring the radio conversations, the two Harriers hovered over the now-stopped flotilla, the pilot speaking with the fleet's leader.

They *were* the Freedom Navy, a combination Sicilian-Italian force that had apparently heard all about the *Saratoga*'s mission to the Suez.

But what did they want?

"We are here to join you!" the fleet leader kept saying over and over in very broken English. "Compadres! We sail with you!"

An hour later the Freedom Navy boats were floating beside the *Saratoga* fleet. Several Norwegian frigates repeatedly sailed through the *Liberte* boats keeping an eye on them. A half-dozen helicopters buzzing above them did the same. The BBC video crew was hanging off the side of the carrier deck, diligently capturing all the action on film.

Hunter was back on board the *Saratoga* by the time the Navy's leader had been airlifted aboard. He joined Heath, Yaz, and Captain Olson in the carrier's stateroom, where they questioned him.

His name was Commodore Antonio Vanaria. He was a short, stubby character complete with knee-high boots, a feathered Napoleon-style hat, a mean-looking double-barreled carbine strapped over his shoulder, and bandolier ammunition belts crossing his chest.

He had come to offer help.

"Everywhere people are talking about the *Saratoga!*" he said in broken English, gesturing expansively. "They say, 'The men on the *Saratoga* will stop Lucifer in his tracks!' The men on the *Saratoga*—they the bravest in the whole world!

"We—my men of the *Liberte Marina*—want to join such brave men. We too will fight the devil, Lucifer!"

"Commodore," Heath calmly began, taking the place of Sir Neil. "We are on a very, very dangerous mission here. You can see the type of ships and weapons we had to hire for protection. I'm afraid your, well, boats, would be very vulnerable to weapons such as the Exocet, especially—"

"We no care," the Commodore broke in. "We want to fight. We want to fight with the brave men of the *Saratoga!*"

With that, the strange little man walked to the stateroom's typically round porthole window, opened it, and screamed at the top of his lungs: *"Viva la Saratoga!"*

His cry was immediately received with a return chorus of *"Viva! Viva la Saratoga!"* Amazingly, it was coming through loud and clear from the men on his boats nearby.

"It appears we have a fan club," Yaz said in an aside to Hunter.

"I guess so," Hunter said, shaking his head. "And this was supposed to be a secret mission."

The Commodore returned from the porthole. "Me—my men—we have been waiting. Preparing. Training to sail with you. We know our stuff, *signori*. We are good fighters. Sea fighters."

"Sea fighters?" Heath asked.

"I believe he means 'pirates,' " Olson, the Norwegian commander, said.

"Good pirates," the Commodore quickly injected. "We no raid women and babies. We raid the Sardinians. We raid no-good Sidra-Benghazi. We raid Russians—"

"What a minute." Hunter stopped him. "You've seen Russian ships in these waters?"

"Si, signor," the man answered excitedly. "Reds. Armed trawlers. Destroyers. Even some submarines and cruisers."

"Heavy-duty stuff." Yaz whistled.

"Between them and whatever the hell Lucifer's

allies have floating around," Hunter said, "we're going to have our hands full."

"*Si, si, signor!*" the commodore said, bounding over to Hunter. "We help. We know the waters!"

Hunter, Yaz, Heath, and Olson all looked at each other. The Commodore's enthusiasm was contagious. And Hunter could just tell by the nature of the man that he was trustworthy.

"But how could we feed them all?" Heath said. "You know what the food situation is on this ship."

"Yeah," Yaz said. "The bad news is the food is terrible. The good news is that no one can cook it and there's not much to go around."

The Commodore's eyes lit up. *"Food?"* he said, a wide grin revealing a tooth-gaped smile. "We have plenty of food! Good food! And we can cook. My men and I are the best-fed sailors in the whole Mediterranean!"

Whether the little man knew it or not, his value had just gone up a few notches.

Once again the four principals exchanged looks and a round of "what the hell" shrugs.

"We'll have to blow it by Sir Neil," Hunter said. "Though I know he could stand a few good meals —"

"And he's not averse to adding every fighting hand we can get," Heath said.

Hunter turned to Olson. Really the final decision would be his. "Captain, you would have to coordinate the Commodore's boats with yours. Can it be done?"

The craggy, proud-looking Olson rubbed his chin in a habit of thought. "They could provide a fine protection for our flanks and rear, of course."

"Of course!" the Commodore yelled in glee, waving his hands.

"If it's okay with Sir Neil," Olson said, "it's okay with me."

A quick meeting was held in Sir Neil's intensive-care room. Heath slowly and deliberately whispered the situation into the British commander's ear. Hunter could hear the key word "food" repeated several times. Finally they saw Sir Neil nodding his head, before falling back into semiconsciousness.

"The Commodore can throw in with us," Heath told Hunter, Yaz, and Olson afterwards. "If Captain Olson can shepherd them for a while — who knows, they might bring us some luck."

"Luck, hell," Hunter said. "I'll be glad to have one thousand sea pirates on my side any day."

"Plus they can cook," Heath said, raffishly twirling his huge red mustache.

The Commodore soon made good on his promise for edible food and decent cooking. That night he and 100 of his men fed the entire crew of the *Saratoga* a huge pasta meal. Similar feasts were prepared for the men on the other ships in the carrier's entourage. But, privately, Hunter, Heath, and Olson agreed that the Norwegians would keep a close eye on the pirates — although, judging by the Commodore's fervor, the likelihood of one of his men being a spy for Lucifer was remote.

In the meantime, the Italian communications team continued monitoring long-range radio transmissions emanating from Lucifer's Arabian Empire. Hunter was constantly kept informed on critical messages. Most of the radio intercepts had to do with movements of Lucifer's Legions and coordinating their transfers to troop ships anchored near his base at Jidda on the Red Sea.

201

But then, on the afternoon following the appearance of the Commodore's fleet, Hunter and Heath were called up to the *Saratoga's* CIC. The communications people had eavesdropped on a conversation between the pilot of Lucifer's only airplane—a captured US-made P-3 Orion—and the captain a fleet of mercenary ships sailing in the Red Sea. The ships were discussing instructions to head toward the Suez Canal and "commence operations."

"What kind of operations?" Hunter asked Giuseppe, the leader of the Italian communications team.

"It's hard to say, major," the man told him as he sat working over a sophisticated radio set. "But, judging by the strength of the mercenary's radio signal, we can approximate the size and type of the ships they are using."

"And?" Heath asked.

"And, if I had to guess," Giuseppe said, "I'd say they were minelayers. Russian-built minelayers."

"Blast!" Heath spat out. "Soviet mines! That's all we need."

"Mines in the canal could definitely crimp our style," Hunter said.

Heath tugged at his mustache with worry. "Should we consider an air strike, major?" the Brit asked.

"I don't think we can risk it," Hunter replied. "We could lose some very valuable aircraft to SAMs, especially if they have a P-3 Orion flying around out there. With the AWACs gear on that airplane, they'd see us coming for miles.

"Plus we can sink the minelayers, but that wouldn't take care of the mines themselves."

"So what are our options?" Heath asked.

Hunter shook his head. "I'm afraid we don't have any right now," he said. "We'll just have to deal with

202

it as we go along."

"Christ," Heath said. "Just one more thing to worry about . . ."

Another day passed. Slowly. Tension was building on the carrier, Hunter could feel it in his psyche. Even the Med seemed to be working against them. They were running into strong head winds. The resulting currents were making the towing operation more difficult.

Hunter spent most of his time this day supervising the rewiring of the Swedish Viggen fighters to carry heavy ordnance. The constant, more noticeable pull-push of the carrier in the rough seas made the precise work required twice as difficult.

After the long day finally ended, Hunter walked alone to the stern of the *Saratoga*. He stood close to the edge of the mighty carrier's deck, watching O'Brien's tugs churn up the Mediterranean in front of him, their thick towlines taut and vibrating like a too-tightly-strung violin.

As always, his mind was going in a million different directions. Life was so strange, he thought. He loved the USA. He missed his friends back home. Anna had filled a nice niche in his life, but he yearned for the sweet touch of Dominique. Yet here he was, out in the middle of the Mediterranean, on a disabled flattop, being towed into "the Gates of Hell," as Sir Neal liked to describe it. Chasing the super-criminal who had so ruthlessly destroyed the fragility of America.

But was it worth it? Was it more like chasing a phantom? Punishing one man certainly wasn't going to rebuild America from the ruins of The Circle War. Was the fact that Lucifer—then Viktor—had kidnapped Dominique and had used her in his devious plans the *real* reason why Hunter was so intent in tracking down the madman? Was this crazy adventure simply nothing more than a personal vendetta? Hunter shook his head — he just didn't know . . .

The pilot heard someone behind him. He turned to see that it was the strange man Peter.

The prophetic looney-tune had been calmer than usual in the last few days; one of Yaz's corpsman had injected him several times with a sedative, so Heath had told him. The drug was working; Peter spent most of his time lying in his wooden box-bed, placidly ranting. The Brits had even reduced the man's four-man SAS guard to just two. Now, as these soldiers took a smoke break nearby, Peter walked to the edge of the deck and sat down, completely oblivious to Hunter, who was standing no more than ten feet away.

He didn't speak. It appeared to Hunter that the strange little guy was working his way into a trance. He was sitting in an authentic cross-legged swami style, his palms open on his knees, his eyes closed tight. Hunter expected him to start moaning the magic word "Om" at any minute. Instead the man just sat there rigidly, the ever-present stream of drool running out of the corners of his mouth and on to his disgustingly moist and dirty beard.

Hunter moved a little closer to the man. Who the hell was he? he thought. How could anyone so obviously fringed out see the future so clearly? How did the man function from minute to minute, day to day? What spirits haunted him?

Suddenly Peter opened his eyes and turned his strange gaze right at Hunter. The eyes were almost red with intensity. The stare absolutely haunting.

"You . . ." he said, as if Hunter had just suddenly appeared. "You are the pilot. The Wingman. I see you. In my dreams. Battling the Angel of Death . . ."

Hunter knew the man was about to go "off" once again. But he also knew that it was in Peter's most disordered moments that he was at his most prophetic.

He knelt down beside the man. "What else do you see, Peter?"

The man put his hands to his face and rubbed his eyes in his agitation. "Lucifer," he said, his voice trembling. "I see him in my dreams too. His face. In the sky. The color of blood.

"Lucifer's minions will attack us. I see them now. Their boats can fly on the sea. The storms do not bother them. They are protected by the Death Angel's face in the sky."

Peter took his hands away from his eyes and looked again right at Hunter.

"The multitudes turn away when they see his face. But you, The Wingman, do not turn away . . ."

Suddenly Peter was on his feet and grabbing Hunter by the collar. His face was desperate. Tears rolled out of his wild eyes and down his soiled face. *"You do not turn away!"* he said, tugging at Hunter's flight suit. "I can no longer help you! Don't you understand? I've done all I can!"

The man let out a long, unearthly, agonizing wail.

"This ship," Peter said, more tears flowing. "This ship was once mine. I tried! I tried to defeat the Red demons. But I abandoned it! Yes, abandoned it!

"Now it's up to you. It's your ship now. You must use it. You must defeat the great Evil sent to this world. You! The Wingman. My dreams . . . Your battles to come. God help me! *Why was I cursed this way!"*

By this time, Peter was screaming at the top of his lungs. His SAS guards were on the scene and dragging him away. Hunter was stunned. He couldn't move. A strange feeling had completely wrapped around his body, holding him rigidly in place. It wasn't so much what Peter said—to anyone else it was only so much raving, drooling malarky. But it was *how* he said it. A psychic link existed between him and the strange man. Peter's words had penetrated the deepest recesses of Hunter's soul. The place where *the feeling* came from. Now an ice-cold chill enveloped his body as he watched the SAS men lead Peter into a hatchway in the carrier's superstructure.

Do not turn away. The words echoed in Hunter's ears. *Do not turn away!*

Chapter 24

One of the Commodore's boat captains saw them first . . .

The carrier fleet had passed through the Strait of Sicily and was about 100 miles due east of the island of Malta. Captain Olson had decided the best way to utilize the *Liberte Marina* was to deploy them forward of the carrier. This way they could serve as lookouts and warn the *Saratoga* of any treacherous waters ahead.

So now the proud fleet of armed yachts, converted workboats, ferries, and trawlers plowed the sea, spread out anywhere from ten to fifteen miles ahead of the carrier force.

It was mid-afternoon. The day had dawned hot and nearly breezeless. Hunter was in the CIC, catching up on the latest radio intercepts from Lucifer's Empire, when a frantic call came in from one of the Commodore's lead boats.

"Emergency! Emergency!" the heavily accented voice cried out from the radio speakers. "We are under attack! Enemy aircraft! We are under att — "

The radio suddenly went dead.

"Christ," Heath said to Hunter. "What the hell was that?"

Hunter didn't reply. He was already out of the CIC, and up on the ship's bridge. There, the six men of Yaz's group charged with keeping the carrier on course had also heard the message and were already reacting. Yaz himself was crouched over the bridge radar. It had momentarily picked up several blips just as the panicky call had come in from the Freedom Navy boat. Now Hunter was peering out of the ship's powerful telescope, searching the horizon for the boat that made the call.

The first thing he saw was a faint wisp of smoke off to the northeast.

"Yaz, can we establish contact with any of those boats out there?" Hunter called out, zooming in on the smoke.

Yaz moved over to the bridge radio and started punching buttons and twisting dials. "We've only got radio linkup with a few of them," he said. "I'll try the Commodore's boat itself. He's in that area."

At the same time, a call came in from one of Olson's frigates. "We've got enemy aircraft out here," the calm, cool, Norwegian-accented voice reported via the bridge radio speakers. "They have sunk one Freedom Navy boat. They are attacking others. We are moving in to engage . . ."

Hunter gave up on the telescope — the action was too far away from them. Instead he moved to the bridge's backup radio set and called the frigate commander. "This is Major Hunter. Please ID number of enemy aircraft and type."

The radio crackled with a burst of angry static. Then the same Norwegian voice came back on, this time a little less calm. "We are now under attack ourselves!" the radioman reported. "At least twenty-five aircraft! They are firing on us with cannon and missiles . . . We are . . ." Another burst of static drowned out the man's word.

Yaz was at Hunter's side as the pilot tried to raise the frigate again. "How can there be aircraft out there, major?" the American sailor asked. "We would have seen it on the radar before it was a hundred miles near us."

Hunter jumped up from the radio and ran to the radar set. "I don't know," he said, shaking his head. "You got a few blips when they first attacked, but now, there's nothing. Unless . . ."

"Unless?" Yaz asked.

"Unless, they are flying too low to be picked up on our screens," Hunter said, quickly.

Heath had by this time appeared on the bridge, quickly assessed the situation, and yelled into a microphone, "Battle stations!" Immediately, the carrier's warning klaxon began blaring. Men were running around the ship in controlled pandemonium. While deck sailors were feverishly working on Hunter's F-16, preparing it for launch, others were using the carrier's massive elevator to bring up the Harriers from below decks. Similar emergency sirens could be heard from the Norwegian escort ships cruising on either side of the carrier. Even the men on O'Brien's tugs were reacting.

Once again the bridge's radio speaker came to life. "SOS! SOS!" the Norwegian voice said. "May Day! May Day! We have been hit. Ship is on fire. May Day! May Day!"

Hunter was back at the radio in a flash. "This is the *Saratoga*," he called. "Please ID attacking aircraft . . ."

There was no reply.

"That does it," Hunter said, running from the bridge. "I'm going out there . . ."

With that, he disappeared from the bridge and was soon climbing into his F-16.

In less than a minute, the jet fighter's engine was hot and its missiles fully armed. Hunter gave the launch officer the thumbs-up sign, and in a flash of fire and a burst of steam the F-16 was catapulted off the deck. It seemed to hang in the air for a moment. Then Hunter booted it and instantly the jet throttled forward and soon disappeared over the northeastern horizon.

He was approaching the battle a minute later. It was a wild, confused scene, one that took him a few seconds to sort out. There was smoke and flames everywhere. White, streaky missile contrails crisscrossed the sky. Long streams of returning gunfire were coming from the many smaller boats of the Freedom Navy, but the direction of the fire looked to be almost horizontal. Gunners on the two Norwegian frigates on the scene—one of which was smoking heavily—appeared to be doing the same curious thing. At first, it looked as if the ships were firing at each other.

Then, as he drew closer, he saw what was happening. He had guessed right; the enemy aircraft *were* flying too low to be picked up on radar. But it was the kind of aircraft that startled him.

"Christ," he whispered. "They're seaplanes . . ."

Then Peter's words came back to him. The man had said the enemy would have "boats that fly."

Hunter shook off a chill, then flew directly over the battle. He banked to the right to get a good look. There were two kinds of enemy aircraft that he could see. One type was a large, rather lumbering seaplane, the size of a small airliner. It looked like a bizarre variation of the US-made Albatross Air-Sea Rescue plane of the 1960s, yet it was bigger, with a longer snout and a long, thin, tube-like appendage protruding from its tail.

It took only a few moments for him to identify the strange seaplane: it was a Beriev M-12, a Soviet-built amphibian used years before for antisubmarine duty. But whoever was flying them now had made some major modifications. The original two Ivchenko Al-20D turbo-prop engines mounted on the over-the-top wing had been increased to four. Hunter knew the protrusions on the front and back of the airplane were for radar, but these airplanes were also bristling with literally dozens of gun ports and carrying many wing-launched missiles.

Their tactic was simple and easily recognizable. They would come in just a few feet above the water, passing between the target ships. Their on-board gunners would then blast away from both sides with guns ranging from .50-caliber machine guns to M-61 20mm cannons. Hunter even recognized the distinctive black puff of smoke characteristic of small howitzers.

Against these big flying boats, both the frigate and the Freedom Navy gunners were depressing their gun barrels as low as possible to shoot at the attackers. But many of the antiaircraft guns simply weren't made to shoot at such a low angle. The enemy flyers had found a weakness and they were exploiting it.

"Ingenious," Hunter muttered, grudgingly giving the attackers credit.

The other type of attacking aircraft was a small, swift, jet-powered seaplane—a type Hunter had never seen. These airplanes looked almost as if they

211

were assembled from a kit of some sort. They were smaller than the smallest service-type jet, just barely fifteen feet in overall length. Their jet engine was fitted above the boat-like fusilage, sitting centered on the short, slightly sweptback wing. These fighters were also carrying missiles and cannons.

Working in tandem with the larger boats flying, the fighters too were operating at wave-top level, zipping in and out of the passages between their targets, pumping missiles and cannon shells into the Freedom Navy boats. All of the seaplanes, big and small, were painted in the same off-green ocean-camouflage color scheme, indicating an organized unit was in action. And they were performing a highly specialized, coordinated attack. Custom-made, it would seem, to stopping a large flotilla in its tracks.

Hunter was in amongst them in seconds, streaking down low between a frigate and an armed Freedom Navy trawler. A large, rather sluggish flying boat was making its way in the opposite direction when its pilot, obviously very surprised to see an F-16 coming right towards him, pulled up sharply. Hunter could hear the big plane's engines scream as it sought altitude. In doing so, the pilot had exposed his undefended belly to Hunter. He promptly deposited a Sidewinder into its hind quarters—the missile's heat-seeking system apparently finding something to its liking there.

The enemy airplane continued to climb for a few seconds after the missile exploded inside it, its gunners still diligently firing away at the frigate below them. Then—most likely—a fuel line ruptured, caught fire, and sparked some ammunition. The airplane was just 500 feet above the water when it disappeared in an enormous explosion, showering the ships below with a rain of fiery debris.

Hunter was already picking out his next target—one of the smaller sea fighters. A lone jet was zooming in on an armed Freedom Navy trawler that was desperately zigzagging to deny the attacker a clear shot. Hunter was on the fighter's tail in seconds. A short squeeze of his nose-mounted 20mm cannon Six Pack proved more than enough. The sea fighter exploded instantly, pieces of flaming wood and metal bouncing off the F-16's nose as it swept up and over the rescued trawler.

Hunter put the 16 on its ass and did a 360-degree loop. At once, he was on the tail of a large seaplane just as it was beginning its attack on a Freedom Navy converted workboat. All of the ship's hands were on deck firing at the slow-moving airplane with everything from a shotgun and rifles to pistols. Yet the ship's fairly sophisticated deck gun just couldn't get a clear shot at the flying boat. The airplane's gunners, meanwhile, were delivering a punishing barrage upon the workboat. The stream of fire coming from the starboard side of the airplane was incredible.

Hunter opened up the Six Pack once again, chopping off the big plane's tail as well as its radar tube. The airplane immediately hit the water, bounced up once, then twice. Hunter stayed on its tail, lowering his flaps to slow the F-16 down. He pressed his cannon trigger again, catching the airplane coming up off its third bounce and ripping away one of its port engines. The Beriev bounced once more, then plunged nose first into the sea, sending up a fiery stream of water and steam.

Still, the attackers pressed the battle. While they were no match for his interceptor, their sheet numbers proved devastating to the Freedom Navy boats.

There were at least twenty of the big flying boats passing in and out of the *Liberte Marina* flotilla, with just as many of the smaller jets. The Freedom Navy had already lost at least eight boats and several more were burning uncontrollably.

Hunter was glad to see two Harriers arrive on the scene. He briefly discussed the situation with the jump-jet pilots, then the three fighters went to work.

The Harriers proved especially nimble in fighting the big flying boats. They would hover at 150 feet above the water, waiting for one of the lumbering seaplanes to commit to making a pass. Then the Harrier would pounce, ripping apart the slow, large craft with withering bursts of cannon fire. The big Berievs thus occupied, Hunter chased down the smaller, swifter sea-jets.

The battle raged for several more minutes before the attackers finally broke off and retreated toward the north. Hunter had half a mind to chase them, but a more important job would be to get back to the carrier and report the attack. The Harriers remained on the scene of the battle, directing rescue efforts for those Freedom Navy men still alive and in the water. Before leaving the scene, Hunter counted four large seaplanes downed, as well as eight smaller jets. Still, as many as a dozen of the Commodore's boats were either sunk or sinking. Hunter estimated as many as 100 *Liberte Marina* crewmen were killed.

"Who the hell *were* they, major?" Heath asked, nervously pulling on a cigarette.

"Who knows?" Hunter replied, downing a cup of whiskey-laced coffee. "Whoever they were, they sure knew how the hell to fly those goddamn mothers low-ass-end on the water."

They were sitting in a small dining room that doubled as the *Saratoga*'s pilot-debriefing room. Besides Hunter and Heath, Olson, Yaz, and the Commodore were present. Even the industrious O'Brien was there.

"We lose so many men," the Commodore said. "Those bastards. We must find them. Destroy them!"

"Do you think they were in Lucifer's employ, major?" Olson asked.

"I'm sure of it," Hunter replied. "And the fact they were using Soviet-designed, if not Soviet-built and -piloted, aircraft, is really bugging me. God knows what they have out there waiting for us."

"Couldn't we send out a search plane and locate their base?" O'Brien asked.

"Sure, we could," Hunter said. "But the thing is, I'll bet they don't have a base. Not a fixed, permanent one anyway."

Heath refilled a cup with coffee and spiked it with the bottle of no-name whiskey on the table. "How do you mean, major?"

"Well, they wouldn't really need a fixed land base," Hunter began. "All they need is a source of fuel. They could have a few supertankers filled with JP-8 aviation fuel floating around out there somewhere. They land on the water nearby and fuel up. They could even have some kind of docking works extended from the ship. Some supply ships nearby, where they keep the food, and extra crews. Hell, the crew members could live right on the aircraft without much trouble. They wouldn't have to put into dry land for weeks."

Yaz let out a groan. "God, that's all we need," he said, his Southern accent betraying him. "We got a floating airbase out there, keeping one step ahead of us."

"That's not the only problem," Hunter said. "Those big seaplanes are carrying some very sophisticated radar domes on them. They might be slow and clumsy, but I'll tell you, there's a lot of them and they can probably fight in all situations."

"Like night fighting?" Olson asked.

"Yes," Hunter replied, deadly serious. "Night fighting and even in bad flying weather. If that happens, there's not a fighter on this ship that would be safe going up after them. And I doubt if even the Spanish rocket teams could stop them."

Heath thought for a second, bit his lip, then asked, "So, what if they ever got into us here — on the carrier, I mean — what would happen?"

Hunter looked them all straight in the eye, then said, "They could sink this ship . . ."

Hunter couldn't sleep. His normally fourth-gear-and-racing mind was working overtime now, to the point where he couldn't lay still. He carefully moved Anna's sweet, naked body from his, kissed her, then rose and left his cabin.

It was a calm, cool, moonless night. The Med was like a sheet of glass; hardly a wave rose and fell. Peaceful, yet uneasy. The calm before the storm. He knew the attack that day had been simply a probing action. The flying boats knew they could go after bigger game than the potluck vessels of the Freedom Navy.

And Peter had predicted it, the spooky son of a bitch . . .

Hunter walked through the CIC, speaking briefly with the night-shift crew. They reported everything as normal. Nothing out of the ordinary had been picked up in Lucifer's radio transmissions since the seaplane attack—but then again, Hunter didn't expect anything unusual.

He left and walked about the *Saratoga*'s superstructure. The French anti-ship group had doubled their watch, as had the Spanish rocketeers. Two Harriers and a Viggen were on the deck, ready to launch at a moment's notice. On the frigates surrounding the carrier, he could see more than the normal running lights were burning. Cabin lights were on; figures moved silently on the walkways. He knew all of the ships were on general, first-degree alert.

A quarter-mile off the carrier's stern was the Moroccan troop ship. His extra-sensitive ears could hear the unmistakable drone of chanting. The desert fighters were praying in the middle of the night. Most of the boats of the *Liberte Marina* were now mixed in amongst the frigates and the tugs, although the Commodore insisted that twenty-five of his boats still be allowed to "sail the point." The whole fleet was on edge. Expecting the unexpected. Even O'Brien's tugs had their deck guns fully manned.

He walked into the bridge, where Yaz sat, going over sea and weather charts with O'Brien's second-in-command.

"We could be in Malta in forty-eight hours, Major," Yaz told him. "Currents here are still running against us, but O'Brien says he can put on an auxiliary tug or two."

"God knows what it's like in Malta these days," Hunter said.

Yaz nodded. "It's anyone's guess," he said. "When we were holed up in Algiers, we heard some pretty wild stories about the place. Still, Sir Neil had scheduled it as our first resupply stop. He felt confident at the time that we could get gassed up there."

Suddenly a loud, howling scream split the night.

"What the fuck was that!" Yaz yelled.

Hunter picked up on the last tones of the scream and determined it was coming from below, in the general area of the sick bay. "Sounds like it came from Sir Neil's room," he said, running out of the bridge, with Yaz and two SAS men in tow.

They reached the sick bay to find two more SAS men and a couple of Gurkhas in the process of battering down the hatch door that led to Sir Neil's recovery room. Another scream pierced the night.

"Bloody door's locked from the inside," one of the SAS men grunted as they pounded away at the hatch handle. Finally it gave, and those on the outside rushed in just as another scream was heard.

When Hunter got inside, he was relieved to see Sir Neil, awake and relatively safe, though looking quite confused. Clara, the Madam who had taken a liking to the British commander, was at his side, stark naked. She looked absolutely petrified. She had done the screaming.

It was almost completely dark inside the room and it was oddly cold. Someone tried the light switch, but it didn't work. Still, Hunter could see that Clara was pointing to the far corner. He whirled around and saw a figure sitting there, hunched low, groaning and shaking.

It was Peter . . .

No one dared approach him. And for good reason. The strange man had raised his head and Hunter saw a sight he would never forget. The man's eye were *glowing*. Glowing the color of red. Hunter shut his own and quickly opened them again, just to check and make sure it wasn't him. It wasn't. Nor was it some freak reflection. The man's eyes were actually burning red. It looked like a special effect from a cheap sci-fi movie. But in real life, it was extremely chilling.

"He came out of nowhere!" Clara screamed. "One moment there was no one there, the next he was there. And he's making such an awful, dreadful sounds. And those eyes—"

She screamed once again, causing everyone in the room to jump. Hunter gave the thumb to two SAS guys and they quickly picked her up and literally carried her outside the room.

Then the cabin became very hot.

"Peter . . ." Hunter said, daring to take a step toward the man.

Suddenly, a strange laughter filled the room. Peter's mouth was open, and the deep, booming laughter was coming from it. But it was not Peter's voice . . .

"You fools!" the echoing, graveled voice said, gurgling in mocking laughter. *"You should know better than to dare attack me!"*

At that point, the normally unruffled Gurkhas left. A suspicious lot, they had had enough. Hunter could hear one of them vomiting outside the room.

Goddamn, this is spooky, Hunter thought, taking another step toward the man.

"Don't you dare come come any closer to me," the voice said *"You! Hunter! I won't rest until I see you dead!"*

At that point, all the electrical systems on the ship went out. Hunter knew because the distinctive sounds of the gas-powered generators located in the ship's hold had suddenly ceased.

"Jesus Christ," one of the SAS men swore. "He's knocked out the blooming power."

219

Hunter had experienced some pretty strange things before, but nothing as strange as this.

Still, he drew yet another step closer to the man. "Peter," he said, loudly. "Snap out of it—"

The voice roared. *"Don't you dare come near me!"* With that, a great glob of green, stinking mass came spraying out of Peter's mouth. Hunter deftly moved to the side just in time to avoid the disgusting spit.

Hunter gulped, then in a voice as strong as he could muster, he yelled: "Fuck you!"

A terrifying scream filled the cabin. The sickly Sir Neil put his hands to his ears, as did the two remaining SAS men. Another glob of smelly mess— this one blood red—came spitting from Peter's mouth. Hunter was also able to dodge this.

"So who the *fuck* are you?" Hunter yelled defiantly, stepping a little closer towards Peter. *"That coward, Lucifer?"*

"I am your worst nightmare, Hunter," the deep voice gurgled with ear-splitting volume. *"I am in this wretch's body only to curse you. To condemn you! You fools!"*

Hunter was now three steps away from Peter. His eyes were glowing even more intensely. His beard was covered with the repulsive, sticky vomit. Hunter had to do something. The room smelled worse than anything he'd ever imagined.

"Stay away!" the voice from within Peter screamed. *"Stay away from me!"*

Hunter then quickly moved two steps and planted his boot right against Peter's chest. He pressed hard. Another blood-curdling scream came out of the man's mouth, so intense Hunter could feel the vibrations right through his boot.

He leaned over and with a balled fist laid a strong punch on Peter's left jaw. Another scream. But this one was cut short by a left uppercup from Hunter. Peter's body was lifted up and flung back against the wall, where his eyes went wide. In a microsecond, they changed back to a normal human color. Then they closed and the man slumped to the floor.

A few seconds later, the lights came back on . . .

Chapter 25

The next day dawned cold and stormy. The seas were rougher than at anytime in the voyage and the crews of the *Saratoga* flotilla witnessed the beginning of a savage mid-morning thunder and lightning storm. It was as if Hunter's punches, thrown the night before to break Peter's spell, had dented some fragile fabric of Nature. Now Nature would seek its revenge . . .

The sudden bad weather—none of which had shown up on the carrier's fairly sophisticated meteorological hardware—forced the towing operation to stop. The risk of damage to both the carrier and the precious tugboats was too great to attempt pushing on in the wind-swept seas. Reluctantly, Heath, acting as temporary commander of the operation in Sir Neil's incapacity, asked Yaz to order the carrier's anchor dropped. The other ships in the fleet did likewise.

Hunter was still mystified by the bizarre happenings of the night before. No one could figure out how Peter had gotten inside Sir Neil's room—his

SAS guards once again had left him heavily sedated in his box-bed, and they swore they hadn't left his cabin's door for a moment. Clara, who had been sleeping with Sir Neil, said she simply woke up and Peter was there, crouched in the corner, the frightening glow coming from his eyes. Peter himself would provide no clues either; he was heavily sedated. The SAS guard watching over him was increased again to four.

The whole day was a series of storms, thunder, lightning, and waves so high they crashed regularly on to the *Saratoga*'s deck. One gigantic wave hit the stern of the flattop and carried away a frigate helicopter with it, although the chopper was triple-fastened to the deck. While the Norwegian frigates, the Moroccan troopship, the oiler, and the tugs were rugged enough to ride out the weather, the storms were especially destructive to the smaller boats of the Freedom Navy. Several had already sunk — though the loss of life was slight due to heroic efforts of the Norwegians, who managed to pluck many of the hapless sailors out of the rough seas.

Hunter spent most of the day in the CIC. The radio-intercept operations were at a standstill too. But his major concern — next to being thrown around due to the violent up-and-down motion of the carrier — was to maintain some sort of defensive perimeter around the fleet despite the storm.

Around mid-afternoon, Hunter was trying to drink a cup of coffee in the mess when Yaz came in.

"Well, it's official," the American sailor told him. "We are in the middle of an authentic hurricane."

"I didn't think they had hurricanes in the Mediterranean," Hunter replied.

"They don't. But the winds are strong enough to qualify it as one," Yaz said, trying to drink some

223

coffee himself.

"Any sign of it letting up?" Hunter asked.

"None that we can see," Yaz said. "Of course, it really snuck up on us. Maybe it will go away just as quickly."

At that moment, the ship went through a particularly violent shudder, caused by a gigantic wave hitting it broadside. The lights blinked a couple times, then stayed on, though noticeably dimmer.

"Those poor generators," Yaz said. "If they hold out through this, I want to buy stock in the company that made them."

Hunter spent several more hours in the CIC, then went up to see Sir Neil.

"Recovered from last night?" Hunter asked, slipping the British Commander a small flask filled with wine.

"Aye, just barely," Sir Neil said, keeping an eye on the Italian doctor on watch and taking a quick swig of the *vino* when he was sure the physician wasn't looking.

"Looked like a bad scene from a bad movie, no?" Hunter asked.

"I'll tell you, major," Sir Neil said, "I've heard Lucifer had such powers, but I never believed until now. It really shows you what we are up against."

"Well, if he orchestrated that little spook show last night, he is quite an opponent," Hunter agreed. "But I guess I should be used to it. He pulled some pretty unworldly things back during The Circle War too."

"One thing is for certain," Sir Neil said, struggling a bit to sit up in his bed. "He wants to stop us from accomplishing our mission at all costs. In my mind, that should give us even more reason to push on."

"Hear, hear!" Hunter said, smiling.

Sir Neil feigned a slight cough, expertly sneaking another swig of wine. "What shape are the airplanes in, Hunter?"

"They're in fine condition," the pilot told him. "We're keeping the Tornados, the Jags, and the Viggens secured until we get to the Canal, or unless we need them sooner. The Harriers are always on standby. They're goddamn tough airplanes. The S-3A still needs some armament work, and its engine is just a little cranky.

"But your monkeys are good. They're smart and they know their way around a jet engine, whether it be British, Swedish, or made in the USA. When the time comes, we'll be close to ninety-five percent available. And we'll have plenty of ammo to strap under their wings, thanks to the haul from Sardinia."

"That's all we want," Sir Neil said, resting back down into his bed. "I'm just sorry that I'm laying here, all busted up. Goddamn Sardinians. The hedonistic bastards. Why wasn't that bloke with the machine gun out getting laid or pissed like everyone else on the whole shitting island?"

Hunter eyed a woman's nightgown hanging from a hook near Sir Neil's bed. It was obviously Clara's.

"Well, I see you've at least been making the best of the time you've spent here," he said.

Sir Neil caught his drift. "Aye. Clara." He sighed. "She's a sweetie, to come and comfort an old goat like me, especially with all these bandages and things."

"Well," Hunter said, getting up to go, "if you're bedridden anyway, what the hell?"

Suddenly Sir Neil was sitting up again. "Hunter," he said, extending his hand, "thanks, me boy."

Hunter took the man's hand and shook it.

"Heath is a good lad and doing well in my stead—but he's following orders because he's RAF to the end," Sir Neil said. "But I know you don't have to be doing this. I feel sometimes like I've gotten you in to one hell of a mess. Mixed up in some fool's cockamamy idea of a crusade to save the world. I just wanted to let you know I appreciate it."

Hunter became very serious. He could see in the man's eyes the look one has when a dream is in danger of being lost. The worst fear in the world. The fear of the unfulfilled.

He gripped Sir Neil's hand harder. "Don't worry, sir," The Wingman said. "You can count on me . . ."

The storm continued unabated into the night. If anything, the seas got rougher. There was no need to calculate where the center of the storm was—the simultaneous crack of lightning and boom of thunder proved it was directly over the *Saratoga*.

Once again, Hunter tried to sleep, but found it impossible. He had checked with the CIC one last time, and everything was normal—or as normal as they could be in the middle of a hurricane. Yet something was still gnawing at him—the anticipation of trouble ahead, compounded by the spooky trip the night before. His own fairly extensive extrasensory abilities were buzzing. Would he ever reach a point where he wouldn't have to worry about such things again?

The answer was no . . .

He lay on his bunk and had just closed his eyes when *the feeling* washing over him.

"Oh no," he thought, immediately jumping up from the bunk. "Here we go again . . ."

He was up and running toward the deck in a moment, pausing only to put on his flight helmet and grab his M-16. He was working totally on instinct now—a nether region so baffling for him that in some cases he couldn't explain his actions even after the crisis was over.

He reached the deck and went out into the night. The wind was howling ferociously. Lightning was splitting the sky every other second. The thunder was so loud, his ears began to hurt. Waves the size of buildings were crashing against the side of the carrier. At some points, the frigate nearest the *Saratoga* looked higher in elevation that the carrier itself.

Yet out there, somewhere, he knew enemy aircraft were coming . . .

Suddenly the battle stations' klaxon went off, even though the howling wind and the booming thunder nearly drowned it out. Yaz emerged from the conning tower and, spotting him on the deck, screamed at the top of his lungs, "They're coming, Hawk! The flying boats! There's at least eighty of them!"

Hunter didn't even bother to ask Yaz how he knew this. It simply confirmed what Hunter had been feeling in his bones all along.

"Those crazy bastards," he thought. "Who the hell would come out in a hurricane to pull a mid-sea air strike? *And at night?*"

Immediately, he saw the Spanish Rocketeers and the French Legion soldiers appear on the deck. Hunter grabbed the Spaniards' group leader.

"We're about to be attacked," he yelled to the man, trying to be heard over the pandemonium of noise. "Get your guys to their positions and tell them to strap themselves in. Tell them to use belts, ropes, wire, whatever. But get them secured so no one goes overboard!"

The Spaniard nodded, saluted, and ran off into the night. Meanwhile, Hunter sought out the French antiship company leader. He found the man at the carrier's forward Phalanx gun position.

"We are about to be attacked by aircraft," he explained to the man. "Seaplanes like the ones that attacked the Freedom Navy. Do you understand?"

"Oui, monsieur," the man yelled back.

"Can your guns work against slow-moving aircraft?"

The Frenchmen mustered up a smile. "We certainly will find out, *monsieur.*"

Hunter had to smile too. Talk about *esprit de corps.* He patted the man on the back, yelled, "Go get 'em!" and was off.

That's when he heard the sound of approaching aircraft . . .

He ran towards the front of the ship again, noting that all the carrier's guns were manned and that the Spanish rocketeers were in position. Even the Australians and the Gurkhas were huddled in doorways and bulkheads, ready if needed.

Hunter reached the front of the ship and stared out into the stormy night. His extraordinary eyes picked out first one, then two, then a half-dozen red and white lights coming directly towards him.

"Those crazy bastards . . ." he whispered once again. Although his eyes confirmed it, his mind was having a hard time believing it. "Here they come . . ."

Not ten seconds later one of the huge Soviet-built Beriev-12 flying boats roared between the carrier and the frigate on its port side. It was traveling so slow, Hunter could see dozens of faces peering out of the double line of gun portholes on the side of the Beriev. The huge airplane seemed to hang in the air for a moment then it was gone—disappearing into the storm.

Next a smaller sea-jet came through, its nose spitting cannon fire, which Hunter heard pinging off the hull of the ship. This airplane banked to the right and as it passed, Hunter saw a weapon strapped under its wing that sent a chill through him.

"Jezzuz!" he said to himself. "That was a god-damn Exocet!"

Another Beriev came in. This time every gun was aimed at the carrier and firing. Hunter hit the deck, though the spray from the sea was hard to distinguish from metal splinters flying around because of the vicious barrage from the flying boat.

He was quickly back on his feet. He could see through the rain and sea spray that the attackers were buzzing all over the fleet on both sides of the carrier. He could also see streaks of light piercing the foul night as the flying boats pounded the storm-tossed ships.

"If this isn't the craziest thing," he thought, his uniform and every inch of his body soaking wet. "Battling a bunch of crazy fuckers in seaplanes in the middle of the night in the middle of a typhoon!"

Another Beriev came roaring in, its howitzer pumping out shells that were just screaming over the deck and crashing to the sea on the other side. Still no one on the *Saratoga,* or on the other attending ships that he could see, was firing back.

"Well, fuck this," Hunter said, his temper getting the better of him. Someone had to fight back! He ran up to the edge of the ship, cocked his M-16, and started firing. He could see some of his tracer bullets bouncing off the side of the flying boat, but others were penetrating. He shot out at least one gun port window before the huge plane roared off.

Then a seaplane streaked by and Hunter pumped a few shots at it too. Then, down by the stern of the ship, Hunter saw the flash of a Stinger missile going off. Its tail twisted up and over the top of the flying boat missing it by just five feet. That's better, Hunter thought.

Now he saw more return fire was coming from the attending ships as their sailors began exchanging shots in earnest with the flying boats. Within seconds, the sounds of the battle were overwhelming the roar of the wind and the ever-present claps of thunder.

But now the attackers started to intensify their attack. Changing their tactics, two sea-jets swooped in on the carrier head on, each firing a small antiship missile. One exploded just feet from the carrier's catapult channel, spraying the deck with shrapnel and fire. Another hit the base of the conning tower, the explosion breaking a number of windows and ripping a hatchway door off its hinges and flinging it off into the raging wind.

Hunter pumped half of his M-16's magazine into the two jets as they streaked overhead. As soon as they passed, another two sea-jets repeated the maneuver. Luckily, their two missiles passed right over the carrier's superstructure.

Two more sea-jets came in, but by this time the French Phalanx team had found the range. Firing the modern Gatling gun manually, the French sent up a wall of lead usually intended to destroy incoming missiles. This time, the bullets—firing at a rate of 100 rounds *a second*—perforated both sea-jets. The force of the barrage was so intense, it seemed to stop the two sea-jets in place. Both airplanes simply disintegrated, their fiery debris instantly swept away by the howling wind.

"Jesus Christ!" Hunter yelled out. He had never seen anything quite like that!

The battle became even more intense. The sky was filled with sea-jets — screaming by like banshees, their cannons roaring. The Rocketeers were firing Stingers in every direction — so many that Hunter felt they would eventually start to hit targets. But it was hard to tell because the visibility was so poor around the ship.

Then suddenly, off to his left, he heard a tremendous roar. It was one of the frigates. A large spit of flame was exploding from its center. Hunter knew right away what had happened. It had been hit right in its ammunition bunker by an Exocet. He watched as the ship belched a cloud of smoke, followed by another, larger explosion.

When the fiery mist cleared, the ship was gone.

Now another Berilev appeared on the port side. At least twenty guns were firing from its side. Hunter began firing back, as did the deck gunners on the side of the *Saratoga*. That airplane disappeared and another methodically roared in. Again he fired, but then he noticed that others were also on the deck firing hand-held weapons at the enemy airplane. A line of Australian and Gurkha soldiers had formed on his right and they were sending a barrage of return fire into the side of the attacking airplane. Hunter saw one of its engines cough out a burst of smoke, and erupt in flame. "That's one that won't make it home," Hunter thought as the airplane disappeared from view.

Off in the distance he saw another ship go up — probably one of the Freedom Navy's, most likely to an Exocet. Then, off to his right, he saw a big

Beriev take a hit right on its fuel tank and simply obliterate in the sky. Then two more sea-jets streaked over, the Phalanx catching one on its tail, blowing it away. The flaming airplane dove right onto the deck of the carrier, hit it square, bounced up, and streaked by Hunter's head, before bouncing again and pitching over the side of the carrier. It was instantly enveloped by the raging sea.

Hunter knew the attackers—at least the ones in the sea-jets—were getting desperate. More and more they were abandoning their low-level attacks for straight-over runs.

A Stinger took down another sea-jet off the starboard side, and the *Saratoga* ack-ack crews combined with those of a frigate to blow the wing off a big Beriev. Even the gun crews on O'Brien's tugs were getting into the act, peppering anything that dared fly over them.

Still, the air attackers pressed the assault. But the coordination of the attack seemed to break down. Now the flying boats and the sea-jets were coming in from every direction. Missiles filled the air—both coming from the attackers and being fired at them. Ack-ack shells crisscrossed the stormy sky. Tracer bullets rivaled the lightning in intensity. The firing line of Gurkhas and Australians—with Hunter's gun included—would set up a combined barrage at anything that approached the carrier on either port or starboard side. Every once in a while Hunter could hear the highly distinctive whirring sound of the ship's Phalanxes going off.

But suddenly, above it all, Hunter heard a piercing scream . . .

He looked up and down the deck, but couldn't locate the source of the cry. Then he looked up. Up the superstructure. Up the ladders that led to the next. She was now naked before him. ̲ just a teenager, yet she was very mature. ̲ when to soothe him and when to leave him ̲his was a time for soothing. She climbed ̲ bunk with him and nuzzled her breasts ̲his bare chest. He held her, and kissed her. ̲ he closed his eyes and went back to sleep.

coming tower's antennas. Up there, illuminated by the nearby blinking red beacon light, there was a man lashed to the highest point of the conning tower.

It was Peter . . .

"What the . . . ?" Hunter yelled. "How the hell did he get up there?"

The man looked completely disheveled. His beard and long hair was being whipped by the high winds. His face and body completely soaked by the sea spray. He was screaming, foaming at the mouth, *"You devils! Cursed be you!"* This was not the strange, gurgling voice that had emanated from him the night before. This was Peter's own voice, now in full roar, screaming at the attacking aircraft.

A pair of sea-jets streaked overhead, and Hunter joined in the barrage driving them off. They swept right over Peter's head and he freed one of his arms long enough to reach and shake his fist at them.

"Go back to hell, you heathens!" Peter screamed. *"Go back to hell where you belong!"*

Another Beriev roared by, its guns blazing away. A Stinger shot out from the center of the carrier and caught the big plane on its tail section. At the same time, the rear-end Phalanx opened up and caught the flying boat right in its cockpit. The big plane pitched directly into ocean, blew up, and sank instantly.

"Ha Ha!" Hunter could hear Peter scream deliriously. *"You bastards! Burn in Hell!"* The man was going completely wild, shaking his fist and foaming profusely at the mouth.

Suddenly a missile flashed out of nowhere. "Christ!" Hunter yelled. "Another Exocet." As he watched in horror, the missile streaked right over his head, hit the base of the carrier's mast, and exploded. Hunter heard Peter let out one last blood-curdling cry—a cross between a laugh and a scream.

Then everything from the base of the mast on up—including Peter—was gone . . .

Whether by coincidence or design, the air battle tapered off several minutes later. The Spanish rocketeers were able to destroy a retreating Beriev flying boat, and the Phalanx team got one last sea-jet before the enemy planes cleared the area.

Still, Hunter and the rest of the hands on deck searched the wild skies for any more aircraft. It took about ten minutes for it to really sink in. The enemy was gone.

Exhausted, Hunter walked slowly to the super-structure and collapsed to the deck of the carrier. It may have been his imagination, but the storm seemed to start to die down too. He looked around. The deck was filled with smoking debris and cratered in several places. A good portion of the carrier's communications antenna stand was gone. Several of the Aussies had bought it in the ferocious battle.

A few of the Freedom Navy ships near the carrier were burning and Hunter was sure some were lost completely. He would later learn that two of Olson's frigates were lost, with all hands. Three of O'Brien's tugs were also gone.

Just how many enemy airplanes were lost was anyone's guess. Hunter himself saw at least a dozen destroyed or damaged so much that he knew they couldn't go on.

"Screw 'em," he said, lowering his head to his knees. "Screw 'em all . . ."

He woke up a few hours later in
lovely face looking down on hi
a warm washcloth all over his n
tell at once that the storm had co
The carrier was moving again fo
what seemed like an eternity. He
the nightmarish action. Did it rea
closed his eyes and all he could see
hitting the carrier's mast and carryi
with it.

He tried to get up, but Anna pushe
down again.

"Stay down," she ordered him. "You're
you need to rest . . ."

"But, the ship . . ." he started to protes

"The hell with the ship," she said firmly
storm is passed. The sun is out. Heath and Ya
things under control. They were just here. The
to tell you that they have air patrols out. They
said we'll be close to Malta by this time tomor
So just stay put!"

He stopped protesting. Why fight it? He lay ba
down on the bunk and let Anna wash him. Th
battle was one of the most intense he'd ever been
involved in. Who were the attackers? Did Soviet-built airplanes mean Soviet-manned airplanes? And did anyone win or lose? Did the enemy retreat because of the defensive measures, or did they simply break off the attack for lack of fuel or ammo? Would he ever know? Did it matter?

He looked up and saw that Anna had put the washcloth away and was unzipping her jumpsuit. Underneath she wore a small black-lace bra and similar panties. She removed her bra, revealing her small, pert breasts to him once again. Her panties

Chapter 26

"General? This is Crunch, calling . . ."

The powerful, shortwave radio in the San Diego headquarters of the Pacific American Air Corps was bursting with static.

"Go ahead, Crunch," the general replied. "I can hear you about ten by twenty. Where are you?"

"Sir, we are at an air base on the island of Majorca," Crunch reported, his voice fading in and out. "Its a temporary setup, a staging area. We've traced Hunter to this place. We have people here who saw him here just a few weeks ago."

"Well, what the hell's he been up to?" Jones asked.

"I hope you're sitting down, sir," Crunch called back. "It seems he's hooked up with a bunch of Brits. RAF guys. You see, they claim that the war is still going on over here."

"Yes," Jones replied. "We've been hearing a lot about that lately too."

"Well, Hunter is with these Englishmen and he's going after Viktor," Crunch said, continuing his report. "They call him Lucifer over here, by the way. Lucifer has amassed a huge army in what used to be called Saudi Arabia. They say he's planning to start up the war again and try to take over the Mediterranean.

"There's a bunch of rich guys in West Europe that are raising an army to fight Viktor. So, they tell us, Hunter and these Brits are towing an aircraft carrier towards the Suez Canal to try to head off Lucifer—"

"Towing a what?!" Jones yelled.

"It's true," Crunch replied. "They hope to go in right before the Europeans arrive and bottle up Viktor with airpower."

"Jesus H. Christ!" Jones said, his voice rising a notch in excitement. "Leave it to Hunter to get himself mixed up in that kind of crazy adventure."

"Well, he probably feels that if he's going after Viktor, he might as well go with some help," Crunch said.

"It sounds like to me that he'll need even more help, Crunch," Jones replied. "What do you think?"

"That's a definite," Crunch answered. "Because our boy Hunter is very well-known over here. And the place is lousy with Russians, spies, mercenaries that will work any side, anytime. And there's a lot of bounty hunters roaming around. All of them would love to track down Hunter and collect one billion in gold."

There was a short pause on the end of the radio, then Jones said, "I've heard enough, Crunch. You stay put. I'm sending over some help. Will the airfield there handle F-20s and a few AC-130 gunships?"

Crunch looked at Elvis and gave him the thumbs-up sign.

"Affirmative, sir," the F-4 commander replied. "Fuel might be a problem, though."

"Well, we can take care of that too," Jones replied. "We've just taken delivery on two 707s converted for tanker and AWACs duty. This will give one of them a good workout."

"I understand, sir," Crunch said. "We'll expect to see some familiar faces in a few days' time. In the meantime, we'll try to get a fix on exactly where Hunter and his friends are."

"That's a roger," Jones replied. "I don't have to tell you how valuable Hunter is to us and to the rebuilding of this country. We've got to protect him like a natural resource. Over and out."

Crunch signed off and turned to Elvis. "Well, looks like we're stuck here in paradise until reinforcements arrive."

Elvis smiled. Majorca was beautiful this time of year. "Somehow," he said, "I think Hunter would want it this way . . ."

Chapter 27

The Beriev-12 flying boat Number 33 came in for a bumpy landing, its port wing shredded from a direct hit by a Phalanx Gatling gun. Its crew — twelve of which were wounded — was glad to be back down in friendly waters. The murderous air strike the night before had sapped them of all their strength of purpose.

Now the flying boat taxied up to its holding berth at the movable docking facility. The docking area was made up of a converted ocean-drilling platform that had been previously moved down from the Aegean Sea to its present position one mile off the Mediterranean island of Panatella. A shallow reef provided a natural breakwater, while long heavy-duty pontoon bridges served as docks and walkways between the berths and the platform. Three super-tankers — all filled with aviation fuel — were tied up nearby; the returning strike force had flown over a fourth tanker as it was steaming toward the facility. Next to the supertanker docking area were fifty Berievs and as many sea-jets, each in its individual berth.

The pilot of Number 33 was an East German mercenary, as were just about all of the pilots at the base. But now he counted twenty-two empty berths at the mid-sea facility. He knew that was more than one-quarter of the entire force remaining. His employers had told them that an all-out attack on the *Saratoga* flotilla would be a piece of cake, that the inclement weather would prevent the fleet from firing back. The twenty-two empty berths proved that boast a lie. This on top of the handful lost in the initial earlier attack. The men running the *Saratoga* flotilla were obviously people to be reckoned with. Now the mercenary began to question whether this docking facility was as "attack-proof" as its operators had said it was.

The pilot of Number 33 made a mental note to ask his employers for a raise the first chance he got . . .

A few hours later, the S-A3 reconnaissance jet with the Australian pilot E.J. Russell at the controls circled the facility at an unseen height of 60,000 feet.

The fourth supertanker—a ship still carrying its prewar name of *Exxon Challenger*—was about an hour away from the Panatella base when it picked up a distress call from a Sicilian workboat that was taking on water five miles dead ahead. The captain of the supertanker didn't want to stop to aid the sinking ship. He was concerned, though. The workboat was directly in his path, and if he were to change course, he would have to hurry. Turning a filled-to-the-brim supertanker just a few degrees to port or starboard was a major project and one that took time to accomplish.

Soon the burning ship was in sight. It was belching so much smoke, one-half of the horizon was completely clouded on the otherwise clear day. But that wasn't what bothered the tanker captain. More serious was the fact that the smoking ship seemed to be moving toward a direct collision course with the supertanker.

The captain called down to his navigation room. "Are we going to hit it?" he asked, a slight panic rising in his voice.

"We're deflecting, sir," the reply came back, "but it keeps moving as we do."

Goddamn, the captain swore to himself. It was too late to call ahead to Panatella to have them dispatch a couple of sea-jets to blow the boat out of the water.

"Hard again port!" the captain yelled to his steering unit.

Slowly the tanker began to heave to the left. But as the captain watched through his electronic binoculars, the burning ship continued its collision course.

"Hard port! Hard port!" the captain screamed. Again the tanker swayed to the left. Again the burning ship moved in its way.

"Jesus Christ!" the captain yelled. He had no choice, he had to slow down. Even then, there was a danger he'd ram the boat. With a belly full of highly volatile aviation fuel, the slightest bump could spell disaster. "All stop all engines!"

Five miles still separated the two vessels, yet there was panic among the tanker crew. They knew the danger of hitting a burning ship with a load of gas. Secretly the crew chief ordered the lifeboats struck and ready for lowering.

Then the captain got a call from his radar man. "Sir, we are picking up several more blips — smaller boats — in the vicinity of the burning vessel."

Instantly the captain began to smell a rat. "What the hell is going on here?"

He knew soon enough.

Breaking out of the smoke screen laid down by the burning ship, two dozen high-speed craft streaked towards the supertanker. Then, off to the north, he saw four helicopters approaching.

Within a minute the tanker was surrounded by the boats and the choppers were buzzing angrily above. As the captain watched dumbfounded, six of the boats came up to the side of the tanker and started throwing grappling hooks up to its side rails. Soon men from the boats were scaling up the side of the tanker hull.

Most bizarre of all, one of the helicopters had come in low and a man with a camera was hanging out of its hatchway, filming the action.

"What the fuck is this?" the tanker captain screamed. "A pirate movie!?"

He was close . . .

As he watched the dozens of men scramble over the sides of his ship, he ordered the men on the bridge, "Stop those bastards!"

His second in command turned to him and asked, "How?"

The captain looked at him in a rage. "Shoot them, asshole."

The officer glared back at him as the film chopper passed right by the bridge. "Shoot them? *You're* the asshole. You start firing on this ship and we'll go up like an atom bomb."

The captain knew he was right—one spark and the whole ship would go up. There was nothing he could do but watch helplessly as the sea-jackers continued to swarm over the side of the ship. Within a minute, they had overwhelmed his crew.

Five men burst into the bridge, one of them a small man dressed in strange uniform, carrying a saber and wearing a hat like Napoleon.

"I am Commodore Antonio Vanaria!" the little man roared. "I declare this vessel captured and claimed in the name of the Freedom Navy!"

The supertanker captain and his eight crew members were put in a lifeboat and set adrift. Twenty minutes later they heard a great roar coming from the north.

"Christ! What the hell is that!" one of the crew members cried out.

Another spotted a series of dots materializing on the northern horizon. "Look! Out there, low over the water."

The captain and the crew were stunned. Heading right for them were four chevron waves containing four jet fighters each. The airplanes were flying so low, their tails were nearly touching the wave tops.

"Who are they?" someone asked.

The supertanker captain knew his airplanes. The majority of the ones approaching him were swingwing Tornados—eight of them in all. The green camouflage jets were loaded with antiship bombs. One chevron was made up entirely of cream-colored Swedish Viggens, each carrying two deadly racks of air-to-surface missiles. But it was the first formation of jets that was most impressive. This lead wave was made up of three Harrier jump-jets and a fighter that the captain didn't think existed any more.

"Christ, is that an F-16?" he asked himself.

"Get down!" someone yelled. "The fuckers are going to swamp us!"

In a moment the first wave passed right over the lifeboat. The roar was deafening. The hot exhausts did stir up the sea enough to make the surface

244

foaming and choppy, but not enough to capsize the boat.

In enviable precision, each wave passed over the lifeboat and disappeared over the southern horizon—heading directly for the "hidden, air-strike-proof" sea base off Panatella.

"Start paddling," the captain said after the jets had disappeared from view. "Head northeast. We might make the shipping lanes off Malta."

Then, looking back to the south where the exhaust trails of the jet fighters were still visible, he muttered, "We're lucky those sea pirates hijacked us. The last place I'd want to be right now is Panatella . . ."

The jets attacked without warning. As the helicopter containing the video crew hovered from a safe distance, the Tornados went in. Flying in pairs, they headed right for the neat line of Beriev flying boats. Cannons blazing, the British jets methodically ripped up the amphibians. After two passes with cannon, the Tornados commenced their missile attack, using modified antiship rockets. One by one, those flying boats not destroyed in the strafing runs exploded with missile hits. At the end of three missile passes, the Tornados withdrew, and climbed to 10,000 feet to provide air cover for the rest of the strike force.

The Viggens went in next. They concentrated on the converted oil platform, sending a murderous barrage of small air-to-surface rockets into the huge, ten-story structure. The missiles were penetrating the tough outer core of the floating building, crashing through to its center, and exploding within. Soon the structure was rocking back and forth with the power of the blasts. Its massive struts—connected to concrete counterweights below the surface—started to bend in the ferocity of the attack.

Still the Viggens attacked relentlessly. A huge fire broke out on the platform's upper stories. Its topside crane came off in one direct hit, coming down with a mighty splash. Soon the platform was noticeably leaning to the port side, all of its floors belching fire and smoke. Bodies could be seen falling from the upper floors.

Two trailing Viggens swooped in and delivered the *coup de grace*, a pair of direct hits on the platform's left-side struts. They took the full weight of the explosions, tottered for a moment, then gave way. The whole structure collapsed, falling over on its side in a massive, fiery crash. The four Viggens regrouped and flew over the utterly destroyed platform, each jet performing a 360-degree victory roll.

In the confusion, several pilots attempted to take off in the small sea-jets. But the Harriers were on hand to prevent that. Two sea-jet pilots gunned their engines and tried to make a break for it, ripping across the sea surface, hoping to escape in the pandemonium.

But the sea-jet pilots were terrified to see two Harriers hovering over them, watching their every move. The Harrier pilots waited for the sea-jets to lift off. Then two Sidewinders flashed out from their wings. Scratch two seajets.

"Strike Leader, this is Group Commander Heath."

"Go ahead, Group," Hunter answered. He had been orbiting the action at 5000 feet, on the lookout for any antiaircraft weapons. There were none.

"Major objectives hit and destroyed," Heath reported. "We will clear the area now for your run."

"Roger, Group," Hunter replied.

The three supertankers were moored at the edge of the facility, somewhat isolated from the rest of the action. The other jets had purposely left them alone—there was no way the attackers knew if the tankers were loaded with fuel or not. Had they had that information, one jet with one missile could have swooped in, fired on the tankers, set one ablaze, and the whole facility would have gone up.

But as Strike Leader, Hunter decided to play it safe. An attack on the empty tankers would have been a dangerous waste of time. That's why the strike force systematically destroyed the base's airplanes and headquarters before going after the supertankers.

That would be Hunter's job . . .

He was carrying a Shrike missile, an antiradiation "smart" bomb that was usually targeted against radar installations. They had retrieved several from the Sardinians and Hunter had done some last-minute modifications on its guidance system.

He had wired the missile so its warhead would home in on any kind of radio signal, even one as small as a ship's intercom. But in doing so, he knew, the missile would have to be fired at close range, not the usual fifteen-mile "fire-and-forget" firing distance intended for the Shrike.

Once Hunter was sure the rest of the strike force had cleared the area, he brought the 16 down to wave-top level. He streaked along the surface, lining up the first tanker—a rust bucket with a large, faded orange Gulf ball on its smokestack.

Fifteen seconds out, he armed the missile. Everything went green on his weapons-control displays—the missile was now "hot." Ten seconds out, he raised the 16's nose slightly, and throttled down.

Five seconds out he hit the Launch button . . .

He felt the jerk under his left wing as the Shrike took off. He instantly put the F-16 on its tail and booted it. If even one of the tankers had any fuel in it, he wanted to get as far away from the explosion as possible.

He was at 3500 feet when the missile hit. Looking back on it, he theorized the Shrike must have gone right through the first tanker, out the other side, and into the middle vessel. The explosion was delayed by five seconds. But when it went off — it went off big . . .

Hunter felt the shudder as the heat wave rose from the exploding tankers. He put the jet over onto its back at 5500 and was surprised to see the flames were licking at his tail.

"Christ," he said, having to flip down his sun shield to look at the mighty explosion. "What the hell were they carrying? Nitroglycerin?"

The explosion was so powerful, the fireball so intense, it knocked out about a third of his avionics plus his UHF radio. He looked back once again and saw the shock wave had created a whirlpool in the sea. A mini-hurricane swirled around the remains of the base, sucking in and pulling down everything around it into a maelstrom of fire and smoke. He could feel the artificially created winds rock the jet fighter from side to side. It only took fifteen seconds — then everything — the burning airplanes, the cratered tankers, the collapsed oil platform — was gone, drawn into the vortex and quickly covered over by the sea.

"That's what you get for screwing around with us," Hunter said defiantly.

Chapter 28

The tugboat approached the island of Malta and set anchor about a half-mile off the partially fog-shrouded coast. Three hooded men — Heath, Hunter, and O'Brien — were crowded into the boat's high mast, sharing a pair of powerful binoculars. Off in the distance was the island's capital city of Valletta. At the moment it was being plastered by an aerial bombardment.

"Blast, this is the last thing I expected to find going on here," Heath said, passing the spyglasses to Hunter. "Is there anyplace in the Med that isn't at war?"

"Welcome to World War Three, the fifth chapter," Hunter said dryly.

"Any idea what kind of airplanes are doing the job, Hunter?" O'Brien asked.

"It's hard to say," Hunter said, scanning the cloudy sky for any sign of the anonymous attackers. "By the rate the bombs are falling, I'd almost guess they were old-timers. Jets. First-generation jobs. Not a lot of them — maybe six, maybe seven. No fighter escort either."

"Well, this puts a crimp in our plans to resupply here," Heath said. "The way it looks, the Maltese won't have a thing to sell."

"Good thing we solved our aircraft fuel problems," Hunter said, referring to the Commodore's daring sea-pirate attack and capture of the *Exxon Challenger*. The ship, now part of the *Saratoga* flotilla, was filled with JP-8 aviation fuel.

The three men waited for the bombing to stop, then pulled anchor and entered the harbor.

There was no one on the docks, no one in the streets. The three men cautiously got off the tug and headed toward the center of the city, avoiding areas that were still on fire. They had been walking for a few minutes when the sounds of air-raid sirens went up all over town.

"Not another raid," Heath said.

"No, probably more like the all-clear signal," Hunter said.

Sure enough, as the sirens wailed away, people began emerging from cellars and hardened buildings. The citizens routinely went about their way, some pausing to discuss the latest destruction. Hunter asked for directions to the nearest military facility and was told to head for the city's municipal building.

The structure, itself partially damaged, had a strange flag flying from its top above the sign that read: "Malta Self-Defense Force."

They went inside and were soon introducing themselves to the commanding officer of the MSDF.

"Yes, we've heard of you and your carrier," the officer, a man named Baldi, told them. "But resupply? We're just barely holding on here ourselves."

"Who's doing this to you?" Hunter asked.

"Those bastards of the Sidra-Benghazi Gang,"

Baldi said, spitting out the name. He was a large man, possibly a weight lifter in his younger days. He wore a red-and-brown camouflage uniform and a vintage World War I helmet.

"The Sidra-Benghazi Gang?" O'Brien asked. "The name sounds familiar. Are they Libyans?"

"Yes, they are based on the coast of Libya," Baldi said. "But they're from all over. Bandits, thieves, cutthroats, murderers. The dregs of the Mediterranean. They all wind up with the Sidra-Benghazi."

"Don't you have any antiaircraft capability?" Hunter asked. "Or fighter protection?"

Baldi shook his head. "When the Big War started, the British were here in force. Then, as the battles heated up, they gradually were drawn away. Soon we were without any protection at all. Sidra-Benghazi know this. They've been bombing us regularly for about a year and a half. We hear they are trying to raise an army of paratroop mercenaries to invade us, but as you guys know, good help's hard to find these days. We can't pay as much as Lucifer or your own Modern Knights can.

"In fact, our only armed forces now are some ex-Royal Navy UDT guys."

"UDT?" Hunter said. "Underwater demolition teams? That's interesting . . ." His mind flashed back to the report they'd received about the Russian ships laying mines in the Canal at Lucifer's bidding.

"What kind of bombers are they using on you?" Hunter asked.

"Russian-built, what else?" Baldi said in disgust. "Old Bisons, mostly. What you must understand is the Russians are everywhere in this part of the Med. They are in league with that demon Lucifer. Their armies may be depleted, but Lucifer has the manpower now. The Russians supply the instruments of

251

death, then let their lackeys to the fighting."

"What's their SAM capability back at their bases?" Hunter asked Baldi.

"The best," the man replied. "We did hire a mercenary group about a year ago. Bunch of Finnish guys flying some old shitbox Italian fighter-bombers. They reconned the Sidra-Benghazi coastline, flew back here, and gave me our money back. Too many SAMs. They didn't want any part of it."

"What's their bombing timetable?" Hunter asked.

Baldi thought for a moment, then said, "It's like clockwork. Every other day, just before noon. They awake, eat breakfast, fly here at a leisurely pace, bomb, and get home for a late lunch."

Hunter was getting an idea. "Mr. Baldi," he said, "how would you like to make a deal?"

Two days later, just before noon, radar operators on one of Olson's frigates stationed off the southern coast of Malta picked up eight blips on their radar screens. The news was flashed to the *Saratoga,* where Hunter sat in the F-16 waiting for launch.

"Okay, major," he heard the launch officer say over the radio. "They've got eight bogies coming in at two-niner Tango. Airspeed three-four-six knots."

"Roger, Launch," Hunter answered.

He felt the steam pressure build up under the fighter. The launch officer twirled his finger, then pointed an emphatic signal. In an instant, Hunter was hurled back against the cockpit seat and the jet was roaring off the carrier.

"From zero to one hundred twenty MPH in two seconds," Hunter thought. "I'm beginning to enjoy this."

His launch was quickly followed by the three Harriers, taking off the conventional way to save fuel, plus two Viggens. Once all the airplanes were aloft, they formed up into two three-plane groups and headed southeast.

Hunter began monitoring all radio frequencies immediately, searching for the band the Sidra-Benghazi bombers were using. After five minutes, he finally got lucky. The pilots were talking in Arabic, but he recognized enough flying terms to know it was the Bisons.

He called back to the carrier. "Monitor one-two-five-six UHF," he radioed to the CIC radio operators. "We've got some Med Arab dialect."

"That's okay, Major," the reply came back. "We've got an expert standing by."

Hunter smiled. He knew that the commander of the Moroccan desert fighters was in the CIC, ready to translate.

They tracked the bombers as they routinely swung around the northeast side of the island and prepared to start their bombing approach. While the CIC monitored the routine chatter between the bomber pilots and passed the translation on to the *Saratoga* pilots, Hunter activated his radar-monitoring system. Unbelievably, the Bison pilots hadn't switched on their long-range airborne radars. In fact, he was willing to bet the cost-conscious mercenaries didn't bother to carry an air-defense radar man. "Boy, they *are* leisurely," he thought.

The Bison group pilot began to drop down through a thick cloud bank to his bombing altitude. As soon as he broke through the overcast, he noticed a glint of light off to his left. He was startled to see a F-16 fighter jet riding just 200 feet off his wing.

He looked to his right, hoping to turn that way to

253

escape when he saw a Harrier riding on that side too.

He was trapped and he knew it.

Suddenly a strange voice broke in on his group's frequency. It was the Moroccan troop leader. The pilot listened to his ultimatum: follow instructions or all eight of his airplanes would be shot down. The pilot — a hired mercenary with no real loyalty to the Sidra-Benghazi faction — agreed.

As instructed, he followed the F-16 . . .

One by one the eight Bison bombers circled the abandoned RAF Malta base and came in for a landing.

Hunter was there to meet the bombers, having landed before the mercenaries. There was also a battalion of Moroccan Marines on hand to surround the Soviet-built bombers once they reached their taxi stations. Unexpectedly, the troops were needed to keep away angry Maltese citizens, who showed up to throw rocks, bottles and, in one case, a fizzled Moltov cocktail at the bombers.

The pilots were immediately handcuffed and led away to a Maltese jail. "If they are worth anything," Baldi said, "we'll be able to ransom them."

Now Hunter and Heath and six other carrier pilots climbed into the Bisons, along with other assorted members of the carrier force. Each airplane carried a Moroccan officer, plus a bombardier, a navigator, and a radar operator who knew what he was doing. The airplanes were refueled and their bomb loads checked. Within ten minutes, the Soviet-built airplanes were roaring off the runway, heading south for the Libyan coastline.

The hired-hand radar officer stationed at the SAM base at Tripoli yawned. It was almost the end of his shift. His assistant — a corporal just hired for the station — called his attention to the eight blips on the radar screen. They were approaching from the north, he said, flying at 340 knots.

Don't worry, the officer told him. That was the regular bombing force returning from Malta. But they were breaking up into eight separate flight courses, the corporal told him. The officer yawned again. Don't worry about it, he told the rookie. It was probably some training maneuver, or the weather, or something. Besides, it was end of the officer's shift.

Soon the corporal was alone in the SAM radar station. He didn't get too concerned when he noted that one of the blips was heading right for his position.

A minute later, he heard a curious, whistling sound. Almost like a bomb . . .

Up and down the coast, the Bisons attacked the eight major SAM installations. Once the antiaircraft sites were destroyed, the Tornados swept in and hit troop concentrations, oil-storage tanks, and port facilities. The Viggens, carrying antirunway bombs, cratered the Gang's only workable landing strip in the area. The final insult came when the four old Jaguar jets, on their first mission, swept in and destroyed the Sidra-Benghazi headquarters with delayed-fuse iron bombs.

The attack was a complete surprise — and an overwhelming success. Not only were no aircraft lost — none of the attackers were even fired upon. Why? The Sidra-Benghazi Gang had committed the cardinal sin of warfare. They'd become lazy. They had assumed that well-paid mercenaries would compensate for the lack of loyal, homegrown soldiers. The opposite was true. Hunter knew by the way the *Saratoga*'s aircraft carried out the raids with such impunity that many of the Gang's hired hands simply left their posts at the first sign of trouble.

It all came down to a fighting for a cause. The *Saratoga* force was made up almost entirely of paycheck soldiers, but they believed in what they were doing. They recognized that Lucifer had to be stopped and that they were in the vanguard of that effort.

It made all the difference in the world . . .

They returned the Bisons to Baldi. "Our plan," he told Hunter, as they shared a bottle of Maltese wine in Baldi's office, "is to sell them on the open market. They should bring a pretty penny, I should think. Then we'll buy some decent fighter protection and some SAMs."

"Malta has always been fought over, invaded, disputed," Hunter said. "Yet it has never capitulated. It's a tribute to your people."

"We couldn't have done it without your help," Baldi said. "Now, when we first met, you mentioned a deal. Well, you've fulfilled your part of this unspoken bargain. Now what can we do for you?"

"Lend us your UDT unit," Hunter told him. "We got a report that the Soviets have mined a good part of the Suez canal. We'll need frogmen to clear a path for us."

Baldi slapped his hand down on his desk for emphasis. "Done!" he said in a booming voice. "And, by the way, we will be able to scrape up some supplies for you. Not much, but we want to show our appreciation."

"You've already done that and more," Hunter told him, shaking his hand and rising to go.

"Well, please stop by here on your way back," Baldi said, smiling.

Strange, Hunter thought as he left, it was the first time anyone had said anything about *actually* coming back . . .

Chapter 29

The *Saratoga* Task Force got underway shortly after midnight. On-board were a half-ton of supplies from the Malta Defense Force—provided free of charge—plus twenty "volunteers" from the island's underwater demolition team.

Now, as the chugging symphony of O'Brien's tugs' engines started up once again, Hunter and Heath held a late night meeting with Sir Neil.

"Well, I think it was a bloody good trade!" Sir Neil said, after hearing the details of the Sidra-Benghazi operation. "I'm sure that once we reach the Canal, those UDT boys will come in handy."

"Plus, I think we gained valuable experience for our pilots and planes," Heath said. "First, we were successful against the Panatella floating base. And then to go into action just a short time later against the Libyans, well, that's quite a statement on our readiness."

"This is true," Hunter said. "I can't think of two better targets I would have wanted for our first and second missions. But we can't lose sight of the fact that we had virtually no opposition in either case. We can't expect to have it so good from here on out."

"Yes, Hunter," Sir Neil said. "The American is coming out in you now."

The British Commander expertly took a belt of wine from a flask he now routinely hid under his covers. The man was looking better every day and the doctors had told Hunter that the chest and shoulder wounds were healing well. But he would still be bedridden for quite some time.

"The fuel on the supertanker," Sir Neil asked. "Quality stuff?"

"A-1 quality," Heath answered. "We can use it in all our aircraft, including the Jags, thank God."

"We've got a rotating crew of Olson's guys piloting the tanker," Hunter continued. "But its officially under the command of the Freedom Navy."

"As well it should be," Sir Neil said. "Those brave bastards! Hijacking a supertanker on the high seas! Their ancestors would be proud of them."

"They really are good fighters," Hunter said. "And they've proved themselves. They took a beating during both flying boat attacks, especially in the hurricane battle. Lost a lot of men. They could have easily turned back at that point. But they're proud men. They're as committed to beating Lucifer as we are."

Sir Neil rested his head back and sighed. "And that poor beggar, Peter . . ."

There was a long silence, none of the three wanting to talk. Peter had been so strange, yet so chillingly accurate with his predictions. His passing couldn't be taken lightly.

"*Something* was there," Hunter said finally. "He tapped into a part of the collective psyche like no one I've ever heard of."

"Somehow, Lucifer is wired into it too. Call it long-range brainwashing, or mind over matter, or whatever, I'm convinced that Lucifer was responsible for that horror show in here the other night."

"I am too," Sir Neil confirmed. "It just shows you how much we threaten him.

"He'll try anything to turn us back . . ."

The next few days passed uneventfully for the carrier task force as it cruised the sea east of Malta. The Italian communications team was able to replace the antenna lost during the hurricane battle, and they were soon listening in on Lucifer's Empire again. The latest radio intercepts indicated that Lucifer's troopships would embark in force sometime in the next two weeks. That was the same time frame projected for the carrier to reach the northern end of the Canal.

They saw a lot of odd sights during this part of the journey. As it was easier to push and pull the carrier in stiller water, the task force moved northward and sailed into the calmer regions of the Ionian Sea, southwest of Greece. Along the way they passed many islands surrounded by blue-green water.

In many cases where the islands were inhabited, the people burned fires on their beaches or on their highest points when the flotilla passed by. At first these actions mystified Hunter and the others. Were they signals to Lucifer's allies? A means of tracking the task force? They had no way of knowing.

Then, one morning, a small fleet of fishing boats was intercepted heading for the task force. The captain of the fleet said his boats were filled with fish to give to the flotilla's men. He said the Med was abuzz with the news of the *Saratoga*'s mission, and their victories against the flying boats and the Sidra-Behghazi Gang. These groups had terrorized the people in the central Med for years, and they were grateful that the task force had dealt with them. From then on the reasons for the fires on the beaches and on the island peaks was clear. They were signs of support. As the fishing fleet captain put it: "My enemy's enemy is my friend." And just about everyone in the Med considered Lucifer and his allies—the Soviet ones especially—as their enemy.

The area itself was hardly at peace. In one case the flotilla came upon a pocket cruiser flying a strange flag, anchored off the coast of an island. For whatever reason, it was firing away at the island, lobbing shell after shell into the forest-shrouded spit of land, some incomprehensible action in an unknown war.

Hunter used the lull in the excitement to finish work on rearming the S-3A to carry Sidewinders. Also, as a favor to Sir Neil, he began paying regular visits—via a frigate chopper—to the commanders of the other groups in the task force—Olson, O'Brien, the Moroccans, and The Commodore—to get status reports on their units.

The Moroccans intrigued him the most. They were the silent partners of the voyage, enduring its dangers without a word of complaint. Their commanders kept the 7500 troops in fighting trim with a daily regimen of physical workouts and group training. The soldiers took it all very religiously—which was not surprising. On quiet nights, one could hear the droning of prayer and chanting coming from the Moroccan troopship, although it was usually tucked into the back of the battle formation.

But the Moroccans had a more personal bond with Hunter. Although he hadn't been aware of it, Peter at one time had apparently had a long talk with several of the Moroccan troop commanders. The subject of the discussion had been Hunter, his exploits during the outbreak of World War III, and his adventures in the fragmented New Order America. The tales fascinated the Moroccan officers, who, in turn, told their subordinates, who went on to recount the stories to the enlisted troops.

So Hunter, without any desire to do so, quickly became a hero among the Arab desert fighters. Whenever he saw one or a group of them—whether it be on the carrier or on their troopship—they would greet him by displaying a unique two-hand gesture. Made by putting two "V-for-Victory" signs together, their fingers would form a W as in Wingman. A deep bow would follow. When he inquired as to its origin, he heard that Peter had instructed the Moroccans to do it, as a sign of respect and luck. When he mentioned to Heath that he intended to ask the Moroccans to stop, Heath, a man with much knowledge about Arab ways, suggested otherwise, as the request might be interpreted as an insult or even a sign of impending bad luck.

Another reason for talking to the group leaders was to formulate a concrete strategy for what would happen once they reached the Canal. It was a difficult task, as conditions at Suez were virtually unknown to them and recon flights over the area could only begin when the carrier was within some kind of reasonable range.

Nevertheless, the commanders agreed on some tactics. The whole idea was to plant the *Saratoga* somewhere in the northern half of the Canal, then take possession of the land immediately on both sides of the carrier's position, creating a strong buffer zone. The bulk of the land-occupation duties would go to the Moroccans. The Australian Special

Forces would handle the "weak side" of the Canal. The area around the canal was itself fairly demilitarized, so Hunter and the others didn't expect any opposition upon first arriving in the area.

As the plans stood, the *Saratoga* task force would only have to hold the position for three days at the most. By that time, the advanced units of Modern Knights would be in the area.

As agreed, there had been no radio contact with The Modern Knights since shortly after the *Saratoga* was refloated. This was because any messages between the carrier and the Knights were liable to interception by Lucifer or his allies. At the time of the last radio transmission, the vast mercenary army was being loaded on troopships and was expected to set sail within a few days.

But Hunter continued to ask himself over and over: exactly just when would The Modern Knights arrive?

He got his answer one morning as they were cruising past Cape Tainaron on the southern tip of Greece. Working on the bridge, he got a call from Yaz to come down to the CIC.

"Major, we've just received a message from our rear-guard frigate," Yaz told him. "They report contact with an unidentified aircraft coming our way from due west. Slow-moving, maybe a biplane."

"Have they raised the pilot?" Hunter asked, checking the CIC's electronic plotting board for the intruder's position.

"Yes," Yaz replied. "He claims to be a friendly."

"Well, if he isn't, he's got a lot of guts blowing in on us like this in a biplane," Hunter said. Then he asked, "Who's hot on the deck?"

Yaz did a quick check. "One Harrier is about to transfer to the control frigate. Should we divert him?"

"We'd better," Hunter said. "And tell the frigate to contact us when they get a visual."

This happened three minutes later. The captain of the frigate reported a slow-moving biplane, flying with its landing lights blinking. Hunter knew this was the universal sign of nonaggression. He asked the frigate captain to watch the airplane but not to fire unless the pilot initiated an aggressive action.

The Harrier intercepted the biplane less than a minute later. He reported the pilot was waving and displaying a small Union Jack in the cockpit. The Harrier's weapons-check system detected no advanced armaments aboard the airplane, nor was it flying in such a way that it might be carrying a kamikaze-type load of explosives. The only thing unusual was that the plane carried extra-large fuel tanks under its wings. The pilot was also requesting permission to land on the carrier.

Hunter put in a call to Heath, who was up in the CIC in seconds.

"God knows who he is or what he wants," Hunter told him. "But it may be important. The large fuel tanks tell me he's flown a long way."

"He's taking one hell of a risk if it's all just a joke," Heath said, twirling his red mustache in thought. "I vote let him come down. If he's not cricket — well then, over the side with him!"

A few moments later, they watched from the bridge as the mysterious airplane approached. The Harrier was right on the tail of the aircraft — an ancient Gloster Gladiator — as it bounced in for a landing. The pre-World-War-II antisubmarine airplane coughed and clanked to a stop, its undercarriage almost being ripped away by the tautness of the arresting cable. The pilot pulled back his makeshift canopy to find himself staring down at fifty stern-looking Gurkhas.

"Friend!" he yelled at them in an unmistakable Cockney accent. "I'm a subject of the Crown!"

This didn't make a dent in the Gurkhas. They crowded in even closer. Hunter and Heath were down on the deck and beside the airplane immediately.

"Who are you and what do you want?" Heath yelled up to the man.

"I have a message for Sir Neil Asten," the man said. "And for no one *but* Sir Neil Asten."

"Well you're not in a position to make demands right now, are you?" Heath countered, spreading his arms to emphasize the large Gurkha contingent of the Australian Special Forces.

"I got me orders," the pilot answered defiantly. "I'm carrying Top Secret information that can only be given to Sir Neil Asten by me personally."

"And who *are* you?" Hunter said, reasking Heath's question.

"I'm Lieutenant Mike Stanley," the man replied with a touch of pride in his voice. "First Recon Wing. First Division of the Royal Airborne Lancers."

Heath shook his head. "Royal Airborne Lancers?" he said. "What the hell is that?"

The man had reached his limit. "For God's sake, man!" he called down. "I'm with the *blooming* Modern Knights! And I might add I am also a personal friend of Sir Neil's son Roderick!"

Five minutes later, Lieutenant Stanley, Heath, and Hunter were in Sir Neil's room. Clara was there and, upon seeing the unexpected guests arrive, quickly

265

clothed herself and left, returning moments later with a pot of steaming Moroccan tea.

"Ah, Stanley," Sir Neil said, warmly shaking hands with the man. "My son Rod has mentioned you often. How is the lad?"

"He's quite well, sir," Stanley replied, in a somewhat curious awe at seeing the great Sir Neil laid up with a mile of bandage wrappings around him. "He would have come here himself, sir, but he's needed back home, you understand."

"Yes," Sir Neil said sadly. "Tell us news of home."

Stanley got excited. "There's much of it, sir!" Stanley said, removing a document from his pocket. "Here's the Order of Battle."

Sir Neil took the document, read it over quickly. "This is splendid!" the commander said. "Infantry. Motorized divisions. Desert troops."

Stanley bit his lip. "Well, there is a down side of it, sir," he said, his voice dropping a notch. "We had a bit of a delay in departing."

"A delay?" Heath asked Stanley. "How long of a delay? We're going to be in the bloody Canal inside of a fortnight. And so is Lucifer."

"That's why they sent me, sir," Stanley said. "They've told me to ask you to hang on a bit longer than they thought."

"Longer?" Sir Neil asked, his voice sounding stronger than at any time since his wounding. "I expected you to tell me they were two to three days behind us. How long do they think a few bloody ships and twenty-five airplanes can hold off one million of Lucifer's men?"

"Two weeks, sir."

Hunter thought Sir Neil was going to expire on the spot. His face went crimson. His uncovered eye bulged out. *Two weeks!* he roared. "Are they

266

daft?"

"I'm sorry, sir," Stanley said. He knew he carried unpopular news. "The real holdup is that a number of the soldiers are asking for payment in advance. And most of them won't move until it's in the bank, so to speak. I'm afraid it's a question of money, sir."

Money? Hunter thought. Whatever happened to fighting for a cause. Fighting to save the world from Lucifer. What happened to heading off a relighting of World War III?

"But I thought The Modern Knights had plenty of money," Hunter said.

"Oh, they do, sir," Stanley answered. "It's just making the arrangements to disperse it to the soldiers that takes time."

The situation was all too clear to Sir Neil.

Through gritted teeth, laying back down on his bed, he said: "*Damn* them all . . ."

That night Hunter returned to the spot at the front of the carrier where he usually went to think.

A question of money. So much for heroism, he thought. So much for glory. He was well along to convincing himself that his worst fears were justified. This was a fool's errand. Towing a disabling aircraft carrier to the Suez? What the hell did that have to do with America?

He should have stayed home. He was needed there. The country he loved was in danger of dissolving completely and he was here, in the middle of the Med, playing crusader with a bunch of half-mad Brits. The original plan had only an outside chance of working. They might have stemmed the tide for four or five days, tops—and provided air cover for when The Modern Knights arrived. But two weeks

267

was impossible.

Even if they were able to bottle up Lucifer's troopships at the far end of the Canal, what would prevent him from disgorging his troops and marching them up both sides of the waterway? It was only a hundred miles or so. Less than a day's journey by truck, five days by foot. The Moroccans — as good as they were — could not hold off a million of Lucifer's troops for more than five minutes. And eventually, Hunter knew, he would start to lose aircraft — to SAMs, to accidents, to one of the many calamities that always accompanied military operations. Once the airplanes were gone, what good was the carrier?

He reached inside his pocket and drew out the American flag he kept folded there. He turned it over and over in his hands. It was beautiful. He was never at a loss for amazement when he looked at it, felt it, kissed it. This is what he should be fighting for. Not some crazy foreign adventure where the bottom line was not the cause, or freedom, but how to pay nearly a million paycheck soldiers up front.

He should have stuck to his original plan. Track down Viktor wherever the hell he was. One man. One plan. It could have been infinitely easier than this! He took out his second prized possession: the photo of Dominique. He loved her. He wanted her. He should be with her. Back home. In America.

He looked up at the night sky. It was brilliant with stars. Billions of stars and billions of galaxies. He once thought he would ride among them someday. His ticket to pilot the space shuttle was already punched. He had the Russians to thank for screwing up that dream.

In fact, they were at the heart of all this darkness. He saw their hand everywhere. Russian cruise missiles fired at the desert highway base, the Red Army Faction opposing their refloating of the *Saratoga*. Robot-controlled Soviet Ilyushins, Soviet-made flying boats, Soviet-made Bison bombers. Soviet mines bobbing in the Canal. No doubt radio-controlled and activated mines, being attended to by Soviet technicians that would allow Lucifer's troopships to pass through unhindered, while anything else would be blown up. Everywhere was the Red Star. The Hammer and Sickle. The same old, robot-like mentality of "Either we control the world or no one does." He was getting sick and tired of it.

Yet what could he do now? Desert Sir Neil? Jump ship from the *Saratoga?*

He looked back up at the stars. Dominique. Jones. Dozer. His friends: Twomey, Ben Wa, and the others. Would he ever see them again?

Yaz was pulling duty on the bridge that night. The sea was quiet, as was the entire flotilla. The only noise was the constant drone of O'Brien's tugboats.

"Coffee, sir?" the other sailor on duty with him asked.

"Sure," Yaz answered. "Could you run down and get a pot?"

"Back in ten," the sailor said, leaving Yaz alone on the bridge.

The dull green light of the bridge's computer screens and the wide windows of the room allowed Yaz a great view of the Mediterranean night sky. He took a seat next to one of the windows and studied the twinkling wash of galaxies, trying to pick out his favorite constellations.

But something was wrong. Yaz was an astronomy

buff. He knew the star formations were slightly different in this part of the world. But should their colors be different too? He stared at one particular star that was glowing blood red. Was that really Mars? He knews the planet often appeared a hazy shade of red, but it was not at this high angle this time of year. And nowhere this bright.

While he was trying to figure this out, he saw another red star. Then another. And another.

"What the hell is going on here?" he said aloud, standing up. As he watched, as many as 100 stars suddenly went red.

He started checking for location. All of the stars were in one general area of the sky—about seventy degrees to the east, way, way, off in the distance. He strained his eyes to look closer.

Were they moving? It appeared that they were. "Damn!" He wished the other sailor was on the bridge with him now, just to witness the event and convince him he was not crazy. He kept his eyes glued on the group of crimson stars. Now they were forming a pattern. Spinning, twisting, circling, now moving in all directions. Slowly, something was forming.

"Jesus Christ," Yaz swore as he watched the incredible scene.

It was a face. A dastardly face. A familiar, yet distorted face. This was crazy, he thought.

It was the face of Lucifer . . .

Yaz closed his eyes and rubbed them. He was thinking too long and too hard. He counted to five and opened his eyes again. The face was still there— unbelievably, an enormous, horrifying caricature of Lucifer's face formed by the interconnection of the "red stars." It was leering, mocking, laughing . . .

Then it disappeared.

Yaz spent the rest of the night searching the sky for the vision. He decided not to mention it to the sailor who returned with a steaming pot of coffee, so bizarre was the vision. Only briefly did Yaz question his sanity. It was only one of many possible explanations. He knew Lucifer was powerful—but was he powerful enough to project such an illusion over thousands of miles? Or was it an illusion at all?

Hunter was the first one to see the boats . . .

He was up before dawn and on the carrier deck when he saw them, just as the sun was lifting out of the calm, aqua-blue Mediterranean. Out on the horizon. First a group of five, sailing together. Then another group. And another. He looked close. There were fishing boats, sailboats, skiffs. Hundreds of them, maybe thousands. All different. All packed to the railings with people. All heading west.

The boats didn't slow down or change their course to avoid the eastbound ships of the *Saratoga* flotilla. They just wended their way through the task force, braving the wakes of the huge warships and tugboats.

Soon, Heath and many of the other sailors on the *Saratoga* appeared on the deck to witness the strange parade of ships. The BBC camera crew was also on hand, recording the scene.

Five sailors were dispatched in a small boat to stop and question some of the people. They returned with a strange report.

"The people are from Crete," one of the sailors said. "They say they are fleeing for their lives."

"Fleeing from what?" Yaz asked.

The sailor, a machinist's mate, shrugged. "Sounds crazy. Some kind of god, a giant from the netherworld. Named something like Bry-a-roos . . ."

Hunter thought for a moment, then asked, "Could it be Briareus?"

"That sounds more like it," he said.

"The name doesn't ring a bell," Heath said. "Is it from Greek mythology?"

"I think so," Hunter said. "Briareus was one of the giants. He supposedly had a hundred arms. Some of his friends — the Cyclops, Orion — had more familiar names. The giants were so bad-ass, they chased the top gods — Jupiter, Apollo, Venus, Mercury — out of Greece. Chased them all the way to Egypt."

"Tough cookies," Heath said.

The machinist's mate spoke up once again. "The people we talked to swear he appeared to them."

"Appeared to them?" Hunter said. "How?"

The man shrugged again. "They said they saw his face," he said. "In the sky, last night . . ."

Yaz was much relieved when Hunter later found him sitting alone in the messhall and told him about the boat people and their claim of a vision.

"I saw the same goddamn thing!" Yaz said. "I thought I'd gone around the deep end. The frigging thing spun itself right out of the stars. All red. Strange. Like a movie."

"And you're sure it was Lucifer's face?" Hunter asked.

"One hundred percent, major," Yaz said, downing his third cup of coffee. "It was weirdly distorted. Like it was changing back and forth. But it was definitely Lucifer. I'd know that face anywhere. And it was horrifying. I'll never forget it."

Hunter shook his head. Yaz was a tough kid and

still the vision had chilled him. Was there no end to Lucifer's psycho-weapons?

"He's somehow convinced the people of Crete that he is this giant Briareus," he said, anger building inside him.

"But why?" Yaz asked.

"Well, he probably wants the island as a base of operations," Hunter theorized, downing a cup of joe himself. "He can control a lot of the eastern Med from that island."

"But we haven't heard anything from the radio intercepts that Lucifer has gone anywhere," Yaz pointed out.

"And he probably hasn't," Hunter said. "This is probably something he's entrusted to his allies. It's a preinvasion tactic, spooking the population to get them out of the way."

Yaz shook his head, then said, "But the question is, how the hell does he do it? How does he make his face appear in the sky like that?"

Hunter could only shake his head. "Right now, it beats the hell out of me . . ."

Chapter 30

It was about noontime when Hunter got an urgent call to report to the CIC.

Heath was there, looking very worried as he and the rest of the CIC group stared into a radar set.

"We've got big trouble," he said as Hunter entered.

"How big is big?" Hunter asked, looking down at the green screen. He soon had his answer. The radar sweep indicated a large concentration of vessels off to the east, coming out of Crete and heading right for the *Saratoga*.

And as if that weren't bad enough, another, similar-sized force was also heading right for them, approaching from the southwest.

"Christ . . ." he whispered. "They ain't fishing boats, are they?"

"They're warships," Heath told him. "Everything from cruisers to frigates to missile boats according to their radar signatures. Probably some armed supply ships and tankers too. Everything but a battleship and a bloody carrier."

"The way they're formed up, they must be acting in concert," Hunter observed.

"And not a peep out of them on the radios," Heath said.

"Damn!" Hunter swore. "They're coordinating an attack and we're caught in the middle."

"This might have something to do with those escaping civilians," Heath said. "These ships could have been what really scared the hell out of them, along with Lucifer's face-in-the-sky bit, of course."

A thought suddenly leaped into Hunter's head. "How many ships?" he asked. "How many . . . exactly?"

The radar operator took ten seconds to count the blips. "Fifty coming from the east," the sailor told him. "And another fifty from the southwest. Exactly a hundred ships, major."

"The hundred arms of Briareus maybe?" Hunter theorized.

Heath thought for a moment. "Could be," he finally drawled out in his British accent. "Ready to put on a stranglehold. We're in trouble if we are in the noose. Those small missile ships alone could really muck us up."

"And we have to assume they are allies of Lucifer," Hunter said. "No one with fleets of this size could survive this far east in the Med without playing footsies with that snake."

"They are still twenty-five miles off in each direction and moving fairly slow," Heath said. "If we start turning to the southeast now, and tell O'Brien to go full speed up, we might avoid the major warships for the time being."

"And we'll most likely blow out most of the tug engines," Hunter said. He thought it over for a moment, then said, "But we've got no choice. I'd rather have these guys on our tails than on either side of us."

He reached over to the ship's radio and buzzed the lower deck where the carrier's aircraft were stored.

His voice was calm, steady, forceful. "Prepare all aircraft for standby to launch," he said. "Get the Jags fitted with antiship missiles. They'll be the first to go, if we have to go. Put the radar-homing air-to-surface jobs on the Viggens. Harriers get the same thing."

"Aye, aye, sir," the reply came back immediately.

Heath then hit the battle stations' klaxon. Instantaneously, they could hear the emergency bells and sirens going off on the nearby surrounding ships.

"I hate to risk our airplanes and crews on something we can avoid," Hunter said. He turned to one of the CIC technicians and asked. "What kind of a course do we hit going southeast?"

The man punched a handful of computer buttons, then read out the answer from his computer terminal. "On a straight southeast course, we would pass right by an offshore oil facility, major," the man reported.

"God, that's just the kind of place we want to avoid," Hunter said, adding, "Got any more info on it?"

The man pushed more buttons and waited for the lines of words and numbers to jump up on the screen.

"Turkish-controlled, apparently," the tech said. "Crude oil. Unrefined, of course. No good for fuel. Their refinery is back on Crete."

"Turkish, you say," Hunter said, hand on chin. "Why do I have the feeling that those platforms are the real target of these hundred ships?"

"It's a good theory," Heath said. "The Turks have been strictly neutral since the big battles died down. Neutral meaning they'll do business with anyone.

They also control a lot of the oil in this part of the Med. Lucifer and his allies have dealt with the Turks before. But it's strictly business."

Hunter nodded. "That means that Lucifer would attack them in a second if it suited his needs," he said. "Those oil platforms would be very valuable for his warships once they've broken out into the Med. They've probably already taken over the refinery of Crete.

"Lucifer could have hired these hundred ships — the arms of Briareus — to take both Crete *and* the oil. And that light show last night could be part of the plan. I mean, what better way to secure those facilities than by not having to fire a shot?"

"You mean spooking the platform crews?" Heath asked, shaking his head. "Making local fishermen and old people think you are a reincarnated god with some kind of nighttime projection is one thing, Hunter, old boy. But are the men on those platforms so easily fooled?"

"It's hard to say," Hunter replied. "Fooled might not be the right word. The face of Lucifer — as Briareus or not — still is quite a powerful psychwarfare weapon. If the platform guys are just hired help, Lucifer's ugly face appearing to them in the middle of the night might be just enough to convince them of his overwhelming power. Cause them to just throw in the towel. And quickly."

He thought for a moment then added, "Of course, then again, for all we know, the platform crews are probably armed to the teeth."

"Aye," Heath concurred. "I imagine it would be easy to slap a couple of Exocets onto a oil rig."

Hunter was worried. There were too many unpredictables in this one. His mind flashed back to Peter. They could use his blathering but accurate

277

foresight right now. Oddly, it seemed as if he'd been gone for ages.

"The problem is," he continued, "that once the Briareus ship captains get smart and realize that we've squeezed through their pickle, and realize who we are, they might hold off on taking over the platforms, by guns *or* words. If they do, they'll be after us in a second."

"And if we lose any number of O'Brien's tugs, it will be the briefest escape in history," Heath said.

Hunter ran his hand through his long hair. "One thing I know," he said, excitement welling up in his voice. "We don't have any friends on either side. Those Turks would attack us just as sure as Lucifer's allies would."

"You're getting an idea?" Heath said.

"It's a longshot," Hunter said. "But the important thing now is to get the hell out of their way."

He turned to the CIC radioman. "Sparky," he said. "Get O'Brien on the horn, will you?"

Paddy O'Brien sat in the control room on his lead tugboat, his eyes glued to the vessel's speed indicator.

All of the Irishman's tugs were now at full speed ahead, on a course that would take them due south. The tow lines on the dozen "pull" boats were singing. The powerful diesel engines on the six remaining "push" boats were belching loud clouds of smoke as they strained to keep up speed. Even though Olson had pressed two of his frigates into pull duty, O'Brien knew the desperate bid to get out of harm's way would soon deplete his beloved tug flotilla.

"Sorry, girls," he said, referring to the boats in his fleet. "You'll be busting up and all over soon. But I guess it's better than being sent to the bottom by some swine's deck gun."

A pang of sadness exploded in his heart. He could actually feel strain of his engines. "You bastard, Lucifer!" he said under his breath.

High above the tugboats, on the deck of the *Saratoga*, Yaz's sailors were working at a feverish pitch, getting the carrier's aircraft up on deck and ready for takeoff should the bold "slip-through" maneuver not work.

Boats of The Commodore's Freedom Navy had gathered around the flattop for protection, giving the carrier the appearance of an enormous, gray mother goose surrounded by her chicks. The captured supertanker and the oiler were about a half-mile behind the carrier, surrounded by four of Olson's frigates, their anti-missile defenses on high alert. Behind them was the Moroccan troopship, it too surrounded by the Norwegian bodyguards. The rest of the Olson's ships were bringing up the rear, their radar systems keyed in on the approaching pincers of the mysterious fleet.

Hunter sat in his F-16; the airplane would be the first to launch if the plan went awry and the Briareus ships turned toward the *Saratoga*. The entire fleet was now under strict radio silence. As far as they knew, the Briareus ships had not detected them yet. An uneasy tension settled over the fleet. All of the carrier fleet's large ships were ready for battle, yet it was up to O'Brien's small workhorse tugs to get them out of the squeeze.

The BBC video crew roamed the *Saratoga*'s deck, its cameraman taking shots of opportunity. Launch officers fingering their radio buttons. The French anti-missile gunners at their posts chain-smoking. The Spanish rocketeers going over their firing tubes.

279

The Italian communications experts with their ears pressed against their headphones, straining to hear any sound that would indicate that the jig was up and the *Saratoga* fleet had been detected. It would be dusk soon. Hunter knew that, with the gathering darkness, the chances that they would "slip through" would increase.

"Major Hunter?"

The voice knocked him out of his trance. It was the video crew chief, yelling up to him from the carrier deck.

"Can we ask you a few questions, major?" the man, whom Hunter knew as "Chips," called up.

Hunter nodded. What the hell? he thought.

The crew's cameraman was instantly up the 16's access ladder and rolling. The film crew chief started yelling up questions.

"Major, we're in a bit of a jam right now," Chips began. "We've apparently got two fleets converging on us and we're trying to get out of their way undetected. Any idea who the enemy is, major?"

"Lucifer's allies, we figure," Hunter called back. "There are a hundred ships in all, and a force like that could not have been put together in this part of the Med without some help from Lucifer."

The cameraman moved in a little closer.

"We've been through some pretty intense action already, major," Chips said, continuing the interview. "We've done battle against the Red Army Faction, some robot-controlled Russian aircraft, the Holy Sardinians, the Panatellas, and the Sidra-Benghazi Gang. And now this. It doesn't seem to be getting any easier, does it?"

Hunter shook his head. "We don't expect it to," he answered. "It seems like the further we sail into the Med, the stranger things become."

"Major, we all know that you are somewhat of a celebrity back in the States," Chips said. "And we also know that America is going through some particularly tough times right now. What are you doing over here?"

Hunter bit his lip. He'd been asking himself the same question ever since the voyage started. Push-pull. He felt as if he were being tugged in many different directions. "Well, the cause of all the recent troubles in America is Lucifer," Hunter answered. "We know him as Viktor Robotov. But whatever he chooses to call himself, he has brought about untold suffering for many people, back in the States and here.

"Just as American troops came here in World War Two to stop Hitler, I feel my help is needed here in to stop this madman. There are also more than three hundred other Americans on board. US Navy personnel who are in charge of running this ship. I'm sure they feel the same way as do the men of all the other nationalities in the fleet. It's an international, allied effort to stop Lucifer."

"But what will happen if this bold maneuver—this 'slip-through'—does not work?"

"Well . . ." Hunter searched for the most diplomatic answer he could think of. But the situation defied any mincing of words. "We'll be in a for a fight that would significantly hinder our ability to carry out our ultimate mission, which is holding the Suez Canal—through our airpower—until The Modern Knights and their armies arrive."

"One last question, major," Chips called up. "What if The Modern Knights don't arrive in time?"

Hunter found himself tongue-tied. He knew that it was a very real possibility, especially since hearing the disturbing news from Stanley, the biplane pilot.

The man had been dispatched back to England, carrying a bitter message from Sir Neil admonishing The Modern Knights for their delay and telling them in no uncertain terms to get their act in order.

The cameraman moved in very close now, the camera-mounted microphone just inches away from Hunter's face.

The delay in Hunter's answer caused Chips to reask the question. "What will happen if The Modern Knights don't arrive in time?" Hunter detected a hint of nervousness in the questioner's voice. He wasn't surprised; they were *all* in this together.

"No comment," Hunter finally answered.

Hunter never had to launch. Night fell and they could see the flares and blue lights of the oil platforms off on the southern horizon. The trailing Norwegian frigates reported the mysterious fleet had linked up and was also heading for the platforms. Yet they were now a good fifty miles behind the *Saratoga* fleet and moving slowly. The carrier flotilla then steered as one to the starboard for a few degrees to avoid the oil platforms. Another correction maneuver would take place in a few hours, putting the fleet back on course towards Suez.

They had dodged the bullet.

But not without a price . . .

Hunter, Heath, Yaz, and Olson sat in the carrier's messhall holding an impromptu strategy session. O'Brien was also there, giving them the bad news.

"We burnt out five tugs," the Irishman said slowly. "Engines completely blown beyond any repair. Four others are in real bad shape, being held together by God-knows-what."

Hunter shook his head. "We owe you a lot,

282

Paddy," the pilot told him. "You saved us from a very dangerous situation."

"I know," the Irishman said, the pain obvious in his voice. "It's just that it happened so quickly, after all this time. And you can't find a good tug these days. No one makes 'em."

The room was completely silent.

"What's worst is we can expect slow going from here on out," O'Brien finally said. "One-third the speed we were making, and even that will take a toll on the remaining tugs."

Heath looked at Hunter. "That is *very* serious," the Englishman said. "We need to get to the Suez as quickly as possible. Lucifer's troops are already aboard their invasion ships—so the radio intercepts tell us. They'll be sailing very soon."

O'Brien could only shrug. "The more strain we put on the tugs now, the more they'll blow. As it is we won't have much to maneuver with once we get to the Suez."

Heath turned to Olson. "Captain, could we hook up a couple more of your ships for towing duty?"

"By all means," the Norwegian said in heavily accented English. "But if we run into any more trouble, we'll have to cut loose and respond to it."

Hunter shook his head. "We'll be in real danger of leaving the carrier dead in the water," he said. "In which case it will be a perfect target."

"A proverbial sitting duck, as they say," Heath added.

"Exactly," Hunter replied.

Again, the room was silent.

"But we've got other problems right now," Hunter said finally. "Whatever the Briareus fleet does, they'll eventually be on to us. Even if we make it to the Canal, they could come right in after us and we'll *really* be squeezed between them and Lucifer's forces."

"What have you got in mind, major?" Heath asked. "We certainly can't fight them on our own."

"No way," Hunter agreed. "But let's think for a minute. This entire 'face-in-the-sky, hundred-arms business' is probably all an attempt to intimidate the Turks into handing over the oil platforms—and Crete—without a fight. These tactics have worked for Lucifer before all over the Mideast. He's probably just assuming they'll work here again. Just like during The Circle War, anything he can get by using mind over matter he'll try for."

"So what can we do?" Yaz asked.

"Well," Hunter said. "We can screw up his little psych-out party. Get some real fireworks going."

"An air strike?" Heath asked.

"No," Hunter answered. "I'm thinking of something a little more subtle. If those ships out there take a little hostile fire, it just might dissuade them from coming after us. All I'll need is one of Paddy's ailing tugs, a few of Yaz's electrical boys, and a couple of Harpoons."

Chapter 31

The tugboat could hardly get up enough speed to carry them all. O'Brien spent most of the trip fretting over the boat's gearbox and the lack of RPM's coming from the engine. The motor—its rings and valves completely shot—would only provide sporadic bursts of turning power, causing the tug to lurch forward for a few seconds, then float for a few minutes, before another unpredictable surge would push them forward again.

Of course, this was exactly what Hunter wanted.

"If they have any close-in sonar listening devices on those ships," he said, referring to the Briareus fleet, "they'll be picking up our screw-turn vibrations. But the way we're going, they'll never suspect that a boat this shitty would be floating around out here in the middle of the night. They'll probably be ripping apart their machines, looking for a glitch or something."

The ships of the Briareus fleet were just two miles away, sailing southward at a leisurely pace. "They're taking their time," Hunter said to Yaz as they stood on the bow of the tug. "Probably waiting for the face in the sky to make its appearance."

Four miles in the other direction was the cluster of Turkish oil platforms. Hunter had counted at least twenty of the rigs as they'd slipped by earlier in the night. By monitoring the radio transmissions from the platforms, he knew the men aboard them were armed, dangerous, but somewhat unsure as to whether they should fight the approaching, overwhelming fleet or just surrender the whole operation.

In all the confusion, the *Saratoga* flotilla had managed to slip on by them, undetected, fifteen miles to their southwest. The flotilla—with the lone exception of a single frigate—was now moving away from the potential battle zone, slowly but surely.

"I have to ask you again, how the hell does Lucifer do it?" Yaz said to Hunter as the tug went into yet another drifting mode. "This face-in-the-sky stuff? I mean, I've seen fireworks displays back home where they've made flags or whatever hang up in the sky. But nothing like this."

"I'll know more when I see it," Hunter said. "But my guess is that he's using laser projection. It would have to be pretty sophisticated, to be sure. Beamed from some distance away, maybe even bounced off a satellite or even his P-3 Orion."

"Well, whatever it is, it's effective," Yaz said, adding a whistle. "Anyone the least bit superstitious is guaranteed to jump right out of his shoes."

"Well, Lucifer's nothing if not clever," Hunter said. "I mean, the face in the sky is the *coup de grace*, but he also had to have his agents do a lot of legwork on Crete and in this area in order to convince the people of the Briareus connection. You saw the horror show back around Casablanca—

people trying to get the hell out of the way of the war. I'm sure that panic was for the most part caused by tactics like this. Intimidation. Rumors. Disinformation. Playing on people's paranoia. Fleets popping up here and there. Faces in the sky. He managed to evacuate most of the whole frigging Med of unwanted citizens — and probably more than a few would-be soldiers — again, all without firing a shot."

Just then, one of Yaz's men appeared. "We're ready when you are," he said. The sailor was talking about the Harpoon antiship missile-launch system he and his crew members had just finished installing on the old tug.

Hunter and Yaz looked over the launcher. It was jimmy-rigged for sure, and its only power was a five-pack of small automobile-type batteries they had carried along. But a quick look at the electrical connections told Hunter that the launcher would probably work the two times they would need it.

Now they waited. O'Brien cut the tug's engines and let the boat drift between the platforms and the slow-approaching Briareus ships.

"Any minute now," Hunter said to Yaz and O'Brien as they searched the brilliantly star-washed sky.

"There it is!" Yaz shouted, barely able to contain himself. He was pointing to the eastern horizon.

Hunter scanned the area. Sure enough, he saw a single red star, burning brightly. "Definitely a laser," he said, matter-of-factly.

Then another red star appeared. Then another. Soon, one part of the sky consisted of nothing but the red stars. Then they started moving. Circling. Changing positions. Forming patterns. Sure enough a face started taking shape.

"Well, I'll be damned," Hunter said. He had to admit the special effects were superb.

But not only that, the illusion was so real it almost appeared to be holographic in nature. It alternated between Lucifer's devilish face and what Hunter imagined to be Briareus, the giant.

"I can see what you mean," Hunter told Yaz as they and all of the sailors on the boat—O'Brien included—stood in awe of the gigantic vision. "It's a very powerful image. Just enough to throw a lot of people over the edge, I would think."

"Getting a radio message," a sailor watching over the tug's communications set reported.

Immediately Hunter, O'Brien, and Yaz were inside the tug's bridge.

"What language is it in?" Hunter asked.

The sailor adjusted his headphones. "If I had to guess, I'd say Arabic," he said.

"Strange," Hunter said. "I didn't expect they'd be broadcasting in Arabic. Unless . . ."

"Unless what?" Yaz asked.

"Can you try another frequency?" Hunter asked the radio operator.

The sparky twisted a few dials, then said, "Yes, here's another broadcast coming through. Same source, but in a different language."

He kept trying other frequencies and picking up other languages.

"They're all over the band!" he said, excitedly.

"Let's hope there's one in English," Hunter said.

No sooner were the words out of his mouth when the radio operator cried out, "Bingo! We got English!"

He flipped a switch and put the broadcast on the tug's tiny speaker. The person talking—a strange, whining, chilling voice—was in the middle of his message.

"—the dawn of Briareus. You cannot resist this inevitable power. The age of Lucifer is here. Briareus, he of one hundred arms, is here. Here to do Lucifer's bidding. Do not resist—"

"I can't believe someone would fall for something so hokey," Yaz said.

"I know," Hunter said, marking down yet another instance that seemed right out of a bad horror movie. "But he's touching a nerve somewhere."

They listened to the message repeat several more times before O'Brien asked, "He doesn't even give them a chance to reply."

"That's all part of the plan," Hunter said. "They have no recourse. Either surrender or go down fighting."

"Well, let's see if we can influence that decision," Hunter said, bounding out of the cabin and onto the deck.

He took a quick position check. The oil platforms were now about three miles to the south, the first elements of the Briareus ships were one and a half miles to the north.

"Okay," he said. "Let's prepare the first missile. Sparky, put the call into the frigate helicopter crew. Tell to wait ten minutes, then take off."

Everyone pitched in to load the Harpoon missile onto the makeshift launcher. "This is a heavy bastard, isn't it?" Hunter said. They all struggled somewhat until the rocket was finally in place. Then the launch crew started wiring the missile in place, followed by an orgy of button-pushing.

"Ready to fire," one of the sailors finally said.

"Roger," Hunter said. "Now, the first target . . ."

He was peering through powerful electronic binoculars. The spyglasses had a fairly elaborate night-

289

scope capability, just enough for Hunter to pick out the biggest ship in the lead section of the Briareus fleet.

"That one looks like a good-sized missile cruiser," he said, handing the binocs to the launch sailor. "Can you get it?"

"At this range, it should be no problem," the man answered.

Hunter double-checked through the scope, then said: "Okay. It's your show. Fire when ready."

All those not involved in the launch retreated to the cabin. Suddenly, there was a burst of flame on the deck and the Harpoon flew off its launcher.

Hunter watched it climb, level off, and head straight for the missile-launching cruiser. "When that baby hits," Hunter said, "everyone from the fleet captain to the cook will be convinced the Turks launched it."

Ten seconds later, the missile impacted right into the cruiser's bridge, causing an explosion that lifted the beam of the ship right out of the water.

"Jee-suz," Hunter exclaimed as a ball of fire rose from the ship. "You Navy guys know how to pack a missile."

Immediately after the explosion, they heard a cacophony of klaxons and warning bells coming from the enemy fleet.

"That's one," Hunter said. "Now let's get two off."

Once again they struggled to put the Harpoon in place, while O'Brien coaxed the engine to chug one more time, just enough to turn the tug around.

Less than forty-five seconds later, the second Harpoon was launched, this time right at the Turkish oil platforms. Hunter followed this missile's flight with the binoculars. The Harpoon skimmed along the ocean surface as advertised, rising up when needed.

Suddenly, its warhead homing device locked onto to a target and it veered to the left.

"It might have found some kind of radar set," Hunter said as the tug crew watched the Harpoon twist and turn through the platforms. Finally it streaked right into a large rig in the middle of the pack. Another enormous explosion followed. When the smoke and flame cleared, nothing remained of the platform except some scattered, burning debris.

"Wow!" Hunter exclaimed. "Good shooting, guys!"

But now they heard other noises. Turning back to the fleet, they saw by the light of the burning cruiser that five of the Briareus ships had turned broadside to the platforms.

"Oh boy," Yaz said. "Here we go."

No sooner had he spoken than the first volley of shells streaked over their heads and came crashing down around the platforms. As soon as those shells hit, another barrage was tearing over their heads.

"Paddy!" Hunter yelled, "can you get this baby going just one more time?"

"I'll give it a try," the Irishman said, scrambling down the ladder leading to the boat's engine room. "But I think she's had it . . ."

Now the oil platforms began their revenge. Suddenly two Exocets zoomed by the tug, no more than twenty feet out.

"I'm glad we've got nothing those bastards can home in on," Hunter said. He watched as the two rockets streaked off toward the Briareus ships, blue flames spitting out of their tails.

Bang! Bang!

"Two direct hits!" Yaz yelled out as the Exocets slammed into a destroyer and a missile-launcher corvette. The explosions were so powerful, a shock wave rippled back to the tug.

Now, less than a minute after the Harpoons had hit, the sky was filled with flaming ordnance. Incredible naval gunfire from the fleet, dozens of Exocets from the platforms. The dark night had now become like day in the reflections of the explosions. Hunter looked up at the face of Lucifer, still hanging in the sky, the expression oblivious to the sudden violent battle that had broken out.

"Well, we've certainly started something," Yaz said excitedly as a trio of Exocets raced by. "Now where the hell is that chopper?"

At that moment, O'Brien emerged from the engine room. "She's dead, major," he said. "Can't get her to even cough."

"Don't worry," Hunter said, closing his eyes and listening. Ah, yes, *the feeling* was coming over him. It had been a long time. Too long. "The chopper is on its way."

Exactly one minute later, the frigate copter was hovering above the tug, its winch line lifting the first two crew members up to safety. Despite all the missiles flying around and the shells streaking overhead, the Norwegian chopper pilot held steady. He didn't flinch when a stray round from a destroyer fell within a few hundred feet of the tug.

Hunter and Yaz were the last to go up. No sooner were the crew members dragging Hunter on board then the chopper pilot dropped to nearly wave-top level and throttled up. In seconds, the copter was dashing out of the battle zone and heading for the carrier flotilla.

There were handshakes all around as the tug crew congratulated each other for a job well done.

"They'll be battering each other all night," Hunter said, watching the flames of the battle still visible fifteen miles away.

"And they'll probably never figure out who got the first shot in," Yaz said, the glee evident in his voice.

Hunter craned his neck and looked up to where the face of Lucifer was. Just as he spotted it, he noticed it was losing some of its glimmer. Then he watched as it slowly faded away . . .

Chapter 32

Their jubilation didn't last very long . . .

As soon as they touched down on the deck of the *Saratoga,* they saw Heath was waiting for them, an extremely worried look on his face.

"Don't tell me," Hunter said, holding up his hand. "More bad news?" He knew something was up because the *Saratoga* was barely moving.

"I'm afraid so," Heath said, nodding. "While you were gone, we were attacked by two submarines."

"What?!" They all said in unison. Hunter couldn't believe it.

"They got three of your tugs, I'm afraid," Heath said to O'Brien.

"Mother of God." The Irishman's face went crimson. "How about my men?"

"Only one lost," Heath said, brightening a little. "The choppers got into a running gunfight with the subs so the Commodore's boys went in and plucked your guys out."

"What kind of subs?" Hunter asked as the Norwegian chopper took off and headed back to its frigate.

"That's the even worse news," Heath said. "They were Soviets."

"Soviet-built?" Yaz asked.

Heath shook his head. "No, I mean, Soviet-manned."

"How can you be sure?" Hunter asked.

Heath nodded his head grimly. "Because the chopper guys managed to nail one with a depth charge while it was close to the surface. We fished two of its crew members out. They're as Russian as *borsch.*"

"Are they in any shape to talk?" Hunter wanted to know.

"Yes, one is," Heath said. "They're both up in sick bay."

"Well," Hunter said, his voice angry. "Let's go see what he has to say . . ."

Ten minutes later, Hunter was sitting in the Soviet crewman's room, staring down at the man. He had resisted bringing in a whole gang of people, though he was tempted to scare the man rightfully out of his wits. But for now, he decided on a different tactic.

The man, an oldster about fifty, opened his eyes and was startled to see Hunter hovering over him.

"Dobriy vyehchyeer, comrade," Hunter said. "Understand any English?"

The man looked at him suspiciously, then slowly nodded his bandaged head.

"Understand good?" Hunter asked.

The man shrugged.

Hunter clapped his hands twice. The cabin door opened and one of the call girls—a friend of Anna's named Beatrice—walked in. She was lovely. Blonde, well-proportioned, and very alluring, she was the youngest of the group except for Anna herself.

"Okay, Boris," Hunter said to the Soviet sailor. "This is how we'll work it. Tell me what I want to know and you not only go free, you get to get acquainted with Beatrice."

Now a look of complete surprise came across the Soviet's face. Hunter's statement begged the question. "What if I no talk?" the Soviet asked.

Hunter slowly drew out a borrowed .45 Colt automatic. In a half-second it had found itself just a quarter-inch away from the Russian's nose. "We either shoot you or you go overboard."

The man gulped. Hunter turned to Beatrice and nodded. She smiled and slowly undid her blouse. Five buttons later, she revealed her see-through black-lace bra.

The Soviet began to sweat.

"Where's your base?" Hunter asked.

The man shook his head. "They kill me if I tell."

"There is no more 'they,' " Hunter told him. "Your ship is gone. Except for another guy who is busted up in the next room, you are the only one left. Face it, champ. They think you're dead."

Hunter nodded once again to Beatrice. She seductively removed her miniskirt and shoes, then walked to the other side of the Russian's bed.

"Okay, where's your base?" Hunter asked.

The Russian's eyes were fixed on Beatrice's well-rounded breasts. She did her best to further inflame him, slowly shaking and stretching her beautiful body.

"I cannot tell," the Soviet said, though never taking his eyes off Beatrice.

Hunter winked at her. She smiled and slowly removed her bra. The man's face turned five shades of red. These sub guys, Hunter thought. Always horny and always deprived.

Beatrice moved in very close to the man, so much so her nipples wound up just inches from his face.

"Listen, pal," Hunter said. "There's an Englishman out there that would just as soon cut you up and feed you to the fishes. Then there's an Irishman who is very pissed off that you and your buddies sank his tugboats. He's taking it *very* personally. He'd as soon drag your ass around on a fish hook until you fall apart into little pieces. And I won't even mention what the Moroccans would do to you.

"But you see, you're lucky. You're dealing with an American here, okay? All I want is information. Once you're done, we chopper you to the nearest land and you can walk back to Moscow for all I care."

While Hunter was talking, Beatrice had moved her breasts right into the man's face. It was clear that he was breaking down.

"Now," Hunter said a third time. "Where's your base?"

"Alexandria," the Soviet answered.

"Very good," Hunter said, watching as Beatrice rewarded the man by sticking her lovely right nipple into his mouth. The man made a half-hearted attempt to suck it briefly, before Beatrice teasingly withdrew.

"Okay, how many subs?" Hunter continued, as Beatrice zoomed in with her left breast.

"Two squadrons, ten boats in each," the Russian said, gasping. Beatrice inserted her left nipple into his mouth and left it there. The man, a little more greedy this time, sucked it for a good three seconds, before Beatrice again moved away.

"Why are you stationed in Egypt?" Hunter asked.

"That I cannot tell you," the man answered, his eyes never leaving Beatrice's chest.

Hunter again nodded to her. In a second, her hand was resting on top of the blankets right above the man's crotch.

"Why are you in Egypt?" Hunter asked, calmly.

The man gasped. "We are protecting the pyramid."

"A pyramid?" Hunter said. The answer surprised him. Subs protecting a pyramid? "Which pyramid?" He watched as Beatrice's hand began to feel its way around and under the blankets. It soon found its mark.

"The Great Pyramid . . ." the man burst out. "The Great Pyramid of Cheops . . ."

"Besides your subs, who else is protecting the pyramid?" Hunter asked.

"Two helicopter squadrons," the man answered quickly, anticipating Beatrice's next move. "Also ten each. Plus soldiers on the ground."

He fell back onto his pillow as Beatrice snuggled in closer. Hunter could see a jerking movement begin under the man's covers.

He drew close. He had to ask the all-important question. "Why are you guarding the Great Pyramid?"

Hunter nodded to Beatrice and she suddenly stopped all movement. The man, who had settled back onto his pillow with his eyes closed, was suddenly up again, eyes wide open. He looked at Hunter.

"Why are you guarding the pyramid?" the pilot asked again.

The man looked confused. At first he shook his head, but a slight tickle by Beatrice delivered an unmistakable message. Finally the man broke down.

"It's part of an agreement," he said in broken but understandable English.

"An agreement with Lucifer?" Hunter asked.

"Yes. There is something, 'the valuable,' hidden in the pyramid," the man continued. Beatrice had begun her hand movements once again.

"What is it?" Hunter pressed.

"We do not know," the man answered quickly, closing his eyes again. "They don't tell us submariners. Why would they? We are small pawns in big game."

"You must have some idea," Hunter said. "What was the scuttlebutt on your ship? Gold? Jewels?"

"Nyet, not money valuable," the man said, the passionate strain showing on his face. "Very valuable as a weapon of some kind. But we would never know. And neither do the soldiers on ground."

"Why not?" Hunter asked. "They're right next to it. Don't they see it?"

"No, no, no!" the man said, gasping for breath. "You cannot get near it. It is in a tomb. Stone tomb. It is blocked off by doors, stones, and metal. We ship special doors in for them."

Beatrice's hand movements were now reaching a climax. Hunter needed one more question answered.

"What kind of special doors?" he asked quickly.

The man looked like he was about to explode. He grimaced and said with great effort: "They . . . were . . . made . . . of . . . lead."

At that moment, Nature took its course. The man bit his lip, his eyes were pressed shut. He shook once, then slumped down onto his pillow. Beatrice quickly reached for a towel.

"Lead?" Hunter asked, more to himself. Then it hit him. An agreement with Lucifer. A valuable weapon. You can't get near it. *Lead* doors.

It all added up to one thing: there was something *nuclear* in the Great Pyramid of Cheops.

Chapter 33

The F-16 roared in at wave-top level, its whole airframe almost drooping from the weight of ten specially fitted Sidewinders on its wings and the weapons dispenser that was attached to its belly. Hunter checked the time. It was an hour before sun up. He checked his coordinates. The land he saw on his radar scope some fifteen miles ahead was probably the tip of land near the old Egyption city of El Alamein. He did a radar sweep of the area. No hostile weapons were indicated. So far, so good.

He switched on his cockpit's specially adapted SLQ-32 radar detector. This would warn him with a low tone if anyone on the ground happened to get a radar lock on the airplane. If the device detected that a radar was switched to a fire-control mode, a higher tone would be emitted. This meant a missile was about to be launched at him. At that point, he would have to take evasive action.

But for the time being, everything seemed to be quiet on the ground. He made landfall and streaked over El Alamein. Site of a famous World War II tank battle, the place was now deserted. In seconds he was on the other side of the city and heading into the barren area of Egypt known as the Qattara Depression.

He had left the *Saratoga* dead in the water about

150 miles northwest of Alexandria. The tugboat fleet was now history. Those vessels that hadn't burned out their engines had been sunk by the subs. Now the Norwegians formed a protective ring around the carrier, as did the Freedom Navy boats. The frigate choppers were continuously circling the area looking for subs, while four of the carrier jets were in the air at any given time, watching out for any flying threats.

Despite all the protection, Hunter knew that the carrier would be discovered and eventually sunk — by the Soviets, by Lucifer's other allies — if it stayed still for very long. Yet, with the loss of O'Brien's tugs, moving the carrier was impossible. All of the other ships in the *Saratoga* flotilla combined could not generate enough sustained push-pull power to move the carrier very far.

"Son of a bitch," he muttered to himself for the hundredth time. "So goddamn close to the Canal and we run out of gas."

It got worse. Just before he took off, the Italian communications team intercepted a message right from Lucifer's Arabian Kingdom headquarters. His Legion troopships had set sail. They were making their way up the Red Sea and would be in the Gulf of Suez — and at the very threshold of the Canal itself — in a matter of days, if not hours.

He pressed on. He had to find out just what was in the Great Pyramid. For two reasons. One, there was a possibility that "the valuable" was nuclear and therefore could be fissionable plutonium. This meant that, with very little effort, Lucifer would have a nuclear bomb — or *bombs* — courtesy of the Kremlin. If that were the case, "the valuable" would have to be destroyed at all costs, and that included blowing up the whole goddamn pyramid if he had to.

But there was a second reason he had to find out exactly what "the valuable" was. It was a granddaddy of longshots to be sure, but there was a possibility that the nuclear material might be UB-40 grade uranium.

If that was the case, then it would be a whole new ballgame . . .

He swung around to the east and headed for the Nile. He had visited the Great Pyramid once before while touring with The Thunderbirds. He knew there was a long strip of highway—newly constructed at the time—which ran fairly close to the ancient site. He knew the Soviets were using a stretch of highway for their helicopter base. Although the choppers didn't need any length of runway to take off or land, their supply airplanes did. And, just as with the RAF base near Casablanca where he first met Heath, highway bases were the only way to go in the desert. They saved the time and effort of building new bases out in the middle of nowhere. Plus, should something go wrong—like a sneak air attack—the survivors could always drive—or walk—out.

Hunter knew there were no Soviet fighters or fighter-bombers in the area. How? Because he knew they would have attacked the *Saratoga* by now. The Soviets knew the carrier was in their area—their subs had confirmed that. But they would never mount an all-out attack on the fleet with just choppers. Thus sub attacks would be the only way to go.

He also knew that he couldn't just set the 16 down on an isolated piece of asphalt and walk to the pyramid. If the thirst and sun didn't get him, the

Soviet soldiers guarding the place would.

So the situation would seem to call for an air strike. But again, there were problems. He was certain the Soviet troops around the pyramid and flying the choppers would be equipped with SAMs. No matter how many airplanes he could send against the chopper base and the troop site near the pyramid, he would have to expect the loss of at least three aircraft. And that was too many.

So he had decided to do the job himself. Before leaving he had discussed the whole scenario with Sir Neil, who pronounced him "daft" while at the same time crushing his hand with an almost tearful good-luck handshake. Hunter left one instruction behind. Should he not return by a specified time, the Tornados would bomb up and destroy the pyramid. Simple as that.

His plan was to catch as many of the Soviet choppers on the ground as possible. That's why he chose sunrise for the one-man attack. He doubted the Soviets were into doing dawn patrols these days. In fact, knowing the Soviet military mind as he did, he would have bet the chopper pilots and the pyramid guard force would be just about fed up with desert duty right about now. They had obviously been guarding the pyramid for some time—waiting for Lucifer to make his grand entrance through the Canal, no doubt picking up his "valuable" along the way. The sand does crazy things to soldiers—gets in their eyes, their hair, their chow. They come to hate it very quickly. Sand also does crazy things to machines—especially helicopters. It gets into the oil, the fuel, the gears, the grease. It's a bitch to clean out, and as soon as you do, some more will blow in anyway.

So, he figured the Soviets were just about at the

end of their rope about now. This would also work to his advantage.

He found the Nile and turned north. This would be a backdoor operation all the way. The weapons dispenser attached to the 16's belly carried hundreds of small but deadly bomblets, each packing the punch of a large HE grenade. The dispenser—a device custom-made for destroying runways and such—would be particularly effective against the Soviet choppers, provided he could get low enough. The Sidewinders would have to deal with any choppers that might be in the air at the time or that managed to get off the ground during the attack.

A warning light began to blink on his control board. It was the SLQ-32, telling him that radar devices were straight ahead. He eased the 16 over with the side-side controller so it was now flying directly above the highway that ran parallel to the Nile and would eventually run past the Great Pyramid itself. This was the highway he knew the Soviets were using for their chopper base.

He armed his weapons and checked the dispenser triggers. Everything came back green. His SLQ-32 tone got a little higher, hinting that radars ahead were close to going to fire-control mode. No matter, he thought. He'd be on top of them in seconds.

He rose up slightly and peered over a small set of mountains he knew was just south of Giza, the location of the Great Pyramid. Sure enough, his radar sweep indicated sixteen choppers lined up in two neat rows along the highway. In the distance, the massive outline of the Great Pyramid was dominant.

"Okay, gang," he said, dropping down to attack level.

A Soviet sergeant walking to the latrine saw the F-

16 first. His initial thought was that the fighter was either a Soviet airplane or one belonging to one of their myriad of allies.

"Maybe Lucifer finally got himself an airplane," the sergeant thought as he saw the red-white-and-blue jet streak across the desert, a mean-looking exhaust stream trailing behind it.

But almost immediately the sergeant realized the airplane wasn't coming in for a landing. He saw the outline a little more clearly. Being a chopper pilot, he was not totally ignorant of airplanes. "Is that an F-16?" he thought.

He soon knew the answer was yes. The airplane was above the base in a flash, a sputtering noise coming from its belly. The sergeant also knew a weapons dispenser when he saw one. Just seconds before the first tiny parachutes carrying the bomblets landed, the sergeant realized the base was under attack. He also realized it was too late for him to do anything about it. The bomblets began landing and exploding and spraying huge amounts of deadly, burning shrapnel in all directions. Three seconds later the sergeant was obliterated along with two Hind helicopters sitting nearby.

Hunter completed the first bombing run, then pulled up and put the jet on its side so he could survey the damage. He counted seven choppers burning, plus a good portion of the runway torn up. Not bad for the first pass. But the easy part was over. They'd be waiting for him when he came around again.

Sure enough, his SLQ-32 started squealing — two lock-ons were indicated. This would call for special measures. He completed his 360-degree turn and came in again. Suddenly a shoulder-launched SA-7 missile flashed up from a perimeter bunker. No matter—he was by it in a flash. He hit the weapons-dispenser trigger and quickly let go the rest of the bomblets. At the same time, another SA-7 started up towards him, this one shot from a lookout tower near the center of the base. This was where it got tricky. Once he knew the dispenser was empty, he put the F-16 into a quick succession of rolls—six of them in all, enough to confuse the most intelligent homing system.

At the end of the maneuver, he put the fighter on its ass and got the hell away from the base. Only when he was at 10,000 feet did he turn over and look back at the runway. Again, the bomblets had done the job. Scratch eight more choppers, plus another large chunk of runway. As a bonus, he had also set a fuel tank for the base on fire.

He climbed again, up to 60,000 feet. The two-pass air strike had accomplished more than he had hoped for. But at the same time he knew there were still five more choppers to contend with . . .

The Soviet troops stationed next to the Great Pyramid had heard the commotion at the chopper base several miles away. With a pall of smoke rising above the facility and calls to the base going unanswered, the Soviet troop commander ordered three truckloads of his men to drive over and investigate. Because no one at the troop base had actually heard an airplane—another plus gained by Hunter for attacking at dawn—the Soviet troop commander thought the chopper strip's ammo dump might have gone up.

The ride to the air facility usually took twenty minutes. But as the three trucks started out along the deserted highway, they suddenly heard a nightmarish scream coming from behind them. Out of nowhere an F-16 had appeared. Its nose looked as if it was on fire, but this was just an illusion. The spits of flame coming from Hunter's specially installed Vulcan cannon Six Pack were simply converging into one long fiery tongue.

One sweep was all it took. In a matter of seconds, all three trucks were ripped into small, bloody pieces. It had happened so quickly, many of the men went into shock. Those who had been lucky enough to survive, and who still had their wits about them, simply fell to the ground and prayed the F-16 wouldn't return.

Now the troop commander knew what he was up against. He cursed himself for exposing half his troops on the desert highway like that. He literally shook his fist at the jet fighter as it roared overhead, at the same time screaming for troops to break out the shoulder-launched SAMs.

But even this order was issued too late. The F-16 had flashed around the pyramid and was now bearing down on the Soviet soldiers as they scrambled for cover. The Six Pack opened up once again, spraying the dusty ground with an incredible barrage of cannon fire. The Soviet commander watched in horror as his men seemed to explode before his eyes. The jet streaked directly over him and turned to go around again.

"This pilot is a madman," the Soviet commander thought. This time his men were able to man their SAMs. One was launched, then another. But the jet was twisting, turning, darting away from the rockets. All the while its ferocious Vulcan cannons were blazing away. More targets were hit. More men horribly perforated by the awesome flying death.

Suddenly the troop commander's mind flashed

307

back to a time several years before, when the war was going full tilt in Europe. He remembered seeing an F-16 acting in a similar way. That airplane too had ripped up a battalion of troops in a matter of minutes, dodging everything the Soviets soldiers could throw up against it. "That man is crazy," the Soviet commander thought at the time. "Crazy because he keeps coming back for more."

Now, suddenly jerked back to the present, the Soviet officer watched as the F-16 approached for a third time. "It's the same pilot," he thought. "It's the crazy man." This legend he'd heard about even after the battles in Europe had died down. "The pilot, his name is Hunter," he said, surprised he had remembered it after all that time.

The F-16's third pass was the deadliest. As it weaved back and forth, the airplane's guns sprayed the flaming bullets all over the already burning base. The cannon shells seemed to have a mind of their own; everyone of them either hit a man or something flammable, which instantly caught fire.

The troop commander was frozen, unable to move as the six separate streams of cannon shells walked right up to him. His last thoughts seemed to last forever. "This madman is an American," his mind flashed for the last time. "They call him The Wingman."

A second later the commander was caught up in the murderous barrage. He felt the shells enter his chest. Surprisingly, there was no pain. No sensation at all. As he fell backward, his last sight was the bottom of the attacking airplane.

It was red, white, and blue . . .

Hunter flew over the site of the burning Soviet

camp several more times, the adrenalin pumping through his body at breakneck speed. No one fired back at him and his SLQ-32 was silent. Anyone who might have survived the attack was laying low. He cleared the area after one more pass, allowing anyone still breathing to make good their escape.

Within minutes he found a stretch of highway suitably long and straight enough for him to set down on. The search didn't take long; telltale aircraft tire marks up and down the asphalt indicated that aircraft had used this particular juncture of roadway as a landing strip before.

The 16 was down and cooling in five minutes. Trouble was, he had no place to hide it and he didn't have time to worry about it. He pulled out his M-16 and checked its clip. It was full. Then, carrying a canteen full of water and a backpack of special gear, he set out for the Great Pyramid.

Chapter 34

"Sire?"

The man sitting behind the large, black desk did not respond.

"Excuse me, Your Majesty?"

Again no response.

The general gulped. The ship's cabin was dark, the only light coming from a half-dozen flickering candles and the tint of the orange video screen in the corner. Masks, paintings, and other artifacts of the occult were everywhere about the gloomy room. The man behind the desk was dressed completely in black — robe, boots, tunic, and hood. His face was hidden in the dark shadows. Even his hands were covered with black-leather gloves. How did he do it? the general thought, wiping the sweat from his brow. It was 110 degrees outside the ship and easily 15 degrees warmer inside the cabin. Yet the man behind the desk did not appear to be sweating . . .

The general tried a third time. "I'm sorry, Your Highness, but — "

Suddenly the man looked up, his scorched, angry face reflected in the dim light. "What do *you* want!?" he growled at the officer.

"Sire, you asked me to give you a status report at 0800," the general said meekly.

"And?" the man in black asked, barely containing his anger.

"And, it is now 0800, sir—"

"So what are you waiting for?" the man asked in a chilling voice.

Still standing at attention, the general gulped once again and started talking. "Our fleet is now completely underway," he began, trying not to look at the man's horribly scarred face.

"How many goddamned boats?" the man nearly screamed at him.

"Three hundred and twelve, sire," the general answered.

"Were any men left behind?"

The general hesitated for a moment, then answered, "A few, sir—"

"How many?"

Another gulp. "Approximately seven hundred, Your Majesty," the general answered.

There was a long, tense silence.

"Seven hundred men?" the man finally said. "You call that 'a few'?"

"Begging your pardon, Your Highness," the general said. "But seven hundred men out of a total of nine hundred sixty-seven thousand is an exceptionally low dropout rate—"

"I beg *your* pardon, general," the man said sarcastically. "But in this Legion, one malingerer is not acceptable."

"But most of those men are suffering from heat exhaustion, sire," the general replied. "They were among the first troops to load onto our barges. They have been waiting at the dock in the hot sun, with nowhere to move, for four days."

"They are cowards!" the man screamed. "Shoot them all!"

The general started to protest, but thought better of it.

"Anything else, general?" the man in black asked in his strange voice.

The general shifted uneasily. This would be the hard part. "Yes, sire," he began. "We have received a report that the carrier is still operating."

The man's eyes became just slits, anger turning his ashen, scarred face to fire. *What . . . did . . . you . . . say?*

"The carrier, sire," the officer replied, his voice but a whisper. "It is still heading for the Canal."

"Those fools!" the man screamed. "They sent *ten* submarines after it and they didn't sink it?"

"I . . . I'm afraid not, Your Majesty," the general answered. He wanted to get out of the dark room very quickly, yet he felt glued to the spot. "Actually, they lost two submarines."

"Get out!" the man in black roared.

The general was quickly out the door, leaving the man alone. The man rubbed his disfigured face. He knew the scars did not show up when he was "projecting." No, his image was electronically "cleaned up" long before the laser beams flashed it into the sky.

But now, alone, as he ran his fingers over the burns, his face stung. The pain was miniscule compared to the horrible flash of fire that had scarred him that night, back in New York City, when Hawk Hunter had brazenly rescued the beauty named Dominique. He could still see the small miniplane crashing through the window of the top floor of the World Trade Center. The incredible wind that followed sucked out objects and humans alike into the darkness. The fire—caused when the fuel in the miniplane exploded—had leaped across the room and caught him full in the face. Almost as if Nature had intended it that way.

When he woke up that night, under a pile of rubble and dismembered bodies, his face was hot pulp. Everyone else was gone—those not killed had fled. He remembered finding his troops in the Trade Center's lobby looking horrified as they saw his face. There he had collapsed again, a soldier covering his face before loading him onto a waiting helicopter. Those that had seen the act thought he was dead, and later, after he recovered, he did nothing to dispel the rumor. The battles of The Circle War had been long lost by that time.

But his goal had been achieved. America was torn to pieces. The first step of his plan had been fulfilled brilliantly. After all, he couldn't start World War III up again if the Americans were unified.

Those assholes back in Moscow. He needed them for The Circle War, and they were helping in his latest endeavor. But not for much longer. They were already afraid of him—he was one of their kind and they had come to fear him. Soon he would be rid of those old men on the Politburo. Soon *he* would be the Politburo. He would call the shots. He would possess their remaining ICBMs and not screw around with an ounce of nuclear material here and there.

He found his hand inside his pocket, fingering the photograph he always kept there. Against his better judgment, he pulled it out and unfolded it. It was a photo of Dominique. She was completely naked. He had taken it a long time ago, after filling her with drugs. She was beautiful. Now she was gone—the only thing he had really lost. He didn't love her—he just wanted to possess her.

If only . . .

He shook off the thoughts and took his hands away from his face. "Revenge will be mine, Hunter," he whispered. He reached for a bottle on his desk and poured out a handful of painkillers. Swallowing them one at a time, he began to laugh uncontrollably. "The whole world will pay!"

As the pills started to take affect, he began ranting to himself again. "These crazy Englishmen? *Towing* an aircraft carrier? They are *fools* who have been out in the sun too long! There are a million of us!"

He looked at the photo again.

"There is only one hero left in this world, my dear!" he screamed. "And if millions of people have to burn and die for everyone else to realize it, so be it!

"You might have your precious fly-boy, Hunter. But how many men can ignite a world war?"

They didn't call him Lucifer for nothing . . .

Chapter 35

It was cold inside the pyramid. The walls had a strange, clammy feel to them, the opposite of what Hunter had expected from a structure standing in the middle of the desert.

He had no trouble finding the entrance to the massive Cheops—the Russians had carved a large door out on one side of the base. Trudging up to the doorway, Hunter came upon a trove of abandoned Soviet equipment scattered about in front of it. He found AK-47s, grenade launchers, mortars, and even a few SA-7 shoulder-launched SAMs. There was no one around. Just as he had hoped, all of the Soviet troops had fled.

"Well," he thought, taking the knapsack off his back, "time to get dressed."

Ten minutes later he was inside the pyramid, his powerful searchlight in one hand, a small Geiger counter in the other. He found walking in the bulky antiradiation gear to be torturous, especially in the cramped passageways. The suit—he looked more like a beekeeper than anything else—had been found along with the Geiger counter in a locker on the *Saratoga*. Obviously, it hadn't been designed with comfort in mind.

"Who the hell built this place?" Hunter muttered to himself as he moved along the pyramid's dark tunnels.

The passageways ran through the structure at the oddest angles, none of them conducive to walking normally. When he first entered the structure, he was walking downward. Now he was climbing. He held the Geiger counter out in front of him, but so far he had yet to get so much as a peep out of it.

After what seemed like an endless ascent, he finally reached what he knew was the Grand Gallery—a relatively spacious passageway that was thankfully equipped with a stairway installed by archeologists years before. It was at the top of these stairs that the Geiger counter started beeping.

By directing the microphone-like device, Hunter was able to find the source of the beeping. He climbed down into a small room off the Grand Chamber and scanned the walls with the radiation meter. He got nothing but the monotone beeping. But as soon as he pointed the device to the floor, it started buzzing like crazy.

There was a dilapidated trap door at the far end of the chamber. With much effort, Hunter was able to squeeze down through it, dropping several feet to the dusty floor. As soon as he adjusted both his light and helmet, he saw he was in a room quite different from the polished walls of the pyramid's passageways.

He knew at once it was a ritual chamber. Its walls were covered with ancient Egyptian paintings and writings—many of them at first glance apparently

316

relating to burial ceremonies. But Hunter knew this to be misleading — despite popular belief, no one had ever conclusively proved the pyramids were built as burial chambers for the Pharaohs.

At the center of the chamber was a large, tomb-like structure. Again, he knew this was not as it appeared to be. The box, which looked to be carved from a single block of alabaster, didn't contain a mummy. Similar empty, coffin-like coffers had been found all over Egypt.

However, even if no body was in the box, something else was. It was highly radioactive — Hunter's Geiger counter was buzzing so loudly it hurt his ears, despite the bulky anti-radiation helmet.

"This must be the place," he thought.

He approached the box cautiously. Soon he was close enough to peer in. Sure enough, sitting in the middle of a bed of straw was a metal box. An instantly recognizable radiation symbol — like those that once marked the entrance to 1960s bomb shelters — was emblazoned on its top.

"Thank you, Mr. Cheops," Hunter said to himself, smiling. "Wherever you are . . ."

Less than 100 miles away and to the northeast, a half-dozen yachts sailed into the mouth of the Suez Canal. At the controls of the first boat — a sixty-five-foot cruise beauty — was Commodore Antonio Vanaria. The Commodore was not wearing his usual Napoleonic-style uniform. He had replaced the colorful garb with a black frock and a Roman collar. For this mission, the Commodore — like his five lieutenants on the other boats — was disguised as a man of the cloth. To add to the illusion, each boat carried two of the call girls, dressed in nun's habits hastily sewn from dyed bedsheets.

Each yacht also carried a large crucifix on its bow, flags and flowers adorning its base. Large, hastily painted cloth signs hung from the boats' sides, extolling the one thing the Mideast — like the entire globe — had not experienced in a while: "Peace."

The yachts had sailed about fifteen miles into the Canal when they were intercepted by the three gunboats.

"Everyone below decks," the Commodore had called out after first sighting the three boats heading for him. "Except the women. Keep it quiet down there. Not a word."

The patrol boats were of South African manufacture. Large and swift-looking, they carried powerful rocket launchers and .60-caliber machine guns. As the first one pulled alongside the Commodore's lead boat, he saw the decks were crowded with Arab soldiers, armed with Soviet-made AK-47 assault rifles. Each man was wearing a distinctive white uniform, with gaudy gold trim, and a Soviet-style helmet. Each had a patch on his left arm: a triangle containing a field of red and a design of two interlocking Arabic letters.

The Commodore recognized the emblem immediately. It was the coat of arms for Lucifer's Legion.

"At last," the Commodore thought, fingering the .357 Magnum he had hidden in his smock. "No more dealing with surrogates and stand-ins. Now we meet the Devil's men themselves."

"Prepare to be boarded," the Caucasian officer on the patrol boat called over to the Commodore in a heavily accented English. The Commodore knew that the man, like the patrol boat, came from South Africa.

The Commodore had cut all his engines at this

point and, standing on the deck with the two nuns, raised his hand in a sign of peace. He called out, "You may board my ship, but leave your weapons behind. This is an instrument of peace."

The patrol boat commander ignored the Commodore's request and six of his men jumped onto the yacht, their AK-47s at the ready. Next the commander himself came aboard.

"You are in a restricted military zone," he said to the Commodore. "We could have sunk you on sight."

"We are on a mission of peace, sir," the Commodore told him with a straight face. "The sisters and I are sailing to the south to meet with this man Lucifer, to urge him not to make war."

The patrol commander laughed. Meanwhile, his other two boats had taken up positions on either side of the small fleet of yachts. Their guns were manned and ready.

"I don't think you can change his mind," the patrol boat commander told the Italian.

"With prayer, my son, all things are possible," the Commodore intoned. "Please, let us through. We have traveled the entire Mediterranean to come to this place. We have taken up collections all along the way from people who want peace."

"Collections?" the patrol boat commander asked.

"Yes, sir," the Commodore answered. "For we heard that there are tributes to be paid—perhaps to someone like yourself—to pass through here, sir. A tariff of free passage, so to speak."

In other words, a bribe.

The Commodore motioned to one of the "nuns," who came forward with a small burlap bag. "Do we turn these collections over to you, sir?"

The patrol boat commander looked inside the

bag, saw it was filled with gold, and didn't hesitate. "Yes, that is true," he said. "You may give me such a payment."

At the same time he motioned all his soldiers back onto the patrol boat, with a look that said: this never happened.

"Thank you, my son," the Commodore said. "You have done your part for peace today. Now, with your kind permission, sir, we shall continue our voyage."

The commander laughed again. "Go right ahead, padre," he said, stepping back onto his boat. "But be careful of the mines."

Now the Commodore laughed. "Thank you, kind sir!"

The three gunboats pulled away and were soon gone. Below the decks of the six yachts, there was a collective sigh of relief. For the members of the Maltese underwater demo team and Australian Special Forces hiding in the yachts, it had been a brief but dangerous encounter.

The radio in the *Saratoga*'s CIC suddenly sprang to life.

"Delta-Tango-Maxwell," the static-filled voice announced. "Package retrieved. Need pickup. Over."

That was the entire message. Still Heath, who had heard it, smiled broadly. He twirled his huge red mustache and clapped his hands.

"Sparky," he called to the CIC radioman. "Please call over to Olson's flagship and give him the go code."

As the sailor instantly started sending the prearranged signal, Heath turned to Yaz and gave him the thumbs-up sign. There were smiles everywhere in the CIC. Even the BBC video crew, who were capturing

320

the event on film, had to smile.

"I must go tell Sir Neil the good news," Heath said to Yaz, shaking his head in admiration. "If Hunter pulls this one off, I'm going to have Sir Neil recommend him for the Victoria Cross . . ."

The S-3A roared off the deck of the carrier and climbed. E.J. Russell, the Australian mercenary pilot, was at the controls, and one of the Tornado pilots—a Scotsman known as "Gump"—was sitting in as the navigator-photo man.

The big jet reached 6500 feet and did a quick 360-turn before heading south. The maneuver was necessary to test the S-A3's sophisticated cameras. Below them sat the stationary *Saratoga*, Olson's frigates and ninety-odd boats of the Freedom Navy surrounding it like covered wagons drawn into a circle. Above them, four Jaguars circled in slow patterns, each pilot on the lookout for airborne threats. Closer to the surface, a half-dozen of Olson's helicopters buzzed around the collection of ships, their sensitive electronic devices listening for the distinctive sounds of approaching enemy submarines.

"Camera and lens all check out," Gump reported to E.J.

"Okay," the pilot said, increasing the jet's speed to 350 knots. "Let's go get us some pictures of submarines."

Just twenty minutes before, another flight had taken off from the *Saratoga*. Two Harrier jump-jets had lifted off and, linked up with two of Olson's choppers, had headed south. One of the choppers contained twelve members of an elite Moroccan strike team. They were armed to the teeth. Everyone inside the other copter was wearing antiradiation suits similar to the one Hunter had carried with him. These men were all Yaz's guys, former crew members from the USS *Albany*. Hanging from a net underneath their chopper was a crate.

Inside the crate was a specially lead-lined box.

Hunter had finished the last of his canteen's water when his head started buzzing.

"At last," he said aloud. Friendly aircraft were approaching. He knew it — he could feel it in his bones. He ran outside the entrance to the pyramid just in time to see the two Harriers appear out over the northern horizon. They were intentionally moving slow, this to enable the two frigate choppers to keep pace. Sure enough, appearing out of a large white cloud came the two specks he knew were the copters.

Now, as the first chopper, the one carrying the Moroccan troops, came in for a landing next to the pyramid, the two Harriers immediately started to circle the structure, keeping an eye out for any unwanted company. The troop-carrying copter touched down, and immediately the crack Moroccan troops piled out. With enviable precision, they double-timed it to preassigned positions around the pyramid's base, dodging the hot and decaying bodies of the Soviet guards killed in Hunter's one-man air raid.

Hunter greeted the Moroccan commander and the man returned the gesture with the special "W-for-Wingman" hand sign. Hunter then served as the landing officer for the second chopper. Its pilot deftly lowered the net containing the crate so it hit the ground with no more than a slight bump. The pilot then disengaged the net and landed the chopper nearby. Instantly, six men, all wearing antiradiation suits, emerged from the chopper and walked toward Hunter.

The squad leader, a black man named Marvin, came up to Hunter.

"Greetings, major," he said, with a smile Hunter could see through the visor of the man's radiation suit. "Looks like we missed the fun." He was looking around at the still-burning remains of the Soviet camp.

"Oh no, Marvin," Hunter said. "For you guys, the fun is about to begin."

He then quickly gave the man instructions as to the location of the chamber containing the metal box.

"It's going to be cramped, crowded, and complicated," Hunter said in conclusion. "I will personally give you a case of Sir Neil's homemade scotch if you guys can get the box out of there in less than twenty minutes."

Again, Marvin smiled. "Get some ice cubes, major," he said. "We'll be out in twenty minutes."

Hunter was back to his F-16, up, and flying in fifteen minutes. He joined the two Harriers in circling the Great Pyramid, keeping an eye out for enemy aircraft.

He had just heard from one of the chopper pilots that Marvin's team was coming out when he felt a chill in his bones. *Enemy aircraft were approaching.*

He immediately hit his radio button. "Harriers, this is Hunter," he said quickly. "We're going to have company soon. Arm up!"

The Harrier pilots acknowledged his message. Both were wondering the same thing: how the hell did Hunter do it? Neither of their radars indicated anything in their area, yet they knew Hunter didn't give such instructions lightly. Instantly, both pilots started arming their Sidewinder missiles.

Hunter began arming his own missiles, at the same time giving his nose-cannon Six Pack a very brief test burst. He was low on ammo for the guns, having used a quantity ripping up the Soviet encampment. But his 16 was still bulging with the weight of the Sidewinders.

He closed his eyes and let his senses go to work.

"Choppers," Hunter said to himself. "A lot of choppers . . ."

He radioed the frigate chopper pilots and told them that enemy helicopters were approaching and that he needed a status report on the recovery operation.

One of the pilots, a Norseman named Erik, returned the call.

"They've got the 'valuable' inside their lead-lined box," he told Hunter. "It's at the entrance of the pyramid now. Next they have to crate it and then put it in the net. At that time I'll make the pickup."

"We don't have time," Hunter said, eyeing for the first time the blips on his radar screen which confirmed his extraordinary senses. He wasn't surprised they were coming from the southeast. "Tell Marv and his guys to take cover in the pyramid. The Moroccans should set up a defense line just inside the opening."

"Roger, major," Erik radioed back. "What should we do, sir?"

"What's your weapons status?" Hunter asked, his eye scanning the horizon for the approaching enemy force.

"The troop carrier is unarmed," Erik reported.

"But I've got two TOWs and a cranky .30-caliber machine gun on my door."

"Okay," Hunter said. "Grab one of Marv's guys and tell him he's now a waist gunner. Get airborne, then you and the troop carrier get the hell out of the area. We don't want to lose either of you."

"Aye, aye, major," Erik radioed back.

Hunter changed frequencies. "Harriers One and Two," he called. "Do you have radar lock?"

"Radar lock confirmed," both pilots answered almost simultaneously.

"Okay," Hunter said. "Visual will be in about twenty seconds. I count about thirty choppers. Some of them are gunships, probably Hinds and maybe even a couple Havocs. Others might be carrying troops. They might even be dispatched from Lucifer's fleet ships. I'm sure they are coming to investigate what the hell happened to their comrades."

"I've got a visual, major!" one of the Harrier pilots called out.

Hunter looked to the southeast just in time to see the thirty specks riding out of the clouds.

"Just as I thought," he called to the Harriers. "Hind gunships escorting troop carriers. Okay, let's meet them halfway. Remember, those Hinds are bad news with their nose cannons, and the Havocs might be outfitted with Aphid air-to-air missiles."

With that, the two Harriers and the F-16 formed up into a triangle pattern and streaked toward the incoming chopper force. Hunter put his hand to his left breast pocket as he was wont to do before going into battle. The reassuring folds of the American flag and Dominique's photo were still there.

The Commodore's three yachts were thirty miles

325

into the Canal when they spotted their first Soviet mines . . .

They had been moving very slowly down the waterway after encountering the gunboats. Just twenty minutes before, they had seen a large force of helicopters — Russian helicopters — pass right over them. They were heading towards either Cairo or Giza, but they didn't pay any mind to the yachts.

"Screw you, you bastards!" the Commodore had yelled up at them, all the while waving at the aircraft as if he were a friendly native.

Once the Commodore was certain no one could see them, he had put six of the UDT swimmers into the water. They were acting as point men — scanning the waters ahead of the yachts, their eyes peeled for mines.

Now they had found what they were looking for.

"How many?" the Commodore asked the leader of the UDT swimmers as he surfaced next to the lead yacht.

"At least one hundred," the frogman answered. "More than enough for our purposes."

"Deo gratias!" the Commodore said with a slap of his side. "But can you disarm them quickly?"

"It will take the rest of my men and some Aussies in two rubber boats," the diver said. "But then we are talking about an hour's work."

"Then go to it!" the Commodore said excitedly. "I will get your other men in the water as well as the Aussies."

The man slid beneath the surface once again, leaving a trail of air bubbles breaking the surface.

The Commodore checked his watch. It was almost 0900. He had just an hour to fulfill this first part of his mission. Then he would have to get back out of the Canal and start phase two.

He raised his eyes toward heaven. They had been lucky so far. "Please, Father," he whispered. "Remember us today . . ."

The S-A3 continued to circle the port of Alexandria, its elaborate cameras clicking away.

"We've got enough film for three more passes," Gump reported to the pilot, E.J.

"Okay," the Aussie pilot said. "Let's drop down a hair, mate, and try for some closeups."

The recon airplane had been flying way up — at nearly 70,000 feet — for nearly a half hour. Now it slowly slipped down and leveled off at 62,000.

Their target was the Soviet sub base installed at the Egyptian base. Through the jet's long-range telescopic camera lens, Gump had counted at least thirty subs of all sizes and configurations, docked out in the open in the port.

The city of Alexandria itself had been long ago abandoned — its ordinary citizens had either sailed or trekked across to Algeria months before. The richer ones had flown out. They were the first of the calvacade that had descended on Casablanca airport, avoiding the war they knew was to come. Just when the Russians had moved in was anyone's guess. But the subs posed a significant threat not only to the *Saratoga* flotilla, but also to the ships of The Modern Knights — should they ever arrive.

But the problem was, the men of the *Saratoga* couldn't afford a battle with the Soviet subs right now. They had to marshal all the energy and reserves for the battle that lay ahead in the Canal.

That's why these photos of Alexandria were so important.

Five minutes into the swirling air battle, Hunter had personally shot down five helicopters. The Harriers had accounted for three more each. But, as the allied pilots were soon to find out, this would be a numbers game. Despite their victories, there were still nineteen enemy choppers to contend with.

Hunter had decided to concentrate on the troop-carrying Mi-14 Haze-A helicopters first. He methodically pumped four Sidewinders into their loose formation, downing three of them and causing a half-dozen of their comrades to quickly execute 180-degree turns and head off in the direction from which they had come. That's when Hunter went after the Hind gunships that had pressed on, trying to get to the pyramid.

Meanwhile the Brits were facing off against the potentially troublesome Havocs . . .

The small choppers, about the size of a US AH-64 Apache attack copter, were quick, maneuverable, and outfitted with the Aphid missile—a Soviet equivalent to the Sidewinder. If there was a helicopter in the world that could give most jet fighters a run for their money, it was the Mi-28 Havoc.

But, like the F-16, the Harriers were not ordinary jet fighters . . .

On first confronting the Havoc, the two jets immediately went into their "vectoring" or hover mode. The two Havocs did the same. For a moment it looked like an Old West gunfight was shaping up—the two Havocs in the black hats squaring off against the two Harriers in the white hats.

The standoff lasted almost a minute—an eternity in the middle of a battle. But then it was the Havocs that blinked first. One of their pilots let off a short burst of cannon fire. The two Harriers—both pilots highly trained and in sync with each other — instantly lowered their airplanes to avoid the volley. In doing so, they were able to get cannon shots of their own at the unprotected belly of the choppers. One Havoc took a full Harrier burst on its tail. The punctures vibrated the rear of the enemy aircraft so much, the tail rotor snapped off in an instant of smoke and flame. Scratch one Havoc . . .

Meanwhile the other Havoc had climbed, banked, and then turned towards the hovering British fighters, firing two Aphids in rapid succession, hoping the missiles would home in on the VTOL jet exhaust. No such luck. This time, the Harrier pilots simple jumped up and out of the way of the deadly rockets. Then, quickly, both jets turned and fired long, accurate volleys at the helicopter. When the smoke cleared, there was nothing left of the Russian chopper but a rapidly falling cloud of burning metal cinders.

Now the games were over. No more face-offs. The Harriers put the thrusts back on forward and tore into the remaining choppers.

Meanwhile, Hunter was systematically battling the Hind gunships. He had lowered his flaps and his landing gear to slow down enough to fire on the copters with his Sidewinders. Many of the remaining troop-carrying choppers, after seeing the F-16 twist and turn about their loose formation, opted to land and disgorge their troops. This tactic put the friendly troops taking cover inside the pyramid in imminent danger.

The Soviet reinforcements started moving towards the Cheops monument, already drawing fire from the outnumbered Moroccans. Hunter dove in and strafed the Soviets, expending the last of his cannon ammo in three passes. The action served to delay the

Russian advance—but not by much, he knew. He had to call in the Harriers to strafe the advancing troops.

While this was happening, the surviving Soviet Hinds began a curious tactic: the copters circled the pyramid in both directions, firing down on the troops hiding near the entrance. Again, it looked like a scene from the Old West—this time, the old Indians-surrounding-the-wagons ploy. One Harrier, seeing the situation, backed off from the strafing operation, climbed, then screeched down out of the clouds and stationed itself, in a hovering mode, right over the entrance.

"Okay, I've had enough of this bullshit," Hunter said. He put the F-16 into the same orbit as half the circling choppers and started pumping out Sidewinders. The missiles had a liking for the hot exhausts spewing out of the choppers' main rotor engines. First one, then two Hinds went down. Then another. And another.

The other Harrier, having chopped up the Soviet ground troops, joined him in the tactic. Soon the sky was filled with streaking Sidewinders and long, fiery contrails. Hunter could only imagine that the Soviet in charge of the copter attack was pressing his pilots to continue the battle at all costs. As a result, the fighters had a turkey shoot. After seven copters were finally downed in the circling battle, the survivors—barely five of them—finally broke off and fled.

"That was the balmiest goddamned battle I've ever been in!" one of the Harrier pilots radioed.

"Same here," Hunter echoed. He saw it as a portent of things to come.

Now the recovery operation could proceed. The two frigate copters reappeared and, as the Moroccans climbed aboard the troop carrier, Marv and his men, still dressed in their antirad suits, loaded the precious crate into the chopper net. His men then scrambled aboard the copter, which took off and made a successful grab of the net. Marv jumped on the troop carrier for the ride back. The two Harriers fell in behind the copters and, with Hunter's F-16 in the lead, the force headed north, out over the sea, and toward the *Saratoga*.

It had been an exciting morning . . .

Chapter 36

The S-A3 spy plane—its mission high above the port of Alexandria complete—landed on the *Saratoga* right after Hunter's F-16. Once the deck was cleared, the two Harriers and the frigate choppers came in, Yaz's men carefully handling the crate containing the radioactive material found in the Cheops pyramid.

Ten minutes later, Yaz, Marv, and Hunter were standing in the "Clean Room" of the *Saratoga*, dressed in antirad suits. Before them was a huge, thick, plate-glass window which looked in on another smaller room. This "Critical Room" was entirely surrounded by lead—a foot thick in some places. It was a place where most nuclear materials could be handled safely. This was where the metal container had been placed.

Using long, robot-like appendages controlled from the safe side of the window, Yaz managed to open the metal casing. Inside were as many as two dozen short tubes, each one sealed at both ends with a large dob of lead.

"This is interesting," Yaz said as he manipulated the left hand of robotic fingers to pick up one of the tubes. "This lead-end-sealing procedure. I've seen it used for UB-40 uranium. If this were plutonium, I would guess the entire tube would be covered in lead."

"How can you find out what's inside?" Hunter asked.

"There's really only one way — open 'em up," Yaz answered as he began using the right metal arm to carefully scrape off the lead end-seal of one of the tubes. "It will take me a few minutes to get all this lead off, though."

So here it was, Hunter thought, looking at the tubes. "The valuable" the Soviets were guarding for Lucifer. Had they themselves been tricked? Thinking the radioactive stuff could be made into bombs? Or was it he and Yaz that had fallen for a ploy? Could the tubes contain some ultra-high radioactive substance that would instantly contaminate the ship despite protections like the Clean Room and the Critical Room?

Or did the tubes contain the answer to all their prayers?

"We'll know in a few moments," Yaz said as he skillfully worked the lead off the end of the tube.

A lot rested on those few moments. Hunter knew it. Yaz and Marv knew it, everyone on the ship and in the fleet knew it. They were dead in the water. Just 150 miles from their goal. After the long, arduous push-pull journey, the battles, the mind games of Lucifer, the wounding of the valiant Sir Neil, the shows of support from people along the way, the frustration of waiting for The Modern Knights. And now all that could change. Change with the simple identification of the atomic structure of whatever the hell was in those tubes.

Hunter closed his eyes. *Dare he evoke the spirits*

just one more time?

"Okay," Yaz said, completing the operation. "The seal is off. I'm going to put the tube down and shake it a little. Whatever pops out, we'll have our answer. Here we go."

Hunter and Marv watched in silence as the robot arm lowered the tube to the table. Then Yaz swung the tube around to the end and deftly nudged it two times. Nothing came out. He hit it two more times. Still nothing.

"Christ," he swore. "I hope it's not plutonium sealed in some kind of plastic or glass. If it is, it will melt within minutes of the air hitting it."

He nudged it again. Then twice more. Still absolutely nothing.

"Screw it," Yaz said as he clamped his fingers back around the tube. He picked it up and started to shake it.

Suddenly something dropped out of its end . . .

Marv was the first to cry out. *"Hallelujah!"*

"Yeah!" Yaz joined him.

Hunter looked at the small object. It looked like a pellet. Although he didn't have the trained eyes of Marv and Yaz, he caught on quickly as to what the pellet was.

"It's uranium, isn't it?" he asked, a grin spreading across his face. "UB-40?"

"It sure looks that way," Yaz said, pushing a few buttons on the control panel in front of him. It was a device that determined the origin and strength of radioactive elements. A few seconds passed, then lights blinked, meters started registering, and, finally, a buzzer went off.

Both Yaz and Marv started frantically reading the meters and taking notes. A brief orgy of calculations followed, then the two men looked at each other and smiled. Then they slapped each other with high fives. Then they hugged.

"Oh *baby!*" Yaz proclaimed. "It's enriched UB-40 . . ."

"And that means . . ." Hunter said, prodding him.

"And that means we put it into the carrier's reactor," Yaz said, not trying to contain his excitement, "and we'll be at full power. Engines, propulsion, electrical systems, weapons. Everything will work."

Hunter felt an excitement build up inside him. Then he asked the critical question: "How long?"

Yaz thought for a moment. "Normally, it would take a week to ten days," he said. "With my guys and some help—twenty-four hours."

"Solid," Hunter said, giving him the double thumbs-up sign. "Let's get to work . . ."

The Commodore looked through the binoculars and swore. *"Son of a bitch!"*

Approaching his three yachts was a single gunboat. It was still a mile away, but The Commodore knew it was the same patrol boat that had stopped them earlier in the Canal. Perhaps the South African captain would try to extract another bribe from him. Perhaps worse.

The gunship was soon alongside the Commodore's yacht. The Commodore struggled to tighten up his Roman collar as three soldiers jumped on board. The gunboat captain was the next to come across.

"Well, my good holy man," the captain said sarcastically. "Have you decided no one wants his soul saved today?"

"Our prayers are with the people in this area," the

Commodore said, feigning his best angelic voice. "The power of prayer can save men's souls."

The captain laughed. He appeared to be drunk. His soldiers—the three on the yacht's deck and six more waiting on the gunboat—seemed tense.

"And how about the souls of women?" the captain asked, looking past the Commodore at one of the "nuns" on the bridge. "Do you have a means for saving them too?"

The Commodore knew the patrol boat captain wanted more than money this time.

"How many of the good sisters do you have on your boats, holy man?"

The Commodore didn't have a chance to answer.

"Search the boats!" the gunboat captain said, walking right up to the Commodore. "Search them all!"

Well, we're lucky, the Commodore thought. At least he has only one boat this time.

The Commodore fired the .357 Magnum right through his smock. The bullet tore a hole so wide in the gunboat captain's chest, the Commodore actually saw a speck of daylight coming from the exit hole in the man's back. The captain looked at the Commodore in a horrified, quizzical way, before falling forward and hitting the deck with huge thud.

In an instant, Australian Special Forces troopers on the Commodore's yacht as well as the other two boats were up and firing at the gunboat soldiers. They were all cut down in a matter of seconds, the Aussies being careful not to let stray bullets hit the hold of the Commodore's boat.

When the smoke cleared, a strange silence settled over the scene. One of the Maltese UDT men appeared on the deck and spoke to the Commodore. "Close one, sir," he said.

The Commodore kicked aside the dead captain's body, spitting on it for emphasis. "Bastards," he said, then he laughed. "Would he have gotten a surprise if he'd searched our boats!"

The UDT man nodded and returned to his work below the deck, cleaning seaweed and debris from the 100 retrieved Soviet mines.

The sailors on the bridge of the battleship snapped to attention as soon as they saw the black-cloaked figure and his entourage of guards heading down the walkway toward them.

Two red-uniformed Storm Troopers roughly opened the bridge's door and burst inside, eyeing the sailors with contempt. "If they treat their allies like this," one sailor, a Brazilian mercenary, thought, "how do they treat their enemies?"

A second later, Lucifer strolled in, dressed entirely in the heavy black garments, his thin face oozing pain from the burned-in scars. He too viewed the sailors disdain. He immediately sought out the watch commander, an Austrian lieutenant.

"What is our position?" Lucifer demanded.

The lieutenant squared his shoulders and began: "We are at thirty degrees latitude and—"

"No! You fool!" Lucifer raged. "Where are we in relation to the Canal? How long until we enter it?"

"That's very hard to say, sir," the man stammered. "We are about forty miles south of the southern entrance of the Canal. But as to when we'll enter it depends on the currents we'll encounter."

Lucifer's eyes became very thin. "And what about the ships in front of us? Are there not dozens of ships that have already encountered these currents?"

"Yes, sir . . ." the lieutenant replied. "I guess so,

sir . . ."

Lucifer's scarred face became a deeper shade of red. "Then why don't you know when we will enter the Canal? Is it not the most important part of our mission? Is it not what we've been training for? Planning for?"

"Yes, sir . . ."

Lucifer turned to one of his Storm Troopers. "Shoot him," he said calmly.

The other sailors all forgot they were at attention and looked at Lucifer, not quite believing what he had said. Dutifully, the guard pulled his pistol, walked up to the terrified lieutenant, put it beside his head, and pulled the trigger. Half the man's skull flew across the room, followed by a spray of blood. The man fell to the floor. Without a moment's hesitation, two troopers picked up the still-twitching body, walked out the door, and nonchalantly threw it overboard.

"Now," Lucifer said, walking by the other trembling sailors. "This is my flagship. It is the flagship of the greatest fleet ever assembled. How can we light the world on fire if the flagship of this fleet is under the command of a man who cannot answer a simple question?"

A deadly silence fell upon the bridge.

"You are all well-paid," Lucifer began again. "Well-paid and cared for by me. To fight for me. To die for me. You have the honor of being part of the greatest military force the world has known since the Big Battles."

Lucifer's face was getting redder by the moment. He was shouting now, in his irritating whiny voice.

"There are almost *one million* men in this army!" he screamed. "And when I ask any one of them a question, they'd better know the answer."

No one on the bridge dared breathe. Even Lucifer's bodyguards were tense, afraid he might ask one of *them* a fateful question.

"Now," Lucifer said in a voice barely above whisper. "Who is next in command?"

A young North Vietnamese ensign stepped forward. "I am, sir!"

Lucifer looked him over. "All right," he said. "When will we enter the Canal?"

The ensign hesitated one second, then cried out: "In approximately two hours, sir. Shortly after sunset, sir!"

Lucifer looked at him, then at the other sailors, and smiled.

"Now," he said. "That's better . . ."

Then he turned and walked out, unknowingly dragging his long cloak through the pool of blood left on the bridge's floor.

Chapter 37

"Well, that's the best news I've heard in ages!" Sir Neil said, clapping his hands and trying to sit up in his bed. Clara, ever at his side, helped him.

"Yaz said they'll get the reactor to go hot any minute now," Hunter said, continuing to explain the turn of events to Sir Neil. "Then we'll start seeing real electricity. Those generators we've been using are about to burst at the seams. Now we'll be able to power up all the radios, the on-board weapons. Everything."

"Aye, but when can we get underway, Hunter?" the Englishman asked.

"Yaz has a team of propulsion guys on it right now," Hunter replied. "That's the first priority, of course. We'll know more as the night goes on."

"How about the Commodore?"

Hunter smiled and shook his head. "He's a trip," he said. "He fulfilled his mission just as he planned. Docked up to one of the frigates about an hour ago. He's got more than a hundred Russian mines in his hold. Just like he said he would."

"Good Lord, the man is intrepid! Isn't he?" Sir Neil was clearly delighted. However, he quickly turned serious. "Those bloody Modern Knights. Where the hell are they!? We come back from the dead and they're probably still lollygagging around."

"Heath told the Italian communications guys to turn one of their antennas west for a few minutes each hour," Hunter said. "I know the Knights would never send us an open radio message, but our gear on board might be powerful enough to pick up their ship-to-ship communications. At least we'll get a fix on where they are."

"Good plan," Sir Neil said, calming down a bit. Just as he spoke, the lights in his cabin suddenly tripled in intensity. It was as good an indication as any that Yaz's guys had the reactor up and working.

"Lights!" Sir Neil cried out. "Real lights! No more dim bulbs!"

Hunter nodded. For the first time he felt like he was sailing on a real ship.

The next day passed slowly but quietly.

Hunter had six aircraft in the air at all times, providing the carrier fleet with an air cap as well as serving as an early warning system for any approaching Soviet subs.

Hunter could only describe the mood on board the carrier itself as one of "serious jubilation." Serious in that the air crews and the support people, plus the allied mercenaries, went about the duty of preparing for war. But there was jubilation too, every time some previously useless device or machine clicked back on thanks to the revived currents of electricity running through the ship. Hunter was thankful the carrier's catapults were finally working as they should. Launching the half-dozen aircraft earlier in the day had taken one-tenth the time of previous launches.

"The whole goddamn ship feels alive!" Hunter told Emma that morning.

But the real celebration came about mid-afternoon. This was when Yaz's men had boiled up enough steam using the reactor to open the valve which led to the *Saratoga*'s powerful propulsion turbines. Those aboard felt a sudden, almost violent jolt. Then all were aware of a very strange sensation. They were moving. Evenly. Smoothly. No more push. No more pull.

A spontaneous cheer went up all over the ship. Crewmen on the ships nearby, all unaccustomed to seeing the *Saratoga* move under its own power, joined in with applause. Hunter happened to be on the bridge at the time and watched in awe as all the multi-colored lights on all the control panels blinked on. Heath and O'Brien were also there to witness the display.

"Good God," Heath yelled. "They've actually done it!"

"I never thought I'd see the day . . ." O'Brien said, speechless for probably the first time in his life.

"We couldn't have gotten this far without you," Hunter told the Irishman.

"Hear, hear!" Heath echoed, shaking hands with the tugboat skipper. "In fact, on special orders from Sir Neil, I am now naming you the commander of the *Saratoga*."

As those sailors present on the bridge gave him a round of applause, O'Brien pointed to himself, genuinely surprised, and asked, "Me? Why me?"

"It's just logical," Heath told him. "Of us all, only Olson, the Commodore, and yourself are real sea captains. I'm sure you'll agree they've got their hands full right now. Yaz's job has now increased tenfold since he's got the ship running. So, Captain O'Brien, that leaves you in command."

The BBC crew was on hand, of course, to record the historic moment. As the leader of the video crew came forward, microphone in hand, to interview O'Brien, the old tug man looked at Hunter. But the pilot only smiled and said, "It's all yours, Skip . . ."

That night, as the *Saratoga* was approaching the Canal at a speed of fifteen knots, two frigates pulled out ahead of the flotilla and steered due south. On board was the Commodore, the UDT team, and a squad of Spanish Rocketeers. One of the frigates carried a Harrier, just in case the pair of ships was spotted from the air.

The other frigate was running on a skeleton crew. All of its armament had been stripped off, as had anything of value not bolted down. In the frigate's cargo hold were the 100 Soviet mines.

The two ships plowed silently through the night waters traveling the sixty-five miles to a point just a mile off the entrance to Alexandria, Egypt. It was two in the morning when they arrived. Quickly, quietly, the UDT frogmen slipped into the calm seas and went about the task of planting the Soviet mines in strategic, predetermined places.

Later on they would report that, while the mine-laying operation was going on, they had observed the holographic face of Lucifer projected off in the distant eastern sky.

Hunter spent most of the night in the CIC, sitting with Heath, a Moroccan translator, and Giuseppe, the head of the Italian communications group, listening to the multitude of radio broadcasts coming from Lucifer's fleet.

The carrier flotilla had lost time crossing the Med. The battles, the storm, the loss of the tugboats, and other distractions had put them days behind Sir Neil's original schedule. For Hunter, it was a miracle they had made it at all, but the delay had presented some problems.

Originally Sir Neil had intended to sail the carrier through the Canal and plant it — and the soldiers sailing with it — at the northern entrance, thus denying the entire gateway to the Med to Lucifer's ships. But, as the intercepted communications indicated, the first elements of Lucifer's fleet had already entered the Canal. And, in fact, gunboats allied with the madman had been patrolling the Canal for days.

Now it looked as if a mid-Canal confrontation were imminent.

"It's going to be tight," Hunter told Giuseppe and Heath as they moved markers around the ship's plotting map. "The Canal is only about three hundred feet across. That's wide enough to accommodate two major ships going in opposite directions and that's about it."

"We are lucky that the Egyptian Navy dredged the blasted thing before the Big War," Heath said. "Otherwise, we might have scrapped the bottom."

"We still won't have much room to maneuver, if any," Hunter said.

"Well, I imagine if we were still using the bloody tugs!" Heath said. "I guess our best bet is to crank it out, get to a good position in the middle of the Canal, disperse the troops, and launch an air strike immediately."

"I agree," Hunter said, studying the map. "We can tie up a lot of his ships if we just sink a few early, thereby sealing off the Canal midway, at least temporarily. I'm sure his Soviet mine-laying group is equipped with a UDT. They can clear one sunken ship in about six hours. But if we ice six or seven ships, those guys are going to get real tired real quick."

"Look here on the map," Heath said, directing a pointer to an area about halfway down the Canal's 100-mile length. "Here's the only place where the Moroccans would have some kind of cover to meet Lucifer's troops — granting that, if we sink his ships, he's going to throw his foot soldiers off the transports and make them walk."

The group was silent for a time, until Heath spoke up again.

"The question is," he said, "can we get to that point before Lucifer does?"

Hunter finally retired about three in the morning. Tomorrow would be a busy day, he knew, and even three hours' sleep would help.

He found Emma as he always did: curled up naked on his bunk as a candle flickered away on the bed table. He took off his boots, zipped down his flight suit, and crawled in next to her. She immediately drew herself up close to him, one of her small delicate breasts falling right into his hand. He squeezed it softly. Then he looked at her sweet face. *She's so much like a young Dominique,* he thought.

Right away his thoughts flashed over the Mediterranean, across the Atlantic, and back to America. Dominique. He yearned for her as much as he yearned for his country. Although he knew he was changing his mind almost every other day, right now he had somewhat settled whether his being here, on this "crusade," was really the most productive thing to do. In the long run, he felt the answer was *yes*. Whether Lucifer was in the picture or not, his Legion would keep moving if they weren't checked in some way. It sounded old hat, but there was a good possibility that, if the madman's army was not stopped here, in the eastern Med, the day would come when they'd be landing on the shores of America. And the democratic forces in America might not have their shit together enough to mount a decent defense. It was a question of where and when to battle the enemy.

For Hunter, the place was here and the time was now.

He reached into his pocket, pulled out the American flag, and felt its threads with his fingers. He always gained some power from the act. *Someday,* he said. *Someday* the flag will fly again. Mean *something* to millions again. It was his life and he knew it and he accepted it. *"America,"* he whispered to himself. *"I am an American . . ."*

He had drifted off for a couple hours, only to be awakened by a sharp knock on the cabin door. This was getting to be a habit. He would finally start to get some sleep when something would happen and he'd be back in action again.

This time the person at the door was one of Giuseppe's men. "Message," he kept saying, as if it were the only English he knew. "Message . . ."

Hunter was in the CIC inside of two minutes. Heath and Yaz were there, along with Giuseppe.

"What have you got?" Hunter asked, reaching for a mug of coffee.

"An intercepted radio message from the western

Med," Heath said.

Hunter stopped in mid-sip. "The Modern Knights?" he asked.

"Could be," Yaz said. "Listen for yourself . . ."

He reached over to the large radio set and turned on the built-in tape recorder. There was a burst of static, then an indecipherable chatter. Then, gradually, individual voices could be heard. They had definite British accents.

"Lancelot, Lancelot . . . " one voice repeated. "Fueling time for you is 0830."

"I copy you, Galahad," another voice said.

More static went by, then another moment of clarity.

"Godfrey, Godfrey," a distinctly French-accented voice said. *"Repondez. Repondez."*

"Oui, Norman," the reply came back. *"Nuit blanche. Repete. Nuit blanche."*

The tape ended with a final burst of static.

"Nuit blanche," Hunter repeated. "I think that means 'a white night,' like in 'a sleepless night.' "

"It's got to be some kind of code," Yaz said.

"Could be," Hunter said, rewinding the tape and listening to it again.

"Maybe it means they're working overtime," Heath offered.

"Any idea where they are?" Hunter asked.

Giuseppe nodded and pointed to a map of the Mediterranean. "Near Majorca," he said in his best English.

"Really?" Hunter was surprised.

"I felt the same way," Heath said. "I thought, 'My God, at least they've pushed off.' Maybe Stanley's return got them into gear. But then I realized they are still some distance away. That is, if they manage to avoid all the problems we encountered."

"Christ," Yaz said. "We did our best to clear the way for them."

Hunter looked at the map. Majorca. Where it all started. It seemed like a year ago, when it was only a matter of a couple of weeks. How things had changed in this New Order World. At one time, crossing the Med was a lark on a cruise ship, or a flash in a jet airliner. Now, the other side of the Med — and those ships — might as well be a million miles away.

They listened to the messages one more time, then walked out into the open air, Hunter looked out on the horizon and saw it first.

"Jezzuz," he exclaimed. "Is that really it?"

Heath shielded his eyes against the glare of the rising sun. "I believe it is, old boy," he said excitedly.

A voice above them confirmed what they were thinking.

"That's it, lads," O'Brien called down from the bridge railing. "That's the entrance to the Suez Canal . . ."

Chapter 38

Hunter watched the S-3A roar off the deck of the carrier, climb, and turn south. Inside, he knew, the pilot, E.J. Russell, would be flying the most dangerous mission of his life.

Fate had dictated that the carrier, several days behind schedule, would reach the northern entrance of the Canal just as the advanced elements of Lucifer's fleet were entering the southern end. Now only about 100 miles separated the two opposing forces.

So, although the Italian communications team was working round the clock intercepting messages from the enemy fleet, Hunter and the others still lacked an accurate reading as to just how many and what type of ships Lucifer had under his command. That's where the Aussie pilot Russell came in. The pilot's mission was to overfly the southern end of the Canal in his S-3A, unescorted, and photograph the enemy with the plane's sophisticated belly cameras. For good measure, the BBC cameraman volunteered to go along. Videotapes of the fleet would also be very helpful in the battle to come.

The two mine-laying frigates rejoined the *Saratoga* flotilla just as it was preparing to enter the Canal. Before the task force entered the waterway, all of the ships had spent time with the flotilla oiler. Watching the refueling operation, Hunter wondered when they would get a chance to fuel up again. If ever . . .

He spent the morning hours with O'Brien, Olson, Heath, and the Commodore determining the order of battle for the flotilla. They agreed that six of Olson's frigates would enter the Canal first, followed by the carrier itself. The Moroccan troopship would come next, along with the oiler and the captured supertanker. The rest of Olson's frigates would protect the rear. Twenty of the Commodore's armed yachts, carrying members of the UDT, would sweep for mines beyond the area they had already cleared. The rest of the Freedom Navy would be scattered throughout the flotilla.

Hunter had already worked out the air operations. The eleven Tornados were the heart of his squadron. The versatile airplanes were very valuable to their cause, so he divided them into two units, Alpha and Beta, and instructed that only in the worst possible scenario would both units be off the carrier at the same time. The Tornados would comprise the main bombing force. They would go after the enemy ships with everything and anything they could carry.

The Viggens too would serve exclusively in the attack role. Hunter had the Swedish airplanes fitted with overstuffed "Greendog" bombs—so heavy that the airplanes would have to skim the surface of the water for their initial attacks.

The creaking Jaguars would be given the pinch-hitter role. They would be loaded up with aerial bombs, cannon ammo, and Sidewinders. They could either take the measure of the lead enemy ships via dive-bombing attacks and strafing, or protect the bombers from any enemy interference in the air.

The most difficult assignments fell to Hunter's F-16 and the three Harrier jump-jets. They would have to free-lance for most of the air strikes. That is, be on station quickly, unleash whatever bomb loads they might have, then loiter over the battle area and apply force—whether it be Sidewinders, cannon fire, or air-to-surface missiles—as needed.

The S-3A would provide armed recon. Olson's choppers would serve in the air-rescue role.

The flotilla sailed into the Canal quietly, without incident. Moving more or less in single file, the frigates and the Freedom Navy advance ships went in first, then the carrier, the troopship, the tankers, and the rest of the frigates. The only thing they encountered on the waterway was the still-smoldering wreckage of the gunboat that had made the mistake of stopping the Commodore twice.

Hunter had never sailed through the Canal. As he watched the passing shoreline, he knew that in peaceful times the channel would have been bustling with merchant ships big and small. Now it was quiet, eerie. The shores were lined with wreckage everywhere, all of it slowly disintegrating in the mercilessly hot Mideast sun. He saw downed airplanes of all sizes and types, bows of sunken ships, demolished tanks, jeeps, trucks, pontoon bridges. Rusting, sand-blasted reminders of Mideast wars too numerous to count. It was almost as if war were attracted to the area, like tornados to the American Midwest or hurricanes to its East Coast.

"What the hell is the big attraction?" Hunter

asked himself. "Why have so many people died over a bunch of sand?"

There were human skeletons everywhere too. Some still dressed in uniforms, helmets still strapped onto bare jawbones. There were clutches of them, here and there, like the wreckage, victims of wars past and forgotten. Watching them, Hunter got the distinct and unnerving impression that he was floating through a graveyard.

The S-3A returned after the carrier had been in the canal for about an hour. Hunter met Russell as he emerged from the jet and immediately noticed the battle-hardened veteran was visibly shaken.

Hunter ushered him to a remote corner of the *Saratoga*'s mess hall and signaled one of the cooks to bring them some "strong" coffee.

"Jezzuz, Hawk," E.J. told him. "I've never seen so many ships in my life! I thought The Modern Knights were stacked!"

"What kind of ships?" Hunter asked as the cook dropped off a steaming pot of laced coffee.

"You name it, they got it, mate," E.J. answered. "Battleships, missile cruisers, armed freighters, rocket-launcher ships. They must have fifty or sixty destroyers alone. Plus a helicopter assault ship. One of those crazy half-battleship-half-carrier jobs."

"Russian?" Hunter asked.

"Through and through," E.J. said, swigging the coffee. He felt the whiskey-laced mixture slide down his throat. "Still got the hammer and sickle on it. A lot of the ships do."

"Well, Lucifer is an equal-opportunity employer," Hunter said. "He'll hire anyone to help him destroy the world."

"They must have sixty Hind gunships on that flattop," E.J. continued. "The BBC guy has a lot of good footage. And the troopships! They got LSTs, steamers, converted cruise liners, barges, tugs, you name it! All of them stuffed with soldiers. Those guys must be chomping at the bit to get to the Med just so they can spread out."

"Were you spotted?" Hunter asked.

"Maybe, maybe not," the Australian answered. "I didn't get any radar-lock indications, but that doesn't mean they didn't spot us visually."

"No aircraft flying above or near the fleet?"

"Just one airplane," E.J. said. "This P-3 Orion. It's an old Navy job, still with the long, pointy ass-end, you know?"

"Yeah, we intercepted some radio transmissions from it a while ago," Hunter said. "That's how we knew the Sovs were laying mines in the Canal."

"That's right," E.J. replied. "This must be the same airplane. Yet, if anything was going to spot us, that plane would have. They're usually jammed with enough gear to rival an AWACs, aren't they?"

"Yes, usually," Hunter said, after thinking for a moment. "Unless they are carrying some other type of gear on board now . . ."

They left the mess hall and went to the CIC. There the BBC crew had set up a large-screen TV and videotape-playback machine. Heath, Yaz, Olson, O'Brien, and The Commodore were all on hand. Without much fanfare, the cameraman switched on the TV and inserted the freshly shot videotape.

Even though Hunter knew what to expect, he was still stunned. Spread out on the Red Sea near the southern entrance to the Canal, Lucifer's fleet looked like one of the huge armadas the US had thrown against the Japanese in the South Pacific.

"My God," Heath blurted out, speaking for everyone. "How in hell can we expect to hold up that whole bloody thing?"

"Between Lucifer and The Modern Knights, they must have hired just about every ship in the world," O'Brien said.

Even the normally stony Olson was slightly rattled. "This is a formidable force . . ." he said with typical understatement in his Scandinavian-accented English.

"Their biggest problem will be getting all those ships through without causing one hell of a traffic jam," Yaz said, dejectedly.

"No," Hunter said, stemming the tide of negatives. "Their biggest problem is going to be us . . ."

The Jaguars took off first, four of them catapulting into the air with a rush of steam and a scream of jet exhaust. The quartet climbed and began long circles around the carrier.

The Tornados launched next. Six of them, each carrying 18,000 pounds of anti-shipping bombs, streaked off the carrier and joined the Jags orbiting above. Then the carrier's elevators brought up the spaceship-like SAAB Viggens. The fighters, their delta wings bulging with overstuffed bombs, went airborne in less than two minutes. Unlike the other airplanes, they stayed in a ground-hugging holding pattern.

Hunter launched next, the *Saratoga*'s rejuvenated catapult flinging him hard and fast out over the water. Meanwhile, two of the Harrier jump-jets were lifting off vertically from the stern of the carrier. The remaining Harrier as well as the Beta group of

Tornados would be left behind in order to protect the flotilla if necessary.

The air group finally formed up, went through a series of armament and communications checks, and then headed south. The first direct attack on Lucifer was about to begin . . .

The lead ship in Lucifer's fleet was a cruiser manned by crew of Chilean mercenaries. A squadron of destroyers and corvettes, all carrying crews of mixed nationalities, was next in line, followed by the first group of troop-carrying vessels — tugs, small freighters, and barges.

Although Lucifer knew the *Saratoga* was heading for the Canal, his lack of reliable intelligence and recon led him to believe the carrier was still dead in the water in the Mediterranean. A powerless ship, surrounded by a bunch of yachts and frigates, posed little threat to his vast fleet, so he thought. Though he was upset that the Russian Navy subs hadn't finished off the disabled carrier during their first attack, he wasn't worried. When his armada had traveled through the Canal, he would send his own warships to do the job themselves. This message he had foolishly passed on to the commanders of his fleet, who, in turn, bragged about it to their crews.

That's why it was with great surprise that the lookout on Lucifer's lead cruiser spotted the flight of four Viggen jets approaching at wave-top level and heading directly for him. Were the airplanes allies? Free-lancers that Lucifer had hired to protect the fleet through its Canal passage?

He knew the answer was no as soon as when he heard the anxious voice of his comrade in the cruiser's communications room. He was screaming through the intercom that "unidentified enemy aircraft" were heading for the ship. Instantly, the lookout knew a big mistake had been made.

The four Viggens roared right over the cruiser, so close the lookout felt the need to duck. As the jets screamed by he saw their wings were jammed with strange-looking bombs. He watched as they continued up and over the destroyers behind his ship and soon disappeared around a slight bend in the Canal. His first thought was one of relief. "At least they didn't drop those things on me," he whispered.

Then he turned around and saw the Tornados . . .

The British swing-wing fighter-bombers were right in front of him, six altogether, flying in pairs. Their underwings also carried clumps of bombs. But unlike the Viggens, two of the planes were zeroing in on the cruiser. And the lead Tornado was firing its cannon at him.

The lookout felt the cannon shells rip up his right arm, take a chunk of his shoulder off, and graze his head. Suddenly he couldn't move; he was in shock. Everything was moving in slow motion. He saw the lead Tornado drop two silvery cannisters. Both struck the forward gun housing on the cruiser, passed through the compartment, and tore two side-by-side holes in the deck. A tremendous explosion followed, so powerful it lifted the bow of the ship right out of the water.

Only the lead Tornado dropped any bombs; like the Viggens, the six airplanes streaked overhead and continued down the canal.

The lookout, half his body already covered in blood, was now hit square in the face with a wave of flame resulting from the explosion. Suddenly his hair, his uniform, his very skin was on fire. In fact, the whole ship was instantly covered in flames.

He screamed, but no sound came out . . .

By this time, the warning klaxons were blaring on the dozen destroyers and corvettes sailing behind the ill-fated cruiser. The startled crew members, roused by the sound of the approaching jets, first watched the four Viggens pass over, then saw the Tornados deliver a devastating blow to the lead ship.

They knew they were next.

The guns crews were not yet at their posts when the Jaguars appeared. The small, aging jet fighters were flying very slowly four abreast and coming in on a slight angle. After passing over the blazing cruiser, they simultaneously opened up on the first four destroyers with their powerful nose cannons. The combined barrage caught one ship broadside, perforating it, killing any sailor unlucky enough to be on its starboard side. A succession of secondary explosions followed immediately.

The four jets passed over their first victim, and started riddling another—a smaller destroyer escort. The rain of deadly cannon shells walked up the side of this ship and quickly found their way to its magazine. The vessel's ammunition went up, obliterating everything from its forecastle to its stern. The explosion was so quick and so sudden, two of the Jag pilots had to yank back on their sticks to avoid being caught up in the conflagration their cannon fire had caused.

One by one, the destroyers were attacked by the slow-moving Jaguar foursome. Those ships lying directly in the jets' line of attack were caught helpless and with no room to maneuver. No return fire was offered in defense. They were chopped up like lambs in a slaughter.

Further down the canal, word had reached the group of twenty troop-carrying vessels that the fleet was under attack. But these ships too suddenly realized their vulnerability.

Two armed tugs were leading the troopships, followed by fifteen large, open, square river barges of the type used to carry wheat, coal, or garbage in peaceful times. Now they were filled with the advance troops of Lucifer's Legion. The soldiers, already weary from spending so much time packed like sardines on the barges, panicked when they heard the approaching sound of jet engines. Out of the blazing Middle Eastern sun, they soon saw the outline of the four Viggen jets.

The overstuffed bombs, also known as Greendogs, were just that. Cannisters filled with HE, wrapped in an overstuffed layer of plastic explosive. The devices, an old trick Hunter had picked up along the way, precluded the need for a fuse or any kind of sophisticated arming mechanism. The bombs simply exploded on contact with anything, be it the metal side of a barge or the water nearby.

The Viggens had arranged themselves in a single file and separated themselves by a quarter of a mile. The flight leader passed over the armed tugs, routinely ignoring the feeble gunfire coming from the boats' machine guns, and bore down on the river barges.

"Stingers!" the troop commanders on all the vessels began yelling at their air-defense teams. But a Stinger cannot be fired immediately. Time is needed to prepare the shoulder-held antiaircraft missile for launch. And time was running out quickly for the barge troops.

The first Viggen swooped in on the lead river barge no more than fifteen feet above the water. Its pilot flipped a switch and one Greendog bomb fell from its bomb rack. The high-explosive-packed cannister hit the lip of the barge perfectly, igniting the plastic explosive. This in turn set off the 200 pounds of HE inside the bomb instantaneously.

The Viggen pilot had never seen a green explosion before, but now, as he pulled his jet up and turned to look back on his target, he saw a spectacular ball of emerald flame enveloping the river barge. When the smoke and fire cleared, even the Viggen pilot was startled to see that nothing — absolutely *nothing* — was left of the barge.

By this time, the second Viggen was screaming in on another, even larger river barge. Below, the helpless soldiers could only cower as the greendog bomb landed in their midst and exploded. The terrifying green fire instantly splashed all over the men, igniting them like human matchsticks. At the same time, the bomb blew out a huge hole in the bottom of the barge. The water immediately rushed in, for a moment extinguishing the burning soldiers, but also sucking them down to their deaths. The barge went under in two seconds. As with the first barge, no one survived.

Chapter 39

By the time the Tornados reached the barges, the area looked like a scene out of Hell.

The Viggens had done their work — gruesomely and efficiently. The Tornado pilots were shocked to see the Canal water had turned red and the shoreline was covered with smoldering pieces of bodies. Three of the barges looked to be unhit, yet they were doing circles in the Canal, as if their skippers had gone mad. Many of the soldiers had jumped overboard in fear. Those who didn't drown instantly were forced to swim through the bloody, torso-filled water. By the time they reached the shore, the stink of burning flesh had overwhelmed most of them and they dropped, frozen in shock. Only a few hardened souls made it up and away from the shoreline, only to run crazy into the scorching desert.

The Tornados continued on, noting that the Viggens, their heavy bomb loads expended, were now cruising at 15,000 feet providing aircover.

Five miles down the canal was the next group of

Lucifer's ships — four large guided-missile frigates protecting two cruisers. These six ships were the main targets for the Tornados.

The enemy vessels were by this time well aware that the fleet was under air attack, so their gun crews were at their stations when the first two Tornados appeared over the northern horizon. The two British jets, moving slowly as if at attack speed, bore down on the six ships. The frigates at this point had maneuvered so they formed a diamond-shaped pattern around the cruisers. However, all six of the ships' radars were concentrating on the two Tornados approaching from the north.

In the heat of the impending action, their radar operators didn't see the four other Tornados approaching from the west.

The sound characteristic of a jet engine is a strange and unpredictable thing. Wind direction, temperature, speed, location, and many other factors determine not only how loud the engine is, but also whether a person can hear it approaching or not. Sometimes, soldiers in trenches can hear the sound of enemy aircraft approaching from miles away.

Other times, they simply look up and an enemy jet is right on top of them . . .

The captain of one of the protecting rear frigates looked up from his bridge console to see a Tornado was right on top of him. He had no time to shout out a warning or alert his gun crews — they, like everyone else on the six ships, were awaiting an attack by the two Tornados slowly approaching from the north.

But this Tornado was so close, he could see the pilot's face as it streaked by. It was all happening so quickly. In a second, the Tornado had already dropped two bombs on one of the cruisers, broad-siding it with a tremendous one-two punch of explosions. The frigate captain, an ex-Argentine-navy man, felt his jaw drop in surprise as he watched the British jet pull up and away. "How?" he asked himself.

He didn't see the second Tornado until it was too late . . .

The bomb crashed right into the frigate's bridge, exploding on impact. The captain was blasted into a thousand pieces, as was everyone on the bridge. The explosion carried on down to the frigate's guided-missile storage room, ignited two missiles, which in turn blew up. A third missile actually launched itself and traveled a crazy flight path before impacting on the shoreline. The blazing ship turned over immediately, a huge hole on its deck belching dirty, black smoke.

By this time, the two Tornados coming in from the north had banked westward to avoid any opposing fire, then twisted back so as to attack the ships on an easterly course. With one frigate destroyed and a cruiser heavily damaged, the smoke surrounding the ships was thick and obscuring.

This made no difference to the Tornado pilots; they were bombing on instruments anyway. They streaked in and simultaneously unleashed their loads on the other cruiser. Five of the eight bombs were direct hits. Two were near misses, and one skipped across the water to slam into one of the frigates. The cruiser, its structure unable to withstand the five massive explosions, cracked in two places. One break came near its stern, the other right below on its bow. More explosions followed as water reached its engine room. Its sister cruiser, already mortally wounded, tried to spin away from the devastated ship. But it was too late. The doomed cruiser's main ammo magazine erupted, exploding with the force of a hundred bombs, sending out a wall of fiery shrapnel that hit the sister ship head on. Its steering facilities destroyed, the crippled cruiser rammed its sister ship, and together they were sucked down in a whirlpool of fire and water.

The remaining frigates knew now was the time to escape. But two more Tornados were waiting for them. Three screeching bombing runs later, one frigate lay destroyed and two were beached and burning.

Their work done, the Tornados turned northward and headed back to the carrier.

Hunter had watched the destruction of the enemy ships from a height of 10,000 feet. Now it was his turn. He linked up with the two Harriers and proceeded even further down the waterway.

His target-identification device indicated two large ships approximately fourteen miles away. Judging by their electronic signatures, Hunter determined one was probably a helicopter assault ship, the other possibly a battleship.

He armed his payload and, with the Harriers in tow, dropped down to 1000 feet. He kicked in his target-acquisition system and armed his Sidewinders just in case. Sure enough, ahead of him was the distinct outline of a flattop.

"It's a Moskva helicopter carrier," he radioed the two Harrier pilots. "We can expect it to be jammed with antiaircraft weapons, maybe missiles. The other ship looks like an old pocket battleship. It also is probably well-covered with AA."

"What do you have in mind, major?" one of the

Harrier pilots, a man named Chester, asked.

Hunter thought a moment, then said, "Well, we could give them the old 'one-two, out-of-the-blue trick.'"

There was a burst of static, then Chester replied, "We're game, if you are . . ."

"Okay," Hunter radioed back as he dropped to 500 feet, "Just watch out for those choppers . . ."

He turned to see the two Harriers go into steep climbs. Meanwhile, he dropped down even lower. His radar-lock indicator was humming—the chopper carrier's air-defense radar unit had him on their screens. But it didn't matter—this would not be a surprise attack.

The sailors on the Soviet helicopter carrier saw the F-16 coming. It was low, just twenty-five feet above the water, and traveling at an incredible rate of speed. They turned their antiaircraft batteries toward it and opened up immediately. But as their tracer bullets flew out at the fighter, they saw its pilot do a strange thing. He started to spin, rolling the jet over and over like a cockscrew.

"Keep firing!" the gun crew commander yelled into his microphone. But the crazily gyrating jet streaked by them, raking the carrier's deck with cannon fire while passing cleanly through the AA barrage. It then turned east and disappeared over the horizon.

No sooner had it vanished when it appeared again. This time it was heading for them broadside, still very low, still spinning at an incredible rate. Again the ship's AA team opened up. Several antiaircraft missiles flew towards the jet. But it was useless. The gun crews could not get a fix on the wildly revolving jet and the missiles' target-homing systems were at a loss to pick up anything they could lock in on.

The jet spun right towards the ship's center, firing its cannons and knocking off both the primary and secondary radar dishes. Now the radar operators on the Russian ship were effectively blinded.

The F-16 did a quick loop and came back over the carrier superstructure. At the same time, one of the Hind helicopters on board started to take off. In a blinding flash, the F-16 fired a Sidewinder missile that traveled only twenty feet or so before slamming into the Russian chopper, destroying it.

Shocked at the split-second destruction of one of the Hinds, the gun crews still pumped AA fire at the fighter as it streaked towards the east again. But now pandemonium broke out on the ship.

Two more helicopters were ready to lift off as the jet came around a third time. The chopper pilots hoped only to get airborne and possibly launch their own air-to-air missiles at the jet.

But they weren't that fast. The F-16 was on them in a second, still spinning, still firing its cannons. One chopper got it full in the cockpit, splattering its pilot and copilot and causing the helicopter to slam against the ship's superstructure. The other Hind found its rear rotor blade had been neatly sheared off from the rest of its airframe. Now unbalanced, its main rotor still going, the Hind flipped up and over the side of the ship, smashing into the water below.

In all the confusion, and with its radar effectively knocked out, no one on the ship noticed the two Harrier jets that had descended slowly from a great height and were hovering directly over the ship . . .

It was just a matter of flipping two switches,

which the Harrier pilots did. Their entire bomb loads dropped right into the center of the flattop's deck, causing explosions which rocked the large ship back and forth. Instantly, two huge fires broke out, followed by many secondary explosions. As the two Harrier pilots shifted their thrust nozzles to forward and streaked off, the Soviet ship went into a series of fiery convulsions as fuel, weapons, and ammunition were touched off below its decks.

The ship, most of its crew killed in the "out-of-the-blue" bombing, would burn for all day and into the night before finally sinking.

In all the action, Hunter still noticed that the nearby battleship had reversed its engines and was quickly backing out of the battle area. He reluctantly let it go, knowing that the Harriers were out of ordnance and he was only armed with Sidewinders. He knew it was more important for him and the Harriers to get back to the *Saratoga* and rearm.

One by one the jets returned to the *Saratoga*, their bomb racks depleted, their fuel tanks near empty. They found the carrier had moved further south while they were carrying out the air strike. Now it was anchored in the middle of the Canal off a deserted Egyptian city called Ismailia.

The Canal was a little wider at this point and the ground on either side of the waterway was relatively defensible. Already, the Moroccan troopship had landed most of its 7500 troops on the eastern, Sinai side of the Canal. In the meantime the contingent of Australian Special Forces took up positions in an abandoned power plant on the western side.

The returning pilots gathered in the situation room and discussed the air strike with Heath.

"The S-3A is up now and taking pictures of the damage," Heath told them. "But, from your reports, it sounds like we've accomplished our first objectives — that is, hitting them hard on the first try and blocking the canal."

"That we did," Hunter said, speaking up. "By my count, we sank or disabled more than two dozen ships. And we bottlenecked the canal at two points.

"But we still have two problems: one, they've got more than three hundred more ships; and two, they can clear the Canal in very little time."

"That's correct, Hunter," a voice boomed from the back of the room. The pilots turned to see Sir Neil, sitting in a wheelchair being pushed by Clara. "That's why we must hit them again, hard!"

"My God, Sir Neil!" Heath about shouted. "Are you well enough to be moving about?"

"Well enough?" the jaunty Englishman asked, motioning Clara to push him to the front of the room. "I've never felt better!"

His bandages and accompanying intravenous bottle notwithstanding, Hunter did notice that the Brit looked better than at any time since his wounding.

Heath stepped down as Sir Neil took center stage.

"All aircraft returned safely?" Sir Neil asked.

"Yes, sir," Hunter answered.

"And the Moroccans have landed?" the British commander asked. "The Aussies and Gurkhas deployed?"

"Yes, suh!" Heath called out.

"Smashing!" the Englishman said. "And we've taken a measure of them in our first attack. Then we've done what we came here to do."

The group of pilots broke into a spontaneous round of applause. It was Sir Neil's show all the way.

"Now, let's get serious," the Englishman continued. "Hunter, what can we expect if they counterattack?"

Hunter thought for a moment, then said, "I think it's really not a question of if, but when. They've got at least four squadrons of Hinds and I'm sure a lot of small surface-attack craft."

"Any guess as to when they'll strike back?"

"Could be within the hour," Hunter said, slowly looking around at the assembled pilots. "Could be tomorrow. Could be as soon as night falls."

Chapter 40

"Ready! Aim! *Fire!*"

The firing squad obeyed and unleashed a barrage at the four men standing on the stern of the battleship. The bullets hit the men in the heads and chests with enough force to knock them off the back of the ship and into the water.

High above, looking down from one of the ship's catwalks, were Lucifer, three of his bodyguards, and the captain of the battleship. Lucifer was absolutely livid with rage.

"Do you see that, captain?" he asked, sneering at the naval officer. "That will happen to you and any other officer who betrays me!"

"I understand, Your Highness," the nervous officer answered. "But surely you know that *I* had nothing to do with what happened to our ships—"

"I understand *nothing!*" Lucifer spit back at him. "You are supposed to be naval officers. Yet did any of you at least *mention* to me that the cursed carrier was in the middle of the Canal, and not floundering somewhere off the coast of Egypt?"

"But Your Highness," the captain, a heady Brazilian, came back. "We don't have the air-recon capability that the carrier has. Plus they must have found some way to propel the ship. Surely, they didn't tow it that distance in such a short time."

"Excuses!" Lucifer screamed at the top of his lungs. His bodyguards had seen him swallow a handful of pills earlier and now they knew the amphetamines were taking affect. "We are the most powerful fleet in the world. They are a bunch of misfit, underpaid mercenaries, foolish enough to haul a carrier across the Med. We should be able to crush them! Yet, because of this . . . this conspiracy of ignorance among my top officers, these English glory boys sink some of the best ships in our fleet!"

"But, Your Highness," the captain pressed on, perhaps foolishly. "We are certain they have this pilot — Hunter — with them. His airplane has been spotted. The . . . ah, action at the pyramid might have been his doing. If this is true, he is a formidable foe."

"More excuses!" Lucifer screamed. "Don't tell me of this Hunter! *I've fucked his woman!* Understand? He's no match for me. For the power I have at my disposal.

"Now immediately launch a counterattack! You are personally in charge, captain. Send the Hinds! Send our fastest ships up past the wreckage of those fools and attack! Attack! *Attack!* Wipe out those comic-book heroes. Send all of our battleships after them if necessary!"

The captain looked at Lucifer strangely. "All the battleships?" the captain asked. "Including this one?" For all he knew this was the first time the leader had mentioned putting himself near the battle.

"If necessary, captain," the man answered snidely. "I will tolerate no more delays!"

The black-cloaked man was pounding his fist on the battleship's railing.

"And if you don't succeed, captain," Lucifer continued, "you can be sure you'll be down there next!"

The captain gulped once and watched as four more officers were lined up and executed, their bloody bodies dropping into the water like four stones.

Chapter 41

"Here they come!" the radar man in the Saratoga's CIC called out.

Instantly, Hunter and Heath were looking over the man's shoulder.

"Fast attack craft, just as you guessed, Hunter," Heath said, hitting the carrier's battle stations' klaxon as he spoke. "Looks like about sixty of them! Thirty miles and closing."

It was an hour past sundown. The flotilla was under strict blackout rules. Photos from the S-3A had confirmed twenty-three ships were sunk or damaged in the air strikes, but also that there was enough room between the hulks for the smaller fast-patrol craft of Lucifer's fleet to squeeze through. And now they were here . . .

Heath was on the radio immediately, sending a predetermined coded message to the Commodore. He knew, as soon as it was sent, the Freedom Navy would be on the move. Four of Olson's helicopters would also go into action.

"They're off," Heath reported as he heard the

confirmation messages coming back from the armed yachts of the Commodore's fleet. "The choppers too."

Hunter shook his head. "Now, all we can do is wait . . ."

Hunter stood on the bow of the carrier and watched the flashes of the spectacular battle off in the distance. He knew the fighting would be at too close quarters to risk sending any of the jets into action. They had to hope that the Commodore's "reformed" pirates could stop the attack.

He watched the flares and explosions off to the south for the entire night, knowing that each hour that passed indicated an increase in the brutality of the fighting. He saw pieces of debris and bodies float by the carrier, even as the fires on the horizon grew brighter. He heard loud blasts similar to sonic booms, and occasionally, when the air was calm, the sound of high-powered deck guns chattering back and forth at each other.

Finally, just as the sun came up, the noise to the south ceased. Now dozens of separate funnels of smoke rose to meet and create one huge black cloud. He waited, scanning the horizon for returning survivors of the Freedom Navy. Heath and Sir Neil joined him and still they waited, saying that many of the Commodore's ship's were probably low on fuel and therefore returning at the lowest speed possible.

A full hour went by and still they waited. They shared a powerful pair of binoculars and took turns scanning the horizon. But all they saw was the smoke.

Finally, Hunter spoke the words none of them wanted to hear. "I don't think any of them are coming back . . ." he said slowly.

One of Olson's choppers confirmed it. Launched

to survey the battle area, the pilot landed on the *Saratoga* less than twenty minutes later and reported to Sir Neil directly.

"There is nothing, no one left," the Norwegian pilot told them. "None of them. None of us. Ships burning everywhere. Some jammed together. Like they were ramming each other. Our helicopters all gone too."

"*No* survivors at all?" Sir Neil asked, not quite believing it.

The Norseman shook his head.

"The Commodore gone?" Heath said, thinking of the colorful, Napoleonic figure.

"Those brave, crazy bastards . . ." Hunter said, sadness in his voice.

"They died for our cause," Sir Neil said. "So did those chopper crews. We've got to make sure they didn't go down fighting for nothing!"

"One more thing," the chopper pilot said. "They have crews further down the waterway, clearing it from the battle yesterday. Big ships right behind them. It looks like what they can't tow out of the way, they are blasting. With their deck guns."

"They're making their move," Hunter said. "We've got to go after them, right now!"

Hunter bore down on the cruiser, four Shrike missiles strapped to his wings. He was somehow flying through a wall of fiery lead as it seemed every gun on the ship was firing at him. He didn't care. He knew he wouldn't be shot down. Not yet.

His body was rippling with intensity. His eyes were burning with hate. The valiant demise of the Freedom Navy had lit a fuse inside of him. Suddenly his questions were all answered. Fighting for freedom knew no bounds or borders. There were no degrees of liberty or desire in dying for it. He was here, fighting Lucifer, but he had no doubts that if the demon weren't stopped here, America again would be on his target list—and many more would die in the process. Now the Commodore and his comrades were gone, fighting for freedom on a bunch of armed yachts in the middle of the Suez Canal. They had showed them the way. *Hit! Hit hard!* Do everything possible to stop tyranny in its tracks.

Or die trying . . .

He launched the Shrike and pulled up, feeling a half dozen AA shells pepper his starboard wing. No matter. The missile homed in on the cruiser's radar-control room and exploded. Two secondary explosions soon followed. Judging by their intensity, Hunter knew he had put the cruiser out of action.

He had sent twenty of the *Saratoga*'s airplanes out to attack the large contingent of ships moving up the Canal toward Ismailia. Ten of them were with him; the other ten were attacking targets further down the Canal. When Hunter's force had arrived over their target area, they had seen that Lucifer had sent no less than four battleships, eight cruisers, a dozen frigates, and many more destroyers and corvettes. Behind this task force were dozens of troopships of all kinds and shapes.

At once Hunter had realized what Lucifer was doing. He was concentrating on destroying the *Saratoga* and its flotilla. It was a typical emotional decision by Lucifer, totally devoid of any military value. It was the same kind of thinking that the madman had displayed back in The Circle War.

So, in a way, Sir Neil's dream of a delaying action was coming true. The time and effort that Lucifer had apparently decided to expend on the small carrier force would delay his breakout into the eastern Med, possibly long enough for The Modern Knights to arrive in the area. The bad news was that now the *Saratoga* flotilla would bear the brunt of an attack by a fleet many times its size and carrying close to 900,000 soldiers.

Hunter was back down at wave-top level in seconds. Ahead of him was a guided-missile frigate. Its gunners too had him in their sights, but he pressed on. One hundred and fifty feet out he launched his second Shrike. He followed its path as it rose and struck the ship's mast, exploding with a great *blam*! and raining flaming death down on the compartments below.

Hunter pulled up, did a tight turn, and came in on the ship again, his Vulcan cannon Six Pack going full blast. The ship was rocked with the withering, concentrated fire, hundreds of puffs of fiery smoke indicating hits all over the vessel. He turned once again, saw he had started at least a half-dozen fires on the frigate, then turned his attention to the troopship next in the line.

He knew by the radio chatter on his intercom that many of Lucifer's troopships further down the canal were landing their troops on the eastern side of the Canal rather than be caught out in the open by *Saratoga*'s attack planes. This troopship in front of him was a converted tramp steamer. He could see the terrified troops were firing their rifles at him as he screeched towards them, his cannons blazing. Once again he felt some of the enemy fire find its mark, bullets pinging off his canopy and nose. But, still, Hunter ignored the enemy fire.

His cannon shells found the ship's boiler room and destroyed it, causing the rear end of the ship to blow up and break apart. The ship went down quickly, horribly, carrying at least 2000 of Lucifer's soldiers to their deaths.

All around him, the *Saratoga*'s airplanes were attacking the ships. The waterway was a mass of confusion, ships exploding, missiles being fired, AA guns going off.

Suddenly one, then two of the Tornados got hit. The battleships were loaded with antiaircraft missiles and it appeared to Hunter that the gunners were launching their rockets in waves, hoping to hit something.

He felt a pang in his heart as his saw the two precious Tornados go down in flames. Two Jaguars bravely attacked the guilty battlewagon, and they too found themselves in the midst of a rocket barrage. One went up from a direct hit, the other caught a missile on its wing and then kept right on going, slamming into the big ship.

Four airplanes in one minute. Christ, Hunter thought, All this way to lose a sixth of his air force in sixty seconds.

But the battle went on. He turned and lined up a cruiser. He pushed his launch button and a Shrike streaked out from under his wing. The missile impacted just behind the ship's bridge, destroying it immediately. Its captain and steering crew dead, the ship caught fire and was soon burning out of control.

He was out of missiles and running low on cannon ammo. So were some of the other aircraft. He hated to leave the battle area. The two remaining Jags had the longest loitering time, so Hunter knew they would be able to stay on station a while longer. He and the remaining attackers — two Viggens and two Tornados — would return to the *Saratoga*.

He put the F-16 into a screaming loop and rocketed away from the fight, the four other planes right on his tail.

As they followed the Canal back to the ship, he saw the effects of the recent battles were giving the waterway a nightmarish quality. Everywhere there seemed to be burning ships, floating debris, dead bodies. The area where the Freedom Navy made its last stand was particularly gruesome—wreckage was scattered along the Canal banks for miles.

But now, although he was still forty miles away from the carrier, his instincts told him something was wrong. Dead wrong. He switched his radio to the carrier's frequency and immediately heard a confusion of chatter he knew meant only one thing: the carrier was under attack.

"It's those goddamn Hinds," he swore.

He radioed the other pilots and made them aware of the situation. They took a quick inventory of their weapons' status. All five airplanes had some cannon ammo left and Hunter had two Sidewinders. Trouble was, both Tornados and one Viggen were dangerously low on fuel. Hunter's tanks were also low; the AA hits he'd taken on his wing had started a moderate fuel leak.

He knew immediately that they would have to perform what had to be the most difficult maneuver in warfare: landing on a carrier that was under attack.

Soon they could see the carrier off in the distance and sure enough a fight was going full tilt. The Soviet Hind helicopters—more than three dozen of them—were buzzing around the carrier like bees. A wall of defensive fire was being thrown up at them by the Spanish Rocketeers, the French Gatling team, and the AA crews on the Norwegian frigates. Hunter knew that, somehow, they would have to dodge all that fire and lead and set their airplanes down.

The five jets roared into the middle of the battle, surprising the attacking Hinds. A melee broke out, with the Hinds dropping down to a lower attack level, and the jets following them. Hunter dispatched two of the choppers instantly courtesy of his two remaining Sidewinders. One of the Viggens blasted another Hind with a cannon burst. The scattering choppers made easier targets for the Rocketeers and the Phalanx crews. Several more enemy choppers were downed.

But still there were at least twenty-five more Hinds pressing the attack. Hunter could see more than a few fires burning on the carrier, and one of the frigates was burning out of control. The Moroccan troopship, docked on the eastern side of the waterway, was also burning.

Hunter shot down another Hind, but now there were buzzers and lights going off all over his cockpit control panel. He wasn't just low on fuel—he was running out. He radioed the four airplanes to check on their fuel supply. He determined that the two Tornados would have to go in first, then the 16. The Viggens could stay up just a little longer and give them covering fire.

The first Tornado landed without much trouble—concentrated fire from the Rocketeers held off the Hinds long enough for the British jet to set down. But the second jet ran into trouble immediately.

As the plane was making its final approach, a Hind shot an air-to-surface missile at one of the frigates. The missile crossed right in front of the slow-moving jet, clipping its nose and forcing the pilot to abort the landing. Its nose smoking, the pilot had trouble controlling the airplane. As Hunter watched, the jet shot straight up, its engine straining. An opportunistic Hind laced the plane with a burst of cannon fire. The pilot ejected. Seconds later the airplane exploded. "Damn!" Hunter seethed. "There goes another one!"

Now it was his turn to land. He made his way through the buzzing Hinds and the smoke, rockets' glare, and AA fire and set the 16 down. The deck was a scene of mass confusion. The deck hands were struggling to get the first Tornado onto the carrier elevator to get it safely to the hangar area.

In the meantime, the Spanish rocketmen were launching missile after antiaircraft missile at the attacking helicopters. The French-manned Phalanx super-machine guns were going off with businesslike regularity. Even the Moroccan troops on the eastern side and the Aussie-Gurkha force on the western side were getting into the act. They were launching Stinger missiles and firing at the Hinds with their rifles. The action was as intense as anything Hunter had ever seen. Yet, despite all the danger, the BBC crew was rushing about the deck, recording all the action on video.

Two deck monkeys rushed up to Hunter. "No time to take it down," he yelled to them. "Fuel me up right here! And load up the cannons! Hurry! Those Viggens got about ten minutes of fuel left and then they're coming in!"

The two monkeys were joined by five others and together they broke the record for servicing the F-16. Within five minutes he had a full tank and about eighty percent ammo for his Six Pack. Then he and the monkeys literally pushed the 16 to the catapult and hooked it up.

All the while the confusion of the battle swirled around them.

"You got a bad fuel leak on your starboard, major!" one of the monkeys yelled to him.

"I know," Hunter yelled back, climbing back into the cockpit. "But I don't have time to worry about it now!"

He strapped in and immediately fired up the engine. His instruments went "hot" in forty-five seconds and he was ready to go. The deck officer, ducking the debris from a near-miss explosion, gave Hunter the go sign. The next thing he knew, he was thrown back against the seat of the 16 as it rocketed off the deck.

He immediately found himself on the tail of two Hinds as they swooped in to attack one of the frigates. He twisted once, then sent a long stream of cannon fire into one of the tail rotors. The chopper immediately broke up, spun out to the right, and smashed into its partner. The midair collision caused a spectacular explosion. As one, the two burning choppers fell into the water.

Then Hunter saw one of the Viggens get it. Three Hinds had ganged up on the slow-moving Swedish fighter as it was coming in for a landing. The airplane was simply obliterated by a concentration of cannon fire. Hunter immediately started pumping cannon fire back at the trio of Hinds, scattering them and allowing the remaining Viggen to set down.

Finally, the Hinds started to back off. Hunter got two more as they were fleeing off to the south, and a Moroccan Stinger team took down two more. Just in time too, as it turned out, for seven aircraft from the second attack force, plus the two Jags, were now returning to land on the carrier.

These pilots had bad news. Not only had three of their jets — two Viggens and a Tornado — been downed. They also reported that a large combined land and sea force was moving toward the carrier.

"Three battleships are just twenty miles away, coming on fast," one of the pilots told Hunter as he orbited above the carrier. "Also, there are at least ten divisions coming up on the eastern side. Lucifer landed a bunch of his troops and they got transport."

Ten divisions. That meant more than 150,000 men. If they were on trucks, they'd be in the area soon. So would the approaching battleships.

And Hunter knew, in his gut, that Lucifer was on one of those battleships . . .

Chapter 42

The Moroccan troop commander looked out over the trench line and saw a nightmare.

Focusing his electronic binoculars, he at first thought the vision was a mirage. But as it became clearer he realized that what lay before him wasn't a trick of the sun. "Allah have mercy on us," he whispered.

There were more than 100,000 foot soldiers heading right for his line. He knew by reports from the carrier planes that there were 50,000 more troops somewhere behind those he saw. He looked at his own troops—all 7500 of them. They had battled the Hinds fiercely—now they would battle this approaching enemy with the same tenacity.

"Troop, attention!" the commander yelled. His soldiers all the way down the lines were suddenly bolt upright. The commander then stood up, a sword in hand, and yelled: *"Troop, forward!"*

Hunter had seen the approaching troops of Lucifer's army too, through binoculars from the very top of the carrier's conning tower.

He had been forced to land shortly after the Hinds departed the battle area, as the fuel leak in his wing had grown worse. Now, he was having the quickest patch job on record being done on the fighter. He had told the monkeys to forget about the nicks and dings on the 16's nose and canopy and the fact that more than half his avionics was not working. "Just get it in flying condition," he had told them.

The carrier was in rough shape, he knew it. A quick conversation with Yaz confirmed it. "All our work," Yaz had said, "half of it went down the drain when the Hinds attacked."

Many sailors had been killed or wounded in the attack. Heath had taken a cannon shell directly on his shoulder and was now wearing bandages rivaling those of Sir Neil. To his credit, Sir Neil had stayed on the bridge throughout the attack, directing the carrier's defenses, an effort that brought down more than half of the attacking Soviet choppers.

But the *Saratoga* itself had paid dearly. The catapult was just barely working, as it had taken several direct rocket hits from the Hinds. The carrier's communications room was in a shambles, and O'Brien was having trouble just keeping the controls working in case the carrier should have to move quickly. Power was again intermittent, and they were running out of ammunition of all kinds.

One question that Yaz posed to Hunter was why the Hinds didn't attack the oiler or the supertanker filled with volatile jet fuel. Hunter knew why. "Because the Hinds were under Soviet command," he told him. "Their orders were to attack the carrier and the frigates and that's what they did. There's no freedom of thought in the Soviet military. Just follow orders, even though, in a military sense, a well-placed rocket into the supertanker would have blown us all sky high. And they would have been rid of us. But they are too rigid, too robotic."

Now, as Hunter watched the Moroccan troops, he felt another kind of military strategy take over. That of self-sacrifice . . .

Although he couldn't believe it at first, he watched the Moroccans climb out of their trenches and, with bayonets on their rifles, walk out on the desert and toward the approaching multitude of enemy troops.

"Christ . . ." Hunter said in awe of the Moroccans. He knew the advance was suicide, but there was nothing to be done. No airplanes from the carrier could take off in time to help them. Not that it would have done much, so overwhelming were the odds against the brave desert fighters. He knew the Moroccans believed strongly in freedom. They were the most vocal anti-Lucifer element in the flotilla. Now they were sacrificing themselves in order to sting the madman's Legion.

" 'Into the jaws of Hell . . .' " Hunter whispered. As he watched, the Moroccans slowly walked into the cloud of dust being raised by the approaching enemy troops. Soon the air crackled with the sound of gunfire. He could see explosions rising up as the two forces clashed. He could almost hear the cacophony of shouts that usually accompanies fierce hand-to-hand combat.

It was over in a matter of thirty minutes. He saw the Moroccans had stopped the Legion advance, at least temporarily. But he was also sure there were no Moroccan survivors.

Things got worse. Now there was a new threat on the horizon. He could see the smokestack trails of four major ships sailing up the Canal. These were the battleships. Above them flew an escort of at least two dozen Hinds.

"Fuck it," Hunter said, climbing down from his perch. He was going to get airborne whether the 16 was ready or not.

Chapter 43

One by one the aircraft launched off the *Saratoga*. Many of the pilots knew it was for the last time. Hunter had assigned half the remaining jets to bomb and strafe the approaching Legion troops, the other half—his F-16 included—would take on the Hinds and the battleships.

The battle lasted for more than two hours. The swirling dogfight between the slow but maneuverable Hinds and the supersonic jet fighters was both incredible and bizarre. The missile-firing Soviet choppers got the worst of it, to be sure. But it had turned into another numbers game. Despite the best efforts of the fighter pilots, there were so many Hinds that some inevitably got through and were able to deliver devastating blows to the *Saratoga* and the frigates. Luckily, by this time the supertanker and the oiler had withdrawn further up the Canal.

Hunter was in the thick of it, blasting endless waves of choppers. When the opportunity presented itself, he strafed the lead battleship for good measure. The jets attacking the Legion ground troops had succeeded in mauling the soldiers to such a point they temporarily retreated. Now these planes joined the air battle above and around the carrier. But then, as if on cue, more Hinds appeared.

Hunter felt a chill run through him. There were

387

just too many Hinds and they were attacking with suicidal ferocity.

Suddenly his radio crackled. "Flight Ops to F-16," the caller said. Hunter instantly recognized it as Sir Neil.

"Go ahead, Flight Ops."

"Hunter, we are really taking a beating here," the British Commander began. "I can't risk any more lives in this . . ."

Hunter then waited for the words he thought he'd never hear from Sir Neil.

"I'm giving the order to abandon ship," the Brit said slowly. Even through the impersonal radio speaker, the pain was evident in the man's voice.

Hunter was stunned. He knew that, in the strictest military sense, the time to withdraw was long ago. But this was not a true battle in the strictest military sense. Wasn't this a *crusade?* With a sense of purpose? How can one retreat from that?

But Hunter knew that Sir Neil was giving the order simply to stop the bloodshed. The Canal was now so blocked up with wreckage, both around Ismailia and at its southern entrance, that it would be a slow process indeed to move Lucifer's huge fleet up and out of the waterway. The *Saratoga*'s mission was thus complete. Perhaps if The Modern Knights arrived on time, they would meet Lucifer's ground forces just as they reached the northern end of the Canal, or even before that. Hunter knew the battle that would take place then would make this "holding action" look like a squirt-gun fight.

Sir Neil continued the transmission: "Can you hold them off until we get most of the people ashore, Hunter?"

"You can count on it," Hunter replied.

So this is how it ends, the pilot thought, watching

the sea battle continue in the narrow confines of the Canal. So typically British. Magnificence in defeat . . .

The word was passed on the carrier to evacuate. Now Heath's job was to get everyone off. And quick. Emma, Clara, and the high-class call girls were the first to go, transported in life rafts to the western side of the waterway, where they were put under the protection of the combined Aussie-Gurkha force. The ship's many wounded went next, then the surviving Italian, French and Spanish mercenaries, and then Yaz's sailors.

Back in the air, Hunter knew his pilots were running low on fuel and ammo. In addition, the Legion troops had been reinforced, and now they had reached the area of the Canal opposite where the big ship lay. They began mortaring the carrier, despite two of the frigates blasting them with their deck guns.

In the course of two minutes, Hunter saw three more of his jets go down — whether by Hind air-to-air missiles or AA fire from the battleships, he never knew. Now he too felt as if he had tripped into the jaws of Hell.

Then he saw that even the evacuation was in jeopardy. Two of the battleships had been disabled by the fighters, but two were relatively healthy and were now steaming right toward the carrier. The huge guns began to open up on the flattop, one-ton projectiles splashing nearer and nearer to the carrier.

Between the battleships and the Legion troops pouring up the eastern shoreline, Hunter knew a "strategic withdrawal" was close to impossible.

That's when he looked up and saw Lucifer's face in the sky . . .

"Flight Commander, this is Eagle Strike Force Command aircraft, come in please."

"Go ahead, Eagle," Captain Crunch O'Malley answered, turning up the volume slightly on his F-4's radio intercom.

"Flight, we have indications of aircraft at Two-Delta-Tango, your south heading zero-three-seven," the voice from the KC-135 AWACs ship replied. "This puts some kind of activity in the vicinity of Ismailia, right on the Canal itself. Over."

"I copy, Eagle Leader," Crunch said, checking his position. They were now just over the deserted city of Cairo, the local pyramids casting strange shadows in the early afternoon sun. "Have you got a report on the situation at Alexandria yet?"

Crunch was at the head of a nine-aircraft convoy—three F-20s were directly behind him, as well as four C-130 gunships and KC-135 in flight tanker that was doubling as an AWACs plane. The airplanes, all belonging to the Pacific American Air Corps or their allies, were the force that General Jones had promised him when he had radioed the US less than a week earlier to report that Hunter might need help.

The Eagle Strike Force had set down on Majorca the day before. The crews had rested briefly, refueled, and took off early the next morning. Their destination: the Suez Canal.

It was an interesting flight. Shortly after taking off from Majorca, the members of the Eagle Strike Force passed over the devastated floating platform near the island of Panatella. They could only guess what had happened there, until they put down for a refueling stop on Malta. There, a man named Baldi told them how Hunter and the others had destroyed the flying-boat base and defeated the Sidra-Benghazi Gang.

Soon afterwards, they passed over the scene of another battle, this one located around a group of oil platforms south of Crete. Every platform was either destroyed or burning, and the sea around it was littered with dozens of burning and sinking ships. Though he couldn't be sure, Crunch was certain that Hunter had something to do with this battle also.

Then, an hour later, they had passed over the enormous convoy of The Modern Knights . . .

While Crunch and Elvis were on Majorca waiting for the American airplanes to arrive, they had learned that the huge Modern Knights' convoy had departed Portugal several days before and was enroute to the Canal zone.

The Strike Force finally caught up to the convoy just off the coast of Egypt. Through the sophisticated communications setup on the KC-135, Crunch had talked to the convoy commander and learned that Hunter and the *Saratoga* force had somehow made it to the Canal and were engaging the enemy halfway down the Suez.

While the Knights were still at least a day away from the war zone (and they had told Crunch they were actually *ahead* of their original timetable), they had suggested that the American aircraft immediately go into mid-Canal. It was a suggestion the Americans would have taken anyway. Though Crunch and the others weren't 100 percent up on the reasons or the purposes of the anti-Lucifer crusade, they did know their friend Hawk Hunter was caught up in the middle of it. His enemy was their enemy.

"Concerning the Alexandria situation," the radio operator in the KC-135 continued. "Our best guess is that those subs were sunk by mines. We have not seen or heard any opposing aircraft or surface ships in the area. Over."

"Well, that's a strange one," Crunch radioed back to Elvis, in the rear seat of the F-4. The Strike Force had just flown over the area and witnessed yet another curious sight. "A bunch of Russian subs, floating on the surface like a bunch of dead mackerel."

"And no one fired a shot at them?" Elvis asked.

"That's what the eavesdrop boys say in the AWACs," Crunch replied. "No opposing craft anywhere near them. I mean, they could have done a number on that carrier. And they would have wreaked havoc on the Modern Knights convoy. But it's like the Russians ran into their own minefield, as crazy as that sounds."

"Well," Elvis said, "whenever I hear anything crazy nowadays, I also just assume that Hunter was behind it."

Crunch rechecked his position, then radioed back to the Strike Force Command ship. "Command, I suggest we turn to that Two-Delta Tango, zero-three-seven heading and check out that action near Ismailia," he said. "It may involve Major Hunter."

"We copy, Flight Leader," the reply came back. Within seconds the nine-plane force was turning south.

"Whether you know it or not, Hawk," Crunch said, "help is on the way."

The huge, grinning face of Lucifer hovered over the battle area like a cruel vision from Hell.

The resurgent Legion ground troops were swarming all over the eastern side of the canal, the Norwegian frigates blasting away at them. The carrier was desperately trying to reverse its engines to back out of the area, but the battleships had now found the range and their enormous shells were hitting all over the big ship. The ship was so battered, it was impossible for any aircraft to land or take off from the carrier now.

On the western side of the canal, the Aussies and Gurkhas were already moving the evacuated soldiers and noncombatants toward the north. However, they knew it was a matter of time before the enemy troops would cross the waterway and pursue them. What was worse, some of the gunners on the battle-ships were firing on the smaller boats that were taking the last of Yaz's sailors from the carrier.

There were only six fighters left now, and the others either shot down or crash-landed due to lack of fuel. The remaining airplanes — the F-16, three Harriers, and two Tornados — were continually bombing the battleships and the Legion troops. But the intensity could only last for another five minutes or so. Then the surviving jets would also fall victim to low fuel.

And above it all, Lucifer's obscene image laughed, as if the soldiers fighting and dying below were his playthings.

It only took Hunter a few seconds to finally figure out the trick behind Lucifer's illusion. High above the battle area, Hunter saw that Lucifier's black P-3 Orion airplane was circling directly above the face in the sky. Hunter deducted that a video image was being beamed up to the P-3, which in turn was projecting a laser image of Lucifer's face. He had seen similar laser-video displays before. Such projections could be beamed hundreds of miles away. Thus, Lucifer was able to project his ugliness over Crete while sitting comfortably in his Arabian Kingdom. And this one was red, like the projections on previous nights.

But in Lucifer's arrogance, he was unintentionally tipping his hand. By lining up the P-3 and the image, Hunter determined the source of the original video image was now coming from one of the battleships.

At last, he had found Lucifer . . .

He put the F-16 into a screaming climb, heading right towards the holographic laser image of his nemesis. As the face got bigger, Hunter felt the fire of hate he had for all things Lucifer boil up inside him. This was Death incarnate. All that was evil with the world was embodied in that sneering, devilish face. If it was the last thing he ever did, he vowed to smash it . . .

He streaked right through the image and lined up the P-3 flying 10,000 feet above it. Whether the pilots of the Orion knew he was coming or not, the airplane didn't try to escape. Hunter knew it meant only one thing: Lucifer had ordered them to hold their position no matter what.

Hunter armed a Sidewinder and let it fly. It caught the four-engine propeller plane on its right wing, knocking out its outboard engine. But the damage was not instantly fatal to the laser plane. Hunter wanted more. He let another Sidewinder loose and this one impacted right on the aircraft's midsection, blowing it to pieces.

Just as the missile hit, Hunter turned over quickly and saw the image of Lucifer blink once and fade away . . .

Chapter 44

The *Saratoga* was being rocked by the deadly accurate fire from the two battleships now just a half-mile away. The remaining principal officers — Sir Neil, Heath, Yaz, and O'Brien — were hurrying the others aboard to lifeboats at the rear of the big ship. The American sailors and Spanish Rocketeers were the most difficult groups to convince to go. But with every shell that hit the flattop, the argument for leaving the carrier grew.

Heath, bandages and all, was running back to the bridge when he heard a strange sound behind him. He spinned to find that, unbelievably, the F-16 was coming in for a landing.

"What the hell is that crazy Yank doing?" Heath thought.

The F-16 screamed in, caught the arresting wire, and screeched to a halt. Heath ran over to the jet just as another barrage from the battleships struck the forecastle.

"Hunter, are you daft, man?" Heath screamed up at him. "Get the hell out of here!"

"I can't let you guys go down with the ship!"

Hunter yelled back to him. "Tell them to pull the S-3A up here. We can jam at least seven of us into it!"

"Impossible, Hunter," Heath said, ducking from another explosion. "The elevator took a hit five minutes ago. It's gone, ruined. Plus we've got fires below. All the airplanes down there are destroyed."

"Well, what the hell are you guys still doing here?" Hunter yelled back to him. "Get your asses in a lifeboat!"

"No . . ." Heath called back. "I must stay here with Sir Neil. He's too banged up to move . . ."

"You frigging British!" Hunter finally yelled at him. "Will you knock off this crap about going down with the ship! This isn't a goddamn movie!"

Suddenly four huge shells hit the *Saratoga* in succession, two on the conning tower, two on the hull. Hunter felt the flattop rock back and forth. The deck was filled with fire and smoke. Suddenly Yaz ran out of nowhere and was climbing the F-16's access steps. He was carrying two items.

"Not you too?" Hunter yelled at him. "Just because these crazy Brits are willing to go down fighting, doesn't mean you have to!"

"Don't worry about me," Yaz said. "Just take these with you and get out of here!"

He dumped two bundles into Hunter's lap and was gone, disappearing into the smoke. Not Heath nor anyone else was in sight.

Hunter looked at the two bundles. One was a bunch of videotapes, strapped together with a piece of wire. They had to be the BBC videos. The other bundle was the huge Stars and Stripes that Hunter knew belonged to Yaz's unit. It was the flag he first saw flying over their camp back in Algiers.

But then, through the flames, he saw a helicopter

rising from the second battleship. It was white and gold and he knew immediately that it was Lucifer's personal chopper.

He had to go after it.

He didn't have time to look around for someone to hook him up to the burning carrier's catapult. He doubted it was working anyway. Instead he revved up the F-16's powerful engine, while keeping his brakes locked on. He watched the RPM build up and, at the right moment, he popped the brakes. The F-16 burnt up a cloud of smoky rubber for two seconds, then instantly screeched forward. Hunter hit the throttle at full power and yanked back on the side-stick controller. The airplane roared off the carrier, then dipped as its speed was nowhere near that needed for unassisted takeoff. But Hunter coolly kicked in the afterburner, and the engine responded with a burst of flame and power. Soon he was climbing.

Just as the fighter cleared the deck, a barrage of six shells struck the ship square on the flight deck. Two of the high-explosive shots blew out a pair of huge holes in the deck. Four of the shells crashed on through to the below-decks, exploding there. It was the death blow for the flattop. Ammunition left over in the hangar area blew up, causing a raging fire to roar through to the reactor room. Another incredible explosion followed, nearly lifting the mighty ship clear out of water. It settled back down into the thirty-foot depth of the Canal, and continued to explode.

Hunter looked over his shoulder and saw the carrier going through its death throes. He still couldn't believe it was happening; the carrier they had all worked so hard to bring to the Canal was now in the process of blowing itself up. And Sir

Neil. Heath. O'Brien. Probably Yaz. All gone . . .

There were still some Hinds in the area, many of them mercilessly firing on the carrier evacuees. Now the battleships, seeing the *Saratoga* had received enough punishment, also started hammering away at the western shoreline.

Hunter didn't want Lucifer's chopper to get away, but neither could he leave the helpless carrier survivors at the mercy of the Hinds and the battleships. As if to underscore his point, he saw three Hinds swooping in on the beach where the carrier survivors were and start to strafe them.

Suddenly he felt a ringing start in his brain.

More aircraft. Nearby. Heading this way.

He dove toward the Hinds, blasted one from the air with his cannon Six Pack, then sheared the main rotor off another one. But just as he was about to open fire on a third, it seemed to explode on its own.

"What the . . .?" Hunter then spun around and saw that there was a very familiar F-4 flying right above him.

"Hey, Hawk!" He heard Crunch's voice come over his radio set. "Where you been? We've been all over the goddamn Med looking for you!"

"Crunch!" Hunter called back. "I should have heard that Phantom coming a hundred miles away!"

"Well, we got a bunch of friends on the way," Crunch said. "Gunships and F-20s. Now just tell us who the bad guys are."

"You were right the first time," Hunter told him. "The Hinds and the battleships belong to Viktor's armies. Cover those people on the beaches, will you? I got to catch that bastard."

"Go, Hawk!" Crunch called back, diving toward the battleships. "We'll take care of things here!"

With that, Hunter climbed and headed south, adjusting his long-range radar hoping to pick up Lucifer's chopper.

The Brazilian captain, the man who had been in charge of Lucifer's personal battleship, now sat bound hand and foot in the jump seat of the Hind helicopter. They were flying at 7000 feet, heading south toward Lucifer's headquarters at Rub al Khali.

"You stupid fool!" Lucifer was screaming at the captain, the horribly scarred face just an inch away. The captain could see little bubbles of foam forming at the sides of the madman's mouth. "You have personally destroyed half this fleet. You have set back our timetable by weeks!"

"But Your Excellency," the captain said in his own defense. "You approved my idea to bring the battleships up to the war zone. In fact, you suggested it."

Lucifer put his face even closer to the captain's. "How dare you speak that way to me, you bushman!" the black-cloaked man said. "If it weren't for you, we would still have a complete fleet. We would not have lost seventeen thousand men to those goddamn Moroccans, and we would not have lost our only aircraft and my laser imager. That was our most powerful weapon!"

"But Your Highness," the captain plunged on, "I had nothing to do with all that. It was Hunter and those Englishmen. How could I have known they would have stuck it out so long? How did I know they were so crazy?"

Lucifer closed his eyes and rubbed his burned face. "Captain," he said in a slight, whiny voice, "You have just admitted your guilt to me. In front of witnesses!"

Lucifer spread his hands out to indicate his ever-present entourage of bodyguards.

"Because, captain," he continued, "if you say that Hunter caused all these losses and I say that *you* did, then that must mean you were, in fact, *allied* with Hunter and the Britishers!"

"That's preposterous!" the captain screamed.

"Is it?" Lucifer said, turning toward him again. There was more foam coming from the corners of his mouth now. "Then why is it that you keep bringing up Hunter? Why!? Don't you understand I screwed his woman? I have that much power over him."

The captain had had enough. He knew he was to be executed anyway. He decided to cash in his chips.

"Oh, fuck you," he screamed back at Lucifer. "Everyone in the world knows that Hunter kicked your ass in The Circle War *and* got his broad back. In fact, he kicked your ass so bad, *you had to change your name!*"

Lucifer's bodyguards thought the boss was going to pop a vein. No one, but no one, had ever talked to him like that. They half-expected to see steam coming out of his ears.

But Lucifer fooled them all. He simply turned to the nearest bodyguard and offhandedly said, "Get rid of him."

The bodyguards unhesitatingly stood the captain up and pushed him towards the open door of the Hind. Lucifer turned his back as the bodyguard kicked the captain hard in the back. The officer tumbled out of the chopper, screaming as he fell.

Chapter 45

Hunter was losing fuel fast.

He had more than a dozen holes in his starboard wing, and possibly more on his portside. His canopy was cracked in three places and his radio was cutting in and out. What was worse, only a third of his cockpit devices were functioning, all his navigational units were out, and his left rear stabilizer was all but shot off. With all the 16's maladies, Hunter was lucky if he could keep it going at half its normal cruising speed.

Still, he pressed on in pursuit of Lucifer. He had a good idea of where the madman was heading. He knew his headquarters was near Jidda, in the south-west part of old Saudi Arabia on the Red Sea. He was just hoping he'd find out where before his JP-8 gave out.

Flying more on instinct than anything else, Hunter navigated by the Canal and then the Suez estuary itself. Along the entire way he saw the results of the bombing raids by his now-lost air wing. He flew over a gang of ships two miles south of the Canal's southern entrance. An earlier air attack had clogged the entrance. No ship could get in, no ship could get out. The ships on the outside were simply at anchor, awaiting orders. The world's most powerful fleet had fallen victim to a traffic jam.

Hunter continued flying until he saw the outline of a city about forty-five miles to his southeast. His acute vision detected several gas-flare tubes, indicating a refinery was working at the city. Cities were few and far between in the area—inhabited ones especially. He steered toward it.

The closer he got, the more he was convinced this was Lucifer's destination. There were hundreds of military vehicles parked on the roads below him, and even more barracks—all empty, he imagined. He flew over an open area near a dock and saw what looked to be an execution ground. As many as 700 bodies lay rotting in the sun. He didn't even want to think about what had happened there.

He continued on over the typically Arabian city, over the barely working refinery, over its substantial port facilities. Yet he hadn't seen a person or any movement below.

But then he saw Lucifer's helicopter . . .

It was just going in for a landing at what looked to be a military base on the edge of the city. Hunter immediately put the hurting F-16 into a dive. There were definitely people at the base—armed people. And Hunter knew they had spotted him.

The AA guns opened up with a ferocity that surprised him. This must have been a heavy-duty HQ for Lucifer, he thought, as he twisted and turned around the ack-ack shells. At once Hunter knew that he had to prevent the chopper from landing. Because if it did, he'd need an army to get Lucifer out.

He roared in and peppered the two minaret gun posts with his Six Pack. There was a courtyard nearby and that was the intended landing site for the chopper, now hovering about 150 feet above. Hunter swooped down underneath the copter and raked the courtyard with cannon fire. As he streaked by he noticed several barrels sitting on one side of the landing pad. They looked like they contained fuel.

He pulled back up, did a loop, and came back in on the courtyard. A push of the cannon trigger and the barrels of fuel went up like fireworks. The courtyard was instantly enveloped in flames. The chopper got the hint and backed off.

But as he pulled up, a burst of AA fire caught his tail section. He felt the F-16 yaw out of control temporarily, and he nearly lost it avoiding a radio tower. He brought the plane under control, although it took all his might on the foot pedals to keep it level.

He spotted the chopper once again, this time flying out away from the city and toward the desert. Hunter turned the 16 around to pursue, only to see a small SAM flash up toward him. He peeled off instantly, but the warhead exploded close by, shattering his already cracked canopy. Hundreds of pieces of the exploded missile got sucked into his jet's air intake. The plane stalled, but he quickly restarted the engine. It stalled again, and he pumped the emergency fuel-release lever and started the engine again.

"C'mon, baby," he said under his breath. "C'mon, stay with me."

His airspeed now was down to less than 100 knots. The noise inside the cockpit was deafening, and things were flying in and out at alarming speeds. He felt like he was losing his beloved F-16 piece by piece. Still, he kept the chopper in sight ahead of him.

His engine coughed once again, and the 16 pitched to right. He regained control and throttled up a little more. The chopper was going at about the same speed as the crippled jet fighter. He throttled up even more and started to gain on it. He had no more Sidewinders—he couldn't have used one anyway. This was a job for his cannons.

He placed himself on the chopper's tail and fired a short burst. The shells streaked by the white and gold Hind's tail rotor, several of them finding targets.

He closed in on the copter and fired another burst. The force of the powerful cannons going off nearly jolted the 16 out of control, but he quickly regained level flight. This time the cannon fire found its intended target, the chopper's fuel tank.

Now, as the misty cloud of fuel flew back into his open cockpit, he fired a third time. He saw pieces of the Hind's tail rotor fly off. Just as the chopper started to drop, the F-16's engine stalled again. Hunter put the jet into a shallow dive and crossed his fingers. The engine came back on again.

He was now at barely 1000 feet, the chopper was at 700. Its rear end was smoking and its fuel leak getting worse. They were getting farther out in the desert with only an hour of sunlight left—he had to wonder if Lucifer knew where he was going.

He dropped down even farther and put another burst in the Hind. That did it. The smoke started pouring out of the chopper now and it veered out of control. He followed it down. The pilot put the burning craft into a semihover, and Hunter shot by it, his own plane doing a fair amount of smoking.

He did a careful loop and came back just as the copter was going through a controlled crash. It slammed into the side of a large sand dune, bounced hard, and came down for good.

One more loop and Hunter spurted right over the Hind. Two figures jumped out of the chopper, one of them wearing black robes and a hood, the other a standard flight uniform. He had no trouble figuring out which one was Lucifer.

But now the F-16 stalled again, and he knew that this time it was for good. He pulled the nose up and started looking for a level piece of sand to set down on. The engine coughed a couple times, telling him he couldn't get fussy about a landing spot. A fairly flat stretch of desert just below the dune where the Hind went down looked to be his best bet.

He glided in, wheels up, the cracked canopy obscuring his view somewhat. Then he hit — *hard*. He was jostled around the cockpit, as every light and buzzer went off at once. Waves of sand flew everywhere as the jet plowed into the soft ground.

"There goes the paint job," Hunter said grimly.

The battered fighter finally came to a stop. Its nose was buried three feet into the sand, its tail end was smoking. But he didn't have time to think about it.

He jumped out of the cockpit, grabbed his M-16, and looked around. Lucifer and his pilot were climbing the dune in front of him. He couldn't lose them now. He checked his rifle's magazine. It was full. He pulled his helmet visor up and took off after the two men.

The chopper pilot foolishly took a shot at him as he was coming around the back of the smoking F-16. Hunter aimed and pumped off three rounds, dropping the pilot with three bullets through his heart.

Lucifer picked up the dead man's rifle and continued climbing the top of the dune. Hunter double-timed it up the dune, drawing even with the heavy robed man just as they reached the summit.

They stood and faced each other. Hunter in his ripped and worn flight suit and helmet, Lucifer in his black robes right out of central casting. It was the first time Hunter had seen the madman since he had crashed his party on top of the World Trade Center. It was also the first time he saw the horrible facial scars.

Each was holding a rifle on the other.

"Well, Hunter," the man sneered at him. "We meet. Again."

"Yes, Viktor . . ." Hunter felt almost tongue-tied talking to the super-criminal. It started with two military forces heading for a collision in the Suez Canal, and now it came down to this. Just Hunter and Viktor.

"I have to admire your pluck, Hunter," Viktor said in his singsongy whine. "I've been watching you ever since you crossed the Atlantic. There was no shortage of assassins willing to get rid of you. You dodged our missiles. You didn't blink when we sent those robot Ilyushin-28s after you, or when the Panatella air force took you on. And you were very clever figuring out my hundred-arms-of-Briareus idea. And even ghosts don't scare you."

Hunter was silent.

"So what do we do now, Mr. Wingman?" Viktor continued. "Take ten paces and draw? I'm sure you are better at such things than I. You should just shoot me now."

"No, Viktor," Hunter said, barely containing his temper. He hated this man, hated him for everything he stood for. "Shooting you would just inflame all those drooling idiots you've brainwashed into joining your sick, perverted cause. Death is too good for you. What you need is a slap of justice."

"How noble, Hunter," the man said. Hunter heard him try to pull the trigger of the AK-47 he was holding. But it had hit the sand many times in the climb up the dune and now it was hopelessly jammed.

"Nice try, Viktor," Hunter said. "But I'm not about to kill you. What I *am* going to do is march you out of this desert and all the way back to America."

The man seemed genuinely surprised. "America?" he asked. "What in Hell's name for?"

"To stand trial," Hunter said, the anger rising up in his voice. "For war crimes committed against the people of the United States of America."

For the first time, the black-robed man lost his sneering grin. He actually looked worried. "You're mad," he said. "What makes you think you can get me all the way back to America?"

"What made us think we could stop your fleet?" Hunter shot back. "You destroyed a good part of my country, Viktor. And I'm going to see that you pay for it."

"You foolish, idealistic patriot," the man said, his sneer returning. "You have *no* country! When are you and your super-hero friends going to realize that? *You lost the war,* Hunter. There *is* no United States."

Never before had Hunter been so tempted to shoot a man in cold blood. He would be doing the world a favor.

"You're wrong, Viktor," Hunter replied, calmly. "As long as one person can say it, believe it, be willing to die for it, there will always be a United States of America. What you and your kind just can't get through your bullet heads is that men were

407

born to be free. Many brave men died today fighting for that idea, Viktor. Many men died when you unleashed The Circle War. And many men died when the Big War was started, I have no doubt, by your countrymen. Or is it 'former' countrymen, Viktor?"

"Don't stand and preach to me, you flag-waving son of a bitch," Viktor just about screamed at him, a slight hint of a Russian accent creeping into his voice. "What the hell do you have to be so proud about? Your leaders weren't the most honorable men who have walked the earth—"

"Screw 'em," Hunter said. "The difference is that in the USA, when we catch the crooks, they go to jail. In your country, the crooks stay in power and the innocent people go to jail."

Viktor shook his head. "Hunter," he said slowly. "It's the question of power you don't understand. Who else can project their face across hundreds of miles? Defeat entire armies without firing a shot? Who else on earth could have turned that babbling idiot Peter into something from your worst nightmare? Don't you realize the control I have over men's souls?"

"Don't even *try* to bullshit me, Viktor," Hunter said sharply, cutting him off. "You're dead wrong. You might be able to control men's *minds*—with trickery, hypnotism, and laser beams. But you cannot control their souls. All those brave soldiers who died today, fighting to stop your evil—you may have tried to spook them, but they carried on, didn't they? They may have been scared, but in their *souls* they recognized you for what you are: a bloodthirsty terrorist. Nothing more."

Viktor shook his head, troubled that he was losing the debate. "Ah, Hunter," he said, stroking his devilish beard. "You are just untemptable. It's just too bad we don't think alike. Together we could—"

Hunter held up his hand, raising the M-16 with the other. "Don't even say it. I'd rather be brain-dead than think like you. Anyone who would kill, maim, and uproot as many people as you have doesn't even deserve the justice you'll get back in America."

Viktor laughed again. "But, Hunter," he began, "as a military man you should know that I was just following orders—"

Suddenly, a shot rang out. Viktor's throat exploded in a burst of blood and bones. He was stunned. He held up his hands to his throat and looked at his own blood. Then another shot hit him, right in the center of the back, exiting through his breast bone. He looked at Hunter, shook his head feebly, then fell face down in the sand at Hunter's feet. He was dead before he hit the ground.

Hunter immediately hit the dirt. Someone had shot Viktor from the back. He looked out over the dune and saw a vehicle parked about a half-mile away, with two uniformed men standing near it. One was holding what appeared to be a rifle with a long telescopic lens.

Hunter reached down into his flight-suit pants leg pocket and pulled out the small pair of binoculars he always kept there. He put them to his eyes and focused just as the two men were climbing into the truck.

They were wearing brown uniform shirts and dark brown pants with desert boots and chaps. Each man was wearing some kind of military-issue pith helmet. Hunter strained to take in more about the men.

Then he saw it . . .

It was an emblem, displayed on an armband both men wore. A red circle, with a particularly twisted design inside. Despite the raging heat, Hunter felt an ice-cold chill run through him. That emblem . . .

"It's a goddamn *swastika* . . ." he whispered, not wanting to believe it.

As he watched, the two men drove off in the opposite direction. He followed the truck through the binoculars until it disappeared over the eastern horizon.

"Nazis?" he asked himself. Then he looked at Viktor. The dead man's body was exuding blood that was quickly soaking the loose sand beneath it.

"Were they gunning for him?" Hunter asked himself, looking at the body. "Or me?"

He trudged back to the crippled F-16, and was surprised to hear the radio crackling. It was just about the only thing that still worked in the plane's cockpit, and that was only because it powered directly off the 16's batteries.

"Hunter, Hunter, Hunter, F-16, come in . . ."

He recognized the voice. It was Crunch. Hunter reached into the shattered cockpit and retrieved his flight microphone. "Hunter here . . ." he said, wearily. "Go ahead, Crunch . . ."

"Hawk, Jeezuz, where the hell are you, buddy?"

Hunter looked around. "Beats me," he said. "Out in the middle of the desert somewhere."

"Are you okay? Did you catch Public Enemy Number One?"

"Viktor's dead . . ." Hunter replied, not quite believing his own words.

The radio crackled. "Dead?" Crunch too was surprised. "Sounds like a long story."

"It is . . ." Hunter answered, the image of the swastika emblazoned in his mind.

"I can't wait to hear all about it," Crunch went on. "But first, we've got to come and get you."

"Take your time," Hunter said, watching the sun go down. "I'm not going anywhere. Plus we'll need a heavy lift chopper. My airplane is slightly bent out of shape."

"Serious damage?" Crunch asked.

Hunter looked over the battered F-16. "Nothing that can't be fixed," he said, managing a proud smile.

"Well, look, Hawk," Crunch continued. "We cleaned up this mess here at Ismailia. Greased all the Hinds and sank both those battlewagons. Saved a lot of people on the western bank too. A couple of platoons of Football City paratroopers jumped in and they're helping the Aussies and the Gurkhas take care of the wounded. We were able to set the planes down about a hundred miles west of the Canal."

A three-second-long burst of static interrupted the F-4 pilot temporarily. It cleared up and he continued. "Anyway, Hawk. I have some good news for you. First of all, we found one friend of yours, a guy named Yaz. He's alive."

Hunter shook his head in an effort to clear it out. "Yaz? Alive?"

"Yep, he's beat up but safe," Crunch reported. "We found him floating down the Canal in a big, old wooden box. He must have been tossed into the water when the carrier went up and grabbed on to it . . ."

Wooden box? Hunter thought. It had to be the wooden box Peter used to sleep in. How strange that the decrepit piece of pine would turn out to be Yaz's salvation.

"Anyone else?" Hunter asked. "Any more of the British officers from the *Saratoga*?"

"No, Hawk," Crunch reported. "A lot of soldiers and sailors. Some Italians. Frenchmen, Spanish. Quite a few Americans. All those women you guys had on board are safe. Three of the frigates made it and that guy Olson will pull through. But all the Englishmen are gone, I'm afraid. No sign of O'Brien, the Irishman, either . . ."

Hunter felt a pang of sadness rip through him. He wasn't surprised to hear they had all perished. But now the reality was setting in. He knew he'd miss them all terribly.

"Another piece of good news, Hawk," Crunch went on. "The advance elements of The Modern Knights landed at the northern end of the Canal just a little while ago . . ."

Suddenly a major burst of static interrupted the transmission. It took more than a minute of Hunter twisting dials before the connection was weakly reestablished.

"Hawk?" Crunch said, his voice growing very faint. "Hawk, I'm losing this signal. Look, switch on your air-sea-rescue indicator. We got an AWACs with us and we'll pick you up when it gets light again. Okay?"

"Sure," Hunter said, reaching underneath his cockpit seat to retrieve the small air-sea-rescue blackbox. He pushed its sensor button and it immediately began to hum.

"We've already got a lock on you, Hawk," Crunch said, his voice fading out for good. "Stay warm, pal, and we'll see you first thing in the morning."

"Okay, Crunch," he said. "Thanks. Over and out . . ."

Now he was truly alone.

It was already getting cold. He felt his mind start to flood with questions, emotions. But he quickly, calmly blocked it all out. He was too tired to wrestle with it all right now. The time to think about it all would come later, he told himself, staring into the brilliant desert sunset.

With that, he climbed into the F-16's shattered cockpit, and cleared the seat of all debris. He unfolded the large American flag Yaz had given him and wrapped it around himself to keep warm.

Then he lay his head back and went to sleep.

ASHES
by William W. Johnstone

OUT OF THE ASHES (1137, $3.50)

Ben Raines hadn't looked forward to the War, but he knew it was coming. After the balloons went up, Ben was one of the survivors, fighting his way across the country, searching for his family, and leading a band of new pioneers attempting to bring American OUT OF THE ASHES.

FIRE IN THE ASHES (1310, $3.50)

It's 1999 and the world as we know it no longer exists. Ben Raines, leader of the Resistance, must regroup his rebels and prep them for bloody guerrilla war. But are they ready to face an even fiercer foe—the human mutants threatening to overpower the world!

ANARCHY IN THE ASHES (1387, $3.50)

Out of the smoldering nuclear wreckage of World War III, Ben Raines has emerged as the strong leader the Resistance needs. When Sam Hartline, the mercenary, joins forces with an invading army of Russians, Ben and his people raise a bloody banner of defiance to defend earth's last bastion of freedom.

SMOKE FROM THE ASHES (2191, $3.50)

Swarming across America's Southern tier march the avenging soldiers of Libyan blood terrorist Khamsin. Lurking in the blackened ruins of once-great cities are the mutant Night People, crazed killers of all who dare enter their domain. Only Ben Raines, his son Buddy, and a handful of Ben's Rebel Army remain to strike a blow for the survival of America and the future of the free world!

ALONE IN THE ASHES (1721, $3.50)

In this hellish new world there are human animals and Ben Raines—famed soldier and survival expert—soon becomes their hunted prey. He desperately tries to stay one step ahead of death, but no one can survive ALONE IN THE ASHES.

Available wherever paperbacks are sold, or order direct from the Publisher. Send cover price plus 50¢ per copy for mailing and handling to Zebra Books, Dept. 2232, 475 Park Avenue South, New York, N.Y. 10016. Residents of New York, New Jersey and Pennsylvania must include sales tax. DO NOT SEND CASH.

hangar, and it was there they made a gruesome discovery. Not only were there several dozen bodies scattered about, there were also five or six dead vultures lying nearby.

At once Crunch and Elvis were both glad that they hadn't popped the F-4's canopy and removed their oxygen masks.

"These guys were gassed," Crunch said. "We could probably find a SCUD missile casing around here somewhere if we looked hard enough. Painted with a big red star on its side, no doubt."

"The gas killed the people, then the poison in the people's blood killed the vultures," Elvis said.

"That's it," Crunch replied, looking back up at the buzzards circling overhead. "And those guys up there are still trying to figure it out."

Crunch rolled the F-4 closer to the bodies. They looked like base help as opposed to RAF personnel. He was sure that other groups of bodies in twos and threes could be found around the base. But then Elvis pointed out something.

"Captain, look at the bodies closest to us," the Weapons Officer said. "Their pockets have been pulled out. Like they were searched or something."

"Either that," Crunch said, "or they got some pretty smart vultures in this part of the world."

"Who the hell would want to go through the pockets of a bunch of stiffs like these?" Elvis asked. "Looters of some kind?"

"Either that or whoever greased this place was looking to kill one person in particular," Crunch observed.

They were quiet for a moment, then Elvis asked, "Do you . . . do you think they were aiming to kill Hawk?"

Crunch had been thinking the exact same thing.

191

"It would be difficult to say," he answered. "But there is a possibility that's exactly what happened.

"Remember, our boy has a billion-dollar price tag on his head. And I believe the Russians would gladly supply some wacko everything he needed to bump off our good buddy. Even SCUD missiles.

"Or they'd probably take on the job themselves. I don't think the New Order boys would mind turning over a billion dollars to the gang in Moscow."

"It's probably their money to begin with," Elvis said.

Crunch fired up the engine and rolled the F-4 toward the runway.

"I've seen enough," he said to Elvis. "I think it's time to call home and tell them what's going on over here. Between some nutty crusade and the fact that every other weirdo in Europe is looking to bump him off, I think Mr. Hunter is going to need a little more help than just you and I can provide."

coming tower's antennas. Up there, illuminated by the nearby blinking red beacon light, there was a man lashed to the highest point of the conning tower.

It was Peter . . .

"What the . . . ?" Hunter yelled. "How the hell did he get up there?"

The man looked completely disheveled. His beard and long hair was being whipped by the high winds. His face and body completely soaked by the sea spray. He was screaming, foaming at the mouth, *"You devils! Cursed be you!"* This was not the strange, gurgling voice that had emanated from him the night before. This was Peter's own voice, now in full roar, screaming at the attacking aircraft.

A pair of sea-jets streaked overhead, and Hunter joined in the barrage driving them off. They swept right over Peter's head and he freed one of his arms long enough to reach and shake his fist at them.

"Go back to hell, you heathens!" Peter screamed. *"Go back to hell where you belong!"*

Another Beriev roared by, its guns blazing away. A Stinger shot out from the center of the carrier and caught the big plane on its tail section. At the same time, the rear-end Phalanx opened up and caught the flying boat right in its cockpit. The big plane pitched directly into ocean, blew up, and sank instantly.

"Ha Ha!" Hunter could hear Peter scream deliriously. *"You bastards! Burn in Hell!"* The man was going completely wild, shaking his fist and foaming profusely at the mouth.

Suddenly a missile flashed out of nowhere. "Christ!" Hunter yelled. "Another Exocet." As he watched in horror, the missile streaked right over his head, hit the base of the carrier's mast, and exploded. Hunter heard Peter let out one last blood-curdling cry — a cross between a laugh and a scream.

Then everything from the base of the mast on up — including Peter — was gone . . .

Whether by coincidence or design, the air battle tapered off several minutes later. The Spanish rocke-teers were able to destroy a retreating Beriev flying boat, and the Phalanx team got one last sea-jet before the enemy planes cleared the area.

Still, Hunter and the rest of the hands on deck searched the wild skies for any more aircraft. It took about ten minutes for it to really sink in. The enemy was gone.

Exhausted, Hunter walked slowly to the super-structure and collapsed to the deck of the carrier. It may have been his imagination, but the storm seemed to start to die down too. He looked around. The deck was filled with smoking debris and cra-tered in several places. A good portion of the carri-er's communications antenna stand was gone. Several of the Aussies had bought it in the ferocious battle.

A few of the Freedom Navy ships near the carrier were burning and Hunter was sure some were lost completely. He would later learn that two of Olson's frigates were lost, with all hands. Three of O'Brien's tugs were also gone.

Just how many enemy airplanes were lost was anyone's guess. Hunter himself saw at least a dozen destroyed or damaged so much that he knew they couldn't go on.

"Screw 'em," he said, lowering his head to his knees. "Screw 'em all . . ."

He woke up a few hours later in his bunk, Anna's lovely face looking down on him, her hand directing a warm washcloth all over his naked body. He could tell at once that the storm had completely dissipated. The carrier was moving again for the first time in what seemed like an eternity. He thought back on the nightmarish action. Did it really happen? He closed his eyes and all he could see was the Exocet hitting the carrier's mast and carrying Peter away with it.

He tried to get up, but Anna pushed him back down again.

"Stay down," she ordered him. "You're hurt and you need to rest . . ."

"But, the ship . . ." he started to protest.

"The hell with the ship," she said firmly. "The storm is passed. The sun is out. Heath and Yaz have things under control. They were just here. They said to tell you that they have air patrols out. They also said we'll be close to Malta by this time tomorrow. So just stay put!"

He stopped protesting. Why fight it? He lay back down on the bunk and let Anna wash him. The battle was one of the most intense he'd ever been involved in. Who were the attackers? Did Soviet-built airplanes mean Soviet-manned airplanes? And did anyone win or lose? Did the enemy retreat because of the defensive measures, or did they simply break off the attack for lack of fuel or ammo? Would he ever know? Did it matter?

He looked up and saw that Anna had put the washcloth away and was unzipping her jumpsuit. Underneath she wore a small black-lace bra and similar panties. She removed her bra, revealing her small, pert breasts to him once again. Her panties came off next. She was now naked before him.

She was just a teenager, yet she was very mature. She knew when to soothe him and when to leave him alone. This was a time for soothing. She climbed into the bunk with him and nuzzled her breasts against his bare chest. He held her, and kissed her.

Then he closed his eyes and went back to sleep.

Chapter 23

They were at sea for only an hour before they were met by two of the Norwegian frigates sailing off the northern end of Sardinia. The ship's chopper was instantly used to evacuate Sir Neil back to the *Saratoga,* where two Italian doctors — members of the communications group — could attend to his serious wounds. Although Hunter and the Spanish rocketeers had been able to stem the bleeding from the Englishman's wounds, Hunter knew the swaggering Brit would never be the same again.

The loss of Sir Neil was tempered somewhat by the discovery of the load of weapons in the hold of the small Sardinian ship. Back on the *Saratoga* once again, Hunter met with Heath and Yaz and discussed the mother lode he had found.

"Either they were hiding their most valuable weapons in that ship or they were just about to make a huge arms deal and we happened to hijack the delivery truck," Hunter said as he battled his way through yet another plate of ill-prepared food. "Not only are there Sidewinders, but also Shrike antiship missiles and dozens of other weapons."

"If I had to guess, I'd say they were doing a deal,"

Yaz said. "Most likely with one of Lucifer's allies. Probably to be used against us."

"If that's the case, we were more than dumb lucky jumping on that freighter," Heath said.

"Right," agreed Hunter. "Not only did we get more Sidewinders than we need, we kept them out of some unfriendly hands."

The *Saratoga* once again starting sailing to the east in earnest. They entered the Strait of Sicily the following evening—a night during which Hunter closely examined the cornucopia of weapons they'd found aboard the Sardinian ship. Hunter counted more than 150 Sidewinders in the cache, which were moved to the ammunition magazine aboard the carrier. There were also a number of antipersonnel bombs, small napalm rockets, and a few dozen Shrike antiradar missiles, as well as more standard iron bombs and high-explosive devices.

Hunter immediately wired up six Sidewinders to his F-16, and began configuring the Harrier jumpjets to do the same. Of all the jets on the carrier, the Harriers could most easily adapt to the fighter-interceptor role.

Hunter later took an hour off to visit the ailing Sir Neil. The Englishman was confined in the carrier's version of intensive care, the two Italian doctors hovering over him. He was heavily bandaged from his waist to his head. Still, the Brit was conscious and typically plucky.

"Hunter, old bean," the man said when the pilot entered the room. "I hear our mission was a success in the end."

"I would have given it all back if we could have avoided this," Hunter told him, examining his